SHIFTING SANDS RESORT OMNIBUS

VOLUME 3

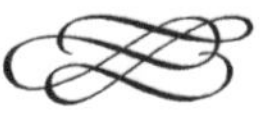

ZOE CHANT
ELVA BIRCH

PO Box 82851
Fairbanks Alaska 99708

ISBN: 978-1-933603-69-8

No generative AI was used in any part of this publication.

For Jake, who has been my unfailing support and soulmate.

SHIFTING SANDS RESORT

Sun, surf, shifters, and secrets!

Escape to a shifters-only resort on a hot tropical island full of secrets and sizzling romance.

Shifting Sands Resort is a complete paranormal romance series with self-standing novels that interconnect in an intriguing mystery.

This omnibus edition is in the author's preferred reading order and includes:

Tropical Christmas Stag (book 7)
Scarlet and the Christmas Kittens (short story)
Run (short story)
Lift (short story)
Tropical Leopard's Longing (book 8)
Her Hellhound Bodyguard (short story)
Pregnancy Knows (short story)
Fake Fur (novella)

CONTENTS

TROPICAL CHRISTMAS STAG

CHAPTER 1

Gizelle paused in the doorway, peering around the doorjamb.

Scarlet was angry.

Scarlet was often angry when she got the thick envelopes from the lawyer who didn't live on the island, the one who wanted to sell the resort so Scarlet couldn't have it anymore.

Everyone else avoided Scarlet as much as they could when those envelopes came in the mail, going about their day-to-day jobs at the resort with their eyes averted.

But Gizelle actually liked it when Scarlet was angry. The prickly feeling made her feel safe, like Scarlet's energy was a shield that kept other bad things away.

The red-haired woman looked up when Gizelle padded into her office, and she pushed the paperwork away to force a smile.

"Gizelle," Scarlet said, carefully gentle.

Everyone was carefully gentle with Gizelle.

Gizelle trailed around the room, touching the potted plants and the spines of the old books.

"My head was quiet this morning," she said, coming to stand

beside Scarlet and look down at the paperwork spread out in front of her. "Can we read that?"

"This isn't very interesting," Scarlet lied with a dry, humorless chuckle. She put it into a pile, tapping it briskly into order. "Let's read another chapter of The Secret Garden and practice some of your letters."

Gizelle fidgeted as Scarlet put the papers back in their dread-steeped envelope and stood up. "Ally says she learned to read as a little kid," she said dejectedly.

"Most people do," Scarlet said. She gave Gizelle a searching look. "You don't have to feel bad, though. I didn't learn to read until I was grown up, either."

Gizelle felt brighter. "You didn't?"

Scarlet shook her vivid head.

"Who taught you?" Gizelle asked.

"A dear friend," Scarlet said softly. "A dear friend who knew that reading would give me what I needed to understand people."

"I'd like to understand people," Gizelle said wistfully.

They walked together out to the open lawn behind Scarlet's office and settled into the grass to read. Other people seemed to prefer chairs, but Scarlet liked to sit on the ground like Gizelle did. Gizelle tucked her skirt neatly under her knees, imitating Scarlet's pose.

"Did you grow up in a zoo, too?"

Gizelle didn't remember the menagerie that she'd been rescued from, but she had heard enough stories to piece together where people thought she came from. A bad man had collected shifters in a prison where he did awful things to them.

No one would tell her what the awful things were.

Scarlet, opening the book in her lap, gave Gizelle an amused look under her eyelashes. Scarlet never talked about her life, not to anyone.

Scarlet's reading voice was low and calm, and there were pictures that Gizelle could look at over her shoulder periodically. When the chapter ended, too soon, the world came back. Then it was time for writing practice.

"Can't I learn to read without learning to write?" Gizelle asked, frowning over the disappointing mess she made copying Scarlet's tidy handwriting.

"It has to do with how you learn," Scarlet assured her. "How *everyone* learns. When you make your hands do it, it gets into your brain better."

"Why doesn't it look like it does in a book?" Gizelle chewed on her lip, trying to make herself finish out the page, but the letters slithered away from how she wanted them to look, and she couldn't concentrate over the sounds crowding her head.

"Scarlet?" She pushed away the noise.

"Yes, dear?" Scarlet was thinking about the lawyer's letter again. Gizelle could tell because of the prickles all around her.

"Do you think I could ever have a mate?"

That earned her all of Scarlet's attention, prickles changing to little rays of surprise. "A mate?"

Gizelle picked at the edge of her paper. "Jenny and Tex and Bastian and Lydia all have mates. And Neal." She missed Neal. Her gazelle missed Neal.

"Do you want a mate?" Scarlet asked pointedly.

"Don't *you* want a mate?" Gizelle countered.

Scarlet was silent with surprise, as if no one had ever asked her that before.

"They seem really happy," Gizelle said wistfully. "Like something they didn't know was missing was found. I've got a lot of missing parts, would a mate fix them?"

"I don't know if a mate could bring your memories back," Scarlet said frankly, but slowly, like she was thinking carefully about her answer. "And I don't know if you'd want them to. And there are… other parts to having a mate."

"Sex," Gizelle said impatiently. "I *know* about that."

"What do you know about it?" Scarlet asked suspiciously.

"I've seen the pictures in the magazines at The Den," Gizelle said defensively, referring to the staff house where most of the bachelors lived. A few of them had mates that lived there now, and those magazines had gotten scarce. "I know how to pleasure myself. And Breck told me all about what people do with each other."

Scarlet made a funny face. "Breck?"

"He's an authority on the subject," Gizelle said confidently, repeating what the leopard shifter waiter had told her. "And he wanted to make sure that I could make up my own mind about it when I was ready. So I wouldn't be surprised or let someone take advantage of me."

"That's... wise," Scarlet conceded. She didn't sound particularly happy about it, though.

"I'm not a child," Gizelle insisted.

"I know," Scarlet said, almost mournfully.

That reminded Gizelle of something else. "Travis said he was decorating for Christmas today, but he didn't have time to explain it to me. And Ally keeps talking about it, but she doesn't make any sense."

"Christmas? Christmas doesn't have to make sense," Scarlet said warmly, following Gizelle's change of topic without hesitation. "Christmas is a holiday we celebrate near the end of the year. People give each other presents, and there is singing, and Chef will make special food."

That sounded nice. "What kind of food?" Gizelle asked. "What are presents? Will Saina sing?"

Scarlet grinned at her, all warm and fuzzy with memories. "I had forgotten that this would be your first Christmas. You'll get to try figgy pudding and sugar cookies."

Figgy pudding sounded questionable, but Gizelle knew she liked cookies and sugar.

Scarlet continued, "Presents are special gifts that friends and family give each other. Usually little things, like books or clothing or candy. They get wrapped in special paper and tied with bows and we all open them together on Christmas Day."

That sounded… baffling, but Scarlet was looking at her with an encouraging smile, clearly expecting some kind of reaction.

"I don't have anything to give as a present," Gizelle said hesitantly. If it was a reciprocal thing, Christmas probably wasn't for her.

"I could help you make something," Scarlet promised warmly. "It's not really about what the present is as much as it is about the giving. It reminds people that we're thinking about them."

"Alright," Gizelle agreed. She thought about people a lot.

They were interrupted by the beep of the resort van at the entrance, announcing that a new group of guests was arriving. Gizelle leaped to her feet, scattering her lesson papers.

"I should go," Gizelle said swiftly. New people were always unnerving and Scarlet would be busy checking them in.

She was concentrating so hard on remembering not to shift, not to be afraid, not to be *weird* that she got all the way down the path to the bar before she realized that she'd left her papers all over the lawn.

CHAPTER 2

Conall scowled at the entrance to the resort. The van ride from the airstrip had been absolutely jaw-rattling. He could guess from the other passengers that it was too loud for anything but shouted conversation and was just as happy to leave the ill-sprung vehicle behind for his own two feet.

He let the other guests rush forward to check in. He moved to the side of the doorway as the driver hurried past with an over-stacked armful of luggage, an apology undoubtedly at the lips Conall anti-socially refused to look at.

At least the place didn't have Christmas decorations up yet.

Since Thanksgiving, Boston had been a gaudy sea of tinsel and obnoxiously blinking lights, reveling in its seasonal snow and silver bells. There were plastic Santas and wire reindeer on every other white-dusted lawn. Even the most understated business had wreaths and fake holly and the air smelled cloyingly like cinnamon and pine.

"You're so lucky you don't have to listen to the music," his secretary had said to him thoughtlessly. "They start playing the carols so early now, by the time we get to December, I'm ready to unplug sound systems in the stores. It's even in the cabs!"

He had pretended to laugh, gone straight to his office, and put his credit card into the Internet form for the last room at the most exotic tropical resort that he could find. Reservations at this place, Shifting Sands Resort, were by approval of the management or invitation only, but he had received his confirmation within a day. He had then filled out the lengthy forms confirming that he was indeed a shifter and agreed to abide by their specific terms, like no predation and no picking flowers. He had been grimly amused by the polite disclaimers that the resort was not ADA compatible and that while they would certainly make accommodations, they might not be able to meet all special needs.

Special needs.

It had taken him several false starts to fill that part of the form out, wrestling with over-explaining, justifying. In the end, he'd put down only three words: Deaf. Fluent lip-reader.

He realized he was starting to crumple the confirmation page his assistant had printed and made his hands relax.

The last guest before him was leaving the little desk in the courtyard and he stalked forward with his matching leather luggage to check in.

The woman behind the desk had improbably red hair, pulled back into a tidy bun, and a sharp, green-eyed gaze.

"I'm Scarlet," she said, looking him square in the face and enunciating with refreshing clarity. "I'm the owner of Shifting Sands."

Conall appreciated an owner who kept their hands actively on a business and handed his confirmation form and credit card across the desk with a nod and a noise he hoped sounded approving and not just unfriendly.

She took both, efficiently running the card first so that a slow connection—which was to be expected on an isolated island in a foreign country—wouldn't delay the check-in process.

"You have cottage seven," Scarlet told him, looking him clearly in the face again. She spread out a map on the desk between him and showed him where it was on the map, on the second tier of buildings from the beach near the edge of the jungle. She pointed out several other features, and Conall had to assume she was saying what they were, as he couldn't watch her mouth and look at the map at the same time. He could read just fine, so he didn't ask her to repeat anything.

She turned the brochure over and pointed out the dining and event schedule.

Weekly dances.

Nightly concerts.

Conall stopped reading and took the brochure abruptly. He looked at Scarlet as politely as he had to as they completed the payment. It was a ridiculous amount of money for more cottage than he needed, but at least it was all-inclusive.

"If there is anything we can do for you, I hope you won't hesitate to ask," she added. "I have let the staff know about your special needs and I hope that your stay will go smoothly."

"I don't need any special concessions," Conall said firmly. *And I don't want them*, he didn't add, though he thought it bitterly.

He gave his final signature on the paperwork and gathered his luggage, half an eye on Scarlet to see if she was going to be troublesome and chatty.

But she only nodded briskly and returned to her own business, leaving Conall to descend down the jungle path to his escape from Christmas.

CHAPTER 3

"You sure about this?" Tex asked Gizelle. He was being carefully gentle, like Scarlet had been.

"I can do this," Gizelle insisted.

Everyone at the resort *did* something. Tex, a bear shifter, was the bartender, and he made drinks and listened to people. His mate, the wolf shifter Laura, did a little of everything, helping out at the spa and making beds and cleaning and serving drinks in the bar.

Bastian, who was also a dragon, was a lifeguard and had saved two people from drowning since Gizelle had arrived almost a year ago. One of those people, Saina, had turned out to be a mermaid and Bastian's mate, and as well as sometimes being a lifeguard, she sang every night in a fancy dress. Gizelle liked the way Saina's voice made her forget how different she was.

Travis, a lynx shifter, fixed things that were broken, if they weren't people. His mate, Jenny, was the good lawyer, and Gizelle had taught her to be better at being an otter shifter.

Jenny was good at shifting now, even better than Gizelle was, so that didn't count as Gizelle doing anything anymore.

They all *did* something, and Gizelle wanted to be that kind of person, the kind who *did* something.

Tex gave her the tray reluctantly.

"It's almost Christmas," Gizelle reminded him as the thought occurred to her. "Isn't that exciting? I'm going to make presents."

She took the tray, holding it carefully flat even though it was empty, and took a deep breath. She was going to do this. She was going to be *useful.*

The first table she picked had a woman sitting all by herself.

"Can I take your glass?" Gizelle offered, like she had practiced with Tex, checking first to make sure it was empty except for ice cubes.

The woman made a careless gesture of approval, not even really noticing her, and Gizelle swooped in to claim her prize.

The glass was returned triumphantly to Tex at the bar, perched on the tray.

"Nice work, cub," Tex said encouragingly, taking the glass casually.

"I'm not a child," Gizelle reminded him, feeling a little let down.

She took the tray back and surveyed the bar. There were three people sitting together by the edge of the deck that looked down over the big pool; they appeared to have extra glasses and possibly even a bottle. Gizelle padded over the tiles towards them, only remembering to keep her tray level at the last moment.

These people looked at her when she approached, momentarily making Gizelle freeze. These were strangers and it wasn't so very long ago that just having them glance at her would have made her shift and flee in her gazelle form.

This time, she reminded herself before her flight instinct kicked in that she was in a safe place. These people would not hurt her. She was *supposed* to be in human form.

"Can I take your glasses?" she remembered to say.

She realized that she was standing too far away, several paces from the table still, but the woman in the group had a friendly smile and gestured her to come closer.

"I'd like another mojito," the friendly-smile woman said.

Gizelle clutched her tray. She wasn't supposed to take orders, just glasses. But really, what was the harm? She took another step closer, eyeing the empty glasses. "Alright," she said slowly. "A mojito." What did Tex usually say when someone asked for that? "Extra mint?"

"Yes, please," the woman said. Gizelle felt like she'd just done something momentous.

One of the men pushed a glass towards the edge of the table. That was an invitation, right? Gizelle swooped in to take the glass, and then bravely took the rest of the empty ones, stacking them carefully around the tray so they were balanced, with the bottle perfectly in the middle.

"I'll take another IPA," the other man said agreeably. "And a shot of Jaeger."

"Whiskey on the rocks," the last person added.

Gizelle smiled bravely. "Mojito, extra mint, IPA, shot of... Jaeger. Whiskey on rocks."

Friendly-smile woman continued to smile and nodded approvingly. The men returned to their conversation.

Gizelle turned back to the bar, tray balanced on one hand like Laura did. She caught Tex's nervous look and returned to holding it in both hands.

"They want drinks," she told Tex happily as she arrived at the bar. "Mojito... with... extra Jaeger. On rocks?"

Her cheerfulness faded with her faulty memory.

Tex took the glasses from the tray with a practiced sniff for each. "Mojito with extra leaf. Pale ale. Shot of Jaeger. Jack on rocks."

Gizelle might have pouted, but Tex swiftly told her, "You did a good job." He didn't call her a cub that time. "I'll make these while you go collect glasses from the tables by the pool," he suggested.

Gizelle took the empty tray, enthusiasm slightly dented, and went to gather glasses.

CHAPTER 4

The first disappointment of the resort was the lack of private kitchen facilities. A note in the brochure explained it away as jungle bug control and played up the fine food available at the restaurant and buffet.

Conall was skeptical of their claims, but hungry after the long plane ride. He left his luggage, still packed, to follow the signs and smells to the central buildings and the promise of food.

The second disappointment was the string of Christmas lights being hung at the restaurant entrance. A rough-looking character covered in tattoos and scars stood on one ladder while a smiling Native American man on a stepladder was handling the other end of the string and directing the placement. There was a box of tinsel and decoration overflowing by the foot of the ladder.

Conall's appetite vanished.

The bar below sounded far more appealing.

It was late afternoon and a sign by the restaurant door claimed it was opening for dinner service in half an hour anyway. Conall had doubts about how strictly they followed schedules at a tropical resort such as this, but maybe a drink before dinner would be just what he needed.

A strong drink.

The bar was manned by a smiling cowboy, complete with ridiculous hat and over-sized belt buckle. At least Conall didn't have to *hear* the Southern drawl.

"What can I get you?" the man asked, mixing something in a shaker and straining it into a glass over mint leaves.

There was a well-worn guitar leaning in the corner behind the bar, completing the man's cowboy image and driving a spike of pain into Conall's heart.

Conall picked up a menu and scowled darkly at it.

It was a seasonal menu, with inane holiday twists on traditional drinks. Holly and Santa hats decorated the margins.

This vacation was starting to look like an expensive mistake, and no kind of escape at all.

CHAPTER 5

The tables on the pool deck were mostly empty; Gizelle could snag the bottles and glasses without having to talk to anyone. In two cases, guests were lounging on laid-back chairs with sunglasses. Gizelle crept up behind them and took their empty glasses without asking, darting away triumphantly without disturbing them.

No one had a chance to ask her for another drink, though one of the women further down the deck gave her a long, skeptical look.

Gizelle realized she was crouching behind a chair and made herself stand up and tilt her chin defiantly.

Her tray was as full as Gizelle trusted herself to carry up stairs. Laura sometimes carried them heaped with glasses, but Tex had made her promise not to stack anything.

She was watching her bare feet as she climbed the grand stairs from the pool deck to the bar above, when the gazelle who was never far from her stirred and gave an unexpected sigh of longing.

Gizelle looked up as she moved off the last step and was struck with a jolt of something like fear, but much, much better.

There was a man standing at the bar in front of Tex, wearing khaki shorts and a fancy silk shirt covered in green leaves. He had dark hair and he was almost as tall as Tex. He was glowering at a menu as if it had offended him.

Gizelle did not realize she had dropped the tray until everyone turned in shock to look at her.

Almost everyone.

The man at the bar did not turn. He was completely unaware of Gizelle as she stepped carefully through the shattered glass and over the upside-down tray and walked towards him, ignoring the chaos in her wake.

He didn't notice her at all until she was right beside him, trying to crane around to see into his fascinating face.

He startled like she had, and then stared back at her with blue eyes like pools of sky.

"I *do* have a mate," Gizelle breathed.

For a long, unmarked moment, they gazed at each other in surprise.

Then the enormity of it all came crashing down on her and Gizelle was shifting and leaping away in her antelope form, scattering chairs and pieces of her sundress as she fled.

CHAPTER 6

Conall was not aware of the woman until she had not only crowded into his personal space, but had wedged herself at an awkward angle against the bar to look into his face.

White-streaked dark hair was wild around her face and falling past her waist, half-obscuring her thin, pale face. Big, dark eyes threatened to swallow him whole.

She said something, but Conall was too busy watching those amazing eyes to look at her mouth.

Ours, his elk told him firmly. *Ours forever.*

Then, before he could even reach out and brush back her tangled hair, she was leaping back, tipping over chairs as she shifted into a gazelle and sprang away in terror.

He sat there, frozen, until a thump that rattled the bar prompted him to turn in a daze to the bartender, clearly at the end of a rant, with familiar words at his scowling lips.

"Are you deaf, man?"

"Yes," he snarled back, silencing the man.

The bartender adjusted his hat in consternation and blinked rapidly. "Sorry," he said, undoubtedly a mumble. "Scarlet warned us."

"Who was that?" Conall demanded.

"That was gazelle," the bartender explained. Conall scowled at him. It had been obvious what her shift form was, of course. Conall wasn't sure what the point of telling him that was.

They stared at each other for a moment and the bartender sighed and ducked under the bar. He came up with a bottle of Tanqueray Ten. "You look like a gin and tonic man," the cowboy guessed. "And you're going to need this."

He was good at his job, Conall had to admit; gin and tonic was his drink of choice. He settled onto one of the stools while the bartender put ice into a glass. His legs still felt unsteady from the shock. "Thank you," he said automatically. "I'd appreciate that."

His *mate*.

Had she run because she realized he was deaf?

What had she said that he'd missed?

"I'm Tex," the other man said as he slid the glass across the counter to him.

"Tex," Conall repeated numbly, confirming that it was a name. "I'm Conall."

"That was gazelle," Tex repeated.

Conall took a bracing sip of the drink and wondered if Tex would prove to be one of those people who assumed deaf meant idiot.

"She's… different. Special." Tex was clearly struggling. When the native man who had been hanging lights brought a tray of broken glass to the bar, he exchanged a desperate look with him. "How would you explain gazelle, Travis?"

Conall turned on the stool, watching carefully. Travis started to answer obliquely as he dumped the glass shards, and Tex stopped him. "He's deaf, you have to face him."

Travis looked straight at him, with the startled, uncomfortable expression that Conall was so familiar with.

"Gazelle is different," Travis echoed Tex's first descriptor reluctantly. "She's… *really* different."

Conall took another drink as Travis sat down on one of the bar stools, raking a hand through his short, dark hair. "Look, to understand gazelle, you have to understand where she came from."

Conall glanced at Tex quickly enough to catch him saying, "... don't really know." They weren't close enough to make watching both of them easy.

"There was a collection, like a zoo," Travis continued. "Shifters in cages, torture."

"... forced to stay in animal form," Tex added.

Conall stared from one to the other. Someone had *tortured* his mate? Rage was not the least of his complicated emotions.

Travis continued, "She wouldn't shift when we found her, or couldn't. She stayed in gazelle form for months after her rescue, and as far as we can tell, she doesn't remember anything before that. The other shifters we rescued all said she was there longer than they were."

"We don't know how old she is, or when she was captured," Tex added.

"She might have been born there," Travis said.

"She's come a long way," Tex said firmly. "But she's still really…"

"Sheltered?" Travis grasped, clearly flailing.

"You have to be careful about startling her," Tex said.

"She doesn't like loud noises," Travis agreed. "I try to warn her if I'll be using power tools."

"She can seem simple," Tex said uncomfortably.

"But she's quite smart," Travis hastened to add. "She picks things up plenty quickly. She's just… missing a lot of really basic education and socialization."

"... is teaching her to read." Conall missed the name Tex gave, but didn't want to ask.

They lapsed into silence, one that Conall wasn't gracious enough to break himself, chewing over everything they'd told him.

His elk was having trouble moving past the part where someone had hurt his mate.

"So," Travis said finally, when Conall had downed the last of his gin and tonic. "You're gazelle's mate."

There was unexpected challenge in Travis' face.

"I am," Conall gruffly agreed. That wild, wounded woman was his, and everything about him was hers.

Travis put his hand forward. Conall stared at it reluctantly a moment, then shook it. "I'm Conall."

Before he let go, Travis said seriously, "If you hurt her, I *will* have to kill you." His grip tightened.

Conall glanced towards Tex, trying to gauge whether this was some sort of joke.

Tex had a grim smile on his cowboy face. "Only if I don't get there first."

CHAPTER 7

"Gizelle? Honey?"

Gizelle flicked big ears at the voice but didn't turn.

Wanting a lot of things at once made her legs tremble, and it was easiest just to lean against the fence here and let the noise in her head turn everything to nonsense.

"Gizelle."

Gizelle reluctantly swiveled her head.

Scarlet was carrying a new sundress. Maybe it was the same sundress and Travis had already repaired it. Gizelle didn't remember what she had been wearing. Had she been wearing clothing? Probably. Tex was always making her put on a dress if she forgot. It was sometimes easier being a gazelle because she didn't have to remember things like that.

She could remember what *he* was wearing.

A short-sleeved silk shirt, with tropical leaves and flowers all over. Khaki shorts, pressed crisp. A silver bracelet on one strong wrist.

Blue eyes.

Blue eyes like a cloudless sky, full of promise and freedom.

"Gizelle." More firmly this time.

Gizelle gave a sigh of defeat and shrugged back into her human form.

"I dropped the glasses," she said regretfully. "They all broke."

"No one is angry," Scarlet assured her as Gizelle slipped the dress on over her head.

"*I'm* angry," Gizelle said unhappily.

"What are you angry about?" Scarlet asked so sweetly that it made it worse.

"*That*," Gizelle said sharply, knowing Scarlet wouldn't understand. "Me. *Every*thing."

Scarlet sat on the grass, her legs neatly together in her narrow skirt. Gizelle circled her twice, warily, then sat cross-legged to face her.

"There are some things you should know," Scarlet said evenly.

Gizelle gave a noisy sigh. "Breck told me about *that*."

"About your mate."

Gizelle held her breath. She wanted to know everything about *him*.

Scarlet had papers. Papers with words that made Gizelle wish she was already good at reading, not barely able to remember the alphabet sounds. But they had pictures, too, and Gizelle looked through them curiously. One of them was a picture of the man with blue eyes. He was sitting on a car holding a guitar and he was smiling. He hadn't been smiling when Gizelle met him.

She liked the smile.

"His name is Conall Wright. He's deaf."

"What does that mean?"

"He can't hear anything."

That sounded *wonderful*.

Scarlet continued. "He can speak and he can read your lips. If you look at him when you speak, he'll be able to understand what you're saying."

"Even in the dark?"

"No, probably not in the dark." Scarlet sounded like she was trying not to laugh, but she kept going. "It's important that he be able to see you, to see your mouth when you speak, so look up; you can't hide in your hair."

Gizelle had been doing exactly that and made herself brush it back from her face and sit up straight.

"What else?" she asked eagerly.

"He's from a city called Boston," Scarlet explained, and she showed Gizelle a map with the city circled. "He owns a chain of high-end music supply stores and a clothing line, among other things."

Scarlet looked like she expected Gizelle to be impressed with that, but Gizelle didn't like the sound that chains made, and the rest of the sentence made no sense to her.

Scarlet continued, gravely relaying things she clearly thought were important.

But only one thing really mattered to Gizelle.

She leaned forward to interrupt Scarlet when the red-haired woman paused. "Will he like me?"

CHAPTER 8

We should pursue her, Conall's elk insisted, pawing impatiently.

We have to give her the space to come to us, Conall reminded his elk and himself equally.

If the resort had seemed like a glittery disappointment before, it was a hundred times more so now that Conall had met his mate.

The grand pool didn't seem as impressive as the gazelle's brief gaze had been and the rich food was tasteless when he made himself eat.

The woman's recognition of him, and her subsequent flight, had escaped no one's notice, and if Conall couldn't hear the whispers, he could see the appraising looks as he woodenly went through the motions of being just another guest at the resort.

He skipped the special dinner menu to pick an unappetizing plate from the buffet and successfully avoided meaningful contact with everyone simply by glancing away if they tried to talk to him.

After dinner he prowled the resort from the salon, where he waved away the cheerful offer of service, through several gardens with too many shadowed places, all perfect for a vacation tryst. The empty event hall had an open box of Christmas decorations that

Conall only barely held himself back from kicking. He stalked past the pool to look down over the dark beach and the ocean, picturesquely reflecting the nearly-full moon.

He told himself he wasn't really looking for her, just getting the lay of the land.

But the disappointment when every shadowy figure or deer-shaped bush turned out not to be her suggested otherwise and he finally returned to his opulent cottage.

The following morning, having failed to find anything resembling rest, Conall went straight to the bar. He did not, technically, plan to ask where the gazelle would be. But he had to know more and hoped to get more of her story from the bartender.

It was too early for the bar to be open, though Conall was briefly tempted by the self-service cooler.

He didn't think he could drink away this pain.

A dark-haired woman and a man who looked like he had a hangover were staring at him from a table across the otherwise deserted bar. Conall scowled at them in challenge and they looked away first.

He probably looked just as hungover, though the gin and tonic hadn't really dented his faculties at all.

Not like her eyes had.

Eyes like escape.

A fist connected with his shoulder and Conall turned with an automatic growl of challenge to find a staff gardener, obvious by the resort polo shirt and the machete he had casually over one shoulder. He smelled like earth.

"You'd be Conall," the stranger said. "Gazelle's mate."

The fist had not been gentle, but Conall guessed that if it had been a genuine attack, he would not still be standing.

We could take him, his elk said confidently.

"I'm Conall," he answered out loud.

They stared at each other for a long moment.

The other man finally said something that must have been his name. He didn't offer a hand to shake. Conall wasn't about to ask him to repeat the name; names were tricky to read.

He was finally rewarded when the other man looked faintly uncomfortable and said, “We’re all quite fond of her.”

Conall, who had never been chatty even before he had lost his hearing, flailed for an answer. “I’m sure she’s…” amazing? Everything? They hadn’t even exchanged words and he knew to the bottom of his soul that she was something incredibly precious and rare. “... great,” he finished lamely.

“If you hurt her, I’m going to have to pound you to a pulp.” The man had the grace to look vaguely chagrined about the threat.

“Naturally,” Conall agreed.

There was another moment where no one attempted to say anything.

Finally, the gardener nodded briskly. “Alright then.” And he turned and went elsewhere with his machete.

As if meeting his mate hadn’t already proved complicated enough without threats of violence.

CHAPTER 9

Lydia looked up curiously from the nails she was painting when Gizelle padded into the salon.

"Gizelle," the swan shifter said gently, the way everyone did. "What a lovely surprise."

Gizelle didn't like the salon much. It smelled delicious but everything she tasted was terrible. There were noisy dryers and it was usually too busy for Gizelle's tastes.

But she liked Lydia. Lydia was quiet and graceful.

"Can you make me pretty?" Gizelle asked. She surveyed her reflection critically in one corner.

She didn't look like other women. She was too skinny, she thought, turning and watching her reflection turn. Her elbows were pointy. "Can you give me soft parts?" she said longingly. "And pretty hands? And maybe purple eyes?"

Lydia finished swiftly with her guest, who looked amused at the interruption instead of annoyed. "What if we start with your hair?" she suggested, rising to stand beside Gizelle.

Gizelle cocked her head at her reflection. Her hair didn't look like other people's. Sometimes they had lighter strands in their hair, but Gizelle's white streaks were unnaturally bold against her dark hair. It was long, like Magnolia's, but it didn't hang in such tidy waves. She wasn't supposed to hide in it, she reminded herself, or Conall wouldn't be able to hear her.

"Alright," she said reluctantly.

Lydia took her hand and led her to one of the chairs by the sinks. With one smooth move, she twirled a smock over Gizelle's dress. Lydia's hands were even more gentle than her voice, stroking over Gizelle's head with clever, investigative fingers.

"Do you want it cut?" Lydia said, a note of hesitation in her voice.

"No," Gizelle said at once, nearly leaping out of the chair. If the smock hadn't been tangled around her, she might have made it further.

"Okay, okay," Lydia said swiftly, with gentle pressure on her shoulders. "We'll just trim a little off the ends to even it up, that's all." She continued to explore Gizelle's hair, and asked, "Have you been washing your hair, dear?"

"I don't like the water falling on me," Gizelle told her. "It's too noisy on my head. So I just go swimming. Bastian showed me how."

"Swimming in a bathtub?" Lydia said hopefully.

"No," Gizelle said frankly. "In the saltwater pool."

Lydia was quiet for a long moment as she tugged gingerly at the knots and tangles. "This is going to take a while," she finally admitted. "And I'm going to need some help."

"I'm ready," Gizelle said.

She hoped she really was.

She let Lydia put entire bottles of scented things on her head and start massaging it in.

Laura came to help, shaking her head over the task. "What did you do to your fingernails?" she exclaimed.

"Nothing," Gizelle said defensively. "They just do that."

Laura put Gizelle's hands in tubs of squishy stuff, then scolded her when she tried to play with it. "Just sit," the wolf shifter said firmly. "Tex told me that you asked him to arrange a dinner date," she added.

"Dinner?" Lydia exclaimed, stilling her fingers for a moment. "Don't you want to start with something… simpler?" she suggested.

"Isn't dinner what most people do?" Gizelle said, squirming. "Maybe we could have drinks, instead."

"Oh, no," Lydia and Laura both said, with voices that edged on horror.

"Stop wiggling," Laura said. "Just sit."

So Gizelle sat, while Laura did things to her fingernails and toes that tickled and smelled bad.

CHAPTER 10

After the encounter with the gardener, Conall went, resigned, to the restaurant. It was lunchtime, which was apparently a meal limited to the buffet.

He was no hungrier than he'd been the night before, but he picked some food he knew would sustain him while he continued to wait.

Conall had never been particularly good at waiting. As a child, the months before Christmas had been a torture of anticipation. More recently, waiting for the awful, ubiquitous Christmas holiday season to finally *end* was the real test of his patience.

As Conall picked at his plate he became aware of someone standing by his table. He looked up to find a waiter hovering.

Probably he had been clearing his throat or some other useless thing. Conall answered with his most off-putting scowl.

But the waiter's unexpected words made him regret it. "Gazelle wants to see you."

It was like an electric jolt directly to his heart and Conall pushed back his plate and started to stand.

The waiter shook his head. "Not now! Sorry to get your hopes up, handsome."

Feeling like he was on some sort of cruel roller coaster, Conall sank back into his chair. "When?" he asked shortly, actively watching for the answer.

"Tonight. She wants to do dinner. We tried to talk her into something more casual, but once she gets her head wrapped around something, it's like trying to stop a runaway train."

Conall looked around. "Here?" Guests at nearby tables were pretending not to eavesdrop and turned away to convenient conversations as his gaze raked over them.

"We'll set you up in a quiet corner out of the way," the waiter promised. "The fewer distractions the better, believe me."

Before he could stop himself, Conall gave a helpless guffaw of laughter. "I imagine so," he agreed.

"I'm…" The waiter's name was probably not Brick. He extended a friendly hand, and Conall shook it firmly.

"Conall," he said, though clearly probably-not-Brick had known who he was. Probably everyone at the resort knew who he was at this point. "What time should I be here?"

"Lydia's got her work cut out for her," certainly-not-Brick said mysteriously. "I think seven is as early as you can hope for."

Conall made a note to be there at six. "Thank you," he said stiffly.

He wasn't sure what to make of the staff who had so clearly rallied around their strange ward. On the one hand, he'd had no fewer than three threats on his continued health if he hurt her. On the other, they persisted in calling her a gazelle, rather than allowing her the dignity of a name and seemed to treat her like a simple-minded child. The barest glimpse into her eyes made Conall sure there was much, much more to her than they were giving her credit for.

"One more thing," not-Brick added. "Chef wanted me to let you know that he has a kitchen full of very sharp instruments and he wouldn't hesitate to use them on you if you let gazelle get hurt."

Make that four threats.

CHAPTER 11

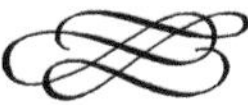

Gizelle sat obediently while Lydia continued to tug gently on her increasingly tender scalp.

"I got an unexpected letter in this morning's mail," the swan shifter said conversationally.

"Do tell," Laura encouraged.

"A great resort in Cabo San Lucas offered me a salaried lead spa position. Numbers before tips to take my breath away."

Gizelle went still with worry. Would Lydia leave?

"Are you going to go?" Laura asked, so Gizelle didn't have to.

"I thought about it," Lydia admitted. "But I like what I have here."

"And your mate Wrench," Laura said, nodding sagely. "He'd have a hard time getting work there, with his criminal record."

"It was enough that he wouldn't have *had* to work," Lydia said in wonder. "And they included a *pretty* top-floor condo."

"Oooo," Laura said, then thoughtfully added. "That's funny. Jenny got an offer from a rival law firm today, too. Said they offered her a partnership and a signing bonus that made her jaw drop."

"Is *she* going to take it?" Lydia asked as Gizelle dug worried fingers into her armrest.

Laura shrugged. "There was no option to telecommute, and Travis has zero interest in living in Los Angeles, so I don't think it will go anywhere."

"Funny that we both got offers, though," Lydia said. "Let's move to the sink."

That was apparently meant for Gizelle and she obediently shuffled to the sink under her crinkling smock, Lydia holding her hair up.

After she was done rinsing Gizelle's hair of the flowery stuff it had been coated in, Lydia told stories about Christmas in Mexico, tales about parties and *piñatas* and Three Kings Day and cakes with toy babies baked into them.

Christmas sounded too weird and wonderful to be true and it made everyone feel fuzzy and warm to talk about it.

Gizelle continued to sit through another round of combing and coating and rinsing, trying not to panic as it seemed like she was never going to be released. She reminded herself not to shift, that she was safe, and she would probably break a lot of things if she shifted and she really, really wanted to look pretty for Conall.

She sat, eyes screwed shut, as she thought about not wanting to look *weird* for him. There wasn't much she could do about what was in her head, or what wasn't, but she could at least *look* normal.

CHAPTER 12

Not sure what else to do in the meantime, Conall finished his lunch and went to the pool.

It was an impressive bit of architecture, with white marble columns and fancy water features at one end. Palm trees lined the far side; deck chairs were arranged along the near side. Several people were lounging in the shallow end, chatting and taking advantage of the dappled shade.

Conall wasn't interested in swimming, but he brought a book and found a lounge chair overlooking the beach to pretend to read it in.

A cheerful dark-skinned waitress offered him a bottle of water that he gravely accepted. He supposed it wouldn't make a good impression on his mate to pass out from dehydration halfway through dinner.

She looked like she might want to talk, but Conall simply went back to his charade of reading.

It wasn't long before the dragon on the beach noticed him.

Conall knew about dragons theoretically; some of the most prestigious law firms in Boston quietly boasted about the dragon lawyers on their staff. But it was quite different to see a dragon in its shifted form, casually surveying both the beach and the pool with watchful jeweled eyes.

After a moment of unblinking consideration, the dragon got up from where it was curled around the lifeguard's tower and padded towards the resort, laying one claw on the railing between the pool deck and the beach.

He shifted seamlessly as he moved, and became a human figure, vaulting over the railing as if it had been waist-high instead of ten feet above the sand.

He was also a clothing shifter and was fully dressed in a bright lifeguard's uniform, with a first aid kit at his waist.

Without asking, the lifeguard came to sit on the lounge chair next to Conall, facing him. "You're Conall," he said. "Gazelle's mate."

Conall put the book down and gave him a challenging look with no spoken answer. This was starting to become tiresome.

The lifeguard looked chagrined. "I'm Bastian," he introduced himself.

"Conall," he confirmed briefly in response.

"I don't know… what you know about gazelle," Bastian said, running a hand through his short, damp hair.

Not enough, Conall thought, and he sighed and sat up to face Bastian. "A little," he said. "But I'd like to know more." Was someone finally going to be able to fill in the many missing pieces of her story?

"You know about the zoo?"

Conall nodded slowly and his elk snorted in anger at the reminder.

"And how she spent the next few months as a gazelle? We weren't sure if she could shift, or if she ever had."

The waitress was back, sitting next to Bastian. "I'm Jenny," she said, looking friendly. "Travis' mate."

Conall gave his name in return, but was mostly watching Bastian for more of the story.

"She's shy and smart and scared," Bastian said. Or possibly

scarred instead of scared; they looked the same and Conall suspected that both applied. "And she's not like other shifters."

"I'm not expecting her to be," Conall said firmly.

She's better than other shifters, his elk agreed smugly.

"She can… hypnotize people," Bastian said slowly, probably knowing he sounded ridiculous. He glanced at Jenny for support.

Jenny nodded. "I've only had a bit of it… she'll sort of put you off in a trance when she goes, er, off script."

Bastian chuckled. "Well, she's done it flat out to me. Me, Neal, and Travis, plus a handful of goons with guns who were trying to buy the resort out from under Scarlet. Damned unnerving, I'll tell you. Like there was nothing else in the world for a while there."

A third figure joined them, a sultry dark-haired woman with sea-green eyes. Conall only caught fragments of what she was saying until Bastian nodded his direction in reminder.

"My apologies," the woman said without a trace of embarrassment as she sat close beside Bastian and twined her fingers into his. "I'm Saina. Gazelle has hypnotized me, and let me assure you, sirens are not easy to work magic on. I've never felt anything quite like it."

"Sirens?" Conall was surprised into saying. Surely he was reading that one wrong.

But she nodded calmly. "I'm a mermaid," she confirmed. "And my kind knows a lot about entrancement. This was nothing like our magic."

"Basilisk, maybe?" Jenny theorized.

Conall had to see the word on Saina's mouth a second time to make sense of it as she said, "Basilisk? I've heard of those, but I've never met one. And she's pretty clearly a gazelle shifter."

Bastian nodded. "The point is, we don't know exactly what she can do. We're not sure *she* knows what she can do. But you should be prepared."

"... not sure you can prepare him for her with a week of warnings," Jenny laughed.

Bastian's wry smile suggested he agreed. "You have to understand, too, that she's got none of the background you'd expect. She's never… been in a car, or a boat, or even seen a bicycle. She's never used a phone, or browsed the Internet. She's watched maybe six movies in her entire life, and almost no television. She doesn't understand commercials."

"She doesn't get any jokes that rely on modern culture," Jenny said wryly.

Conall's expression amply conveyed how many jokes he had planned to tell.

"She's never been in a city, or traveled anywhere off the island," Bastian said pointedly.

"I'm not sure she's ever worn shoes," Jenny added.

"She doesn't have ID," Bastian warned.

"She spent a few days as a gazelle just a few weeks ago when an earthquake frightened her." Jenny said.

It was Saina who finally said what they were all clearly thinking. "You can't just take her back to Boston with you."

"She'd be so frightened," Jenny agreed. "Crowds? Airports? Oh heavens, can you just imagine her shifting on the airplane when it took off?"

"I could get a private jet," Conall mused. "Bypass most of that. I have a lot of private property." But he could not picture the gazelle grazing on the groomed lawns of his family's land.

"What would she do there?" Bastian asked. "It might be *years* before she could handle being out with people who weren't shifters."

"She wouldn't have to," Conall said defensively. "She would be safe in my home and have everything she needed."

They all looked at him skeptically.

"Would you replace her old cage with a fancier one?" Bastian finally asked.

Conall's elk was outraged at the idea.

A shadow fell over him and Conall looked up to find a great hulking man with tattoos spilling out of his staff polo shirt towering above him.

"Lydia sent me," he said. "I'm…" His name could not have actually been Wrench.

Lydia had been the person with her work cut out for her. "Conall," he replied as curtly. "Is she ready early?"

"Hardly," certainly-not-Wrench said. "Lydia wanted to make sure someone had gotten *you* ready." He nodded at the others. "But I ain't gunna be able to add anything to what they can tell you."

"... n't think anyone can really prepare him for gazelle," Jenny was saying with a shake of her dark hair.

"Thank you all for the vote of confidence," Conall said dryly to no one in particular.

"One more thing." That was the tattooed man who definitely wasn't Wrench.

Conall waited for it.

"I used to hurt people for a living. I don't much like to do that no more, but know that I could, if something happened to gazelle."

"There's a big ocean out there a body could be lost in pretty easily," Bastian added with a cheerful smile.

And, they were back to threats of violence.

Conall honestly wasn't sure if these were serious.

CHAPTER 13

When Lydia's voice had grown rough from telling stories, Jenny and Saina arrived. Saina sang mesmerizing Christmas songs about snow and reindeer and Santa Claus.

Jenny brought snacks. It was dark out, and Gizelle gratefully ate pieces of cheese and circular brown crackers. She had not expected Lydia's work to take so long or make her so hungry.

Finally, Lydia told Gizelle, "You can get up now."

Gizelle barely could. She had been sitting so long that her feet tingled when she stood on them, and her fingers felt numb where she'd been gripping the arm of the chair too tightly. Lydia had turned on the lights at some point and when she led Gizelle to the corner with all the mirrors, Gizelle felt like she was in a spotlight on a stage.

It was like looking at someone else.

Lydia had washed and brushed through all of her hair, leaving it shining and glossy, and so silky that it didn't feel like Gizelle's head anymore. Then Lydia had trimmed it, leaving a pile of foot-long pieces all over the floor. And finally, she had braided it, with the sides pulled up to the top of her head. The braid, dramatically dark and light, swung down to her waist, with a short little swirl of soft hair at the end.

Gizelle's neck felt naked. Her scalp felt tender. Her balance was off, with the weight of her hair tugging her backwards.

She looked at her nails, all perfectly rounded and shining with color. She wriggled her toes and wrinkled her nose.

She looked around, and realized that Lydia, Saina, Jenny, and Laura were all staring at her, waiting.

"You made me look pretty," she said shyly. "Thank you."

They all clapped and broke into happy chatter.

Lydia brought her a red dress. "This one laces up the sides so we can make it fit you," the swan shifter told her as Gizelle shimmied out of her sundress, careful of the swinging braid.

"I won't shift in it," Gizelle promised. If she could sit through this, she'd be able to get through a dinner without panicking.

Probably.

"It's red like Christmas," she said dreamily, as Lydia laced up the dress. It felt different than her usual loose dresses or plain wraps. It hugged her thin form, making her think too hard about her skin where it touched fabric. *That* made her think about other people touching her skin.

She unexpectedly didn't think she'd mind if Conall did.

Her reflection blushed as she felt her cheeks heat, a phenomena that fascinated her.

She was trying to touch her own blush in the mirror, chasing it around the corners, when Lydia asked her, "Are you ready?"

Gizelle straightened, leaving her reflection with a flip of her new braid. "I'm ready," she said with confidence she only sort of felt.

"Breck's set you a table in a private corner. Chef's made you something you'll like," Jenny told her.

"If you need anything, you just have to raise your hand and ask for it," Laura reminded her.

"I'm ready," Gizelle repeated, less sure than ever.

It felt *big*.

It felt one step from terrifying.

She caught her breath starting to quicken and her eyes were already searching for an exit.

No.

She was going to do this. She wasn't going to shift. She wasn't going to be weird.

Well, not too weird.

She let Jenny take her hand and lead her down the white gravel path to the back entrance of the restaurant.

CHAPTER 14

Conall was at the restaurant at six, dressed in a suit and tie. His assistant had packed his clothing and every tie she had packed was a Christmas monstrosity. He was wearing the least objectionable, with muted maroon poinsettias all over it. He tried not wearing the tie, but the result was not what he'd hoped for.

At least he wouldn't have to look at it himself.

The waiter from lunch raised an eyebrow at his early arrival but didn't comment; his table was already prepared.

Fully half of the outside restaurant deck had been cleared for them. The other side was over-crowded with guests, clearly curious, but a barrier of chairless tables fenced them out quite effectively.

At the very end of the deck was a single table with two chairs, not too close to the railing.

Probably-not-Brick led him to the table, smirking mysteriously in return for every curious stare and probable-whisper that they got.

"Can I get you a drink?" the waiter offered.

Conall was sorely tempted, but shook his head. "Just water."

The ice in his water glass had melted and been replaced several times by the time seven came and went. Conall began to wonder if his gazelle was going to be coming after all. Possibly-Brick could only give him a shrug when he looked pointedly at his watch.

Conall ignored the continued stares from the far side of the restaurant and buried himself in work, answering emails on his phone until nearly eight, when his elk gave a snort for attention.

His mate stood in the employee entrance, the waiter smiling at her side as he gestured her towards the table.

Conall felt his heart catch in his throat at the sight of her.

She wasn't looking at the waiter, or at Conall.

She was looking at her feet.

Conall realized that they were bare, but not before he realized that she was the most stunning woman he had ever seen, and he had never wanted anything so much in his life.

In a graceful, effortless way, she was shifting in place like she was ready to bolt away at any given moment. With her hair pulled back away from her face, every perfect plane was exposed to the subdued restaurant lights. She had high, defined cheekbones, and a proud forehead over arched brows. She wasn't short, but she was very slight, with perfectly-shaped, lanky legs.

She was wearing a sleeveless red dress laced tight across her torso that flowed silkily to her knees, and her arms were long and slim, hands nervous at the asymmetric hem of her dress.

Then she looked up and spotted him.

The idea of someone freezing had always been an imaginative metaphor, but his mate actually seemed to; she was suddenly and abruptly utterly motionless, staring at him with wide, dark, unblinking eyes from across the restaurant.

He wasn't sure when she started moving, it was so incredibly slow and deliberate.

One foot padded in front of the other in a smooth, unbroken motion, and suddenly she was standing across the table from him.

"Hello," Conall breathed.

She blinked.

Was it the first time she had blinked since she first spotted him? Conall wasn't sure.

"Hello," she answered shyly.

Conall would have paid his entire sizable fortune to hear her voice, even for just that one word.

He considered standing politely while she sat, but something about the tension in her beautiful body, a slight shiver to her frame, suggested that staying seated was less likely to frighten her off.

"Will you join me?" he asked quietly.

She circled the chair, glancing at it suspiciously, then perched on it with her feet beneath her, cross-legged.

The waiter offered her the napkin from her setting and she spread it out in her own lap like a royal garment as he filled her water glass.

"I've never eaten in the restaurant," she confessed to Conall with a smile that crinkled her entire face as the waiter vanished.

It was a smile like the sun, and Conall felt the corners of his mouth turn up irresistibly. "I'm Conall," he said, and he offered his hand across the table.

The smile, and her entire body, froze again.

"I don't think I'm ready for that," she said frankly, looking him square in the eyes. He could see the conflict there; desire and fear and confusion.

Conall recalled his hand carefully. "You don't have to be," he assured her.

He stuffed his elk's protest down resolutely and picked up his water.

It was going to be an interesting dinner.

CHAPTER 15

Gizelle had never seen anyone as gorgeous and grim as her mate before.

Her *mate*.

Her gazelle gave a happy little caper.

He looked like longing and sadness and loss. Making him smile, even briefly, was a moment of triumph.

But then he wanted to shake her hand, like people sometimes did, and Gizelle wanted his touch so badly that she knew she would come undone if she got it.

"I don't think I'm ready for that," she confessed.

The shape of his mouth remained on his face like a mask but all the smile in his eyes vanished. "You don't have to be," he said, pulling his hand back so gently that it wasn't frightening.

"I'm Gizelle," she said, smoothing the edge of the tablecloth.

"I'm an Irish elk," Conall replied.

Gizelle blinked. "I'm a gazelle," she replied. She had been expecting his name, but perhaps he was aware that she already knew it.

He was looking at her with a confused expression, staring at her mouth.

Had she forgotten to look at him, or covered her face with her hair? Gizelle put a hand to her face to check and remembered that Lydia had put her hair back in a braid, which was why the breeze felt so prying.

"Er, your name is…?"

"Gizelle," she repeated uncertainly. Was she saying it wrong? It would be like her to say her own name wrong.

His confusion resolved into embarrassment. "Oh," he said. "Your name is Gizelle. A gazelle named Gizelle. That explains so much."

"Neal named me," Gizelle added, not sure how it explained anything.

"Who is Neal?" Conall asked.

Gizelle didn't want to talk about Neal. "Neal left," she said. "Do you know about Christmas?"

He blinked at her. "What about it?"

"Lydia was telling me about Christmas in Mexico." Gizelle tried to remember the stories the swan shifter had told. "About cakes with babies in them, and these things you hang up and hit." She was explaining it badly, so she hurried on. "And there are presents and… wiggy pudding…" that wasn't right. "It all sounds very exciting. Do you like Christmas?"

His beautiful brows were wrinkled up next to each other as he puzzled at her mouth and Gizelle very badly wanted to wrap her braid around her face and hide but reminded herself not to.

"I… I used to like Christmas," he finally answered when she could make her mouth stop talking.

"But you don't any more? Why not?"

She regretted the question as soon as she asked, because his face went so sad and cold and complicated.

"I used to like the music most of all," Conall said.

"And you can't hear it now," Gizelle realized out loud.

He winced, and she flinched.

"I'm sorry," she whispered.

She only recognized that she'd looked down when he echoed her, "I'm sorry, what?"

Everything about the situation made her want to bolt. She'd hurt him, and it made her feel terrible to the pit of her stomach. She wasn't doing a good job of remembering to look at him when she spoke. It would be *easier* to run.

"Gizelle?"

She looked up to find Breck holding two plates. "Oh, thank you," she said, because eating would give her something to do besides panic.

Breck served them both and refilled their glasses, then vanished again too soon.

Gizelle picked her fork up in what she hoped looked like a familiar fashion. She didn't use it often, but this was what people were supposed to use, so she was going to.

Chef had made a vegetable omelet, to her delight. Something easy to cut, not too messy. It had less cheese than she considered ideal, but that would hopefully keep her from getting confused by ridiculous strings of it. Maybe she could make it through without embarrassing herself or saying anything else wrong.

Conversation was problematic.

"Your chef is good," Conall said approvingly after only a few bites.

"He sings," Gizelle said cheerfully, before she remembered that singing was music and would make him remember what he'd lost again.

They ate in silence for a while and Gizelle had to stop herself several times from losing track of eating to trace paths in the condensation on her glass.

"You know we don't have to do this, right?" Conall said.

Gizelle could think of too many things they might not have to do. "What do you mean?" she asked, hating that she had to.

"Dinner. Dating. Conversation by candlelight." He put his fork down. "Whatever conventions you think you might need to do, you don't have to. We could go somewhere you'd be more comfortable, do something different."

"Oh," Gizelle said thoughtfully. "Oh! I know where we can go!"

CHAPTER 16

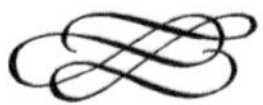

Conall hated how uncomfortable she looked and when her face brightened at the idea of somewhere else to go, he took his napkin from his lap and was prepared to follow her anywhere. He wasn't expecting her to leap to her feet and lean over the table to gaze into his eyes.

He definitely wasn't prepared for the fall.

But the landing wasn't problematic; he was simply standing, disoriented, in a bright field of waist-high grass.

This is unexpected, his elk said, and Conall turned to find his animal companion at his side.

I'm not sure what is happening, he confessed, and he turned again to find Gizelle standing next to him, her gazelle bouncing a little in place beyond her.

This is my safe place, she said proudly. *I can always run here.*

He could hear her, in some bizarre way, but it wasn't really hearing.

Just like he could touch her, when she offered him her hand, but it wasn't really touching.

Her hair was loose, smooth and glossy, and she was standing straight.

Where are we? Conall asked. His words came echoing back.

He had forgotten all about echoes, he realized with a pang.

I made this, Gizelle said proudly. *Only I can open the door.*

Conall looked around in bewilderment. It stretched impossibly in every direction and the sky was black and smooth despite the illumination, without sun or sky or stars. *Where does it go?*

It doesn't go anywhere, Gizelle said. *It goes everywhere. I'll show you.*

Then she was pulling him into a laughing run.

It was like nothing Conall had ever done. There was no effort to it, even when his elk was running flat out beside him, snorting happily. The gazelle frolicked joyfully before them and the horizon never changed.

And finally, Gizelle stopped running and tackled him, rolling him down into the whispery grass.

She was laughing, her whole face and all her limbs more relaxed than Conall had yet seen. He caught her in his arms and wanted badly to kiss her, but it was different than his impulse to kiss her in the other world. There were no demands of his body here, only the curiosity to see what she would do, and the cerebral desire to make her smile and laugh forever.

But he wasn't sure how this would translate back to where they were sitting in the restaurant, and what qualified as consent in imaginary worlds, so he held himself back and she gave a sigh of something he couldn't pin down.

They sat up and his elk trotted over and put his nose in Gizelle's hair, snuffling.

She looked fearlessly up at his great bulk and rubbed his velvety face. *You are very beautiful*, she told him.

Thank you, his elk said back, enormously pleased. Conall was never going to hear the end of his satisfaction with himself now.

The gazelle tossed her long, spiral horns and danced.

You're lovely, Conall told her honestly, lest she feel left out. And she *was* a lovely gazelle, with long, graceful legs and large, expressive ears framing curving, spiraled horns.

The gazelle dipped her head in acknowledgment.

She doesn't speak, Gizelle said, and the gazelle came over and touched noses with her affectionately.

At all? Conall asked. *Or just to other people?*

She has always been silent, Gizelle explained.

You could take a lesson, Conall told his elk wryly.

It was distinctly odd to see his elk flatten his ears and toss his head, not just know that he was doing so.

I like it, Gizelle said, scratching behind the gazelle's ears and laying her forehead to hers. *There's usually too much noise and we know each other better than words.*

How long have we been here? Conall asked. *Does time pass here like it does back there?*

It depends on how wide I leave the door open, Gizelle said, as if it were perfectly logical.

Of course, Conall said, mystified.

Gizelle gazed up, an unexpected expression of dread creeping onto her face.

There's rain coming, she said.

Conall looked up. Above them, it was featureless and black. No stars. No clouds. *How can you tell?* he asked.

Gizelle ignored him. *There's rain coming*, she repeated. *A rain of blood. And the earth splitting and the cage breaking.*

Gizelle?

She looked at him, but it didn't seem like her eyes. *Everything will come undone*, she cried. *It will be* ***my*** *fault!*

Then he was blinking back at the restaurant as couldn't-be-Brick was snapping fingers in front of his face.

Gizelle was gone.

"What…?" He was half-standing, crouched at the table as if he'd been right in the middle of standing. His muscles ached.

"That probably could have gone better," the waiter said with a shrug, gathering up the uneaten food and dishes.

Conall finished standing. "How long?" he had to ask, still feeling dazed.

"Just a few minutes," the waiter said with a shake of his head. "But that was long enough, I guess."

Conall recognized the dark red pools of material on the floor past Gizelle's chair as the parts of her dress.

CHAPTER 17

Gizelle ran and ran and ran until her sides were heaving and the lights of the resort were distant twinkles behind her, and kept running until the jungle closed around her.

Finally, she shifted back onto trembling human legs, staggered a few steps, and sank down into the moss to weep.

She'd made a mistake in taking Conall to her safe place. All she had done was prove what an abnormality she was.

She was such a joke as a human.

She was foolish and awkward and ugly and odd and she couldn't imagine anyone ever loving her.

It hadn't mattered so much before… before Conall.

She hadn't wanted to be loved before she'd seen him and realized what love might be.

He was so beautiful and proud, and he moved so easily through the world that baffled her.

She wanted him so badly that it hurt, deep in her belly. She ached for his touch and was terrified of it. She could feel all the hollow places inside that she wanted to let him into, and she was afraid she would crack apart if she tried to open to him.

And to top it all off, she had probably destroyed Lydia's pretty dress when she ran away.

For some reason, that made her want to cry harder than ever, the hurt pressing against the inside of her eyes, and she was grateful when she felt her gazelle reach out to enfold her.

Wordlessly, the graceful animal offered her distance.

Protection.

Escape.

She didn't have to be Gizelle, she could just *be*.

For now, it was easiest just to run.

CHAPTER 18

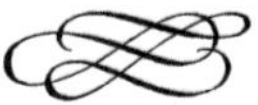

Conall woke, surprised that he'd slept at all.

He didn't feel reste, and he could feel his elk pacing in his head, full of unrelieved need and unhappiness.

He couldn't stop remembering Gizelle: her slight, sweet figure in that alluring red dress. Her expressive mouth. Her ancient, dark eyes, framed in those long lashes. Her clever fingers tracing patterns in the condensation on her glass.

He groaned, willing his body to stop wanting her. He wondered how cold the showers here got.

She's here, his elk breathed, suddenly aware, and Conall rolled over to find Gizelle sitting cross-legged on his tall wardrobe.

"Gizelle," he said, strangled, as he sat up and pulled a decorative pillow into his lap.

"You were sleeping," she said matter-of-factly.

"Most people do," Conall said wryly, and after he said it, he wondered if she did.

"Did you dream?" she asked.

Did it count as dreaming that he couldn't stop thinking about her, even while he was sleeping?

"I don't remember."

She nodded sagely. "There is a lot I don't remember," she said. "But I always remember not remembering. I always remember the place with no sky."

Conall found himself having to watch her mouth carefully. Half of lip-reading was guessing what someone was going to say and there was no predicting where Gizelle would go next.

"Have you had breakfast?" he asked, not sure how to answer.

"I grazed," Gizelle said carelessly. "I wanted to see where you lived." She ducked her head then, and said something Conall couldn't see.

"I couldn't see that," he said, hating the admission.

She looked up in alarm. "I'm sorry! I just…" she blushed, but kept her chin up, clearly with effort. "I just thought maybe I'd show you where I lived."

Her flush was the most adorable thing Conall had ever seen, and his elk persisted in finding it erotic and wondering if he would be able to make her flush like that while lying on the sheets beneath him.

This wasn't helping his efforts to not need a pillow in his lap.

"I'd like that," he said grimly.

To his alarm, Gizelle seemed to think that meant now and she acrobatically vaulted from the wardrobe, plummeting to the floor to land in a crouch.

Her hair was still braided but was starting to fray, with loose strands everywhere. She brushed it back and sprang to her feet. "It's not far," she promised, skirting away from the bed. She clearly still wasn't ready to be touched.

"I, er, can't yet," Conall said, his voice breaking for the first time since puberty. He didn't have to hear it to know, and he clutched the pillow closer.

Gizelle's puzzled gaze, almost hurt, got him partway there.

Thinking about music, about never hearing the songs that he'd loved, that nearly did it.

Realizing that he would never be able to hear the sounds he

longed to make her utter was better than the coldest shower he'd ever taken.

He rolled out of bed and dressed swiftly. "I would love to see it," he said sincerely.

CHAPTER 19

Gizelle scouted ahead of Conall to her cottage. "Scarlet gave this to me," she told him, then remembered that he wouldn't be able to hear her that way. She turned backwards and repeated herself.

Continuing to walk backwards, confident of her path, she added, "Graham let the plants grow up, so no guests will accidentally come see me."

They were at the very edge of the resort, where the jungle whispered its desire to spread roots and trail vines in to take it over again. It wouldn't, of course. It respected the resort boundaries that Scarlet enforced. But here, the white gravel path was allowed to overgrow and Gizelle showed Conall where to duck under just the right branches.

He was bigger than she was, *wonderfully* bigger, and it was a tight squeeze, but he didn't complain, following her willingly to her house.

It was one of the little cottages, not a big one like his, but it still had a pretty deck and shining windows.

Conall started to go to the door, but Gizelle stopped him. "I never go in," she said. "It's too echoing inside. Too much space. And the door shuts too tightly."

Instead, she led him around back to the outside shower. It was under the eaves of the house, walled on three sides, with a wide door that she never shut.

Conall did not fit in it very well, especially since he was trying very hard not to accidentally touch her. When she sat down, he sat opposite from her. He had very nice pants that probably weren't good for sitting in the dirt, but he didn't complain.

"This is where I come when it's too noisy for me but not noisy enough for my gazelle," she told him.

She was glad that Conall didn't ask her to explain that. He just nodded sagely. Maybe his elk was the same way, she thought hopefully.

She showed him her treasures; the brochures she picked up from the lawn, and the sea shells that guests sometimes left near the pool. She rarely went to the beach herself—the sand was too soft to run in.

There was a flower she had picked and hidden from Graham. It was wilted now, but still velvety soft. Scarlet had given her a book, but that was before Gizelle had known that water was bad for books; it was now sadly wrinkled and some of the ink had run.

Scarlet hadn't scolded her, but she also hadn't let Gizelle take any more books.

Gizelle put everything on the ground between them, not wanting to accidentally brush Conall's fingers. If he touched her, she wasn't sure what would happen, but she knew that just the idea of it made her breathe harder, like she did before panic choked her and she had to run.

And she didn't *want* to run.

Conall treated everything with grave admiration, though Gizelle knew that some of it was worthless.

"This is my favorite thing," she said, putting her last treasure between them.

"What is it?" Conall asked, picking it up. It was a twisted and broken bar of steel with dangling electrical wires, bent like it had been torn with a great force.

"It was the lock on Neal's cage. He gave it to me," Gizelle told him, remembering.

She didn't want to remember that.

Neal had *left*.

"No one will ever put you in a cage again," Conall said, and he said it like Neal had, fiercely.

Gizelle realized that she had backed up against the shower wall. "Give it back," she said faintly, but he was looking at the lock, not at her.

He didn't hear her, she told herself. It wasn't that he was ignoring her. He wouldn't ignore her. He wouldn't leave her.

Her gazelle was nuzzling in her ear, trying to calm her, but panic was rising, as sure as strangers, and everything whispered.

She saw an opportunity as he turned the lock in his hands, to safely snatch it away. For an awful moment, he instinctively held it, and she had to tug at it and she could almost feel his fingers, they were so close.

Then he opened his hand and the lock was hers again and she could retreat to her side of the shower.

"No one will ever hurt you again," Conall repeated.

It was better, with the heavy weight of the lock in her hand. Gizelle could catch her breath again, like she had roots and could drink the earth once more. "This is the heart of my hoard." She tucked it back away underneath the shower shelf.

"You're… a dragon?" Conall looked understandably confused.

Gizelle shook her head. "No. But if I were, this would be it."

She got to her feet. "Come on, I've shown you my hoard. Now, the rest of the island."

CHAPTER 20

Conall at several points wondered if Gizelle honestly meant the *entire* island.

The tour she led him on was a completely different experience than prowling the resort the first evening. They didn't spend any time at all at the sites labeled on the brochure, and very little time on the marked paths. One of their routes went right out into the jungle, over tangled roots and following no sort of trail that Conall could identify whatsoever.

They even hiked along the tree-tangled ridge of the island to the abandoned compound on the other end, staying to the edge of the overgrown lawn.

"That is where the cages are," Gizelle said calmly. "I come visit sometimes." But she didn't offer to show them to Conall and he didn't know if he should ask to see them. "I don't eat the grass here," she said, and then they turned and hiked back through the jungle to the resort along a completely different route.

"I don't like the beach," she said, leading him to one of the lawns that overlooked it. She had to repeat herself when she remembered to look at him while she spoke. "The sand is too hard to run in. But the grass here is delicious. Graham says it has to do with the salt water spray and the sun that it gets and the kind of soil. He says even less than you do." She added that last with a thoughtful look. "Did losing your hearing make you talk less?"

She was still better at keeping her face in view when she spoke than many of Conall's friends had been after months of reminders.

They had felt so awkward about interacting with him that after a few failed attempts at staying in contact, Conall hadn't bothered. "I'll call you," they always ended a conversation, forgetting that a phone call was useless.

Conall had to laugh and he wondered if it sounded as humorless as it felt. "I guess it did," he said honestly. "I wasn't what you'd call chatty before the accident, but since it happened, talking can be a challenge. People don't remember to look at me, and I can't tell what I sound like. It's easier being quiet."

"I think you sound nice," Gizelle said swiftly. "You have… sort of a fuzzy voice. Like a cat."

Conall decided to take that as a compliment. "Thank you?"

"We don't have any cats here, unless you count Travis and Graham and" (undoubtedly-not-) "Wrench and" (probably-not-) "Brick. No *domestic* cats. Except sometimes guests, but you aren't supposed to pet the guests." She sounded wistful.

That surprised a real laugh out of him, and Gizelle smiled slowly in reply. "I like it when you laugh," she said.

"Then I shall endeavor to laugh as often as possible," Conall told her gravely.

She almost laughed herself then and leaned so close that Conall thought she was finally going to touch him, but she didn't quite.

Then she was turning away, possibly saying something that Conall couldn't hear.

He followed her, sorely tempted to catch her swinging braid and use it to pull her into an embrace.

From that lawn, they went to another at the exact opposite end of the resort by the most circuitous route. This one was outside the resort gates; soft groomed mounds of grass rose from the jungle to meet the stone wall.

They contemplated the Shifting Sands Resort sign.

Gizelle traced one of the esses, then turned to him and said, "I like letters. I can't wait to learn to read."

Reading would certainly simplify her life. Or possibly complicate it, given the strange rabbit-hole that was the Internet.

"Have you thought about what you want to do next?" Conall had to ask, thinking about the warning Bastian and the mermaid had given him. He couldn't imagine Gizelle in Boston, any more than they could.

She looked at him, big eyes under long innocent eyelashes. "After I learn to read?"

"With your life. Forever."

She will be with us forever, his elk said confidently.

But where did that put *them*?

Her eyelashes might be innocent, but Gizelle's eyes were fathomless and ancient. "Forever is an arbitrary point in time," she said grimly. "And I've already been *there*."

Conall had no answer for that.

Fortunately, she continued, voice light again. "I would like to be useful," she said. "I want to do something that helps Scarlet the way she's helped me. I tried helping at the bar but I dropped all my glasses and bottles. And Chef won't let me help in the kitchen."

"What do you want to do?" Conall pressed. "For yourself. What's something that you like to do?"

Gizelle blinked at him, as if it had never occurred to her before. She was close enough that Conall could have touched her without trying. It took conscious effort to keep from reaching out to her every few moments, to brush the loose hair back from her face, or just to see if her skin was as warm in the sunlight as it looked.

"I like to run," she said slowly. "And I like it when Scarlet reads to me, so I think I will like reading." Her eyes widened with a sudden thought. "Will *you* read to me?" she begged.

At that moment, Conall would have read her the Boston phonebook in one sitting. "Anything you'd like."

Gizelle pointed at the sign.

"Shifting Sands Resort."

She pointed at the smaller sign.

"Authorized Guests Only. No Predation."

Gizelle all but dragged him back down into the resort, dancing ahead of him and gesturing enthusiastically every time he paused. They stopped at every sign. Some of them she had memorized, mouthing along with him.

She made him read the entire staff bulletin board, including notes about shifts in the restaurant that referenced someone named Breck who was surely the waiter-who-wasn't-Brick and repair notes for Travis and Wrench, confirming that as an unexpected name. Graham must be the gardener with the machete.

"I want my name to be up there," Gizelle said, once Conall had puzzled through all the handwritten comments and baffling assignments.

"You don't want to go somewhere else someday?"

Gizelle had to repeat her reply, because she glanced away the first time. "Where else is there?"

"The whole world out there," Conall said. "Paris, maybe? America? Africa? Great Britain?"

"Boston," she said flatly. "You want to know if I'd go to Boston."

Conall rapidly re-evaluated her. Again.

"I have a business there," he told her. "An… important business." But even as he said as much, he had to wonder.

He had poured himself into his business when his music career came to a crashing halt. He'd built it from a niche novelty business into a global chain, expanded it into clothing, and diversified it overseas. *Time* had run a cover article on him that hung, framed, in his office. He hadn't read the article after the lengthy interview, but he knew it had lingered poignantly over his disability and his shattered promise as a musician.

Lemonade from lemons, everyone praised him. The elk antlers that twisted into Celtic knots framing a guitar was one of the most respected logos in the modern high end instrument and supply industry.

Now he was thinking about throwing it all away to live on a

tropical island in the middle of nowhere, filled with the strangest people he had ever met, for a gorgeous wild woman who wouldn't even let him touch her.

And he was *seriously* considering it.

CHAPTER 21

Gizelle looked at Conall in consternation.

Scarlet had shown her photographs of Boston. It was big, and busy, and full of people and buildings and streets and she didn't have to be told that it would be loud.

"Scarlet doesn't even think I should go to the mainland," Gizelle tried to explain. "I don't *want* to go to the mainland." Was Boston on the mainland or was it on another island? She had looked at maps with Travis, as he tried to explain how Alaska wasn't an island even though it was shown surrounded by water. Was Boston like that?

She wondered if she *could* go to Boston. She wanted to follow Conall, but the whole idea of a city made the urge to flee rise in her throat.

She didn't realize she was shaking until Conall reached for her and she jumped back, just out of his reach. His hand fell back to his side.

"I'm not asking you to come to Boston," he said firmly.

"Not now, or not ever?" Gizelle asked suspiciously.

He was silent with consternation.

He didn't know what he wanted, Gizelle realized with unexpected clarity.

He was clearly drawn to her, the same, strange, gut-deep way that she couldn't stop thinking about him, and her gazelle couldn't stop sighing over him.

But he couldn't want the rest of her, like she couldn't want the Boston and business that he came with.

She couldn't bear the idea of traveling over the ocean, or seeing a city, or leaving the only safe place she knew in the world.

He could clearly not bear the idea of leaving his business, and Gizelle knew she was nothing to look at, and that her broken mind would test any bond.

What must he look at her and think?

She was a clumsy disaster, with no memories, no social graces. She looked up at the staff announcement board without seeing it. She couldn't even *read.*

"Gizelle…"

Even his voice was perfect.

She had to look at him, Gizelle reminded herself. Otherwise, he wouldn't understand her.

But when she looked at him, he was so handsome and confusing that all her words got tangled up together and she didn't have anything to say.

She screwed her eyes shut and tried to think. What had everyone else done when they met their mates? Neal led Mary off for a romantic hike in the rain. Tex took Laura to the mainland to visit the market. Travis taught Jenny build a deck. Bastian showed Saina his hoard. Wrench arranged a picnic on the beach.

Gizelle hated the beach.

But she didn't know what else to offer. "Do you want to have a picnic on the beach?" she blurted.

She opened her eyes to find Conall staring. "A picnic?" he said helplessly.

Now she was stuck with it. "It's food, you take it in a basket," she explained. "Like for lunch. And you sit on the beach and eat it. I guess." She had never done it herself.

"That sounds nice," Conall agreed, dashing her hopes that he'd refuse and come up with something better.

"I'll get the basket," Gizelle offered. "You get the beach."

She turned and escaped, wondering what on earth she'd gotten herself into this time.

CHAPTER 22

Conall realized that there was a wry half-smile on his mouth when actually-Wrench wandered by to check the board and he was still standing at it bemusedly.

He pulled his face into a more familiar frown at Wrench's glower, and went off to 'get the beach,' as directed.

Gizelle was… so much. She was so much person packed into her small frame. She was shy, and she was excited, and she was curious. She badly wanted to be helpful and when she was uncertain, she was adorable, and when she was passionate, her enthusiasm and focus were entirely complete.

Conall had never met anyone as unpredictable, or anyone half as fascinating.

It wasn't just that she was beautiful—which she undeniably was—it was that she was a whole world in a tiny bottle.

Dialed up to eleven, his mother used to say. But she had said it about Conall and he couldn't hold a candle to the intensity in Gizelle.

He desperately wanted to know if that intensity translated to the bedroom, but he knew he had to continue being patient. They'd gotten this far, they'd get the rest of the way. Eventually.

Conall paused at the gate to his cottage as he realized that he was considering it a done thing.

He was wholly prepared to set the business adrift and stay here to bask in the golden presence of the strange, wild woman who had captured his own heart along with his elk's. He was ready to wait as long as it took her to accept him, even if that was weeks or months of awkward courtship.

It would make a fine Christmas present, his elk mused.

I hate Christmas, Conall replied out of habit.

There was a neat pile of fabric on the table just inside his cottage door. Conall unfolded it curiously to find a sundress, definitely not in his size.

There was a new bowl on his bedside table as well, overflowing in condoms. There was a second stash in the bathroom.

The staff, at least, had some optimism about this whole complicated affair.

He found two over-sized beach towels in a cabinet and went to 'get the beach.'

CHAPTER 23

Chef was singing in the kitchen.

It was one of the Christmas songs that Saina had sung the day before, when Lydia was taming her hair.

Could I sing? Gizelle wondered. She moved her mouth when Chef got to a chorus she recognized, but she wasn't brave enough to make the sounds.

"What are you up to, buttercup?" Breck asked, suddenly appearing around one of the counters with a tray of dirty dishes. "Can I get you something from the buffet?"

Sometimes, when she wasn't feeling brave enough to go out into the restaurant, Breck would get her a plate of her favorite food and bring it to her behind the restaurant, or out to one of the picnic benches by the lawns she liked.

"Do you have a basket?" Gizelle asked. "We're going to have a picnic on the beach. Me and Conall." Probably that was unnecessary to explain.

"You're moving right along," Breck said approvingly. "You going to let him kiss you?"

"Oh," Gizelle said, stunned by the idea of it.

Conall's mouth, on hers. His lips, touching hers. She was suddenly weak-legged and too hot.

"Don't look like that," Breck teased her kindly. "He's a gentleman. He'll wait for you to wave him over. I'll pack you a lunch you can feed each other. Nothing breakable, so Bastian won't grouse about messing up his beach."

"Yes, please," Gizelle said faintly.

She was still imagining what Conall's lips might feel like when Breck returned with the heavy picnic basket.

"Too heavy?" Breck asked, putting it carefully into her hands.

"Of course not," Gizelle scoffed. Whatever else she was, she was not weak. Even if her knees did insist on feeling a little insufficient when she thought about Conall's mouth.

"Go get him," Breck told her with a wink and a grin.

Gizelle smiled cautiously back, but the leopard shifter was already hurrying back to his duties. She had a moment of envy—not just because he was so easy about things that were so hard for her, but because he was useful.

She wanted to feel useful.

CHAPTER 24

The sun on the beach was intense. Most of the resort guests had retreated to the pool deck, or the shade on their own cottage porches. Only a few were swimming in the ocean, or using the paddleboards, under Bastian's watchful eyes.

Conall chose a spot at the far edge of the crescent, spread out his towels, and stabbed one of the provided umbrellas into the sand. He was tilting it to provide the best shade when he spotted Gizelle coming down the steps and had to suck in his breath.

She walked like a song, every step deliberate and beautiful. When she got down to the hot sand, her pace quickened and she danced to him. The hair that had frayed from her neglected braid glowed around her face, silver and dark, and her sundress molded to her slight curves in the breeze from the water.

"All those lawns made me hungry," she said when she got to him.

Conall took the basket and was surprised by the weight; she had carried it so easily. Gizelle circled the towels and carefully sat on one corner, barely in the shade of the umbrella. She tried in vain to brush off all of the sand that had crept onto it.

Conall tucked the basket into the best part of the shade and offered Gizelle a bottle of water out of it. She took it, but waited and watched as Conall opened his own and drank from it, carefully copying his every gesture.

"A sandwich?" Conall offered, inspecting the contents of the basket. Most of the weight was water and an ice pack to keep it cool, but there were also slices of watermelon and strawberries, and cold noodle salad and kettle chips.

"Yes, please," Gizelle said, eyes shyly down.

Thin slices of cheese and a generous spread of hummus were garnished with lettuce and tomatoes so fresh Conall would have put money on the fact they'd been grown on the island. The bread, too, was fresh: the perfect combination of chewy and light, with a hearty crust.

Watching Gizelle eat was more fun than even enjoying his own food was—and he had worked up quite an appetite from their zig-zag tour of the island. He couldn't understand a single thing she tried to say around her mouthfuls of food and settled for nodding and smiling with a shrug until they'd finished.

He could imagine the contented sigh that she gave, washing down the last bites with her water.

She offered him something from the basket, but her face was tilted down, so Conall couldn't tell what it was. The slice of watermelon that emerged answered that question.

"Sure," he said, but she startled back when he reached for it, and it fell to the sand.

He couldn't hear her exclamation of dismay or apology, but could guess it from her shoulders and her hasty scramble to pick it up.

She tried in vain to brush the sand away, face scrunched in consternation.

"Don't worry about it," Conall tried to assure her, but she continued to worry at the melon. "There's more," he told her. "It's just something that happens on beach picnics."

She didn't look entirely like she believed him, but she dropped the sandy melon into the empty sandwich wrapper that Conall carefully held out for her.

They sat awkwardly a moment, Conall trying to watch her face without staring in case she spoke, Gizelle trying again to brush the inevitable sand from the towel she was sitting on.

Finally, she looked up. "You're wondering what on earth to talk about now, since I know nothing about politics and the weather here is always lovely."

Since that was exactly what Conall had been doing, he had to laugh.

His laugh made Gizelle smile hopefully and he vowed again to do it as much as possible.

"Will you tell me about Boston?" she asked, chin lifted so he could easily see her mouth, but eyes down shyly.

Conall leaned back on his elbows. "Boston is on the ocean," he started. "But it's nothing like this ocean. It's cold water, and busy docks, and city."

"What's a city like?" Gizelle asked.

"Crowded," Conall said, feeling apologetic. "Giant buildings taller than any tree all around so that there isn't much sunlight. Lots of traffic, and people."

Gizelle shuddered. "Why would anyone want to live that way?"

"It has its points," Conall defended. "The culture! There are museums and art galleries and gourmet food. And of course the… music." Once he had started the sentence, he didn't know another way to end it.

"You can't hear the music," Gizelle pointed out. She realized the thoughtlessness of her statement at once and her eyes went large. She bit her lip. "I'm sorry."

"Don't be," Conall said grimly. "But other people can still enjoy it. Boston has some renowned orchestras."

"Did you go to school in Boston?" Gizelle asked desperately.

Conall tried not to wince and failed. "I went to school in New York," he said gently. "Have you heard of Juilliard?"

She shook her head, face brightening until he went on.

"It's probably the most famous school for music in the world. I was in my last year when… I lost my hearing."

"You couldn't finish," Gizelle guessed reluctantly.

Conall laughed humorlessly and it didn't have nearly the effect that his previous laugh had; Gizelle flinched.

"I did, actually," he explained. "I took a semester off to learn sign language and lip reading and came back to complete a degree in composition. The faculty..." *felt sorry for me*, he didn't say. "They were flexible about the application of my previous credits."

"Composition," Gizelle said thoughtfully. "You *made up* music that you couldn't hear?"

"I could play it, too," Conall said. "I performed a guitar concerto for my final presentation. I could feel the vibrations to keep me in time, and the rest is just finger memory and… trust."

The smile he'd been trying to keep on his face felt brittle. "I got a Grawemeyer award for that piece," he said as lightly as he could.

Gizelle was looking at him with sorrow and guilt and confusion, tangling the end of her braid in her hands, but Conall didn't want any of those things.

"It's a big deal," he felt obligated to explain. "An important prize in the music industry." And he'd gotten it out of *pity*.

"I'm… this was a terrible idea." Gizelle abruptly stood. "I'm not good at this. And I *hate* the beach. I'm *sorry*."

Conall, watching her flee across the hot sand, wondered if he should count it a victory that she hadn't shifted before she ran away this time.

He lay back in the sand, feeling defeated. He knew this was his own fault. He was terrible company. And tragedy did not make good courtship.

Stop feeling sorry for yourself, his elk scolded him. *Get up! Pursue her!*

Conall remained stubbornly lying in the sand. *And scare her further away? What would we do if we caught her? Put her in a cage?*

She wants to be caught, his elk insisted.

Not by me, Conall was dismally sure.

CHAPTER 25

Gizelle looked at her feet critically.

The nail polish that Laura had put on was starting to chip. She had three beautiful, red-tipped toes and four that were only half red, and the rest only had tiny flecks of color.

Her fingernails were no better.

She could at least scrape some of the flecks away, so they were all the same color again, and she had done so with one entire hand when the door behind her opened.

"What are you doing out here?" Conall asked, as he settled on the opposite side of the step from her. He was so gorgeous in the sunrise, all gold like a lion, and his clothes were always so fine. Gizelle desperately wanted to see if his skin was as soft and velvety as it looked and it made her breath come quickly just thinking about it.

"Jenny reminded me that I shouldn't go into people's rooms without asking," Gizelle explained.

"It's… generally polite not to."

Gizelle looked carefully at his face. He spoke so *neutrally*. Was he saying that she shouldn't have come in yesterday? He was squinting into the sun at her, so it was hard to tell what he was thinking.

"I could have knocked!" Gizelle realized. Then her face fell. "But you wouldn't be able to hear it."

"How long have you been here?" Conall asked.

Gizelle looked up. "The sky is always changing," she said. "I can never tell."

"Do you drink coffee?" Conall asked, running a hand through his ruffled dark hair. "Probably not," he answered himself.

"I could try," Gizelle offered.

He smiled at that, a slow, tired smile. "You are so beautiful," he said unexpectedly.

"I am?" The words made Gizelle feel unexpectedly warm at the bottom of her belly, and all the way to her toes. That reminded her, "My nail polish is chipping."

"I don't care," Conall said, and Gizelle had to believe him. He wasn't looking at her fingers or toes, but at her face, like he was trying to memorize it.

"Tex has a coffee maker behind the bar," Gizelle whispered, because it was not where guests were supposed to get coffee in the morning. Then she remembered that it didn't matter how loudly she spoke and felt foolish.

"That is exactly what I need," Conall said agreeably.

He stood and offered a hand to help Gizelle up, but she didn't notice it until she had already bounced to her feet.

She wished she had seen it earlier, because she might have actually taken it this time. She thought about how his hand might feel in hers all the way to the bar.

CHAPTER 26

As advertised, Tex did indeed have a single-serve coffee maker tucked away behind the empty bar. Conall, after only a moment of hesitation, made himself a cup of the strongest option, black. He offered Gizelle a sip, but she took one cautious sniff and shook her head.

"That smells like it will wake you up," she said, sitting cross-legged on the floor behind the bar. "But I don't want to be more awake than this."

Conall slid down to sit across from her, cradling the hot cup in his hands.

"What do you want to do today?" he asked.

"Do you like to play backgammon?" Gizelle asked.

"Yes, well enough," Conall said, but before he had finished speaking, Gizelle was scrambling up and gone in a flash of bare legs and bright sarong.

Before he had decided if he needed to stand up, or what to do with his coffee, Gizelle was back, a wooden box in her hands. "Breck taught me how to play," she said eagerly, opening the game between them. "I'll be black."

She deftly set up the pieces and placed dice across the board for Conall. There were no dice cups.

He tossed a die onto the board to roll for first play and Gizelle pushed back into the liquor cabinet behind her, hands over her ears.

"Too loud?" Conall asked in concern.

"Too sharp a sound," Gizelle said, lowering her hands. "It's all triangular and red. We usually roll onto a towel." She crawled over to a drawer—her body tantalizingly close—where she found a bar towel and unfolded it next to the board.

Conall wondered if she had some form of synesthesia, or if she just spoke creatively. He rolled the die again and she won the first move.

She played better than Conall expected, making clever moves and not hesitating to hit him when the opportunity presented itself. He began by playing generously, but regretted it as she swept her pieces from the board while he was still not fully on his home board.

"You weren't even trying," she scolded him. "You thought I couldn't really play!"

"I… wanted you to have fun," Conall said, abashed.

Dark eyes met his, solemn and sorrowed. "I can have fun losing," she assured him.

"Give me another chance," Conall challenged, stung with guilt. "I won't let you win again."

Gizelle's face brightened with a slow smile. "You may not have a choice," she taunted him, laying out the pieces again.

This game was far more even and both of them spent many frustrating rolls trying to get their checkers off the center bar. Conall won by just a few pieces; they were both laughing and alternating curses and praise at their dice at the end.

Gizelle showed Conall where Tex kept the nut mix when his stomach growled in hunger, and they snacked and played a third game, which she took handily despite Conall's best efforts.

It would have been even more fun if Conall hadn't been fighting his urge to kiss her. Several times, reaching for dice, their hands almost touched, and Conall found himself watching her mouth when she concentrated, longing for its taste.

Was her glance up through her eyelashes an innocent look, or an invitation? Did she thoughtfully lick her lips just a little more slowly than she needed to? The sarong she was wearing showed more leg than her previous dresses; was it on purpose?

He wanted her to laugh like this forever and was unwilling to risk the brief easy companionship they had at the moment to test their boundaries, but he wanted her so badly.

"Gizelle," he started, as she put the pieces back into the box, and he put out his hand to her, palm up. "Good game," he said as lightly as he could.

She froze momentarily, checkers still in one hand, and then looked between his face and his hand.

Triumph started to bloom in Conall's chest as she slowly reached for the offered hand with her own empty hand.

Then she startled, snatching her hand back. All of her attention riveted to Tex, who had just appeared around the corner of the bar and clearly said something.

Conall could cheerfully have thrown the board at the bartender, and was able to follow none of the conversation that then occurred; it was too fast, not facing him, and his elk was groaning and stomping in frustration.

Then Gizelle was scampering away as if she'd forgotten him entirely and he was sitting alone with a backgammon board missing a third of its checkers, hiding behind the bar like a boy playing hooky from school.

He swept the remaining pieces carelessly into the board and snapped it shut, rising to find Tex watching him. The bartender looked amused, and worse, pitying.

"Sorry to interrupt," the cowboy said. "Scarlet asked me to see if Gizelle wanted to do some reading."

Conall found the games shelf that the backgammon board had clearly come from and returned it to the empty space.

"Can I get you a drink?" Tex offered when Conall turned briefly back.

"It's a little early for that," Conall declined crossly. His elk firmly reminded him of his manners. "Thanks anyway."

Tex shrugged. "We're on island time. No one will judge."

"I'm paying a fairly astronomical amount of money for meals I keep missing," Conall said with a stiff smile. "I think I'll go try to catch one of them."

Tex tipped his hat to Conall. "Good call. Chef's food is not to be squandered." He paused and then added, "You shouldn't feel discouraged. She's already easier with you than with people she's known for months. We're all actually really impressed."

Without tone to telegraph unspoken things, Conall's sense for truth had dampened into something unreliable.

But something uncoiled in his chest anyway.

Something suspiciously like hope.

CHAPTER 27

Gizelle's reading lesson with Scarlet was a disaster. She arrived to realize that she was still holding the checkers from the backgammon game in one hand, and couldn't concentrate on anything that Scarlet said or read.

She wished that she'd taken Conall's hand when she had the chance—two chances! She wished she was someone different. Someone smarter about people. Someone… else. She thought about how Laura and Tex liked to hold hands across the bar, how Travis and Jenny kissed each other every chance they got. Even Wrench, who didn't like to be touched, got all soft around the edges and reached for Lydia whenever they were together.

"Gizelle?"

Scarlet put the book down and Gizelle realized that at some point she had fallen back onto the grass so she could look up at the sky that was blue like Conall's eyes.

"I'm not all here inside today," she said regretfully as she sat up. Clutching the checkers was making her hand sweaty.

"We can try tomorrow," Scarlet said patiently.

"Tomorrow…" There was something Gizelle was supposed to

remember about tomorrow. "Chef is making figgy pudding tomorrow!"

"Yes, but…"

Gizelle was already gone, flying to tell Conall about the pudding.

Conall, unfortunately, was at the restaurant. Gizelle fidgeted a while at the back entrance, then decided she was not feeling brave enough to join him after a particularly loud laugh from one of the other guests.

Instead, she returned the checkers to the game board on the deck below with a sigh of relief, frowning over the red marks in her sweaty palm from holding them too tightly and too long.

Then she went to graze as a gazelle, because it was easiest, and the sun was warm on her tawny coat and the grass was sweet and the insects made a lovely, restful droning sound that drowned out all the rest of the noise in her head.

By the time she was aware of time again, the sun was starting to set.

She still hadn't told Conall about the figgy pudding, so she went to find him. Her sarong was where she had left it, so she tied it back around herself in one of the clever ways that Lydia had shown her.

Conall wasn't at his cottage, so she went to look for him.

He wasn't on the bar deck, but Magnolia was.

Magnolia was restful to be around. She was the biggest and most beautiful thing that Gizelle knew, as a human or as a polar bear.

When Gizelle approached her, Magnolia tipped her sunglasses down her nose. "Darling, you're looking almost tanned, you've been out in the sun in your human skin so much."

Gizelle envied how comfortable Magnolia was in her own skin.

Not even her gazelle's skin was that comfortable.

"It's just the sunset," Gizelle assured her, putting both pale arms out in front of her. "I'm still more moonlight than melanin."

Magnolia's laugh was like caramel. "I love how unexpected you always are," she said warmly.

"I love that you don't think I'm weird. Unexpected is better than weird," Gizelle said gratefully. She thought that she should sit in one of the tall chairs, but when she did, she was too restless, so she stood again almost at once.

"Want some water?" Magnolia offered, preparing one of her ringed hands to signal Tex from the bar.

Gizelle shook her head. "I had a drink from one of the rain buckets earlier," she explained offhandedly.

"So, tell me about Conall," Magnolia said, with no trace of the discomfort that other people got on the topic. "Because he looks like a dish, and you don't look as happy as you should."

Gizelle decided that sitting would make her more likely to stay through the whole conversation and perched up on the tall chair with her legs crossed. "It's not what I expected."

"Having a mate?" Magnolia prodded.

"Any of it," Gizelle said mournfully. She tried to square the napkin in front of her to the circular table, with futile results.

"Do you like him?" Magnolia asked.

"I do," Gizelle said at once. "He's beautiful and kind and never shouts."

"Then what's the problem?"

Gizelle stared across the table. "I am," she said finally.

Magnolia laughed at her. "You are not a problem."

It was hard not to believe her when she spoke so confidently.

"I'm problematic, then," Gizelle countered.

She sighed. "I've tried all the things that everyone is supposed to do. Dinner at the restaurant. I showed him my hoard. We had a picnic on the beach. Even though I hate the beach."

"And?"

"It's all awful and I say stupid things and remind him of music and it hurts him but when he laughs it's amazing and he's trying so hard and I want him so badly." By this point, she had pulled her knees up against her chest and was clinging to them tightly.

Magnolia offered her hands across the table in that way that she had that wasn't really a request.

Gizelle reluctantly unwound her arms and lowered her legs so she could put her hands cautiously on top of Magnolia's lovely large fingers.

"It can all seem very complicated," Magnolia said gently. She cradled Gizelle's hands, but didn't hold them tight, perhaps knowing that would make Gizelle feel trapped. "A new mate is overwhelming, for anyone, and it can feel like you don't have *choices*."

Gizelle felt her chest squeeze in recognition as Magnolia continued.

"You haven't been making your own choices for very long, darling," Magnolia reminded her. "You never had the chance before. And now, it probably feels like that was taken away from you again, and that must be pretty terrifying."

Terrifying didn't begin to describe the wave that threatened Gizelle as Magnolia's words clarified her discomfort.

"But you like him," Magnolia reminded her. "And your gazelle likes him. You both *want* him." She withdrew her hands and sat back in satisfaction. "So, choose him."

It was like the sun coming through clouds.

"You make it sound so easy," Gizelle breathed.

Her gazelle was nuzzling the back of her mind in amused agreement and she looked up to see Conall across the bar, coming in the back entrance.

He paused there, searching… for her, Gizelle realized, and all the lines in his body changed when he spotted her. He brightened, some of the sadness lifting from his shoulders as he strode forward.

She could *choose* him.

The idea was amazing.

"Coming through!" Just inside the bar, out of view of the entrance, Laura was rushing across his path with a tray of empty drink glasses. *Her* tray, Gizelle had time to note, was stacked high with glassware.

Then Gizelle froze, realizing that Conall hadn't been able to hear Laura's warning, that he was walking forward with eyes only for *her*.

"Look out!" Magnolia called urgently, but Conall couldn't hear that either and Laura was moving too fast to stop herself, and even as Gizelle thought about finding a way to warn him, they collided, the tray flying from Laura's hands.

Conall swore, Laura gave a little shriek, and glass dashed against tile all around them as they just managed to both stay upright.

The crash was too much sound. Gizelle's hands at her ears couldn't stop it and her will shattered with the glass.

Before she could stop herself, she was bounding away on four hooves.

CHAPTER 28

Conall sank onto the barstool in defeat as Laura waved him away from helping to clean up the broken glass.

Gizelle had fled again, and who wouldn't.

She needed someone whole. Someone undamaged. Someone who could *hear* her speak and actually help her heal.

Someone who could avoid a simple collision by hearing the warning.

He didn't look to see what Tex would say, but was not surprised to find a gin and tonic in front of him within a few moments.

A strong gin and tonic, with no umbrella.

A second followed it in short order and Conall loosened his hateful tie and rolled up his shirt sleeves.

It was the third drink before he was drunk enough to look at Tex. "You got an electric tuner?" he asked in challenge.

Tex, surprised, glanced at the guitar that had been taunting Conall from the corner. "No, sir. Always tuned her by… ah… ear."

Conall kept his gaze steady. "Can you tune it to an open G?" Did he sound as desperate as he felt? It was impossible to know.

Tex after a perplexed moment, nodded, and reached up to turn down the radio that must be playing.

Conall watched him sit and bend over the strings with a hunger that only rivaled what he felt when he'd seen Gizelle standing at the edge of the restaurant in the red dress. He didn't comment on Tex's questionable technique, only watched him strum out the chords and adjust the pins until it obviously satisfied him.

Conall understood the reluctance in the bartender's motions when he finally passed the instrument over the bar, and took the guitar with the reverence the favor deserved. It was a worn instrument, mass-produced and of decidedly pedestrian quality, but it had clearly been treated with care.

Conall cradled it into his lap, ignoring the gaudy country strap, and gave it a test scale that told him nothing.

His fingers remembered, after ten years of inactivity. Without thinking, he was falling into a Spanish lament, a song that had always brought him comfort, with its aching trills and slow progressions.

He had learned it as a challenge, for its complicated fingering and changing tempos, but it had become a favored song for informal concerts and for impressing company when his family was entertaining. It rarely failed to draw a tear from the aunts who were visiting and Conall always took the extra time to linger over the last minor runs, squeezing each last emotion from the music.

At the last phrase, he stumbled, and let his fingers stop.

It was useless.

The familiar strains brought no peace when he couldn't hear them, even if his fingers did remember how to coax them from the strings. Probably. He could only judge by his audience, and he had no interest in looking at any of them.

He put the guitar down on the bar, knowing from the vibration in the neck that it had thumped down too hard. He shoved it across at a shocked Tex before he noticed that there were glasses between them. He couldn't hear them shatter as Tex caught the precious guitar and let them fall.

He muttered what might have been an apology as he shoved back from the bar and took a page from Gizelle's book, fleeing the scene.

His feet took him to the beach, away from the hated Christmas lights now strung all along the pool deck. Behind him, the resort was a twinkling cathedral; before him, the dark ocean stretched forever. He could feel the surf rumbling through the sand that threatened to fill his shoes at once.

Gritty socks were nothing compared to the bleakness inside.

Motion caught the corner of his eye as he considered wading out into the water, shoes and all.

Gizelle had followed him, still in her antelope form, and was stepping carefully towards him over the sand she hated. She froze when he glanced her way.

Conall sighed and looked away, hands limp and empty at his sides. Did she feel like he did? Was she impossibly drawn to him, but sure it was a terrible mistake?

Then there was a whiskered muzzle tickling his hand and his world exploded in sounds.

He crumpled to his knees, hands clasped uselessly over his ears, and howled.

CHAPTER 29

Gizelle had never shifted so quickly in her life.

"Did I hurt you? What's wrong? What did I do??" She flung herself at Conall, trying to lift him back to his feet. He took hold of her bare shoulders as she remembered he wouldn't be able to understand her in the darkness. "I'm sorry!" she cried anyway.

"Gizelle," he said roughly, voice cracking. "Gizelle," he repeated in wonder. "Say something!"

Gizelle froze. "I don't understand," she squeaked.

He gathered her into his arms and sobbed into her hair. "Don't stop talking," he begged. "Don't stop."

"You can hear me?" Gizelle asked wonderingly into his chest. Every time she thought she had figured something out, the rules changed. His chest, however, was a very nice place to be. His shirt was thin enough that she could feel the warmth of his muscles beneath it, and his heart beating, fast and strong.

"I can hear everything," he gasped. "Everything. The water, the sky, birds, I… don't even know what I'm hearing. Voices?" He paused and said achingly, "I hear music."

"Saina is singing," Gizelle told him. She could barely hear the strains from here, Saina's magic a faint, distant tickle in her mind.

"What have you given me?" Conall drew back and put his hands at either side of her face. "How did you do this?"

Gizelle wanted to be close against his chest again, but his hands on her face were nearly as nice. "I don't know," she said simply. "I don't know how I work."

Then he bent and kissed her, and all the questions were irrelevant.

Gizelle had never understood kissing. She'd watched others kiss with fascination, not sure what the appeal of touching lips was when touching people altogether was rather distasteful, or what they did with their tongues when their mouths were open. The sucking looked *uncomfortable*, even while they seemed to be enjoying it immensely.

But Conall's mouth explained it all, without any words whatsoever. It was an intoxicating mix of strong and soft and when she instinctively opened her mouth in welcome, his tongue set her entire body on fire. She couldn't be close enough, she couldn't have enough of him touching her, and she whimpered in overwhelming longing as she kissed him passionately in return. His hands weren't on her face anymore; one was at the small of her back, pulling her closer, but not close enough, and the other was tangling in the hair at the back of her neck.

She had her hands on his arms and when he suddenly drew away, she took handfuls of his shirt, trying to keep him close.

"I'm sorry," he said, panting raggedly. "I meant to let you set the pace. I shouldn't have…"

"Do that again," she begged, her breath as unsteady as his was. "Please…"

She threw arms around his neck and he let her kiss him again, bending to meet her hungry mouth with his own.

Every time she thought the kiss was ending, they found some new way of touching tongues, or his fingers found new places to tantalize her. Even his teeth were amazing, when she dared to explore them, and her lips felt crushed and sensitive and ravenous.

"Conall," she breathed, when they broke for breath.

His arms tightened around her, and he made a noise that sounded like grief and happiness at the same time.

"I want more," she said shyly. "I want…" she wasn't sure how to articulate herself and feared looking like a fool. "Will you do sex with me?"

That wasn't right.

"I would like to make love to you," he said earnestly.

That sounded better.

Much better.

He was kissing her neck now, which Gizelle hadn't known was a place that would like to be kissed so much, and it was very distracting. They were still on their knees together in the sand, and it seemed like a poor place to continue what they'd started, so she was delighted when he rather suddenly picked her up and got to his feet with her in his arms.

She could still kiss him this way, and he could carry her back to his cottage.

CHAPTER 30

Conall had fantasized about hearing again, imagined what strains of music would sound like, what noise the wind in trees must be making.

He hadn't imagined a din like this. He wasn't sure if he was hearing insects or frogs, or possibly birds. And the wind was like a thousand whispers, voices just out of hearing, a radio just out of tune. The music was the least of the sounds he had in his head.

And the very best of the sounds was Gizelle.

He could hear her breath catch and her little moans when he found particularly sensitive places. When she said his name, it was like a piece of heaven. She didn't sound like he had expected, and it was a long moment, very distracted by her kisses, before he recognized that he wasn't truly hearing her, he was hearing through *her* ears.

His own voice was somehow distant and different as well, like hearing a poor recording of himself.

She was a scant armful, all long, smooth limbs and hungry mouth, and finally having her in his arms was the answer to every question he had ever had.

His cottage was fortunately close to the beach, because between

Gizelle's demanding kisses and his own desperate need, he would not have gotten much further.

The door was not locked and he fumbled with one hand to open it and then kicked it closed behind them so hard that it bounced back open. He left it open, carrying Gizelle into the bedroom.

This door he kicked closed with a little more finesse and it stayed shut.

Removing his clothing with Gizelle in his arms proved to require more limbs than Conall had, so he finally, reluctantly, put her down to tear at the buttons of his shirt. In that instance, the silence was back like a lightning bolt, and just as quickly, the roar of sound returned as Gizelle pressed up close again. The jolt between hearing and not was enough to stagger him, and the return of the din threatened to overwhelm him.

Gizelle was kissing him again, up on her tiptoes as he bent to meet her mouth with his own. She was touching him everywhere his skin was bare, fingers like the whispers in her head.

Conall wanted to strip out of his pants and lay her down on the bed to claim her at last, but he held himself back with the same iron will that had seen him through his final year at Juilliard without being to hear the things he had composed.

He had waited this long… his noble intentions faltered as Gizelle stopped kissing him and tugged at the waist of his pants, trying to work out how to release him.

"Please," she whimpered. "I want…"

Conall wasn't sure what was more intense; her words, or that he could *hear* them. His hands on her shoulders tightened.

"Gizelle," he said, hoarse to her ears. "Gizelle, I have to…"

She had worked out the button and was puzzling at the zipper. "I know you have to be naked for this part," she said breathlessly.

CHAPTER 31

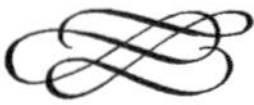

With Conall's help, Gizelle got the pants and the briefs down and the glory within sprang free, causing her to pause.

His cock was beautiful; long and thick and much *more* than she had expected. When she touched it reverently, Conall shuddered and gave a strangled moan.

It was impossible. It could never fit in her.

More impossibly still, she *wanted* it to.

She felt hot and full of need and his skin couldn't be close enough; she wanted to be wrapped around him in entirety.

"A condom," Conall said urgently. "I need a condom. Your friends might murder me if I don't."

Breck had explained these details to her, but it had all been so ridiculous sounding. Once she had started, she could not stop touching the fascinating manhood, reveling in the way it made Conall suck in his breath and tighten all of his muscles.

"I'm going to need five condoms," he said between gritted teeth. "Gizelle…" He took her hands in his own. "Slow down, sweetheart. Just for a moment. It's… been a really long time."

He let go of her, fishing a little crinkly plastic square from the overflowing bowl by his bed. Gizelle watched, fascinated, while he opened it and deftly unrolled the nearly-invisible sheath over himself.

When he turned back to her, she wasn't sure what to do, or where to put her hands.

"I've thought about this a lot," he said gruffly.

"Me, too," Gizelle confessed. Her hands still didn't know where to go and she was glad when he took them, jolting a little at her touch.

He drew her back to the bed, close against him, so his cock was pressing at her belly. He kissed her, gently this time, hands lingering at her face, then lay back on the bed, guiding her up to straddle him.

"You say when," he said, hands soft at her hips. "You say how."

He was so large, jutting up against her waiting entrance, so firm and alluring. She had to hold herself up with her legs to keep the pressure from being unbearable and she could barely breathe for the anticipation that was crowding her chest.

"I choose you," she whispered. "I *choose* you." And she let herself slip onto him, the resistance so delicious and the friction so sweet.

Something so uncomfortable shouldn't feel so *wonderful*, she found herself thinking, and somehow still more fit in, and still more, until she felt so filled up that she might slosh over like a glass of water.

This must be what ecstasy felt like, she realized, but then Conall pulled away a fraction of an inch, lifting her away. She made a noise of protest, not ready to be done, and he moved back in like a wave and there was something more amazing yet, any discomfort barely a memory.

He did that again, and again, and his hands were all over her body, cupping her breasts and running thumbs over her hard nipples, stroking her sides and her arms.

Gizelle felt like a panic attack was building in her whole body, except that it was *exquisite*, and when she fell, she didn't want to run, she wanted to be falling forever.

She realized she was making noise, that she was crying out in pleasure and release, because Conall was too, trying and failing to keep his hands at her waist gentle as he thrust in her with the same urgent need that had just broken over her.

Gizelle did not mind his hands grabbing at her; it was somehow perfect for the moment, and she knew beyond anything else that she was safe here, with him.

She had chosen him.

He was hers.

CHAPTER 32

Conall woke to quiet.

No, not to quiet.

To *silence.*

It was silent again, and Gizelle was gone.

Despair felt like a heavy blanket. There was moonlight through the windows that Conall had never bothered to pull the curtains across and he stared out at the jungle canopy that was moving in a night breeze he couldn't hear.

After an indulgent moment of self-pity, he made himself throw off the blanket and get up, turning on the light beside the bed so he could navigate to the bathroom.

He was splashing cool water on his face when he caught sight of her in the mirror.

Gizelle was curled up in the corner of the tile shower, tangled in a towel, with another draped over her as a blanket. Her eyes were closed tight.

"Gizelle," he said, not wanting to startle her as he approached.

She was shivering.

No, not shivering.

She was trembling, her limbs twitching as if she were trying to flee but couldn't.

"Gizelle," he said again, and he gently touched her, braced for the explosion of sound.

He jumped, releasing her, and spun around at the voices. They vanished as his hand left her skin, and a quick survey of the room revealed no one with them.

Cautiously, he touched her again, laying careful fingers on her bare shoulder.

It sounded like there was a storm, a bone-deep rumbling, screams. A man's voice was saying in agony, "We're losing her!" A wolf howled in agony, and someone… sang.

She was dreaming.

"Gizelle," he called. He couldn't hear his own voice.

Unable to leave her lying there, he gathered her into his arms, towels and all, and carried her back to the bed. "Gizelle," he called, and she continued to dream. He guessed from what he felt through his arms that she was whimpering, but she couldn't hear it, so he couldn't either.

He slipped in behind her, curling close, propped up on a pillow. "Gizelle," he whispered into her hair.

The sounds were awful, drowned in other sounds he couldn't even identify, like radio static or wind, and she wouldn't wake up.

So he sang to her, mouth near her ear, a lullaby his mother had sung when he was a child.

He was no opera singer, but he'd done time in the boys' choir in school and had always been able to carry a tune. He had to trust he still could.

After a long moment, he realized he could hear himself. It was distant and faint, but just enough to confirm his notes were true.

Too sad, he thought. The music was too sad.

Gizelle was excited for Christmas, so Conall took a breath, and sang her the happiest Christmas song he could think of, Santa Claus is Coming to Town. He drew her back from her dreams with his voice until she was lying peacefully in his arms and the voices were gone, swept away in the chaos of the jungle night noises.

Then she opened her eyes. "I remember," she said softly, sitting up.

Conall sat up with her, dreading what she would say next. Did she remember cages and chains? *Torture*?

"I remember that today is the day Chef is making figgy pudding," she said in glee. Then she smiled sunnily and bounced in place. "The bed is softer than the floor," and she was stretching and yawning.

Did she not remember because she didn't want to? Transference or denial or some psychological term? Whatever the reason, Conall was sure it was a mercy.

"Gizelle," he said softly, gently. "You don't have to remember."

She sobered. "If I don't, he might forget to share it with me. Scarlet says I'll like it, and that it wouldn't be Christmas without it. I'd better go tell him right now." She started to scramble out of the bed.

Conall caught Gizelle's hand at the last moment, the silence when their contact was briefly broken a curious, short burst in the din of their shared hearing. "It's the middle of the night," he reminded her, pointing outside to the moonlit porch.

"Oh," she said, disappointed. "I suppose Chef won't be up yet."

Then she smiled, full of mischief and suggestion, and it heated Conall's blood to his toes. "I can think of something we can do. You said you could show me more ways to do that!"

Conall realized he was grinning in reply, and then she was flowing into his arms for kisses.

CHAPTER 33

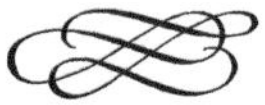

When Gizelle woke again, daylight was streaming in the windows and doors and she was still in the bed.

The bed was far, far more comfortable than the floor had been.

So comfortable that Gizelle was surprised she had slept.

But it didn't feel like cheating, it felt like home, and the pillow beside her still had a dip where Conall's head had dented it.

She rose from the bed and wandered around. Conall wasn't in the bathroom or on the deck.

There was a sundress folded on one of the chairs, so Gizelle put it on.

She was sore, *deliciously* sore, in places she'd never been sore before, and it made her cheeks feel hot.

She scampered to the bathroom to see herself blush, but it was already gone when she got there, so she frowned at her reflection.

Lydia's pretty braid was looking less and less tidy every day. Gizelle supposed she would have to go back to the salon and sit for hours again to have it look nice again. This explained why some people went to the salon every day, she guessed.

Looking good was hard work.

She wasn't sure it was worth it.

Then she remembered that Conall had liked the braid and she thought perhaps it *was* worth it.

There was a note on the counter in the bathroom, strong letters written on a piece of Shifting Sands stationery. Conall had left her a letter, she realized, heart soaring.

Maybe it was a love letter.

She puzzled at it, trying to make the letters resolve into words from sheer force of will until her stomach growled. She considered grazing, because it was the easiest, but probably she should eat like a person. Tex always had a bag of nuts behind the bar if she didn't feel brave enough for the buffet.

As she walked, she continued to try to make sense of the letter. She knew her name had a zee, but didn't see one anywhere. Maybe he had used a different name. What had he called her? Darling? Sweetheart?

"What's that you've got, Rapunzel?" a voice interrupted her.

Her feet had walked her to the pool deck.

"It's a letter," she said, glancing at the man. He smelled like Tex's trash can and his nose was too red for his face.

"Pretty important looking letter," the man said, moving to block her path. "It's got all of your attention. There are better things to do."

Still looking at the paper, trying to figure out its secrets, Gizelle didn't have the energy to spare for him.

"Mmm," she said, trying to skirt around him.

Then, to her horror, the horrible man snatched the paper away from her.

"No!" she shrieked. "That's mine!"

CHAPTER 34

Conall was bent over his phone answering emails with his thumbs when the bar vibrated beneath his elbows.

He looked up to find Tex holding a baseball bat and thumping his fist down.

"I swear, I haven't hurt her," Conall said swiftly. "Why does everyone think I would?"

But Tex pointed to the edge of the bar deck, urgently, and Conall left his phone behind as he went quickly to the railing and looked down.

His hands balled into fists as he took in the scene below.

He couldn't hear Gizelle's cries, but he could see the distress in every line of her body as she frantically tried to grab for the paper that some muscle in a Speedo and a t-shirt was holding out of her reach. The bastard was taunting her, clearly teasing her as she grew more agitated. A few guests in lounge chairs were frowning and looking at each other, but no one was stepping in.

As he stalked towards the stairs, Tex caught his arm. Conall turned to snarl at him, then realized the bartender was offering his bat.

"I don't need that," Conall growled, and he was flying down the stairs as he unbuttoned his shirt.

"Leave her alone!" he hurled in challenge as he reached the bottom, hoping his voice would carry over the water features of the pool.

If the man said anything, he didn't turn so that Conall could catch it, continuing to bait Gizelle with the paper she so obviously coveted.

There were tears in her eyes and it took all of Conall's self-control not to simply shift and destroy the man on the spot. "Leave her alone!" he repeated, throwing his shirt over the back of one of the lounge chairs.

The man turned, just in time for Conall to catch, "...just a bit of fun with her." His eyes narrowed. "You're that deaf moose, aren't you, fancy boy." Apparently, it wasn't just helpless women he enjoyed taunting. Conall couldn't hear if his speech slurred, but he guessed the man was drunk from the flush on his face.

"Moose?" Conall said evenly, slipping out of his shoes. "Gizelle, get back."

"You want to have at it?" the man said in challenge, removing his own shirt viciously. "Maybe you don't know that I'm a grizzly bear, and I can take on any deer. You're all prey to me."

"I'm not a moose," Conall warned. "I'm an elk." He gave a quick glance to see that the guests around them were properly far off and Gizelle had retreated a few steps.

"That's just what you stuck-up Europeans call moose," the man said dismissively, taking off his Speedo defiantly.

"I'm from Boston," Conall told him, unbuttoning his own pants. "And I'm an *Irish* elk."

He shifted seamlessly the moment his clothing was free and the man scrambled back in front of him. Extinct since the ice age, his elk stood seven feet at the shoulder and had a rack wider than a car.

The odious man swiftly turned into his grizzly counterpart but even standing on rear feet, he wasn't level with the elk's eyes.

Conall snorted once, tipped his head, and charged forward.

The bear didn't even have a chance to slash out with his claws before Conall had scooped him up with his antlers and tossed him out into the pool with a massive splash.

Conall shifted back to human and turned to find Gizelle kneeling in defeat at the side of the pool. She raised tearful eyes to him as Conall came to comfort her.

"My letter," she cried, holding the sodden piece of paper. The ink had run, and it was stained in a rainbow of unreadable color. "The love letter you wrote me."

"Oh, sweetheart," Conall said, gathering her up to hug her as she sobbed. "That wasn't a letter. That was a note for housekeeping. I was asking for more towels in case you wanted to sleep in the shower again."

Gizelle cried harder into his shoulder and because he was touching her, he could hear Tex, behind him, saying with satisfaction, "He'll be on the next plane out."

The bear was slogging out of the shallow end of the pool, where Scarlet was standing with her arms crossed, safely back from the spray of salt water as the bear shook itself.

She didn't look amused.

"Good riddance," Conall said sharply.

Then Gizelle was pushing back from him, looking critically at the note. "Do I have to sleep in the shower?" she asked. "Your bed was very comfortable."

"You can sleep anywhere you please," Conall said, still holding one of her hands.

"Oh!" Gizelle said. "You could come sleep at my cottage!"

Conall imagined trying to sleep in her tiny outdoor shower and cringed. "Can I convince you that my cottage is better?" he said hopefully.

But Gizelle was already pulling away and on to her next thought. "I have to go try figgy pudding," she remembered. "And you're not wearing clothes. Tex is always telling me to put on clothes."

Then she wasn't touching him, and whatever else she said was lost to the silence that fell.

Conall turned to glance at Tex in time to catch him shrugging and saying, "I am."

The bartender had the balls to look amused by the whole thing.

CHAPTER 35

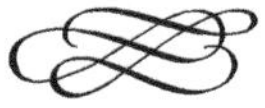

Gizelle paused inside the back kitchen door, bracing herself against the noise and bustle of Chef's domain.

Chef was Magnolia's mate, and he was just as wonderfully large and gentle as Magnolia was, but the kitchen where he loved to be was full of sharp things, and often very noisy.

Chef was singing, of course, and the kitchen was quieter than it sometimes was; the rush of breakfast was over and things were being washed.

"How was your picnic?" Breck asked her, easing a heaping tray of dishes into the soapy water for the dishwasher.

"Awful. It was tense and the watermelon got sandy and I don't like the beach," Gizelle said honestly, after pausing to remember. "But the sandwiches were good!"

"And after…?" Breck said leadingly.

Gizelle blinked at him. "I ran away."

He looked disappointed for her, but Gizelle was quick to add, "But it's all right now. I can make him hear and he can make my whole body sing, and I beat him at backgammon."

Breck grinned at her. "That's my girl."

"Gizelle!" Chef called from further within the kitchen. "They're coming out of the oven now!"

Gizelle darted past Breck down the shiny kitchen aisles and found Chef pulling a tray from the steaming oven. A dozen more were already cooling on the counter.

The figgy puddings did not look like the soft pudding she had expected, but like dark, dense cakes, round and ridged. They were mottled and rather unattractive, and the smell was rich and fruity and a little bit like Tex's bar.

"When can we eat them?" Gizelle asked eagerly.

"Two weeks," Chef said, to her horror. "On Christmas Eve."

"Two *weeks*?" A week was an eternity of moments to wait.

"They have to age a bit," Chef insisted. "Traditionally I should have given them a full four weeks, but they'll do."

"Two weeks," Gizelle moaned. "That's a lot of anticipation."

"Anticipation makes them taste better," Chef said with a booming laugh.

"Something has to," Breck said dryly, beside Gizelle.

"Won't they be stale in two weeks?" Gizelle said suspiciously, glancing between the head waiter and Chef. Was this a joke? The staff was always making jokes she didn't understand.

"It's got too much booze to go stale," Breck scoffed. "It's basically trumped up fruitcake that you set fire to."

Gizelle knew they were joking then. "You're teasing me!"

They laughed then, kindly, but Chef shook his head. "He's basically right," the big man admitted. "It's more like a fruitcake with a lot of brandy than a true pudding."

"And you light it on *fire*?"

"Only for a moment," Chef assured her.

"Not nearly long enough," Breck added.

Gizelle still wasn't sure that they weren't fooling her, but she accepted that she wasn't going to be getting any figgy pudding that day.

"Christmas cannot get here soon enough," she sighed. Then she wandered out of the kitchen to find Conall.

CHAPTER 36

Conall considered the Christmas lights hanging around the bar.

He hated Christmas: the gaudy decorations, the crushing pressure to buy the perfect presents, the memory of music. He had a hundred reasons to detest the whole season.

And now he had one reason to love it.

One wild-haired, wide-eyed woman who'd never done any of it before, whose every tentative smile made him want to move the world for her.

His laptop was open on the bar in front of him, grinding through the sluggish connection to the Internet. A dozen priority emails from the previous few days needed his attention, each one sounding more urgent than the last. Signature needed, approval required, get back to me immediately, are you ignoring your texts?

He grinned, imagining what kind of chaos the emails he'd just sent were going to set off. For once he had a reason to be glad he couldn't manage phone calls. Texts and email at least gave him some buffer.

Not that he was dealing with any of them now.

The page he was loading finally resolved and he scrolled down, impulsively adding anything that appealed to him to his cart.

He was going to make sure that Gizelle had the perfect Christmas. It was going to cost a fortune in express shipping to get things here in time, but he could not imagine a better way to spend the money.

She's here, his elk warned, as excited for the surprise as he was.

Conall shut the laptop as Gizelle tripped across the tiles to him.

"How was the figgy pudding?" he asked as she sidled into his arms with a sigh and all the sounds in the world seemed to crowd into his ears. He kissed the crown of her head.

"Two weeks," Gizelle said in despair. "I have to wait until *Christmas* to taste it."

Conall remembered that exquisite anguish of anticipation. Though Gizelle's voice was sad, her eyes were sparkling and the familiar tension that hummed in her body seemed more like excitement than fear.

"Time will fly by," Conall promised.

Gizelle gave him a puzzled look. "Fly? Like Bastian? Where will it go?"

"It will pass quickly," Conall amended. "It will be Christmas before you realize."

"But I realize *now*!" Gizelle countered.

"You just need something else to do," Conall suggested, tracing her bare arm with a finger.

"Oh," Gizelle said, then, "Oh!" as Conall bent and kissed her neck. "I can think of something," she said slyly. "But Tex is always chasing people out of the bar for trying to do that here."

"Let's not make him do that," Conall chuckled. He gathered up his laptop and stood, offering Gizelle his hand.

She eagerly took it, fingers sliding into his like they belonged there.

They do belong there, his elk reminded him.

CHAPTER 37

"You have your own pool," Gizelle observed much later, standing on Conall's porch.

"It's a Jacuzzi," Conall explained, after she had repeated herself looking at him. "Have you ever been in one?"

Gizelle shook her head, gazing down at the blue water. It smelled… different than the saltwater pool. She dipped a hand into it, but when she bent her head to taste it, Conall stopped her.

"It won't taste good."

Gizelle paused, considering the advice. It was probably good advice. She let the water trickle out through her fingers like rain… like dark rain. Dark red. No, bright red. Like blood.

"Gizelle?"

Gizelle bit the moment in half and was back on Conall's porch. The water in the little pool was blue again. "Can I try it?"

"You can," Conall said skeptically. "But I'm serious. It's pretty nasty tasting."

Gizelle laughed. "Not tasting it. Swimming in it."

"Swimming is an overstatement of what you can do in it," Conall cautioned. "But we could sit if you liked."

Gizelle was already stripping off her dress and climbing up on the steps next to it.

"Do you want the bubbles on?" Conall asked, pulling off his own shirt and stepping out of his pants. He was looking too hard at her face, like he really wanted to be watching the rest of her but thought it would be rude.

Gizelle liked bubbles, so she nodded, then leaped back with a shriek when the little pool gave a rumbling roar and erupted into a volcano of froth and foam.

Conall was quick to slip the switch off and quicker still to come across the deck to her. "It's okay," he assured her. "We don't have to have them on."

She was trembling, something she only realized when his arms came around her and they were solid and still. "Why would people do that?" she asked in horror.

"It feels good," Conall explained mysteriously. "It relaxes muscles and makes people feel better."

"That's absurd," Gizelle said flatly. She could not imagine that sitting inside a blender was relaxing.

"They're off now," Conall reassured her. "We don't have to turn them on."

He coaxed her back across the deck and up the steps, then let go of her hand to sink down into the water. There were still a few foamy swells of bubbles along the edge and Gizelle poked at them cautiously before she put first one, then a second foot into the tub.

It was warm, like the saltwater pool never was. And it was swirly.

She stepped in another step and took Conall's offered hand, sliding down into the water to sit next to him on the submerged bench. He felt good, with the cushion of water like a tease between their skin. His hand in hers was big and safe and strong and when she put her other hand on his chest she could feel his heart thrumming against her palm.

He tugged her closer and Gizelle went willingly for a kiss, squeaking against his lips when she unexpectedly floated.

She could feel him smile beneath her kiss and that was even better than the kiss itself.

CHAPTER 38

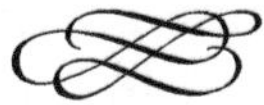

Gizelle was an armful of joy.

Her kisses were the sweetest thing that Conall had ever known, but never cloying. She had a bright, fresh sweetness, wild and intoxicating. She lived more in every moment than he'd lived in a lifetime and when she rose beneath him and cried out in pleasure, Conall thought that perishing from happiness might actually be a thing.

He loved watching her discover things, even when it frightened her. *Especially* when it frightened her, because she was so brave, shaking with fear and fighting down her instinct to flee.

Kissing her in the hot tub that she'd crawled back into after bolting away—it was a triumph on every level.

Ours, his elk agreed in perfect harmony. *Our brave, beautiful mate.*

They dried in the warm sunshine on the porch and Conall drew Gizelle down to sit on the lounge chair in front of him.

A hairbrush had been among the things that had appeared in his bathroom. "May I brush your hair?" he asked, stroking back the hairs that were drying, loose, around her face.

Gizelle tipped her head back to look at him from an impossible angle. "You *want* to?" she said skeptically. If Conall hadn't been touching her, he doubted he would have been able to lipread upside down.

"I want to," he said, and when she didn't protest, he got up from the chair and went to retrieve the hairbrush.

When he returned, she had pulled out the few pins that remained from Lydia's work and was tugging counter-productively at a knot near the end of the braid, trying to untangle it.

"Let me," Conall said, drawing her hair into his hands as he settled back onto the chair.

Gizelle drew her legs up, crossing them in front of her, and put tight hands on the sides of the lounge, clearly bracing for the worst.

Holding only her hair, Conall could barely hear—everything was a distant swish of sound. Clearly whatever magic was at work did a better job skin-to-skin. He moved his leg so that it was touching her hip and it focused again, like rabbit-ears fixing the reception on an old television.

"... might get hungry," Gizelle was saying. "I got hungry when Lydia was brushing my hair."

Conall teased the knot she'd made out of the end of her braid and gently unwove it.

"We can stop any time," he assured her.

But when he began to brush, she slowly relaxed.

The braid had saved her neglected hair from being much worse; though Conall had to stop and carefully coax tangles from several places, he knew that it would have been much wilder if had been left loose.

"I sometimes think about where I might have come from," Gizelle said unexpectedly, and Conall stopped brushing for a moment, holding his breath.

"Where do you think that was?" Conall started brushing again, slowly.

"Do you think I was made? That a man in a white coat made me in a laboratory like some sort of Frankster?"

"Frankenstein?" Conall guessed. He did not correct the

common misconception that Frankenstein was the monster rather than the scientist.

"Frankenstein," Gizelle agreed. "Do you think I'm all parts of different people and that's why I'm so much in little pieces and hear too much?"

Conall had once been good at navigating the usual girlfriend questions like 'does this make me look fat?' and 'do you see wrinkles?' but this was far outside of his realm of comfort. "I don't think you're a monster, Gizelle," he said firmly.

"But could someone have made me to be like this?" she insisted.

"It's possible," Conall conceded. Then he added, "And if I had made you, I would have made you exactly like this."

She tipped her head back to smile at him, then sat in silence for a few moments while he gently tamed another handspan of her dark-and-light hair.

"Sometimes I wonder about my parents," she said abruptly. "Maybe I was born broken and they gave me to Beehag because they didn't want me."

"I cannot fathom anyone in the world giving you up," Conall said firmly. He thought about his own demanding mother and his stern father, and could not imagine even them giving up a baby. "Mothers love their children more than anything in the world."

Beneath his gentle strokes, her hair became soft and glossy, with little waves near the end.

"How did you lose your hearing?" Gizelle asked next, toying with one of the locks while Conall worked another tangle loose.

Conall made his fingers keep going. The pain that the question always woke in him felt distant and muffled, like hearing her voice through Gizelle's ears did.

"I was in a car accident," he explained. "A drunk driver ran me off the road. When paramedics found me, I was unconscious and they took me to the hospital, where I wasn't able to shift until it was too late. I had already healed wrong; there was nothing my elk could do to make it the way it had been."

I tried, his elk said mournfully, full of guilt.

It wasn't your fault, Conall was quick to assure him.

"No, of course it wasn't your fault," Gizelle agreed. "You must have tried very hard."

Conall and his elk both froze, as completely as Gizelle ever had.

"You could hear him?" Conall asked in disbelief.

She could hear me? his elk asked in delight.

"Of course," Gizelle said simply. "He has a very nice voice."

CHAPTER 39

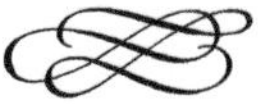

Gizelle could never predict what would surprise people; no one seemed the slightest bit amazed when she realized she could do marvelous things like somersaults. But Conall was absolutely blown away that she could hear his elk.

"Can you always hear him?" Conall asked, trepidatiously. "Can you hear *me*?"

"Not you, but I can always hear *them*," Gizelle tried to explain. "I just never understand them. Doesn't everyone?"

"Those whispers," Conall said in understanding. "I thought it… was the wind. Or..."

"Or just voices in my imagination?" Gizelle nodded, and Conall's brush tugged at her scalp through a knot. "Ow. I thought so for a while. But every so often, when I touch someone, it turns into words. You can't do that?"

Conall shook his head. "It only happens with shifters?" he asked.

"I've only ever known shifters," Gizelle said, and Conall paused in his brushing.

"Are there very many people who aren't?" she asked when he started again.

"Aren't shifters?"

"It must be very lonely," Gizelle explained. "And I wondered if there were very many of them."

Conall actually laughed—his surprised laugh, which was different than his delighted laugh, and much different than the giddy chuckle after sex (that was Gizelle's favorite so far). "There are far, far more people who aren't shifters than who are," he explained. "It's got to be a hundred to one. Maybe a thousand to one."

"How awful for them," Gizelle said in dismay. "Why is that?"

"I have no idea," Conall said frankly.

"Do they have animals sleeping inside of them like Jenny did?"

"It's… possible," Conall conceded, though he didn't sound convinced. "But Jenny came from a family of shifters, and most people don't."

He put down the brush. "I'm going to try to braid your hair," he said, with the air of someone going into battle. "It probably won't be as good as Lydia's braid."

Gizelle braced herself.

He was very careful and gentle. At the end of his ministrations, Gizelle had not one, but two swinging braids. "It was too much hair for one," he said apologetically. "At least at my skill level."

"I love it," Gizelle assured him, letting the braids swirl around as she moved her head. "Will you do it often?"

"As often as you like," Conall promised. "Every day, if you want."

Gizelle considered. "I liked having you brush my hair," she conceded. "But I don't know if I liked it that much."

"I understand that it's easier if you do this every day," Conall told her encouragingly.

"If you think I should," Gizelle agreed reluctantly.

Conall tugged on one of her braids playfully. "I think you should do what you want to do," he said easily.

Gizelle smiled then. "I know what I want to do," she said earnestly. "Every day…"

CHAPTER 40

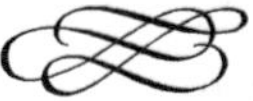

Conall was confused when Travis waved him over to where the staff was sitting near the bar after dinner.

He was more confused when they didn't appear to have anything to actively discuss with him. He was offered a seat and then largely ignored as they continued to chat among themselves, though they politely turned towards him to include him in the conversation.

"It's no real wonder that they'd want me," Breck was saying confidently. "But I've got to question the salary they offered. Before tips, which, no question, I'd be bringing in."

"We've been getting offers that are too good to be true," Bastian explained for Conall's benefit. "A resort in California has lifeguard positions for both me and Saina, with room and board and wages to tempt even a dragon."

"One of those trendy restaurants in New York sent me a letter," Breck added.

"I got a letter from a construction company back home in Alaska. They offered me a management position," Travis said.

Tex put a gin and tonic down in front of Conall and another beer for Wrench. Pointedly facing Conall to include him, he said, "I got a letter offering to front me the money for my own bar in Bermuda. An established place with a great bottom line in a sleepy tourist town. Everything I would have wanted before coming here."

Wrench shrugged. "Nobody's makin' me any offers."

The others all laughed good-naturedly and Conall found himself smiling bemusedly.

"Are you going to take these offers?" he asked.

"Not me," Travis said. "I have no interest in management. I like a job where I can use my hands, and I'm too spoiled by this island to go back to Alaska."

"Saina and I talked about it, but we're pretty happy with our lot here," Bastian said. "And I'd hate to have to move my hoard again."

"I don't think the place in New York is clothing optional," Breck added with a grin. "So what fun would that be?"

"Besides, I wouldn't want to leave Scarlet in a bind," Travis added. "Maybe the pay here isn't the greatest, but I've never had a better job."

Everyone nodded at that.

"I've got my own bar here, basically," Tex agreed. "And I don't have to worry about balancing the books or paying off a debt."

"Kind of weird we got these, don't you think?" Travis mused. "All at once like this?"

"Sounds like a hostile takeover," Conall suggested.

They all looked at him curiously and he frowned at their attention. "It's a standard business tactic," he said stiffly. "Poach the best players away from the competition."

"What competition?" Breck asked curiously. "Scarlet's got a kind of a narrow niche here."

"And our offers were from all over the place," Travis added. "Not just one rival resort."

"Beehag has been trying to sell the island and Scarlet's been giving him nothing but trouble over that," Tex suggested thoughtfully. "Maybe he's trying to whittle away at the resort to get her out of here?"

"Beehag isn't smart enough to come up with something like that," Breck scoffed.

Travis looked concerned. "Jenny says his lawyer is a smart cookie. Maybe it was his idea."

They all sat around musing that idea for a moment and Breck finally asked Conall bluntly, "So can you hear now or what?"

Conall laughed humorlessly, thinking about how oddly he must be coming across—deaf but not always. "I can only hear when I'm touching Gizelle. And it's not really hearing... it's... hearing through her ears. Sort of."

Slow, puzzled nods answered him and he felt compelled to add. "It's honestly not all that comfortable. I thought it was just that I'd forgotten what hearing was like, but she's got a lot more *input* than most people. It's really rather overwhelming, with so many voices. She can hear the voices of our animals. All of them at once."

The silence that met that was clearly each of them consulting with their own inner animals and meeting astonishment.

"It's almost all just whispers, like trying to listen to a hundred radios turned down really low that are just slightly out of tune, all at once," Conall was quick to explain. "It's not like either of us could eavesdrop even if we tried; I've been able to pick out just a few words at all. She says it's clearer if she makes skin contact, but she doesn't like to do that."

"Sweet daisies," said Tex. "No wonder she doesn't like touching people."

"Remarkable," Bastian said.

"I'm not sure I want Gizelle hearing my leopard," Breck said, amused. "He has some very dirty thoughts."

"Dirtier than yours?" Travis needled him.

"You'd be surprised," Breck said with a grin and a wink.

CHAPTER 41

"I'm getting in the shower before lunch," Conall called from the bedroom. He had just returned from using the noisy machines in the little fitness center near the pool. "Want to join me?"

Gizelle was perched on the deck railing, looking out over the tiny lawn. She hadn't put her dress on yet, but that didn't matter if she wasn't wandering about where the guests were. "I'm afraid of showers," she called back. Then she remembered that Conall wouldn't be able to hear her, so she hopped off the railing to tell him.

He already had the water running and it was just starting to steam.

Gizelle crept into the bathroom with her hands over her ears, but when she went to repeat herself where Conall would be able to see her, she stopped and simply watched him.

She had seen him without clothing several times, though not as many times as the other way around.

But she had never seen him quite like this, not looking at her, unconsciously graceful and so incredibly sexy as he groomed himself.

He was so marvelous, with his broad, muscled shoulders and his strong arms as he stood under the cascade of water in the open shower. Talented fingers poured shampoo into the opposite hand, then massaged it into his short hair, causing a cascade of bubbles that followed all the tantalizing planes and crannies of his splendid body.

He turned then and smiled, and if he had been dazzling before, it was nothing to what he was when he looked at her like she had just hung the stars in the sky.

"I'm afraid of showers," Gizelle repeated faintly, but when he put out a hand to her anyway, she tentatively uncovered her ears and followed him into the far end of the open shower, carefully skirting away from the falling water.

The sprinkles from the stream felt cool as they evaporated slowly off her skin. It was noisy, but not as overwhelming as it always had been before.

Nothing was as overwhelming as it had been before Conall and when his hand remained out in invitation, she finally crept a few steps forward and took it.

She braced herself for the worst as he pulled her gently into the stream, then gave a gasp of relief and delight.

It was amazing.

It was like having gentle hands all over her at once, warm and kind and inviting. If the water striking her head was noisier than she liked, it was worth it for the trickle of warm water running down her neck and shoulders.

"This is marvelous!" she said in wonder. "I never knew!"

Conall helped her unweave her braids and she eagerly poured a handful of shampoo into her palm and put it to her head. It lathered into a frothy foam all over her hands and she was fascinated to watch it spilling down over her breasts. It whispered down her cheek and she tipped her head back to see if she could see it above her even as Conall warned, "Careful, don't let it get into your—"

Gizelle gave a cry of betrayed pain as her eyes suddenly burned. She backed up blindly.

Conall's arms were immediately around her and he was angling her face into the water. "It will pass!" he promised desperately. "Let it rinse away! Blink!"

Gizelle had to fight down her instinct to struggle and screw her eyes shut and went limp in his arms, crying pitifully and letting him rinse the soap from her miserable eyes.

Slowly, the agony faded and Gizelle's sobs and shaking slowed.

"I'm so sorry," Conall said. "You were brave to come in, and I'm so sorry that happened."

"It was awful," Gizelle said, feeling wrung out. "How do you keep that from happening?"

Conall showed her, tipping his back under the water so it all flowed back away from his face. "Or, you close your eyes," he suggested.

Gizelle gave a hiccup of a laugh and closed her eyes as Conall helped her rinse the last of the bubbles from her hair.

"We can keep the soap below your chin," Conall suggested, lathering a bar in his hands.

When he began to soap her, Gizelle forgave him entirely for the unpleasant shampoo experience.

Soap was slippery and Conall massaged it everywhere. Then, when she had been rinsed clean, he gave her the bar and let her loose on his own body.

As she had been dying to do since she first saw him standing in the shower, Gizelle laid her hands on all the places that fascinated her. She stood on her toes to soap over his broad shoulders and explored each powerful arm. She scrubbed the muscles of his back and ran her hands over his tight ass cheeks, squeezing them for fun.

Standing behind him, she reached around and soaped his cock, half hard from her attention already. She pressed her breasts into his back as she worked and was rewarded by nearly making him choke.

"Gizelle," he moaned.

"I think I want to try the Jacuzzi with the bubbles on," she told him, rinsing all the remaining bubbles off with her careful fingers.

She wasn't entirely sure why he laughed, but she loved the sound of it.

CHAPTER 42

Conall was sitting on the deck alone when he felt footsteps that weren't Gizelle's. He looked around to see Scarlet walking from the French doors that opened into the living area. She was holding a folder of paperwork and a clipboard with a yellow steno pad.

"I apologize for walking in without an invitation," she said. "But knocking…" She gave a helpless shrug.

Conall stood. "That's one of the things I wanted to talk about. I'd like to get a ringer installed that sets off the lights and vibrates. And maybe an additional light on the deck that is colored?"

Scarlet made a series of swift notes. "That's certainly reasonable," she said with a nod. "I would consider that a covered modification."

"I also want to talk about putting a fridge in," Conall said, walking into the living area with her. "Perhaps make a kitchenette here."

Scarlet looked more reluctant about that. "We have certain power considerations here," she cautioned. "Our generators are not that robust and we're still expanding our solar options."

"A dorm-sized fridge?" Conall countered. "I'm not thinking of full meals, just snacks for days that Gizelle doesn't feel up to the restaurant, and a coffee maker."

Scarlet took more notes. "That's also reasonable. I would expect you to maintain sterile conditions. Sugary items in particular must be safely stowed. We haven't talked about housekeeping."

"Daily is unnecessary," Conall assured her. "Perhaps twice weekly for the linens and floors and supply us with a few basic cleaning supplies."

Scarlet nodded. "I can have a broom and dustpan brought by." She frowned at one of the potted plants that looked less robust than the others and made another note.

"I'd like to remove the glass-topped coffee table," Conall said. "Maybe replace it with something… sturdier."

"That's wise," Scarlet said, with just the hint of a smile.

"The second bedroom isn't really necessary," Conall said, as their navigation arrived at the door to it. "I would like to reserve the right to remodel it into an office in the future. I'll have a better idea of what I want to do with it once I'm back in January."

"At your expense, naturally," Scarlet specified.

"Naturally," Conall agreed.

"Agreed."

Their circuit of the house ended with the exterior. "I would appreciate a slightly larger lawn," Conall said. "But I understand that's problematic."

"I'm afraid we're rather constrained in terms of space," Scarlet said regretfully. "Presuming you do not wish to add the lease of one of the neighboring cottages to this bill."

"I do not," Conall chuckled.

They walked back inside.

"I will change out the coffee table for another and make the other cosmetic changes at no charge. The expense of the kitchenette will be billed to you. I will revise the estimate I shared with you earlier to reflect the reduced housekeeping and increased power consumption."

"It covers meals for both Gizelle and myself," Conall confirmed.

Scarlet hesitated and Conall knew that she hadn't included Gizelle's meals. "I can't charge her for grazing—" she started.

"I insist," Conall said firmly. "I also want a line item for the glassware we've managed to destroy between the two of us."

Scarlet smiled. "Very well."

"The pricing was honestly more reasonable than I expected," Conall said frankly.

Equally frank in reply, Scarlet confessed. "This is a challenging cottage to let; it's a less desirable size and price group than most of the others, and it's not right on the beach. I am also quoting this with the presumption that Gizelle's cottage will be back in service."

"I've talked her into claiming this outdoor shower instead," Conall said with a smile. "She's already moved her hoard."

"She's come so far," Scarlet said warmly. "Just a month ago, I would never have left her alone in my office making Christmas presents."

"Presents?"

"She's drawing everyone's animals for them; I've lent her some art supplies and good paper.

"Have you spoiled the surprise?" Conall teased.

Scarlet looked scandalized. "Of course not. She said she had something else for you and I didn't ask." She said it as if she suspected the worst and didn't want to know.

Conall chuckled, and marveled at how natural it felt to laugh again. "Fair enough."

Scarlet almost smiled, then added thoughtfully. "You should know that she's asked me to have some of my connections start investigating where she might have come from. She didn't want to know, when we first offered to try to find out."

Conall stilled, remembering Gizelle's fear that she was a monster. "That's a big step."

"I don't know how much we'll be able to find out," Scarlet cautioned. "A lot of the information from Beehag's case is classified."

"If it requires money..." Conall started.

He wasn't sure how to take her expression. Was she offended by the idea? Did she think he was implying a bribe?

But she only said, briskly, "I will let you know. We can have the coffee table swapped out in the next day or so, and most of the other changes over the next week. The kitchenette may take a little longer, I'm afraid. I probably won't be able to get the appliances here until just after Christmas."

"I'll be leaving for Boston a few days after Christmas," Conall said, already dreading the trip. "So if they could be installed…"

He turned at an unexpected thump that vibrated up through the floor.

Gizelle stood in the doorway, the box she had been holding at her feet and sheets of paper still falling around her.

"You're leaving?" she said in terror. "You're leaving me?"

"Gizelle, wait…"

But Gizelle was already leaping back and shifting. Conall had one last view of her grief-stricken face before she was a gazelle, her tail twitching as she fled.

When he turned back to Scarlet in dismay, the resort manager was frowning. "Yes, I think replacing the coffee table should be a priority."

CHAPTER 43

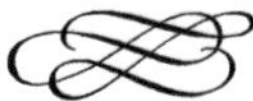

Her world was grass and gravity.

The rhythm of the nearby ocean was the only music she needed, the insects the only chorus.

Her fears were distant, and her human quiet and safe.

If she was lonely, it was a familiar loneliness, and she was free and fearless.

She nibbled at the best of the blades, comfortable knowing that she could run in any direction if danger threatened. She was fast and fleet and the emptiness inside her must only be an empty belly.

So she cropped at the lush foliage and was only a gazelle, in a weighted world of green and grass.

CHAPTER 44

Conall found the gazelle grazing at her favorite lawn, the ocean rippling just over the cliff in the late afternoon light.

"Gizelle," he said, sitting wearily at the edge of the lawn where the garden started. He didn't want to chase her, or make her feel trapped. It was the third lawn he'd checked and he was starting to appreciate exactly how steep the island was.

He was glad to see the gazelle come towards him, head down in the grass as if the grazing was the more serious business. Finally, she lifted her head, within arm's reach if he stretched, and considered him thoughtfully.

For a moment, Conall was confused.

It wasn't Gizelle.

Not really.

It was the gazelle, not Gizelle who looked back at him. It didn't feel the same as the way he looked out from his shifted form.

"Gizelle?" he asked tentatively.

The gazelle tossed her head and snorted.

Conall offered his hand anyway and the gazelle put a tentative nose to his palm and tickled it with her breath. Though he braced himself to hear, no sounds broke through the barrier of silence with this touch.

Gizelle was in there, he knew. Somewhere.

And just as he had waited for her to touch him the first time, he could wait again for her to find her way back to him.

He peeled off his clothing and folded it neatly on a bench, then shifted to graze with the gazelle.

We haven't done this in a long while, his elk said, stretching long legs and tossing his heavy head.

We should do it more often, Conall agreed.

For a long, slow afternoon, he grazed with the gazelle, enjoying the sun that beat on his dark coat and the peaceful, sweet air.

Evening fell, and the sun sank quickly into the sea. Conall marveled at how beautiful it could look, even without being able to see reds. The purples and blues of the twilight that followed were more intense than ever and the lights of the resort behind them were enchanting.

He settled onto his knees, prepared to wait out the mild night, if that's what it took, and to his joy, the gazelle came and curled against his side.

They drowsed that way for a while, then, abruptly, the din of the evening rushed back. The form at his side gave a little sigh and shifted into Gizelle.

Conall kept his elk's form a little longer, enjoying the warmth of her on his hide and the new sounds of the insects and the breeze. Then he shifted and held her close against him as they sat together in the darkness. She trembled against him.

"I will come back," he promised. "I will *always* come back."

"I know," Gizelle whispered. If he hadn't been hearing through her own ears, he might not have heard it at all. "I know you *will*, it just scares me so much that you *might not*."

I would bring him back to you, Conall's elk assured her directly. *He would have no choice.*

"I wouldn't," Conall confirmed. "He's a terrible bully and his is the only voice I can hear without you."

CHAPTER 45

Gizelle wasn't sure if she was trembling or shivering. The night air was cool to her human skin, and Conall's arms were warm. When he kissed her, she forgot to be cold, and his fingers on her bare skin heated her up much more than they should be able to.

There was just enough light from the strings of Christmas bulbs above the bench to see each other with. His shoulders were so broad and full of interesting planes, and his cheek was so fascinatingly covered with stubble.

There wasn't enough light to see the blue of his eyes, but they were bright for her.

"How can you look at me that way?" she asked in wonder.

"Which way?" Conall asked, drinking her in.

"Like I'm… beautiful."

"Because you're beautiful," Conall said without hesitation.

"But I'm so skinny and pale and knobby," Gizelle said in despair. She wanted curves, and comfortable skin, like Magnolia.

"You are perfect," Conall insisted. "And you have clearly not been exposed to many fashion magazines. Let me show you."

He put a finger on her cheek. "Women wear makeup to give

them cheekbones half this beautiful." He kissed them solemnly, one and then the other.

"A swan wishes it had a neck so perfect," he said, kissing down her neck.

"Lydia's a swan," Gizelle giggled breathlessly.

His mouth found her collarbone, and his hands explored lower. "Your breasts are my ideal in shape and they fill up a hand just like they should," he told her, cupping one and using a finger to define the profile of the other. Gizelle had to hiss her breath in as he passed her nipple. It was hard as a pebble, and she knew it wasn't only from the chill that she'd already forgotten about.

Then he laid her back in the grass and kissed them, sucking and nibbling his way down to her belly. "There is an industry of health clubs that make millions from women who dream of a belly so flat and fit."

And after that, he didn't say anything, only worshiped her body with his mouth until she was pulling at his shoulders and wordlessly begging him to take her.

"I didn't bring a condom," he said, denying her whimpered request for the hard cock that was brushing her thighs. "But that doesn't mean you can't have satisfaction."

Then he dipped his head and *licked* into her eager folds and Gizelle arched up in shock and delight. His tongue was agile and impossible and unexpectedly intimate as it explored her, and Gizelle had to grab fistfuls of grass and cry out as he suckled at her until pleasure washed over her.

For a long moment afterwards, she could only lie and pant as he kissed her back to calm.

"But what about you?" she asked, when she had breath again. His cock was hard and thick between them as he lay beside her.

"It can be just about you this time," Conall insisted.

But when she reached to touch him, caressing the length of him, he hissed and flinched.

"Can I kiss you there, too?" Gizelle asked. "Because that was *fun*."

"I'd… like… that." She was still touching him gently and it was clearly causing complications in his speech.

She scooted down until she could kiss it in earnest, first laying butterfly kisses all over it, then drawing the head into her mouth with her tongue.

Conall groaned, shifting his hips and brushing his fingers into her hair.

"Gizelle," he moaned, but Gizelle's mouth was too busy to answer.

He was dauntingly large, but she could lick and suck and coax the beautiful thing further into her mouth than she had thought possible.

Then, while she was still figuring out how best to make it fit, Conall made a guttural noise, and clenched his hand in her hair. His elk bugled in triumph and her mouth was unexpectedly filling with his hot, salty seed.

"Mph," she said, sitting up after the last waves of his release had eased. She licked her lips curiously.

"You," Conall said firmly. "Are amazing."

Gizelle decided that she liked being amazing.

CHAPTER 46

As Conall passed the bar deck the following morning, he was startled by a hand on his arm. "Scarlet needs to see you in her office right away," Travis told him.

"I'll swing by her office after I've…"

"No, she meant now," Travis said urgently.

Conall blinked at him. "Alright," he agreed reluctantly. "But if you see Gizelle, tell her where I am."

Travis nodded, and gave him what Conall thought might be a pitying look. It didn't bother him as much as it usually would.

As Conall took the flight of steps that led to Scarlet's office at the top of the resort, it occurred to him that some of the things he had ordered might have arrived early.

The courtyard outside of the manager's office was indeed, filled with boxes. Conall paused to look at the shipping labels, grinning as he thought about Gizelle's reaction to them.

"I'm sorry I didn't warn you these were coming," he said, entering Scarlet's office. "I'm expecting a few more that…" He stopped in alarm.

Sitting across from Scarlet was a familiar figure, smartly dressed in a lightweight silk pantsuit, her hair done perfectly.

"Mother?!"

"Conall!" she said as she turned and both women stood. She signed, "I've come to help you out of whatever mess you're in."

"Everything is fine," Conall assured her out loud with a glance for Scarlet.

His mother's eyes narrowed. "When everything is fine," she said, abandoning the sign language, "you don't up and attempt to sell a business that made the cover of *Time* magazine and run away to a half-rate foreign island for some little gold digger."

Conall looked past her. "You've met my mother, Aideen?" he said mildly to Scarlet.

"It's been a pleasure," Scarlet said. Her face was carefully neutral in a way that made Conall suspect she was seething. His mother tended to do that to people. "I was just explaining that we didn't have any accommodations currently available for guests to simply drop in. This *is* our busiest time of year."

"And I," Aideen added smoothly, "was explaining that I would stay with you. You can certainly afford any surcharge necessary."

Now both women were looking at Conall and he suddenly understood Gizelle's regular impulse to simply shift and run away.

They abruptly looked past him and Conall turned to find a gazelle skittering into the courtyard. Before he could find some way to warn her—of what he wasn't even sure—she had shifted seamlessly into her human form. "Oh, Conall!" she said in excitement, coming to tug on his arm. "Travis and Wrench are putting the Christmas tree up at the event hall! Bastian is going to put a star on top! You have to come see!"

"Gizelle," he said cautiously, not budging. "This is my mother."

She stopped pulling on him and stared at Aideen. "A mother?" she said in wonder. "You have a mother?"

Aideen stared back at her.

"Mother," Conall said patiently. "This is Gizelle."

"You're not wearing any clothing," his mother said severely.

Gizelle met her disapproving gaze with a lifted chin. "That is the least of my oddities," she promised.

"I see," Aideen said dryly. "It's nice to meet you," she added, and she extended a polite hand to Gizelle, who promptly darted behind Conall.

"I don't do that," she said from behind him.

Conall could feel the tremor in her slight body, pressed up behind him. "You don't have to do that," he said protectively.

That earned him a narrow look from his mother. "You *heard* her," she said in surprise.

Gizelle peered around him and said proudly. "He can use *my* ears, if we're touching."

Aideen's mouth went thoughtfully thin. "How curious," she said, as neutral as Scarlet's face. "That certainly explains some things." To Conall, she added, "I brought the item you asked your assistant to mail. I certainly wasn't going to trust it to a service."

She gestured to an instrument case and something in Conall's chest did a flip-flop. Gizelle trailed behind him cautiously as he went to inspect it, frowning over a scuff on the bag.

He felt as if he was trembling like Gizelle as he knelt to unzip it, though his hands were steady.

Gizelle peeked over his shoulder as he pulled the guitar out, fingers reverent over the glossy neck and inlaid mother-of-pearl.

"What a pretty guitar," Gizelle breathed near his ear. "Will you play it for me?"

A strum across the strings made a terrible noise; even if he hadn't loosened the tension for long-term storage, it had been unused for ten years and wouldn't have been in tune anyway.

Gizelle winced. "I like Tex's better," she said dismissively.

"That's a Zemaitis," his mother said, appalled. "That particularly instrument is insured for a hundred thousand dollars."

Conall didn't have to see Gizelle's blank gaze to know what she looked like. She wouldn't know what a Zemaitis was, or probably what insurance was. She might not even know what dollars were; the resort was all-inclusive and no one here used money.

Scarlet cleared her throat. "If Mrs. Wright is staying, I will need her signature on the policies agreement."

"Fine," Conall said shortly, still caressing his beloved instrument.

He started tuning it, then Gizelle withdrew her hand from his arm and the sound cut off like he'd lost a limb.

Later, he promised the guitar, zipping it back into the case as his mother, triumphant, signed the papers that Scarlet gave her.

"Let me show you the way," he told Aideen. "The staff can bring your bags later." He gathered up the guitar himself.

"And the tree!" Gizelle remembered. "You have to come see the Christmas tree!" She scampered out ahead of them.

"Can she please put on some clothing first?" Aideen asked in a strangled voice.

CHAPTER 47

Conall's mother seemed much more comfortable with Gizelle once she'd found the spare dress that Tex kept behind the bar, and Gizelle was glad for that.

His *mother*.

Gizelle could see that they had similar cheekbones, and she had dark hair like Conall did, but most fascinating of all, she had the same sky blue eye color, even though she was not the same person behind them. Her nose, however, was much different, and her mouth, a perfect shade of lipstick red, was utterly alien.

"Why is she staring at me?" Aideen asked Conall.

"I've never seen a mother before," Gizelle answered for him.

"This will be your room, Mother," Conall said, ignoring both of them. Gizelle wasn't touching him; maybe he hadn't noticed the exchange.

"Isn't it lucky you got a two-bedroom cottage," Aideen said airily.

"It was the last one they had available when I made the reservation," Conall explained shortly.

"This place boasts its fine gourmet food," Aideen said. "And I'm famished. Show me to the restaurant, dear. We can all get to know each other over a nice meal."

Conall looked at Gizelle in alarm. "I don't think that's a good idea," he said reluctantly, and Gizelle knew he was thinking about their first disastrous dinner.

But she'd come a long way since then.

"That's okay," Gizelle insisted. "I can do that."

"Are you *sure*?" Conall asked.

"I'll leave the doors of time closed," Gizelle assured him. "And I promise not to shift."

"What about the Christmas tree?" Did Conall sound slightly desperate?

"They are leaving it up until New Year's," Gizelle said. "I can show you later."

Like a man resigned to disaster, Conall offered each of them an elbow. "Let's go have dinner," he said.

Breck was surprised to see them. "Gizelle," he said slowly. "Conall," even more slowly. Then, "Ma'am?"

"Have you got a *good* table for us?" Conall asked. Gizelle was not sure that he had ever sounded so stiff.

Breck swallowed, looking out over the crowded restaurant. "I'm… not sure."

"Don't be foolish," Aideen said crossly. "There are plenty of empty tables. Put us there!" She pointed imperiously at a table in the center.

"Oh, no," Conall and Breck said together.

"Let me find you a corner," Breck said with a flash of his best charming smile for Aideen. "Only the best for family of our favorite Irish Elk."

Aideen seemed pleased with that as the waiter disappeared into the din.

Gizelle watched the room, fascinated. It was noisy, but it was noisy like the ocean; a rolling din of sound, not sharp and loud like she had feared.

"Are you okay with this?" Conall asked quietly near Gizelle's ear.

She smiled at him. "I can do it," she whispered back.

Breck came back and led them to a table that was not exactly quiet, but was at least on the edge of the room. He held the chair for Aideen, who sat down as gracefully as a swan. Was she a dancer like Lydia? Gizelle wondered.

"Are you all right?" Conall asked, still standing with her as Gizelle realized she was staring again and that Breck was holding a chair for her.

She looked up at Conall. *His* blue eyes were worried for her. She smiled slowly, because she loved the way that they softened when she did. "I got this," she said, and she sat gingerly in the chair Breck was holding and tried to mimic Aideen's effortless elegance. Conall sat last. Breck had cleverly put Aideen closest to Gizelle so that he would be able to see both their faces without looking back and forth and he wouldn't need to hold her hand.

"So Gizelle, my dear," Aideen said, after they had placed their requests for drinks. "Tell me all about yourself."

Gizelle tucked her feet up on the chair with her, forgetting to copy Aideen's manners. "I don't know much about myself," she said honestly. "But I am about this tall and I like to run."

"Mm," said Aideen, not impressed. "Where are you from?"

"Nobody knows," Gizelle said mournfully. "I don't remember anything before Tony and Neal set us all loose from the zoo."

It was Aideen's turn to stare. "The… zoo?"

"There was a collector," Conall explained for her. "He was kidnapping exotic shifters and keeping them in a… menagerie."

"How dreadful!" Aideen said in horror. "You poor thing!"

Gizelle smiled tentatively. "I… don't remember it," she insisted, but when she reached for her water glass, her hand was trembling, so she sat on it instead.

There was a moment of silence that even Gizelle's poor social skills could recognize as awkward.

Aideen politely said, "So, I understand you're a gazelle shifter."

"Yes," Gizelle said softly. "We like to run." She cast about for something interesting to add. "Oh, I can hypnotize people."

"Hypnotize?" Aideen said in shock.

"I could show you—" Gizelle started to offer, but Conall cleared his throat urgently. She looked at his anxious face and added, "Later, maybe?"

"How fascinating," Aideen said, sounding slightly strangled.

Breck brought them a tray of drinks then; something fancy and tall for Aideen, a juice with a straw for Gizelle and a gin and tonic for Conall.

"I didn't order this," Conall said as Breck put his in front of him.

"You're going to need it," Breck said sympathetically.

Gizelle smiled at him nervously and played with her straw.

CHAPTER 48

Conall began to relax as the meal went on.

Gizelle startled once, when someone dropped a fork with a clatter at the next table, but she only made it partway out of her chair before hauling herself back and giving a determined smile to Aideen. She handled her utensils well, and the conversation even better.

His mother was unexpectedly sympathetic; Conall thought that Gizelle's story had surprised and touched her and the subtle barbs and cuts that he had braced for never materialized. She had clearly been expecting a certain class of woman who would be out for Conall's money. But no one could expect Gizelle.

Chef himself served them a tender pork dish in a light glaze, with tender new vegetables and a silky root mash that wasn't all potatoes. Dessert was a creamy cheesecake with a sweet cherry topping. The fine food even impressed Aideen.

After the meal, Conall and Gizelle took her on a brief tour of the resort. He and Gizelle compromised on just one of her favorite lawns, and showed her the spa, the bar deck, the pool, overlooking the beach below, ending at last at the event hall.

The glittering tree had been assembled, in all its tinselly glory, and half of it was dripping in ornaments.

"It's so beautiful," Gizelle breathed. "It looks like *sugar*."

"Don't lick it," Conall felt obligated to warn her.

Aideen laughed uncertainly.

Travis and Wrench were moving the ladder to a bare portion of the tree. "Want to hang a few?" Travis offered Gizelle.

"I find I'm quite fatigued," Aideen said pointedly. "Conall, shall we retire?"

Conall stiffened, looking at Gazelle, who was gazing longingly at the box of gleaming ornaments. She looked reluctantly across him at Aideen and chewed on her lower lip.

"Oh, you won't mind if we leave you to this, will you Gizelle, my dear?" Aideen said sweetly. Conall wanted to step between them; he knew this voice of his mother's and it never meant that good things were happening.

But Gizelle took it at face value and smiled like the moon. "Of course not," she said, and she was off to the box of temptation like a shot.

Aideen tucked her hand into Conall's elbow and led him firmly away.

They could not speak on the walk back to Conall's cottage; between the darkness and the awkwardness of having to turn to each other to make lipreading or sign language work, it was easiest to walk in silence.

But, as Conall suspected, once they arrived at the cottage, Aideen did not simply retire, but waved Conall to a seat on the couch as she took the recliner like it was her throne. Conall noted that the potted plant that Scarlet had scowled at was blooming riotously. Graham must have come and worked his gardening magic on it. The coffee table had been replaced and the rustic wooden piece in its place looked sturdy and had rounded corners.

"Gizelle is certainly… interesting," she said.

"She's my mate," Conall told her firmly, wondering if his mother was going to try to insist that he date someone more suitable to their elite social class or some other nonsense.

"Are you sure?" Aideen asked smoothly. "She said herself that she can hypnotize people."

"She has not hypnotized me," Conall growled. "I mean she did once, but I'm not hypnotized now."

"How would you know?" Aideen asked innocently. "Isn't being convinced of something false what hypnotism *is*?"

Conall stood up, fury rising in his chest. "She is my mate," he insisted. "She is my everything. You may make peace with that, or you may leave."

Aideen stood as well, hands raised in the sign for peace. "Darling! There's no reason to get upset! I'm your mother, I just want to make sure that you are certain about this." She sat again, gesturing that Conall do the same, and after a reluctant moment, Conall did.

"Is she autistic?" Aideen asked, after a moment.

"Is she what?" Conall wasn't sure he had recognized the word correctly.

"Autistic," Aideen repeated. "Has she been diagnosed with anything? She's certainly… not normal. And the trembling, is it medical? I know some very good shifter therapists at a facility in Boston who would be able to help her work through her trauma. Certainly a little… behavior modification would do her a world of good."

"Behavior modification?" Conall asked in horror, trying to imagine Gizelle being subjected to batteries of tests and training.

"Well, you have to admit that she would get along much better in Boston if she kept her clothing on more reliably," Aideen said offhandedly.

"I am not bringing her to Boston," Conall said flatly. "She doesn't need drugs or modification of any kind. If she wants therapy, it will be on *her* terms, when *she's* ready. Right now, she needs love and safety, and she has that here."

"You don't have to be so dramatic!" Aideen protested. "You make it sound like I'm suggesting you put her in a mental institution! She could be perfectly happy at the house and might even be able to go out in public with a little work. You don't have to throw away a lifetime of accomplishment to keep her if that's what you've got your heart set on. I'm not a monster, Conall. I just want what's best for you."

"I'm not bringing her back to Boston," Conall repeated firmly. "She would be miserable and I would never forgive myself."

Aideen's face went through a range of emotions and settled on distant resignation. "Very well," she said. "No one can say I didn't raise a son with conviction." She added, "I won't say I'm not a little disappointed, but you clearly have feelings for her, and… she's a very sweet young woman who is very attached to you. Your happiness is more important to me than your business success."

Conall's smile in return was wry; he knew how important his business success was to her. "Thank you," he said simply.

"I hope you will, at least come visit sometimes?" Conall could imagine the artistically plaintive note in her voice.

"I will need to make several trips to sort everything out," Conall assured her. "And you are always welcome to visit us here."

"It is a lovely place," Aideen agreed with a sigh as she stood and looked around critically. "A little small and lacking in *culture*, but I suppose that it would make an acceptable get-away periodically."

That was his mother. Conall had to chuckle as he also stood.

"Isn't it precious to hear you laughing again," Aideen said wonderingly. Her features were surprisingly soft. "Come, give your mother a hug and I will go to bed. It's been a very long and unexpected day."

Conall enfolded her in a heartfelt hug, feeling the last of his dread melt away. This was going to be fine. His mother could see what a special and amazing person Gizelle was, and would accept that their life was on this island… if not forever, for a very long time.

CHAPTER 49

Conall's mother was not what Gizelle had imagined, but she seemed very nice. Her smiles were careful things of beauty, and she spoke very sweetly.

Gizelle showed her more of the resort and even went with her to the spa to have Laura and Lydia paint their nails while Aideen told her stories of Conall as a little boy, something that was very hard for Gizelle to picture.

Only once did Gizelle shift and run, when Graham upended a wheelbarrow of gravel unexpectedly on the other side of a hedge.

She returned at once, sheepishly, to collect the pieces of her sundress. "I'm sorry," she said. "Travis can put it back together for me. I like to run," she tried to explain. "When I'm frightened, I just don't think about it."

Conall had started to defend her to his mother, but Aideen interrupted him. "That's very sensible, dear," she said kindly. "A perfectly normal reaction."

Her understanding had puzzled Gizelle, because she knew that whatever else she was, she wasn't normal. But Conall had smiled with such a look of relief that Gizelle didn't want to press the matter.

Instead, she asked, "Do you know what pronking is?"

Aideen looked horrified. "Possibly? I don't know what they call things these days."

Because her sundress was already in pieces, Gizelle shifted and demonstrated, springing around the lawn with all four legs perfectly straight and her back arched.

She returned to them, shifting back to two legs between one leap and another and throwing herself into Conall's arms with ringing laughter. He caught her easily, spun her around, and then said merrily, "Let's go get you another dress before you scandalize my mother further."

He carried her to the cottage, Aideen trailing behind them with a hand over her eyes. Perhaps it was too sunny for her.

After she had slipped into her dress, Conall and Aideen decided to visit the pool for an afternoon dip.

Gizelle had other ideas and knew that Aideen would be shocked because she had no bathing suit anyway, so she slipped away to The Den. They still called it the bachelors' house sometimes, even though Bastian and Travis had mates living there now. It was Travis' mate that she was there to find. This time, she remembered to knock on the bedroom door.

"Who is it?" Jenny called after a moment and some laughter that wasn't all hers.

"Gizelle," she answered, wondering if that was an invitation, or if she should wait for something more definitive.

"Just a minute," Jenny said promptly, answering that question.

After a few moments, she slipped out of the door and caught Gizelle turning one of the paintings in the hallway upside down. "I like it better this way," Gizelle said simply.

"Other than rearranging the decor, what's up?" Jenny asked.

"I want you to teach me to shift with my clothes on," Gizelle said.

Jenny blinked at her. "I don't know if I can," she admitted. "It's just something I… do. I don't really know how I do it."

Disappointment swept over Gizelle. "Oh," she said sadly. "I guess I know how that feels."

Jenny's expression turned to pity. "I'm sorry," she said. Then, curiously, "Why do you want to all of a sudden?"

Gizelle twisted her hands in the skirt of her dress. "I want Conall's mother to like me," she said shyly. "And she'd like me more if I wore clothes all the time."

Jenny smiled like the sun. "Oh, sweetie. She seems to like you just *fine*. I wouldn't worry a thing about that."

Gizelle smiled back hopefully. Jenny was a lawyer, *and* she had a sister. She *must* know about things like that.

CHAPTER 50

Gizelle braved dinner with them at the restaurant again that night.

Conall was beginning to genuinely relax; they had been seated without incident, and though Gizelle had jumped nearly out of her seat at a crash from the bar below, she settled at once, and quizzed Aideen and Conall about bridges, puzzled by the idea that bodies of water could be smaller than an ocean but larger than a thin creek that she could leap over.

As they explained lakes and rivers and spits, mocking things up with cutlery and napkins, Gizelle suddenly went very tense.

"There will be a lake of fire," she said in frightened confusion, touching the forks that had been the Tobin Bridge. "The cages will burn, but black wings will bridge it."

"What black wings?" Conall asked gently. "Like Lydia?"

Gizelle shook her head, the moment passing. "Different wings," she said carelessly. "Can we have dessert first?"

Conall carefully put the silverware back in order. Aideen gave him a long, thoughtful look, but only patted Gizelle's hand as if she were a child and suggested that they save dessert as a reward for finishing their meal.

After dinner, they walked back to the cottage.

"Conall, darling, will you play for us?" Aideen asked casually as the lights in the cottage turned on.

Conall felt his chest seize and couldn't identify the emotion that came with it. Was it fear? Sorrow? Anticipation?

Gizelle's hand was on his arm so that he could hear the excitement in her voice as she added, "Oh yes! Will you play Christmas music?"

The one request he might have ignored. The two together were impossible to deny.

He tuned the guitar sitting with Gizelle perched on the back of the couch touching his neck. It took several minutes to bring the strings into tune, a task that used to take thirty seconds at most. His fingers weren't used to the strings anymore and the whispering voices were distracting.

Finally, it sounded right, and he began to pick out Christmas songs from his memory.

It was a far cry from the concerts he had once performed in, and not even terribly similar to the house recitals he had done for family. Gizelle loved everything he played unconditionally; he could feel her delight and satisfaction with every note. Aideen had an odd expression throughout his playing; Conall couldn't put his finger on what it was.

His calluses had softened years ago, so he didn't play long.

"That was wonderful," Gizelle said, letting go of him to clap her hands into the sudden silence that cut off the last notes.

Whatever else she said was lost as she leaped down from the couch and scampered out onto the deck.

When he gave Aideen a quizzical look, she shrugged. "Something about having to visit with the stars," she signed.

Conall reverently put the guitar into its case.

When he looked up, Aideen signed, "It was so nice seeing you play again. If you brought her back to Boston, we could…"

Conall looked away furiously, refusing to watch the rest of what she would say. "I'm not bringing her to Boston." He stood to take the case into the bedroom and Aideen caught him.

"Don't be angry," she signed firmly. "I only thought you might have changed your mind."

"I am not changing my mind," he answered out loud. "Don't ever bring it up."

Aideen bowed her head. "I'm sorry," she signed. When she lifted her head, she spoke. "I won't ask again."

CHAPTER 51

Gizelle was practicing her letters on the couch the next afternoon. She couldn't understand why copying letters was so much harder than copying pictures. She had been so happy with how her Christmas portraits had turned out, actually looking like everyone's inner animals (Saina and Scarlet had stumped her; she'd finally drawn a fish from a picture in a book for Saina and drawn the courtyard full of flowers for Scarlet), and she was so *unhappy* with how spidery and crooked her writing was.

She looked up at the footsteps, already knowing it wasn't Conall, but grateful for distraction.

"Look how studious you are," Aideen said with admiration.

"I want to read everything and understand people," Gizelle said cheerfully.

That seemed to take Aideen aback a moment. Then she said graciously, "Maybe I can help you with that a little."

Gizelle put aside her pen and carefully put the lid on it as Aideen settled beside her. She'd already discovered that she would fidget with things to the point of drawing on things she didn't mean to if she didn't put them away.

"It's about Conall," Aideen said gently. "And about knowing what will make him happy."

"I want to know all about that," Gizelle said eagerly.

"Conall has had a very hard time," Aideen explained. "He lost his father when he was young, and his music career was very challenging. Going deaf was hardest of all, of course. But he was very strong and smart and worked very hard to make the best of everything."

Gizelle listened intensely and nodded because Aideen seemed to expect it.

"He made something amazing for himself in Boston," she continued. "And he won't tell you because he cares for you, but he will be very, very sad to give those things up."

Gizelle's eagerness turned to ash in her chest.

"He has a life in Boston. Family. Success. Staying here with you, he gives all of that up." Aideen's voice was so sensible and matter-of-fact. Of course this was true.

"I can let him hear," Gizelle said in a small voice.

"He's spent years living with his disability," Aideen reminded her. "He turned it into a remarkable asset. And what would you do in Boston? Walk to business meetings with him so you could hold his hand? How would you explain that? Magic isn't something most people in Boston believe in. Normal shifters are still a secret in most circles."

She sighed and rubbed her face, looking suddenly very vulnerable. "Gizelle, you're a sweet young woman. You clearly care about my son, and he's very fond of you, but think about what you'd be asking him to give up. Really think about it. Try to understand it."

Aideen's eyes were earnest and direct and so exactly the same blue as Conall's. "His life. The business he spent so much of his heart building. He has family and so many friends in Boston. He'd be turning his back on all of that, and what are you giving him in return?"

"He said… he said I gave him music back," Gizelle said, trying to remember why that had felt like such a momentous thing when he said it. She tried to recall the other things he said that had made her feel so useful and they all seemed so small and foolish. Making love to him and making him laugh could not compare to a *career*. A career in a *city*.

"Losing music? That didn't break him. Giving up everything he worked so hard on? That could."

Gizelle stared, conflicted and hurting inside. "He'd have *me*," she said faintly.

Aideen patted her hand and didn't have to say how little that was. "He would get over you if you let him go," she assured her. "He is smart and would know that you did the right thing when he thought about it more. This island is the best place for you, of course. But Boston is the best place for him."

Gizelle's antelope was trembling and anxious, pacing in her head, and the whispering all seemed too loud and overwhelming. Gizelle had to resist the impulse to shift with all of her will. She had promised herself she wouldn't flee and right now that was the only thing she wanted to do.

She wanted to run and run because nothing she could do would be right. She would hurt Conall if she asked him to stay. She would hurt him if she told him to go. Was Aideen right, that the hurt wouldn't last for him if she let go? She knew it would hurt forever for herself.

"I don't know what to do," she confessed.

Aideen sighed. "I'm so sorry, Gizelle. I just… don't want him to *resent* you."

"Resent me?" That sounded worst of all.

"If he gave that all up for you, after a while, he'd probably regret it. He wouldn't be *happy* here, and he'd always wonder why."

"Regret," Gizelle whispered.

Regret was a pile of broken glasses and bare feet.

"He'd miss you, of course," Aideen said sweetly. "At first. But he could have a *normal* life back in Boston."

Whatever else Gizelle was, she knew she was not *normal*. Hard as she tried, she would never be anything close.

She wanted to weep, and fling herself into the air and leap away, and she wanted to curl into a ball that wouldn't let the pain in. She wanted to cry, but her eyes were dry and her voice was gone, choked by horror.

"Don't make him choose," Aideen suggested. "Everyone knows you like to run away. That's all you have to do."

Gizelle raised searching eyes to Aideen's lovely face. She was Conall's *mother*. A mother would know the best thing for her child.

"I know you'll do the right thing," Aideen said, patting her hand gently.

Running would be so *easy*.

CHAPTER 52

Gizelle was standing at the French doors, looking out over the deck towards the ocean. The sun was starting to set, making all of her edges golden and soft.

It was tricky light, difficult to lipread in; Conall went to take Gizelle's hand so he wouldn't have to.

To his surprise, she skittered back from his touch and her eyes, when she turned to him, gleamed suspiciously. She wouldn't quite look at him, though she carefully tipped her face so he could easily see her.

"I want you to go back to Boston," she said.

"I am going back," Conall said, puzzled. Had he misunderstood? "But I'll be gone less than a week. I've already got the lawyers drawing up the paperwork I'll need to sign and… Gizelle?"

"I want you to stay in Boston. You shouldn't come back."

Conall stared at her mouth, willing it to different shapes.

"I don't understand," he said. When he reached again for her hand, she reluctantly gave it to him.

If the rush of sound was usually overwhelming, it was even worse this time, making him wince at the scale of intensity. He twined his fingers into hers and when he concentrated, he could tune out the worst of it.

Gizelle raised tearful eyes to him. "I wish I could already write," she said. "I would have written you a letter and gotten it all right and not have to think about how to say things when all I want to do is run."

"Why do you want to run?" Conall had to ask. "What changed? Why do you want me to go away?" The obvious occurred to him. "My mother. My mother convinced you I'd be better off in Boston."

Worse than that, he recognized now that Aideen taken the time to win Gizelle's trust, to best betray it. At that moment, he would cheerfully have throttled his own mother. Maybe he could convince the Shifting Sands staff to make good on their myriad of threats and save him the trouble.

"You have a life in Boston," Gizelle reminded him softly. "An important business. Important friends. Opportunity you shouldn't waste. I... don't want to keep you from better things."

Those were his mother's words all right.

His elk offered to drive his mother from their herd... and Conall was half-sure he was serious.

Conall was more than half-sure he would take the offer at that moment, looking at the raw pain in Gizelle's face.

But she hadn't run.

"My life is on this island," he assured her. "And the most important opportunity I will ever have is right in front of me. As for friends…" he had to laugh dryly, thinking about the curious, quirky staff of Shifting Sands, and the way they had opened their arms to him.

There was no comparison to the callous, self-important dandies he'd thought were friends in the city. They had been his friends when he was a rising star, left him when his world came crashing down, and come crawling back for awkward favors when he rebuilt himself and clawed some success from the ashes of his career. The Deaf community of Boston had been welcoming, but he had been too bitter and angry to accept their offers of friendship.

Here, on this strange island, they didn't care if he was famous, or if he was rich, or that he was deaf. As long as he loved Gizelle, they would accept him without judgment.

And Conall could imagine doing nothing else. "My friends are already here."

"What if I never remember anything?" Gizelle cried. "What if I never find out where I came from?"

"None of that matters," Conall said sincerely.

Her eyes were dark behind the tears: aching, ancient pools. "But I'm never going to be *normal*, Conall. I'm all mixed up in my head, and even if I learn *everything*, I am never going to be ordinary. I'm… broken. And I don't think I will ever be fixed."

"You aren't broken," Conall started.

"I *am*," Gizelle interrupted, as fiercely as she'd ever said anything to him.

Just as fiercely, Conall replied, "You are not a *thing* to be fixed. You are person. A beautiful, clever, caring person who deserves to be loved. And I love you."

He took a deep breath, and tucked a loose lock of her hair back from her face. "No, you may not ever be normal, but I hope I can make you happy, because you make me whole. Just the way you are."

The tears welling in her dark eyes spilled over. "I cry too much," she whimpered.

"Then I will comfort you," Conall promised, and he folded her into his arms as she took a fistful of his silk shirt and sobbed into his chest, all the tension in her body releasing.

CHAPTER 53

"Is this my fault?" Gizelle had to ask quietly, her chest tight and her hands shaking too hard to unwind from each other.

Wrench was picking up Aideen's matching bags and he gave her a sharp look. "He can't hear you," the tattooed man reminded her before he disappeared with all of the luggage.

Indeed, Conall was looking away from her, at Aideen coming out of her bedroom with her hair perfectly done and her chin high.

"There's no reason to be this *melodramatic*," she said with a sniff. "It's incredibly selfish of you to throw me off the island just a few days before Christmas, and so *unnecessary*."

"I find it necessary," Conall growled.

"I'm sure this isn't *your* choice," Aideen said to Conall, with a look like thorns at Gizelle.

Gizelle kept herself from stepping behind Conall's comforting form mostly by being too afraid and sad to move. She had thought that Aideen liked her, that she and Conall and his mother could be a real family. She'd never had a family and it had sounded so pleasant.

But nothing about Aideen's anger and disgust was *pleasant*.

"You should have just run," Aideen said coldly to Gizelle. "You'll be sorry when you break his heart."

Gizelle's heart quailed in her chest. What if Aideen was right? What if Conall regretted her? Or worse, resented her?

Conall stepped between them. "She *gave* me my heart," he snarled. "And I trust her with it."

Gizelle rallied at his words and the undeniable truth behind them. "I'm very sorry you couldn't like me," she said, peering around Conall. "I *had* hoped you could be my mother, too."

Aideen stared at her, clearly expecting some other kind of response, and her surprise gave Gizelle the rest of the courage she needed to step from behind Conall and extend her hand as steadily as she could. He put a firm hand on her shoulder but didn't hold her back.

"I enjoyed meeting you," Gizelle said as formally as she knew how. "And you were nice to me even though you thought I was too weird and I'm glad for that much. I can't be sorry for choosing Conall over listening to you, and I'm not really sad to see you go, but I feel badly for Conall because he is so angry with you."

Aideen took her offered hand as if she could not figure out a way around it, and her elk's distressed voice came clearly into Gizelle's head.

...shame! Bow our head to the alpha female of the herd! Instead we lose everything! Remorse! Run!

"You don't have to run," Gizelle said in sudden sympathy. "I don't blame you. It is a hard thing when you are afraid of being alone, or of feeling trapped. Sometimes we don't make the right choices and we're afraid of facing truths."

Aideen and her elk were both stunned into silence. Sky blue eyes like Conall's but so very different gazed back at her in consternation.

"You don't want to miss your plane," Conall growled, clearly not ready to forgive anything.

Aideen licked her lips and drew back her hand from Gizelle. "No," she said, dazed. "I don't suppose that I do."

But she paused in the doorway. "Perhaps I can come back and visit, some day?"

Whatever gentleness she had hoped to find was not apparent in Conall's stony face, but after a moment, he nodded. "Perhaps," he conceded.

Then Aideen lifted her chin and walked away with the kind of graceful dignity that Gizelle could only aspire to.

When her footsteps had finally crunched away on the gravel to be drowned in the unending sound of the ocean, Gizelle turned to Conall.

This time she was touching him when she asked, "Was this my fault?"

Conall's look was no less intense than his mother's had been, but it felt much better than hers had. "This wasn't your fault," he said fiercely.

"If I had been more normal," Gizelle sighed. "If I had worn my clothing more...."

He put his hands on either side of her face, gentle but irresistible. "You are perfect just the way you are," he said with quiet fervor. "I wouldn't change a single thing."

"Even—" Gizelle started.

"Nothing," Conall promised without reservation. "Not anything."

You are perfect, his elk echoed, and if it was hard not to believe Conall, it was impossible not to believe his elk. *You are all the herd we need.*

Her gazelle took a few springy steps in joy and contentment and Gizelle knew that even if she sometimes had to run, she would never have to run alone again.

CHAPTER 54

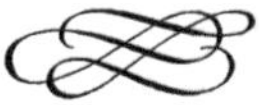

Even if Conall had not actually needed Gizelle for what he was about to face, he couldn't imagine doing it without her.

"Are you sure?" she asked anxiously, a hand on his neck.

Conall wasn't sure at all. "I'm ready," he said anyway.

Gizelle reached over his shoulder, keeping her other hand carefully on his bare skin, and tapped the play-arrow on the screen in front of them.

The file had taken nearly an hour to download; Conall knew better than to try to watch it streaming on the resort's unreliable network.

It was always jarring seeing himself in videos, but it was even more surreal to hear himself.

He stalked onto the stage; he had been so angry then. Angry and undefeated and grim.

He hadn't bothered to acknowledge the audience, though they enthusiastically applauded his entrance. He remembered how gingerly he had carried the guitar, remembered how much trust that performance had taken; had the guitar been tuned correctly, or just barely well enough? Would it *stay* in tune through the entire piece? He hadn't been thinking about performing, he'd been thinking about how the guitar deserved someone who could make music *with* it, not just on it.

The orchestra had already tuned, and once he nodded at the conductor, they swept into the music he'd written.

The music *he'd* written.

The feeling of disassociation only intensified when he began playing.

The music clearly showed that he felt like he had something to prove. If there was a simple progression choice at any point, he had ignored it, preferring to show off his skill instead. There were also points where the song was more about the drama than sound phrasing. He arguably over-used the flutes as a counterpoint to the mellower guitar notes. And towards the end, the guitar might have been just slightly sliding out of tune; understandable after the way he had so ferociously played it.

But on the whole, it was *good.*

It was an emotional piece, with a strong melody and technically excellent harmony. His playing was inspired, if questionably full of angst. If he had been listening to someone else's work, he would have praised the work as excellent, though slightly raw. His recorded version gave the most cursory bow in the history of music performance and fled the stage, leaving the guitar behind as if he had been struck with a case of stage fright, while the audience rose to their feet and thundered their approval.

Conall remembered how it had felt, the silence around him like a fireman's blanket, the despair that he'd tried to recapture in his music feeling distant and unimportant as he tried to shutter away the pain, and all the other feelings that came with it.

"Conall?" Gizelle's quiet voice near his ear reminded him where he was now. "Are you all right?"

"Did you like it?" Conall had to ask, only recognizing the tightness in his throat when he heard how choked he sounded.

"It was beautiful," she said immediately. "So sad and glorious and strong."

Conall folded his head down onto her shoulder and put his arms around her, feeling weak and full of relief. "I… I deserved it," he said numbly. "I actually deserved the Grawemeyer award."

"Of course you did," Gizelle said, as if it was the most obvious thing in the world, and as if she had anything more than his own explanation of what the award was to base her opinion on. She wrapped her arms around him in return. "You are amazing."

"I never felt amazing," Conall admitted. "Not before you. I always felt like I got everything handed to me out of pity or privilege. Everyone felt *sorry* for me."

"Who would feel sorry for you?" Gizelle asked in astonishment. "You're so beautiful and smart and have such a big strong elk inside." She drew back suspiciously. "Is the word you're looking for envy?"

Conall had to laugh at her earnestness, and at his elk's proud assertion that she clearly had a point.

"I want to hear all of your music," Gizelle said eagerly. "Is there more?"

But Conall was looking at her, not at the laptop. Her face was so animated and dear. The white streaks in her dark hair were glowing in the sunlight through the French doors, and her skin was like warm velvet under his fingertips.

He traced the line of her long neck with one finger, then let it wander further, navigating her collarbone and traveling to the enticingly low neckline of her dress. She sucked in her breath and gave a tiny whine of anticipation.

She had given him everything.

And there was only one kind of music he wanted to hear now.

CHAPTER 55

"You can't open anything until Christmas," Conall reminded Gizelle from where he was sitting at the end of his bed, pulling sandals on.

"It's so *tantalizing*!" she exclaimed, bouncing in place.

Conall's cottage—their cottage!—was filled with gifts. They didn't fit under the tiny fake tree, or even on the desk where Conall had set it up. There were colorful wrapped boxes on the floor all around it, and on top of the wardrobe, and on the bedside table, and covering the easy chair in the corner.

"I only have one present for you," Gizelle said shyly. It was sitting in a place of honor in front of the plastic tree, a modest-sized box clumsily wrapped in silver paper and sporting no fewer than five glittering bows.

"I started out with more things," Conall reminded her. "And you have a lot of missed Christmases to make up for. It's all fair."

She smiled, accepting his logic. But when she went to touch one of the smaller boxes, he stopped her. "No touching, now! My mother used to threaten to take them away if she saw fingerprints on them."

Gizelle froze with her fingertips almost touching the box and reluctantly withdrew them. "I don't know how I'm going to wait two whole days," she said with a dramatic sigh. "This is the hardest thing I've ever done."

"You stood up to my mother," Conall reminded her. "You took a shower."

Gizelle considered. "Those were hard," she agreed. "But this is harder."

"You're learning to read. That's hard."

"That *is* hard," Gizelle conceded. "But… *presents*!"

Conall laughed at her earnest excitement, and it felt so good to hear him laugh. Gizelle left the enticing gift to touch his knee and he took her hand to pull her close and kiss the laughter at the edges of her mouth.

She scrambled back at the sound of a knock on the door.

"It's Scarlet," she explained. She walked backwards so that Conall would see her face. "She's angry."

Scarlet didn't *look* particularly angry when Gizelle let her in. Her face was carefully neutral and her smile for Gizelle was gentle. But Gizelle could feel the cold little prickles everywhere and every potted plant in the cottage seemed to shiver.

"I have something for you," Scarlet said.

To Gizelle's surprise, she was not speaking to Conall, but to her.

The resort's owner put a manilla envelope in her eager hands. "Your name is Jessica Ambler. You were born twenty-eight years ago on August third."

Gizelle froze, her fingers just holding the envelope.

Conall rose and walked swiftly to her side.

"What is this?" he asked when Gizelle couldn't. He put his hand on her shoulder and shuddered.

"I received it in the last mail run," Scarlet said, still looking at Gizelle. "A New York postmark, but no return address. Some of the documents are copies of confidential forms from Tony's agency, but he swears he didn't send it."

"Who is Tony?" Conall demanded. "What agency?"

That earned him an appraising look from Scarlet while Gizelle continued to stare at the envelope that her life had narrowed down to.

"Shifter Affairs," Scarlet told him. "It's a quiet branch of the US government. Tony was a guest here, working undercover. He's the one who brought Beehag's zoo to light and helped shut it down."

"I… had a name?" Gizelle shivered and was glad for the weight of Conall's hand on her shoulder.

"Let's sit," Scarlet suggested, waving a hand towards the deck, where a round table had a handful of chairs around it.

They spread the papers out and Gizelle stared at the pictures, curled up on her chair with her knees up tight to her chest.

They were photos of a family; a curly-haired toddler being held by a dark-haired man, then standing proudly holding the hands of a smiling woman. The next photo showed a splay-legged gazelle fawn shaking off a diaper.

"Your parents," Scarlet explained. "Your father was a gazelle shifter like you are. Your mother is noted as possibly a mythical shifter, but nothing was officially known."

"I… had a mother." Gizelle felt dizzy and distant. "A mother of my own." Conall offered a hand. She stared at it a moment, then put her own into it, weaving her fingers into his.

"They died in a car accident. No one could ever prove it wasn't an accident, but you were never found afterwards." Scarlet moved another paper over the photos. "Then there was this."

Conall frowned at it. Then he squeezed Gizelle's fingers until she squeaked.

"What is it?" she asked anxiously.

"A copy of a bill of sale," Conall said reluctantly. "For *exotic livestock*. I presume that is Beehag's signature."

Scarlet had clearly read through the material previously, familiar enough with it that she could show Conall and Gizelle the relevant parts of a sea of pages full of careful handwriting on grid paper.

"Subject Seven, in particular, is mentioned as a gazelle shifter, and the date on her entry to the system matches the bill of sale," she said calmly. "It appears that Beehag was researching the key to shifting. He appears to have been looking for a serum to keep shifters in animal form, to suppress their human instincts and make them… biddable. In most of the subjects, this backfired, turning them human instead."

"I thought Beehag was just a collector," Conall growled.

"I think that was his primary purpose," Scarlet agreed with deceptive serenity. "There is mention of a client or possibly a friend with 'mutual interests' who was driving some of this research. The name Corbin is mentioned in a few private letters." She shuffled through and indicated them.

"Who could even have access to all these documents?"

"I had a… number?" Gizelle asked quietly.

"It appears so," Scarlet said, ignoring Conall. "You puzzled the scientists. They tested you quite extensively. Their final diagnosis is that you went feral at some point. There are a few notes that they may have started with too young a subject, and a few that you had unexpected blood chemistry. Maybe it was the drugs they gave you, maybe it was something from your mother's side; there's a note that they were looking for basilisk blood. One of the scientists mentioned you came in with a head injury, and the brain can do amazing things to compensate if it has to. The special things you can do—it's probably a combination of all these things. I don't know if we'll ever know for sure."

Her gazelle was there at her back, nuzzling protectively. Gizelle didn't have to be here, she didn't have to remember, she could run from this.

Her gazelle had always been there, Gizelle thought fondly. Then it occurred to her: those years in the cage that she had no memory of. Her gazelle had been there.

But not with her.

Instead of her.

You remember, she told her gazelle. *You remember everything. So I don't have to.*

Spiral horns dipped in gentle acknowledgment.

There were no memories buried in her head, waiting to spring out and surprise her. There were no terrible revelations lurking in her mind to dread. She had been asleep through all of it, sheltered and protected.

Like Jenny's otter had been, before Jenny could shift.

Gizelle felt like a band around her chest had been released.

Everyone's stories of the zoo had been so harrowing, and everyone looked at her so nervously when they spoke of it, that Gizelle had unknowingly been bracing herself for all the awful things to someday come flooding back.

Now she knew they never would.

Was it terrible? she had to ask her gazelle.

The gazelle's response was almost a shrug and Gizelle's relief was complete. Animals lived *now*, not in their memories. Everything had happened long ago, and she didn't have to worry about it bubbling up someday and drowning her.

Gizelle let her legs unfold before her and drew all of the paper into a tidy pile in front of her. "Thank you," she said to Scarlet sincerely.

Some of Scarlet's icy anger thawed into sorrow. Sorrow for Gizelle. "I'm sorry I didn't have better news for you. More answers. Happier answers. Especially at Christmas."

Gizelle smiled slowly, looking between Conall, who was clearly holding his elk back from a useless trampling rampage in her defense, and Scarlet. "You don't have to feel bad for me," she said reassuringly. "I'm glad. I know now. I know my parents loved me."

"You don't feel cheated?" Conall asked, clearly feeling cheated for her. "You spent your childhood in a cage."

"I didn't," Gizelle insisted. "I wasn't really Gizelle then; I didn't have to be. I was only a gazelle." She shared her wordless gratitude for that with her gazelle and closed her eyes to share a soft nose-bump in her mind.

Gizelle opened her eyes and looked at Conall. "I wouldn't trade having some sort of normal childhood to possibly not have *you*, to not have *this* place, and *this* life."

Conall made a little indecipherable noise and squeezed her hand more tightly than ever. Gizelle could hear his elk snort, but it was a settled sort of snort. *They are ours forever forward*, the elk told Conall, calming. *They are ours* ***now***.

"Wait," Gizelle said, suddenly recognizing something else. "Wait, you said when I was born."

"August third," Scarlet said with a nod. "You're twenty-eight years old."

Gizelle slowly grinned. "I have a birthday! It will be like Christmas twice but just for me!"

Conall laughed at that, a relieved laugh, and Scarlet smiled and even gave a little chuckle.

"Do you want us to call you Jessica?" Scarlet offered, standing and brushing imaginary wrinkles from her skirt.

Gizelle shook her head. "Jessica and I started the same," she tried to explain. "Just like our names start with the same sound. But we're different people now. I'm Gizelle. There's... not a lot of me if you count things by linear memory, but this is the me that I am. She would have been someone very different."

Scarlet nodded her acceptance briskly, but her eyes were soft and kind. "Very well." With a nod, she turned to leave, then paused.

Her gaze was all for Conall then, and it was much less soft and kind. "I need a moment of your time, please. Privately."

Conall looked at Gizelle, who met his gaze steadily. "I want to look at the pictures," she said, giving him a smile.

He wanted to hover, Gizelle could tell, but he glanced at Scarlet's complicated face and nodded. "I'll be right back," he promised, laying a kiss on her head.

Then Gizelle was alone on the porch, with photographs of her family.

She didn't care about the papers from the zoo, shuffling at once to the pictures of her parents.

Her parents.

It was a dizzying idea.

She'd had a father. She'd had a *mother*.

Neither of them was well-framed in the photographs; the focus had been on Gizelle. Only half of her mother's smiling face showed in the picture, and her father was looking away.

Gizelle gathered them up close to herself and hugged them gently. Scarlet had given her the best Christmas present of all, she was sure.

Then she thought about the shining piles of wrapping and bows waiting inside, and she wasn't sure after all.

Christmas was *amazing*.

CHAPTER 56

Conall grinned at Scarlet as they closed the porch door. "I presume they came through safely?" His last gift for Gizelle would explain Scarlet's secrecy, and her obvious irritation.

"Quite," Scarlet said tightly.

"I'll pay any damages or expenses," Conall said carelessly.

"Believe me, I've already got a list in progress," Scarlet agreed. "But that's not what I wanted to talk about." She handed him a letter, and a brochure.

Conall looked at the brochure first, his eyebrows knitting in confusion. "A mental institution for shifters?" He looked up at Scarlet suspiciously. "Did my mother give you this?" he asked, anger already rising in his chest.

But Scarlet shook her head. "It was in the envelope with the rest of Gizelle's information," she said.

Conall gave her a thoughtful look. "My mother does have connections," he suggested.

Scarlet tapped the letter and let Conall read it without trying to make conversation he wouldn't be able to follow.

It was from the director of the mental institution, and it was a compelling argument for Gizelle's treatment at the facility. It was addressed to Scarlet specifically and diplomatically questioned her capability for Gizelle's care and the danger that she posed. But it somehow didn't sound like his mother's handiwork.

"This doesn't mention me," he finally realized.

"I don't think they know about you," Scarlet agreed, with a thoughtful nod. "And to be frank, if I had gotten this a few weeks earlier..."

She didn't have to finish. The wording in the letter was very clever, complimenting Scarlet and acknowledging her care at the same time it cast just enough doubt on her capacity for truly helping Gizelle.

"A hostile takeover," Conall said thoughtfully, looking over it again.

He looked up in time to see Scarlet's brow furrow in confusion, but not in time to catch her words. "Sorry, what?"

"What do you mean, a hostile takeover?"

Conall considered for only a moment, before admitting, "Your staff, they've been getting offers. Good offers, amazing even. Like someone's trying to poach everyone away from you. Even Gizelle, apparently."

Scarlet's face went dark with anger and her green eyes snapped. If she had been holding something, Conall was sure it would have been broken and he wondered if the change of pressure around them was his imagination.

"*Beehag*," she said. Her clenched teeth made lipreading difficult. "He's *dying* to have our contract canceled. And he'd have access to his father's records, even if they'd been classified. That bastard is smarter than I've given him credit for."

"If it's any consolation, none of your staff are accepting the offers," Conall told her, a little fearfully.

That did seem to settle her. The pressure eased and Scarlet seemed to soften slightly. "I appreciate you telling me," she said gravely.

For a moment so brief that Conall doubted his own eyes, she looked vulnerable, tired, and lonely—then she was drawing herself up, face serene again. "The other matter..." she said coolly.

Conall had to smile despite himself, remembering. "I will make it worth your while."

"Indeed." Scarlet raised an eyebrow at him. "I will bring them by on Christmas morning."

Conall was almost as excited for Christmas as Gizelle was.

SCARLET AND THE CHRISTMAS KITTENS

This story was originally included at the end of Tropical Christmas Stag. It has a line that is one of the greatest puns I've ever written, even though no one would actually understand it until book ten…

"I'm sorry, Mrs. Grant. I simply cannot confirm that Conall Wright is residing here, nor could I promise that he would be available to play at your daughter's wedding if he was." Even though it was a phone call, and Mrs. Jubilee Grant was several thousand miles away, Scarlet kept her face in a perfect mask of polite restraint.

Predictably, Mrs. Grant had protests.

"Yes, Mrs. Grant," Scarlet said calmly. "I realize that you meant Conall Wright the classical guitarist. I cannot—"

She listened a little longer, gambling that she wasn't missing anything critical during the static moments where the spotty long distance connection was lost.

"No, Mrs. Grant, I had not heard the rumor that the island had returned anyone's hearing. You understand that we could of course not guarantee such results for any of our guests."

Finally accepting the futility of the topic, Mrs. Grant turned the subject to flowers and rambled at some length regarding exact species and arrangements. Scarlet patiently repeated exactly the same information she had imparted several times, over several modes of communications.

"I assure you, there will be no problem in supplying exactly what you desire."

Mrs. Grant clearly did not mind the expense of a rambling call to Costa Rica, which did not surprise Scarlet. Someone who was willing to reserve the *entire* resort for a wedding did not have budget concerns. It was worth indulging her desire to discuss every part of the upcoming nuptials in agonizing detail…for the second time that week.

When Mrs. Grant had finally wound down, Scarlet was only listening with half her attention, looking over the end of year expense sheets and bonus calculations.

"Of course, Mrs. Grant!" she said with enthusiasm that probably wouldn't sound too false over the poor phone connection. "We are looking forward to serving you. Have a lovely evening."

It was a relief to finally take the phone from her ear, and turn it off.

A glance at the battery indicator suggested that Mrs. Grant had used nearly half of the phone's charge. Scarlet plugged it into the charger and returned to her paperwork with all of her attention until Graham appeared in the doorway.

Graham had not inherited his grandfather's oratory skills; when he dropped the loose mail on Scarlet's desk, it was without a single word of explanation. The box, however, he was handling with particular care, and he actually grinned when he put it in front of her, right on top of the financial statements she'd been checking over.

"What is this?" Scarlet demanded.

The side of the perforated box was emblazoned with 'LIVE CARGO' and 'HANDLE WITH CARE.'

As she stared at it in consternation, it meowed.

Behind Graham came Travis, grinning even wider than the gardener. "Here's the stuff you'll need for those," he said cheerfully, putting a stack of bulky boxes down in the corner of Scarlet's office.

"Those?!" Scarlet exclaimed. "There's more than one? What *are* they?" The box on her desk wiggled. "Oh, no," she said, suspecting the worst.

Graham was already making a beeline for the door and Travis laughed over his shoulder as they made their escape. "Christmas kittens for Gizelle! Conall wanted you to take care of them for the next few days so it could be a surprise!"

Then they were both hastily gone, and Scarlet was left with a box that meowed at her again, this time in harmony.

She looked at it in uncertainty for several moments while its contents protested, then sighed and carefully opened the box. It wasn't like she could leave them in there indefinitely.

Two curious faces greeted her, with big blinking eyes in juvenile furry faces. One appeared to be a fluffy cream-colored Siamese mix, the other was a faintly striped gray tabby with white feet and ear-tips. They meowed plaintively and reached tiny, furry paws up the sides of the box at her.

"I should have told Mrs. Grant that Conall would be playing an entire charity concert for her damned wedding," Scarlet muttered. She ignored the urge to scoop the kittens out of their box to see if they were as soft as they looked and went to investigate the boxes that Travis had indicated she would also need.

One of them proved to have cans of kitten food and a selection of toys and dishes. The other had a shallow plastic tub and several bags of scented sand. As Scarlet puzzled over the instructions printed on the side of one of the bags, there was a crash and she turned to find that the kittens had toppled the box over on her desk and were spilling eagerly out of it.

"Oh, no," she said, rising to her feet. "There's important paperwork..."

Clearly understanding her, the cream-colored kitten squatted down and began to pee.

Scarlet was across the room in less than a heartbeat, picking the startled kitten up and holding it up off of her desk as it squawked and finished her business over the floor and on Scarlet's shoes.

Swearing under her breath, Scarlet carried the squirming creature to the bathroom, where it could do the least harm, and closed it in.

When she turned back to the desk, the gray kitten was walking through the pee for a pile of paperwork, leaving wet footprints behind her.

"I don't think so…"

Scarlet caught it just as it stepped onto the latest letter from Beehag's lawyer (though she sourly considered that urine pawprints could only improve the correspondence), and tossed her gently in to join the first.

She growled under her breath as she cleaned up the mess, already plotting out the amendment to her contract with Conall. She set up the litter box according to the directions and slipped it into the bathroom…to find only the gray kitten inside, blinking innocently up at her.

A frantic search of the small room with the gray kitten trying to rub against her ankles and twine between her feet led to escalating panic. Scarlet wondered how she was going to explain to Conall that she'd lost one of his kittens within ten minutes of their arrival.

"The *island* isn't that big," she thought fiercely, and just as she settled in to widen her search, the cream kitten launched itself from the tiny space above the cabinet onto her shoulder and alighted with a triumphant trill.

"How did you even get up there?" Scarlet demanded of it, as it purred and rubbed its tiny face against her cheek. She pulled it off her shoulder and held it at arms length while it swung playful paws in her direction. She set it down with its sibling and sidled backwards out of the room, nudging them back into the bathroom with her foot multiple times as she closed the door carefully behind her.

A single peach paw stretched out from underneath the door, investigated everything it could reach, and withdrew.

Scarlet stared, narrow-eyed, at the place the paw had been, and went cautiously back to her desk.

At first, the sound of their play—meows and pounces and scrambling claws—was distracting. But Scarlet soon tuned it out, turning to the pile of mail that Graham had dropped on her desk along with the kittens.

Much of it was to be expected: bills, advertisements, and end of the year license renewals. But there was one large manila envelope, addressed to Scarlet personally, that was a curiosity.

It had a Vermont return address, but a New York postscript, and when Scarlet opened it, it was thick and full of irregular paperwork. A glossy brochure fell out alone.

There was a letter of introduction that Scarlet read twice, growing more and more livid, and then she flipped through the rest of the material.

She was holding Gizelle's past in her hands. An unofficial copy of her birth certificate, a photocopy of the newspaper article involving the car accident that killed her parents, photographs from when she was a child, and the scientists' records of her time in Beehag's zoo.

She picked up her phone, now fully charged, and dialed a familiar number.

"Do you realize what time it is, Scarlet?"

"You've got a lot of nerve," Scarlet snarled, not caring that it was probably three in the morning in Maryland. "I asked you to find out about Gizelle's past, not find her a quiet little mental hospital to lock her up in."

"What are you talking about?" Tony asked at the other end of the line after a puzzled pause.

"This little package that you had your friend at Safe Shifters send me has your fingerprints all over it."

There was another tired and confused moment of silence on the line. "My *literal* fingerprints?" Tony asked. "What is Safe Shifters?"

He certainly sounded innocently befuddled.

"Safe Shifters is apparently a lovely little house with bars on the windows in the countryside of Vermont that specializes in mentally ill shifters. They assure me that Gizelle will have a beautiful life with the finest of medical attention and psychiatric care. I received a letter from their director because we had a mutual friend who cared *very much* for her well being. Are you saying that mutual friend isn't you? Because some of this paperwork regarding her past has *your* agency's letterhead."

Scarlet could picture Tony's furrowed brow in the silence that resulted.

"I've never heard of this place," Tony insisted. "Look, I've been doing some research for you, but it's still in processing to be declassified. I can't send it until the beancounters decide it's not going to negatively impact an active investigation."

Scarlet shuffled one of the pages forward. "So you *didn't* send anyone a copy of the bill of sale for exotic wildlife to Beehag twenty-six years ago? Or the newspaper clipping of her parents' death with your agency's stamp? Or the scientists' notes on the experimental drugs they gave her in Beehag's cages?"

There was a sound like a phone being dropped. A woman's sleepy voice in the background was indecipherable.

"How did you get all that?" Tony demanded then. "You have notes from Beehag's records? We don't even have that. They were classified above our heads directly after my return from the field, before anyone had a chance to go through them."

"If it wasn't you, who could have put this together?" Scarlet was equal parts relieved and disappointed; she was glad that Tony had not been so foolish as to think she would want any part in putting Gizelle into a home, and frustrated that now she had no one to eviscerate.

If Tony had an answer, it was lost when Scarlet dropped her phone to the sound of a loud splash from the bathroom and a shrill yowl of terror.

"I'll call you back," she shouted towards the phone, and she opened the bathroom door onto a scene of absolute chaos.

The cream kitten was paddling around inside the toilet bowl, shrieking her protest and trying in vain to reach up to the seat, claws scrabbling on the hard porcelain. The gray kitten was standing on her back legs beside the toilet, contemplating her own expedition to the toilet seat to save her sibling.

Every towel had been pulled off of every towel rack, including the hand towels by the sink. The washcloth was in the toilet with the flailing kitten. Every bottle on the counter had been tipped over. Most of the lids had proven true, but a few of them were leaking sweet-smelling fluids over and off the counter.

And the entire bathroom was ankle-deep in shredded toilet paper.

The kittens had not only peeled off the roll by the toilet, but also had found and opened the storage cabinet. The plastic had been rent into crinkly shards, and the tubes of a dozen rolls were strewn like the bones of the enemy through the snow of toilet paper clumps that covered the floor.

Scarlet waded through it and pulled the cream kitten out of the toilet by the ruff of its wet neck. She added to its indignity by rinsing it off in the sink, then bent and gathered up a towel to wrap it in, scolding it as she went. "You are a little idiot," she said, as the other meowed and tried to crawl up her leg to join the fun.

"I am not a *cat* tree," Scarlet said, pushing her gently off.

After the third time Scarlet nearly tripped trying to dislodge the gray kitten from her leg, she scooped the persistent beast into her arms and simply toweled them both together, to purrs of delight.

They seemed to consider it a game, squirming and trying to capture the towel with their sharp little teeth and clever claws. Scarlet caught herself smiling as she tousled them in the towel, rolling them over and rubbing them down.

When the kitten was not entirely dry, but at least no longer spiky-wet, Scarlet put her down with her sister. "I've got work to do," she told them regretfully.

The cream kitten meowed pitifully. The gray kitten purred. They both look up at her expectantly.

"I'm going to get back to my work now," Scarlet said firmly.

The cream kitten yowled more demandingly, more than a hint of her Siamese ancestors in her voice.

Scarlet stared back at it. "I can't just play with you all night," she protested.

It meowed again, danced forward, and swiped Scarlet with its paw, all claws retracted.

"You are a little tyrant," Scarlet scolded. It occurred to her that they might be hungry, and she went to the box with their food.

They tried to mob her, constantly underfoot as she found their dishes and peeled open the fragrant can of food. The Siamese mix tried to swarm up her side while she was spooning it out, and the gray and white kitten sweetly made little purring hiccups of joy and anticipation as it patiently sat beside the bowl.

Scarlet gave up working in favor of watching them eat, chuckling helplessly over their clumsy efforts to stuff themselves and nearly drown in their water dish.

Finally, they slowed, and left their dishes to stagger to Scarlet and beg their way up into her arms.

She could not have explained how she arrived in the position, but only a few moments later, the gray one was in her lap, limply covering more space than something so small ought to be capable of. A snoring purr occasionally vibrated through her tiny body. The cream colored one had crawled up further, and was unconscious in a warm curve around Scarlet's neck.

The only work that Scarlet could reach without disturbing them was the mysterious envelope containing Gizelle's unhappy history.

Scarlet sighed, stroking the gray kitten absently. Gizelle's kitten, she reminded herself. They were Gizelle's kittens.

Gizelle.

Gizelle…was complicated.

Scarlet tipped her head against the back of her chair and, now that the rush of her anger had ebbed away, tried to untangle the conflicting emotions that had been dredged up by the paperwork.

Gizelle reminded Scarlet keenly of herself, if circumstances had been only a little different. She could remember herself too easily in Gizelle's confused place, new to a world of human rules and baffling customs. Scarlet had been lucky enough to have powerful and charitable friends, patient enough to teach her the skills she lacked and generous enough to give her a place and purpose.

But it wasn't just empathy for Gizelle's social awkwardness than made Scarlet feel protective of the young woman.

It felt like *her* fault that Gizelle had been in Beehag's zoo.

"No," she protested out loud. "It *wasn't* my fault."

The cream kitten stirred at the sound of her voice and put a paw out to the side of her face, patting her twice and then curling tighter into the side of her neck.

Scarlet couldn't have known about the zoo that Gizelle had been caged in for so much of her life. And if she had, she was under a binding contract not to trespass there.

But she could not convince herself that she couldn't have guessed, couldn't have done something to put a stop to it. Beehag had stolen shifters right out from underneath her nose, from *her* resort. She should have protected them. Should have…

The gray kitten gave a sleepy mrrrr of protest and Scarlet realized she was petting it too roughly. She gentled her hand and the kitten slowly rolled over, exposing her fluffy white tummy.

They trusted her, she thought with a sigh of bittersweet regret. She wasn't sure if they should. She wasn't sure anyone should.

She reached for the letter that had been at the front of Gizelle's packet of secrets, careful not to jostle the kitten sleeping precariously on her shoulder.

It was a terribly convincing letter.

The director of the facility made a compelling argument for Gizelle needing special care. He mentioned her specific challenges with surprising accuracy and proposed methods of treatment that sounded, on the surface, logical and completely humane. He mentioned safe space to run multiple times, and with polite obliqueness pointed out that although Scarlet had the best of intentions, she might not be the person most suited to help Gizelle.

If she had received the letter two weeks prior, Scarlet would have had a hard choice before her. She would have agonized over the truths in the letter, and questioned her own competency.

Knowing what someone was going through didn't make her an expert in helping them get through it.

But Conall was here now, and Gizelle's mate had changed everything.

When she was being honest with herself, Scarlet was not sure which of the two she was more envious of. She was glad, of course, that Conall's patience and love had won Gizelle's trust and her heart, and the young woman had bloomed in his care.

But a small, shallow part of her still wanted to be the person the timid gazelle shifter needed most.

And she'd have to be dead inside not to want someone like Conall; he was that gorgeous broody handsome type who made women weak in the knees with a careless glance.

Scarlet sighed.

She was definitely not dead inside. And it wasn't really that she wanted *Conall*, just that she wanted what Gizelle *had* in Conall.

"Don't you want a mate?" Gizelle had asked her, so innocently.

Scarlet had not had an answer for her.

She wasn't a naive romantic, waiting around for true love to sweep her off her feet, but she would have liked having a man in her life. Not one that got in the way of running the resort of course, but it had been a long time since she had shared her bed, and it was sometimes so lonely and unappealing that she skipped sleeping altogether.

She wanted a hard body to slide up against, a mouth to kiss, strong arms to hold her, clever fingers to — Scarlet stopped her train of thought firmly.

It wasn't like she was going to hook up with a guest, and sleeping with the staff was a level of unprofessional beyond even that, which left…no one. She was on an island she couldn't leave with people who were off limits and if she wanted—if she desperately craved—anything more, she was at least practiced at ignoring her own desires.

She glanced at the kitten in her lap. She wasn't even going to be able to pleasure herself without disturbing her newest unpaying guests.

She smiled despite herself. It wasn't worth doing that.

She reached carefully to put Gizelle's paperwork back on the desk without jostling the kitten on her shoulder, then reached up to scratch her gently, just enough to start her purring faintly near her ear.

Then she settled back in her chair more comfortably and closed her eyes.

She would give all the information to Gizelle, but mention the mental hospital privately to only Conall, without endorsement. Shifting Sands was the best place for the shy gazelle shifter, even if Scarlet was no longer who she needed most.

And if Scarlet had unanswered hungers of her own, it was nothing she hadn't already spent decades avoiding.

Such desires were simply part of who she was…part of *what* she was.

She drifted to sleep with a muted purr near her ear, and dreamed of cooling rains and scorching sun and somedays.

TROPICAL CHRISTMAS STAG: EPILOGUE

The cottage was littered with wrapping paper and filled with laughter.

Gizelle was lying on the bed, surrounded by gifts. New dresses were draped across her feet and an array of hairbrushes and jeweled combs and candies in silk boxes were scattered across the comforter. The bedside table was completely covered in bottles of every kind of hair conditioner Conall had been able to find online that would ship internationally, and several kinds of spray-in detangler.

There were leaning piles of books in a range of difficulties: lush, illustrated volumes of classics, adult-learning writing workbooks, and several instruction guides to braiding and styling long hair. There were two kits of art supplies, open to show a dazzling array of colors and mediums, and a selection of sketchbooks and canvases.

Gizelle was hugging a tablet to her chest and wearing a pair of studio-quality earphones.

"Books that *read* to you," she crowed in delight. "*Hundreds* of them."

"I had your friends help me pick them," Conall told her, leaning over a precarious pile of presents to show her how to navigate.

"There are folders for each person with the books they chose for you."

"I'm going to listen to every one of them," Gizelle sighed rapturously.

"You aren't even going to miss me when I go to Boston," Conall teased.

Gizelle sat up, pulling the headphones off. "Of course I will," she said in sudden seriousness. "A thousand books wouldn't fill that emptiness. Every second will try to be forever and I will have to remember how to run without legs."

Realizing that his teasing had missed its mark, Conall cleared a spot next to her to sit and took her hands. Someone barely in range of hearing was singing a Christmas carol loudly and off-key, but he couldn't bring himself to be irritated about their lack of pitch.

"I will come back," he reminded her. "You have a phone now, and anyone will help you text me whenever you want. I will video call you every evening that the Shifting Sands connection is good enough to make it work and I will think of you every moment that I'm gone and I will come back as soon as I can."

"And then you'll stay forever?" she asked plaintively, dark eyes like pools to eternity.

"Forever is an arbitrary point in time," Conall reminded her. "And you've already been there. But next time you go, I will be at your side."

Gizelle looked at him skeptically, eyes narrow. "Don't be weird," she told him, with a slow smile blooming on her expressive mouth. "That's my job here." She lay back among the gifts again. "I love everything about Christmas," she said with satisfaction. "Everything except the figgy pudding, which was as awful as Breck said it would be."

"I like it," Conall protested. "It's rich."

"You like coffee, too," Gizelle reminded him. Then she sat bolt upright. "Your Christmas present!" she said in alarm. "I still have to give you yours!"

She somehow managed to navigate the heaps of gifts and untangle herself from the earphones without toppling any of the piles. She returned around the bed to drop her gift into Conall's waiting hands.

Not touching her, he couldn't hear the rustle of the paper as he carefully unwrapped it.

Gizelle had wrapped it thoroughly, in several layers of clashing color and she watched him peel through them and bounced on her toes. The weight and density of the package made him guess what it would be before the final layer came off and he opened the box.

"This is the lock from Neal's cage," he said, turning it over in his hands. "Are you sure you want to give me this? It is the heart of your hoard."

"You are the heart of my hoard," Gizelle said, giving it a reverent caress and then closing his fingers around it. "I don't need it to anchor me anymore."

"I will carry it everywhere with me," Conall promised, only belatedly wondering what airport security was going to think of the lump of metal; it had enough heft to be a serious weapon. He smiled at Gizelle. "I love it," he assured her. "I love you."

Gizelle let him draw her into his arms as he put the lock down on the bed beside them. "I *love* you," she breathed.

Then her mouth was on his and her hands were cradling his face. He put arms around her and wondered where on the bed it would be safe to lay her down.

He had just decided to take her to the second bedroom when a knock on the door reminded him. "There's more!" he said, breaking the kiss.

"More than love?" Gizelle asked in confusion, drawing away to look at him.

"More Christmas presents," Conall said, grinning.

"More than this?" Gizelle exclaimed in wonder, gesturing around the crowded room. "What more could there *be*?"

Conall stood, lifting Gizelle and setting her on feet away from him. "Come see," he said.

She scampered to the door with him. "It's Scarlet," she told him. "But she feels *confusing*."

Conall opened the door, and true to Gizelle's prediction, it was Scarlet.

She had company.

"Take them," the resort manager said through clenched teeth. "Just take them."

"Kittens!" squealed Gizelle. "Conall, you got me *kittens*!"

Two kittens were in Scarlet's outstretched arms, one a striped gray with a white belly, the other cream-colored with orange-ish Siamese points.

"I am doubling the price of your lease," Scarlet told Conall.

"A bargain at twice the price," Conall said magnanimously.

Scarlet peeled the gray one gently off her sleeves with a ripping sound as it clung to her, mewing its protest, its tiny tail tucked in tight. "This is the sweetest of the two," she said, dropping it into Gizelle's waiting hands. It immediately started to purr.

The other kitten bolted for Scarlet's shoulder and tried to hide beneath her hair, but it wasn't fast enough to escape her. "I've been calling this one Tyrant," she said, extracting it from her hair.

The kitten mewed and tried to catch her with its needle-sharp claws before Scarlet set it with the other one into Gizelle's arms. "You are of course free to name it whatever you like. My staff is not paid to scoop litter boxes and Graham will not be happy if they use the gardens or planters. Do not flush litter into our septic system. They need to stay out from underfoot and away from guests who may be allergic. And keep your toilet paper out of their reach."

Without waiting for a response, Scarlet turned on her heel and left.

"Kittens!" Gizelle repeated in awe as they scrambled over her, clumsy and eager with their tiny claws and giant eyes.

She looked up at Conall with laughter dancing in her eyes. "*Now* I won't miss you when you go to Boston," she teased.

Conall mimed a knife to the heart. "You wound me!" he said dramatically.

Arms full of squirming kitten, Gizelle still tried to hug him, with very mixed results and squawks of protest from several parties. "Of course I will miss you, my beautiful Irish elk," she insisted.

"And I will miss you, my gorgeous gazelle," Conall echoed.

When they drew apart, the cream-colored kitten was clinging to Conall and trying to scale his shirt to his shoulder.

~

Conall showed Gizelle all about the kittens; how to feed them, where to put their water. They set up the litter box and the sweet one obligingly demonstrated how the kittens planned to use it.

Tyrant, whose name was clearly appropriate and inevitably stuck to her, in the meantime demonstrated why toilet paper needed to be kept out of reach, ripping chunks from the roll by jumping up and tearing at it with her tiny, determined claws and teeth.

After they had laughed helplessly at her antics for a moment, Gizelle pulled Tyrant reluctantly away from the toilet paper roll and scolded her gently. "That's not your toy," she said, distracting the kitten with a plush mouse that chimed.

She and Conall played with the kittens until they grew clumsier than ever. Gizelle was alarmed when they started to ignore the toys that had enraptured them moments before.

"Are they alright?" she asked in concern, when even a ribbon dragged across Tyrant's toes couldn't get her attention.

"They're just getting tired," Conall told her and, sure enough, they shortly collapsed into a boneless furry heap on a pillow. Even lifting the sweet one's paws didn't cause more than a minuscule twitch of her ear. "They're just children," he told her. "They'll do a lot of playing and sleeping at first."

Gizelle tucked the sweet one's paw back into what looked like a comfortable position. "This was the best present of all," she said with a sigh. "Thank you."

"I hope you still feel that way when they destroy something you care about," Conall warned her. "They will require a lot of patience and need a lot of attention and love."

"I am so full of love," Gizelle said, trying to describe how it felt inside her. "It will spill over if I don't give some of it away."

Conall's look said that he understood and, when he took her hands and pulled her close, his kiss said that he felt the same way, too.

Gizelle opened her mouth to him, accepting his love even knowing there couldn't possibly be room for it, because the overflow was so delicious.

It was hard to remember being afraid of his touch. It was so comfortable now, even when comfortable wasn't quite the word for it; it raised a dizzy anticipation in her and his hands were so wonderfully large and nimble as he traced the line of her shoulder and held her in the small of the back like they were dancing.

There was no room on the bed for them among the piles of books and gifts and sleeping kittens, so when Conall might have laid her down, he picked her up instead, his breath ragged near her ear, and carried her out to the second bedroom.

Gizelle started to slip quickly out of her dress but he caught her and did it more slowly than she knew was possible, one strap at a tantalizing time, kissing every inch of her skin as he carefully exposed it.

She took no such care with his clothing, unbuttoning as fast as her own fingers could go; they were trembling with something better than fear, something sweeter than panic.

Then they were naked at last, and Conall was a safe weight over her on the smooth bed; an invitation and a delicious demand as he lifted her legs and drove into her. As full as she was, with joy, with passion, with love, with *him*, there was more, and more, and yet more, until they were sweaty and spent and laughing together in release and Gizelle felt as boneless as her kittens.

He continued to caress her, as if even *afterwards*, he couldn't have enough of her under his fingers.

"You make the most enchanting music," he said, kissing her neck.

"You are the one playing," Gizelle said dreamily. "You know all my strings and tuning pins." He had shown her all the parts of his guitar.

He chuckled at that and gathered her close in his arms. "You write all of my songs," he said into her hair.

"You *are* all of my songs," Gizelle countered, kissing his shoulder.

His elk sighed then, in long-suffering disgust. *You are our mate*, he said simply, as if that explained everything.

And perhaps it did.

RUN

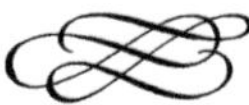

This…is not an easy story.

It wasn't easy to write and it won't be easy to read. It comes with ***all*** *the trigger warnings: it has a tragic ending, there is torture, on-screen character death, child endangerment…all the things my work is usually safe from, in one short, powerful gut-punch of a story. It contains many revelations, but is not at all necessary for enjoyment of the series if you choose not to read it. I wouldn't fault you for skipping it.*

This is the story of Gizelle's parents.

Janine woke in darkness, and had a moment of sheer panic.

She always slept with a light on.

It didn't have to be much…a small nightlight, even a clock radio with a bright face. Anything to remind her when she opened her eyes that she wasn't blindfolded, wasn't in the lab, wasn't a monster…

She had just remembered to start breathing again when the lights came flickering back on and there was a hum of the heater and the fridge again.

Just a power outage.

That's all it was, a power outage. Probably a neighbor had blown the fuse again.

Clammy with fear-sweat, trembling from adrenaline, Janine rolled out of the bed and crept quietly to the crib.

Jessica was sleeping bonelessly, arms akimbo. A stuffed dragon lay next to her.

Janine wanted to wake her up, to reassure herself that she was alright, to have the comfort of comforting her, to have the child's tiny arms wrap around her neck so trustingly.

When Evan came home near dawn, not much later, Janine was still awake, sitting on the floor next to the crib with her arms wrapped around her knees.

He came into the tiny efficiency quietly, subdued, and it took Janine a moment to realize that it wasn't just the wake of her own moment of terror that was making things feel tense.

"What is it?" she asked, crawling over and climbing up to sit with him on the bed that took up most of the room. "What's wrong?"

Evan folded her into his strong arms and Janine let herself go limp in his embrace. "What is it?" she repeated.

"There are people in town," he said, his voice full of defeat. "People in nice clothing, asking about a white-haired woman wearing sunglasses."

Janine gave a keen of sorrow before she could bury her face in

Evan's shoulder. "I thought we'd have longer here," she said, achingly.

"Me, too," Evan said quietly. "I'd hoped…"

They always hoped. They always hoped that *this* would be the place they could be safe. This would be the place they could be invisible. This would be the time they got away.

And every time it wasn't.

"We're down to our last clean ID," Janine said, trying to dredge calm from beneath the waves of despair. She wiped her face and drew in a deep breath. She knew what to do. They'd done it before.

"We'll have to find someone to get us new ones," Evan said grimly.

In her crib, Jessica stirred, not awake, but waking.

Evan stood up and went to the crib, gazing down at the toddler.

Janine busied herself packing. The last IDs were taped in a manilla envelope to the underside of the bed, with a pathetically small bundle of cash. It was smaller every time.

"Do I have time to dye?" she asked, as she put their toiletries into the battered suitcase.

"Better take the time," Evan said calmly. "I'll make us breakfast."

Janine mixed the hair dye and painted it onto her brilliant white roots as Evan bustled around the five feet of counter that qualified as a kitchen. He didn't whistle.

Jessica finished waking up, and was standing in her crib, smiling and bouncing in place when Janine emerged from the bathroom once again completely brunette.

"Mama!" Jessica said. "Bacon!"

"No bacon this morning, kiddo," Evan said apologetically. "But we've got ham!"

"Bacon!" Jessica repeated eagerly.

Janine finished the packing, draping her wet towel over the two suitcases to dry as much as possible. Evan had packed the kitchen as he cooked, making them a feast of everything perishable and putting everything else with their dishes and pans in a box that would probably not survive another move.

They ate swiftly, even Jessica picking up on the urgency. They didn't have a high chair, so she ate on Evan's lap, scattering crumbs that they wouldn't bother to clean up. It wasn't like they would be around to get their deposit back.

They left the lights on to make it look lived in and walked to Evan's shop. Janine tried to look as if dragging suitcases and carrying boxes was a normal thing that normal people did in the early morning through the back alleys of a warehouse district smelling like new hair dye.

"Good thing I got the car done," Evan said cheerfully, bouncing Jessica in his arms.

She crowed happily. "Run?" she asked, pointing down. "Run?"

Janine winced. "No running," she said firmly. "Not now." Even for a regular toddler, the shop yard was not a safe place to run, but in Jessica's mind, *running* was *shifting*, and being able to run around as a little gazelle. She couldn't understand how dangerous it was.

The shop was closed, of course. They had limited daytime hours as a cover story for their nighttime activities.

Evan gave Jessica to Janine and had to wake the boss, who looked disgruntled about the disruption, and even less happy to find out that he was unexpectedly losing Evan's services.

"You do good work," he grumbled. "Don't complain."

"I need money for the last few flips we did," Evan said, too nicely. He was always so nice. Janine might have just taken what they needed, not negotiated…but he wasn't a monster like she was. And sometimes he made her believe that she might not be, either.

"Ain't sold 'em yet," his boss growled, shaking his head. "S'not how we do things."

Jessica started to fuss, wanting down from Janine's arms, and Janine moved further away, trying to distract her by pointing out the dog behind the barbed-wire fence.

"Nice doggy," Janine said.

It snarled at her, but backed away from the fence, sensing what she really was.

Jessica made an attempt at repeating her words, but settled on

"Bacon!" when she couldn't make the sounds to her own satisfaction. "Bacon! Bacon!"

Evan was shaking hands with his boss. He'd gotten something. Probably only a portion of what he was owed.

"Car's this way," he said, taking a suitcase handle and picking up the kitchen box. "You won't even recognize it."

Janine almost didn't. The little junker had a fresh coat of don't-notice-me silver-gray paint, new hubcaps, and the grill was… different in a way that she couldn't quite pinpoint. The off-color door was gone, making it considerably less distinct, and there was even new glass in the back instead of tape and Visqueen. The windshield still had a crack running through it and Evan had not hammered all of the dents out of the hood. It looked like a thousand other cheap little cars, with nothing at all to distinguish it.

It had California plates now, though there were undoubtedly several spare sets that they would be able to swap out as they traveled.

She strapped Jessica into the carseat in the back, and gave her the stuffed dragon. "We're going on a trip, sweetheart."

Jessica babbled happy nonsense back to her.

Janine slipped into the driver seat to take the first leg of driving. "Where are we going?" she asked wearily.

"We're going to find the shifter haven," Evan said optimistically, getting into the passenger side.

Janine gave a humorless laugh. "I suppose they've sent you an invitation with driving instructions?"

Evan smiled at her. "Don't give up, love. It's out there somewhere."

Janine tried to smile back.

"I found some ICQ chatter that suggests it might be in Oregon," he said enthusiastically.

"That's as good a place to start as any," Janine agreed. She started the car and pulled out onto the highway and turned north as Evan reached into the glovebox for a CD.

She knew what it would be before the strains of music started, and Evan skipped right to the song he was looking for: Run Like an Antelope by Phish.

He looked sideways at her, grinning, and Janine had to laugh in earnest. He always did this: cheered her up, made everything better.

They stopped and ate lunch from the kitchen box, focusing on the things that wouldn't last as long: cheese sandwiches and carrots. Jessica ate the bread from her sandwich and wadded the cheese into a ball too disgusting to salvage. They changed her diaper, switched drivers, and drove on.

Janine fell asleep, and dreamed of escape.

~

They got complacent with her. She'd been in the lab almost two years, and she was compliant and agreeable. She never tried to escape, cringed away from any touch, and never tried to use her gaze or shift.

She started by asking for little things; an extra blanket, a favorite food.

She asked for books, as well, but they wouldn't take the blindfold off. It was locked onto her head, and she grew used to navigating around without knowing what time of day it was. They only let her see when they were doing experiments, testing her vision and her talents on hapless subjects. They gave her drugs, trying to dampen the effects, and she let them think it was working, that she could, at least, no longer lock another person's mind away in a moment of time.

She couldn't control the fear response she caused, but they scratched their heads and took notes on clipboards and drew blood and decided that each power was something separate. They talked about infusing other people with the talent, struggling with a formula that would turn ordinary humans into things like her for reasons she didn't understand.

She convinced them she was harmless, a reformed monster, a clawless kitten.

They all congratulated themselves on their progress, and Janine meekly returned to her cell. They continued to test her, she continued to pretend she was helpless, and they eventually stopped strapping her down when they took the blindfold off.

But inside, she was angry.

If they thought she was a monster, she'd *show* them a monster.

She waited until they forgot she was a threat, then trapped them, one-by-one, leaving a trail of white-haired, horrified humans in her wake as she locked each one into a single moment of time—the worst memory she could find in their minds playing over and over in a loop forever. They would die that way, eventually, or live forever in a tortured fugue state hooked up to a machine.

Turned to stone, the legend said, with the glance of a silvery eye.

She raged the hallways, not sure how to get out of the maze of the lab, only knowing she had to, she had to be free, she had to run.

Then she saw Evan.

She'd been freezing everyone without discrimination, not even thinking about it; janitors, technicians, scientists. Anyone in her way felt the blast of her gaze and their hair went as white as hers when she easily, casually, cast them into their own personal hell.

But Evan was different.

He was dressed in service overalls, with a visitor tag at his pocket and an open tool box at his feet. There was a utility access panel open, and he was fiddling with something beyond it. When she came running down the hallway, he looked up, and she wanted to warn him not to, but it was too late.

Brown eyes met hers, and Janine had already opened the door that would trap him in time.

But he wasn't afraid. His dark hair remained free of white frost.

Usually just a glance from her was enough to strike terror into anyone she met, even if she didn't chose to lock them away in their own brain.

She blinked at him.

He looked back at her, utterly unafraid, and said in wonder, "You're beautiful."

Janine felt something happen in the chest where she thought she had no heart and she was as surprised as he was when she opened her mouth and said, "Will you help me?"

Without a second thought for his own life and future, he put his hand out to her. She twisted her hair up under the hat that he gave her, and he put her in his coveralls and sunglasses. Together, they sauntered out under the power of his visitor's badge.

She stared at the sky for the first time in two years, and it stared back.

Her powers of terror had not disappeared, but they quickly discovered that sunglasses muted the effect considerably on people other than Evan.

Evan himself remained immune, and it was the most amazing, beautiful thing in the world to be able to look into someone's eyes and not cause them pain and horror.

Janine had never met a different kind of shifter, had never known it was a possibility. She thought that she and her small family were the only creatures able to change their shape. But Evan was a gazelle shifter, strong and lithe and gentle, and he told her—and showed her—what a shifter could be, and what a mate was, and he loved her with his whole heart.

She reluctantly showed him her own shape, melting a dumpster full of trash with her withering breath, and then stood there, waiting for him to reject her.

But he only looked at her with awe. "A cockatrice," he said in wonder, stroking her dragon-like neck with reverence. "You're beautiful."

Without hesitation, he went on the run with her, and they spent two years with their eyes on the rear view mirror.

They met other shifters, all living in hiding as they were on the fringes of society. Most of them found Janine too uncomfortable to be friends with, but some of them adjusted to her sunglasses and skittishness. Evan made friends like plants drank sunlight, and Janine found herself drawn into the circles of friendship more often than she expected.

They heard rumors of towns where shifters were free to be themselves, and when people—from the lab, or from the equally dangerous Shifter Affairs agency—came sniffing around for the white-haired woman who caused terror, they moved on, looking for such a utopia.

"You're not a monster," Evan told her, when she lamented her gifts and wondered why she had been born this way. "And our child won't be, either."

Janine was far less frightened of childbirth than she was of the child. What if it was a monster like Janine? Worse, what if it was afraid of Janine? It had taken her two days to dredge up the courage to look into the infant's eyes, and when she did, Jessica looked back fearlessly and waved her little fists and rooted for milk, no trace of frost in her brown fuzzy hair.

Janine wept in relief and fell impossibly in love.

Jessica grew a head full of dark, curly hair and her baby-light eyes darkened to brown in just a few months. When she abruptly shifted into a tiny gazelle made of knees just after her first birthday, Janine was so grateful that she wasn't a cockatrice that she didn't even mind all the new hassles that having an early-shifter baby would cause.

It complicated hiding. If Janine was already distinctive, now they also had to hide an increasingly independent child who wanted to run on four legs, in a world that didn't recognize shifters and feared things that were different.

Janine's problems weren't over, by far. They had to move every few months, trying to stay ahead of the people hunting for them. Evan easily got work at auto shops that wanted to pay under the table for jobs of questionable legality, and took odd jobs for mechanical problems of all sorts.

And every day, Janine was terrified that she would look into Evan's eyes and see the fear she saw when she met anyone else's gaze, see him recoil in horror and watch his hair turn white.

Janine woke with a jolt, and made herself breathe slowly again. That hadn't happened. She didn't frighten Evan. He didn't think she was a monster.

By evening, despite a few fitful naps, Jessica was getting restless and bored of being in the car.

Evan pulled off at a diner that looked cheap. "You should probably stay here," he said reluctantly. "I'll get something to go."

Janine knew it was the right choice. It was cloudy and getting dark, and her sunglasses would look odd and obvious. "Take Jessica with you? She'd like the change of scenery."

"Run?" Jessica asked.

"Better not," Evan said.

The only thing worse than Janine being recognized by the wrong people would be if Jessica shifted in public.

Janine fed Jessica animal crackers while they waited, trying to turn it into a game. The little girl fussed, but ate a few handfuls, then fell into a restless sleep.

Janine tried not to squirm, or wake her up. Evan had been in there too long. Had he been caught?

Just as she was weighing her options—leave Jessica, wake Jessica, risk being seen—Evan came bolting, empty-handed, back to the car.

"They're here," he said, slipping into the driver's seat and starting the engine. "Guys in suits, asking questions. I was in the bathroom when they came in. Jerry must've told them which way we went…"

They spun out of the diner parking lot as fast as the little car would go, and Janine was horrified to see a black car pull out to follow them before they got to the first curve in the highway.

Their little gray car was faster than it looked; Evan must have upgraded the inside as well as the outside, and they zipped out through traffic in a way that gave Janine a moment of hope.

But their followers were just as fast, just as brave at cutting through the slower traffic, and they started to close the gap.

Evan turned off on a winding mountain road and floored it, the little car roaring at his command.

Jessica woke up with a brief wail, then quietly watched as the scenery streamed past. They wove in and out of the thinning traffic, risking blind corners and tight spaces to put other cars between them. They were honked at and flipped off, but Janine couldn't bring herself to care.

It seemed like it was working—they were pulling ahead, taking advantage of the other vehicles, and Janine could see the other car dropping back until it was out of sight around the curves.

Evan continued to push forward...and then it happened.

A blind corner on a steep grade, and a truck they hadn't seen coming. Evan could have hit it, or driven the driver he was passing into the ditch, but instead he chose to try to ride the shoulder on the opposite side.

For one brief moment, Janine thought he'd successfully averted the accident; there was frantic honking, and desperate swerving, and a looming grill...and then they were clear...for only a second before they hit the end of a guardrail a glancing blow and the car took a sickening spin and began to roll down the steep embankment with a wild shriek of steel and the crash of breaking glass.

~

Janine came awake in a rush of pain so terrible it felt like her entire body was on fire.

She opened her eyes and found that the car was cold and crushed around them.

The front end had been smashed; the hood was folded up and thrust through the broken windshield, and the footwells had closed to nothing. Evan...Janine turned her protesting head and gave a cry of grief. The steering column was pressed against him. He was breathing, but only barely, and there was blood streaming from his mouth. When she tried to reach out for him, she nearly fell unconscious again, and realized that her own body was pinned.

Jessica was wailing from the back seat.

They wouldn't have been alive if they hadn't been shifters...and even being shifters wasn't going to save them from this.

She made her arms move with sheer force of will, and hauled her unwilling body closer to her mate.

"Evan, Evan, look at me…"

Evan laboriously opened his eyes and Janine knew it would be the last time he could.

She threw herself into his mind, and suddenly, they were sitting together, perched at the edge of a lake. He was nearly transparent, a ghost of himself. Janine didn't have to look down to know that she was in no better shape. Their animal forms sat beside them; something about the transfer to the place with no time separated them like colors of light through a prism.

She knew this place, this memory.

This was a cabin in the woods that they had gone to when they escaped the lab, so many years ago. It was her first taste of freedom, her first taste of love.

And he didn't think she was a monster.

She had shown him what she could do, her terrible form, and he had still loved her.

It didn't matter that Evan was dying. He would be in this moment, in this place, until the life extinguished from his body. He wouldn't feel the pain, he wouldn't know the horror of having the life bleed from him.

It was all she could do for him.

His gazelle, as thin and ghostlike as he was, lifted each of his feet, one at a time, and blew at the grass but didn't graze. There was no hunger here. There were no needs.

"This is it, isn't it," Evan said thoughtfully. "Our last run. We're…"

"We crashed. The car rolled. It's…not good."

"Jessica?" Evan asked anxiously.

"She's crying," Janine said achingly. "I don't think she's hurt badly. The carseat saved her from the worst of it."

"You have to protect her," Evan said urgently. "We can't let them take her…"

Janine bent her head, not wanting to admit how badly she'd

been injured. There was no chance she could escape herself, let alone with a toddler in tow. Her helplessness ate at her.

"I have to go," she said sadly. "But you won't know."

She gave him one last kiss and returned reluctantly to the car, leaving him looping through that happier time, the two of them together forever.

His hair was stark white, his eyes staring sightlessly.

There was a scatter of rocks on the roof of the car, and Janine heard voices, far off. Someone was scrambling down the scree to get to them. She knew better than to hope that it was a good Samaritan.

The car was folded in around them like a crushed can, and there was broken glass everywhere. There was barely room between the two front seats for Janine to wedge herself, reaching back to where Jessica was still wailing.

"Sweetheart, darling, I'm here!" she said soothingly.

Her daughter's crying sounded more frightened than hurt, Janine tried to convince herself.

It was a painful struggle to get herself turned and pressed far enough between the off-kilter seats to get a clear view of Jessica. Her eyes were screwed shut as she continued to cry.

"Jessica, sweetie, I need you to look at me." Janine's voice was harsh, and when she swallowed, she tasted blood. She didn't have long to do this; she could already feel the strength leaching from her body.

Jessica opened her eyes, and Janine leaped into her mind desperately.

The lack of pain was like being suddenly dipped in cold water as she left her body behind.

The place that Jessica took her was nothing like the idyllic memory that Evan had held onto, nothing like anything that existed.

It was a child's composition of reality, and after a moment of confusion, Janine recognized it.

They had once found a secluded mountain meadow, with no one anywhere near, that felt safe enough to shift, all three of them, and spend a blissful several hours pretending they weren't being hunted, running and playing through the waist-high grass in sunlight.

That had been the day Jessica first said 'Run,' and Janine marveled at the way it had been held in her young mind.

There was nothing but grass, in all directions to the horizon, blowing in a gentle breeze that didn't ruffle their hair. She felt bathed in sunlight, everything was bright and beautiful, but when she looked up, there was no sky at all, only a void above like a black velvet canopy. Maybe Jessica had never looked up that day.

She folded Jessica into her arms, but already the little girl had stopped crying and was looking around curiously.

"What a beautiful place you've made," Janine told her, holding her close and stroking her curls. "My clever girl."

"Run?" Jessica asked. She was solid and complete in this place, no hint of transparency.

Janine felt tears gather in her eyes, but they didn't have the same prickle that they would have in reality. "Run, my darling," she said, releasing her.

Jessica smiled as brightly as the sun that wasn't shining and bolted around as only a toddler can, always a breath from toppling forward but not caring for caution. She couldn't shift here; her gazelle capered more sure-footedly at her side and they made big looping, drunken circles, always coming back for Janine's smile of approval.

Janine's cockatrice swished her tail in pleasure beside her, and the grass gave a whisper beneath it.

This is a good place, the cockatrice said, almost gone now. *A good time to be caught in.*

What would it do to the child, to be out of time like this? How long would the lab or Shifter Affairs keep her body alive while her mind was locked away from their meddling and torture? Most of Janine's victims were caught there forever, no chance of escape. But most of her victims weren't shifters, and none of them had ever been able to withstand her gaze like Jessica could.

She stood, scanning the infinite horizon.

This was all she could do. It was a safe place, it was better than a windowless cell and a locked blindfold. Better that her daughter be here until the end, safe and happy in the blink of a moment, than die, terrified and alone in a crumpled car. Better to be *here* than to be found awake by Shifter Affairs agents, or the scientists, and grow up in a prison, believing she was a monster.

"She's not a monster," she whispered, and she gathered herself to leave. She wanted to stay forever, a step out of time, but if her body died while she was here, she wouldn't be able to close the door, and Jessica wouldn't be safe. She could already feel her strength fading.

Would Jessica remember her mother? Janine wondered, gazing through her fading hands. Already, the little girl seemed to have forgotten the car accident, all of her pain and fear washed away in the surety of her safety here. Where time had no meaning, did *memory* even mean anything?

Would she be stuck here forever, without Janine to open the door again? Would Jessica develop her own gifts? Or would another cockatrice find her and release her? The chances seemed so slim.

Doubt washed over her. Was it the right thing to do? To trap her here out of time? Was it a gift, or a terrible curse?

A nose stopped her.

The gazelle had left her human counterpart and was standing at her feet, gazing up at her.

She was too young to speak, but she cocked her head in unexpected understanding.

"Take care of her," Janine said, starting to step away.

To her surprise, the gazelle head-butted her.

Janine stared, as she rarely let herself, and the gazelle backed away, looking up at her and pawing with one hoof.

If she took the gazelle back with her…could the door between times be held open a crack? Could the bond between a shifter and their animal be strong enough…even for that? If she could do that, maybe Jessica *could* open that door someday. Someday when she was safe.

"I love you," she said quietly to Jessica.

Then she scooped the gazelle up into her arms and was gone, all of the pain returning to her broken body in an agonizing jolt.

She had just enough time to see one of Jessica's dark ringlets turn pure white, then the little girl was shifting, and a terrified baby gazelle was bleating and struggling against the five-point harness, tiny legs pointing every direction.

Janine could hear more rocks falling on the battered roof of the car now, and the voices were louder.

"No one could have survived this," one of them said skeptically.

"I heard the brat crying," another answered. "We won't go back empty handed."

Janine tried again to find the strength to shift; as a cockatrice, she could destroy them with a breath or a swipe of her claws.

But there was nothing left. She couldn't shift, she couldn't even make it back to her seat, she just lay there, twisted impossibly, no life left in her limbs. Her eyelids were heavy.

"Run, my darling," she whispered as she closed her eyes a final time. "Run until you're safe." She'd given her little girl *time*. And that was all she could do.

LIFT

Lift occurs after Tropical Christmas Stag, but isn't anchored anywhere in particular in the timeline. I put it here in the omnibus because Run ***really*** *needed a joyful palate cleanser to follow it. I wrote it for my readers and it was available for a short time on my webpage.*

Shifting Sands Resort was made of stairs, it seemed.

Only the beach was flat, and once Mia had made her way laboriously down to it—one painful step at a time, leaning on her hateful cane, waiting for the bad knee to buckle—she honestly wasn't sure how she was going to get back up to her room in the hotel, or if she even wanted to.

The registration form had warned her that the resort did not have accommodations for disabilities, a fact that had been reiterated apologetically by the resort owner who met her at the entrance and gave her the keys to her room.

Why should they? It was a private resort for shifters only, and shifters were faster and stronger than humans and healed more quickly. There were only a vanishing number of shifters with mobility issues, and of those, not many could afford the steep prices of a luxury resort. It was ridiculous to think that such a place would make expensive upgrades like handicap lifts for such a tiny fraction of their target audience.

The owner, Scarlet, had not treated her with pity, but Mia still knew it was there behind her frosty-polite exterior.

"The staff is available to help you if you need anything," Scarlet assured her. "Don't hesitate to ask."

"I don't need any special concessions," Mia told her flatly. She hated asking for help.

But looking back up all the steps she'd come down, she wasn't sure she'd been truthful. She hadn't expected the island to be quite so *steep*. Her long trip, dragging luggage through sprawling airports and sleeping on red eyes in uncomfortable seats had been hard enough.

Mia thought that she was used to navigating inhospitable terrain. Before her injury, she'd loved hiking in the mountains. "Are you sure your shift form isn't goat?" her best friend Lena would ask her, panting up behind her to a view worth the climb. "Some of us can't fly, you know."

But since her life-altering fall, Mia had found that even businesses that made an attempt at accessibility often fell short, and what had once been an easy commute was suddenly a course of obstacles.

Like all those stairs.

Maybe she would just spend the rest of her visit on the beach, Mia decided, settling to a seat on the warm sand and laying her cane beside her. There was a bar that presumably had snacks and shifter-strength drinks and it wasn't so cold that she actually needed the shelter of her hotel room. She could just doze in the sun all day and entertain herself watching the tiny crabs that were scuttling around digging tiny holes with all the focus of their tiny little lives and sleep under the warm stars.

It was less humiliating than asking for one of those big, ridiculously gorgeous guys wandering around in staff shirts to carry her back up to her rented room like a sack of flour.

Mia had to admit that it was a beautiful place and it felt peaceful. There was far-away laughter from the pool-side bar, and even more distant singing—something operatic in a booming bass voice that she could barely hear over the thrumming waves. There was even a dragon at the far end of the beach, craning a gleaming head to watch figures in the water.

She closed her eyes and could feel the sunlight beating down on her eyelids.

It almost felt like magic and she had to swallow around the lump in her throat.

She didn't really believe this was an enchanted island that could cure her injury. Sure, there were rumors that it had brought back the hearing of a famous deaf musician, but she was too practical to listen to ridiculous stories. That wasn't why she had booked her stay here; she was only here for a mundane vacation.

Well, as mundane as you could get at a resort just for shifters.

Just as she was deciding that she had the energy to stand up and make it as far as the beach-side bar for something to drink, there was a sudden commotion in the water at the far end of the curve of the bay and Mia watched in astonishment as an entire pod of dolphins came barreling out of the surf to shift right in mid-leap to human form.

She was struck at once with envy and awe at their sheer athleticism. Even at a resort for shifters, they were remarkable, tumbling and cartwheeling as they laughed and hooted and pelted across the sand. An Olympic gymnastic team would have been impressed at their effortless flips and handsprings. They knelt in pairs and tossed each other up into twists and acrobatic spins, shouting as they went, as unconstrained by gravity in the air as they must be in the water.

And then Mia realized that they were coming right up the beach towards her because she was sitting at bottom of the detested steps to the rest of the resort. She had a sudden impulse to bury her cane in the sand and her stomach gave an unhappy little flip as she saw that they had caught sight of her and were slowing, even as her bird gave an unexpected flutter in her chest.

There were four men and three women, all of them so similar in their golden coloring and lithe build that they must be related, though they ranged in age considerably. They were clearly comfortable in their own skin and enjoying the *optional* part of the clothing-optional beach.

The nearest of them, a man of Mia's own middle age, suddenly bolted forward, outsprinting the others, who laughed and called after him, "Jack! What's in your shoes?"

"Why the rush?"

"Where's the fire?"

"Catapult!" This last was from one of the women, who launched herself at one of the others and was vaulted into the air after him.

She landed in a forward roll across the sand just at his heels as the man who must be Jack came to a stop at Mia's feet, and she realized that she was the center of all of their attention and not one of them mattered except him. He was glittering with saltwater, his hair too dark with wet to guess a color, and his eyes were piercing blue and crinkled with laughter. He had golden-tanned skin and a straight nose. His mouth was slightly parted in a wide grin.

Yes, her bird sighed in contentment. *Yes, this is right.*

He was their mate.

~

Jack wasn't sure why his dolphin would drag him up the beach at some poor sunbather who appeared to be fresh off a plane, but he went along with the compulsion as cheerfully as he did everything. There was no point in dragging his feet if they had somewhere to be!

The urge didn't abate the way it sometimes did when his dolphin found something else to be fascinated with, and about halfway to where the woman was sitting, the draw became a singing certainty.

She was his true mate! She had to be! This was the moment he'd been longing for since he first heard hushed stories about soulmates and destiny.

And naturally, he wasn't alone. He was never alone.

As much as he cared about his boisterous cousins and siblings, at that moment, he would have cheerfully buried every one of them in the sand. He was going to meet his mate, and he was going to do it with an opinionated audience, and he was never, ever going to live down all the stupid things he was about to say to her.

He came to a halt at her feet, staring down at her, wondering why she didn't rise to meet him, until he saw the cane in the sand beside her.

She was gazing up at him, huge dark eyes in a pale, round face, her lips just parted as she must be coming to the same realization that Jack just had.

"Hello! I'm Jordan," his oldest cousin introduced cheerfully. "This is Jack, Julie, John, Jonas, Josh, and Jenny..." Jenny was balanced flat on her back between the shoulders of John and Jonas.

"M-Mia..." the woman said, still looking only at Jack.

"Jack looks like he's just come up for air under a boat and knocked himself stupid," Jonas snorted.

"He always looks like that," Jenny teased.

"Why are we introducing ourselves to a stranger on the beach?" Julie asked skeptically.

Jordan chortled, "Isn't it obvious? Jack's found his mate!"

Julie hissed in shock, and Jonas and Josh cheered and clapped Jack on the bare shoulders.

"You guys know I can do this by myself, right?" Jack asked, keenly aware that they were probably not helping him make the greatest first impression, looming around his poor mate like they were trying to make a naked replica of Stonehenge. "Can we get a little space?"

"C'mon," John said sternly. "Let's give them some privacy."

"Thank you," Jack said gratefully as his brother dragged their protesting cousins away. Jenny rolled off of her brother's shoulder to land lightly on her feet.

They each gave Jack a firm punch in the arm as they left, cheering and speculating loudly about wedding plans and the number of children they'd have.

"I'm so sorry about them," Jack said, dashing to reach up onto the pool deck for a towel hanging on the railing and wrap it around his waist in chagrin. "Can I…can I sit with you? I'm Jack, and those jerks are my closest family. They mean well, but they have a weird idea of personal space. I'm a dolphin, we tend to stick to our pods, and I'm sorry, I'm talking too much, you're Mia?"

Mia. His *mate,* Mia. His dolphin was whistling in joy.

"Yes, I'm Mia," she said, making a vague gesture to the sand beside her that wasn't entirely an invitation but definitely wasn't a protest. "I'm a loon."

Jack started to laugh as he fell to a seat beside her, expecting a joke, then quickly said, "Oh, you meant that literally? A loon? That's amazing, they're so beautiful. You're beautiful and it must be amazing to be able to fly."

He knew in a split second that he'd said something terrible because her face fell into misery and despair. *Fix this!* his dolphin wailed. *What have you done?*

"What's wrong?" he begged, leaning to take her hands, wanting desperately to pull her in close, to do anything to make her smile at him again, only at the last moment remembering to ask, "May I? Can I help? Let me hold you?"

Tears welled up in her beautiful eyes. "I can't fly anymore," she said in agony. "I'll never fly again."

~

It would never work, Mia thought in regret. He was the happiest thing that she had ever laid eyes on, his joy like a light in his pale eyes and in every line of his fit body. But she was dark and broken and she might drag him into the pit of regret that she lived in and she could never forgive herself for doing that to him.

"You should go," she said, over her loon's protests. "I'm sorry, I'm sure you're great, but I'm not really a fit m-m-mate."

Jack looked at her with nothing but adoration on his face. "Why don't you let me decide that," he said gently. "Will you tell me about it?"

"Tell you what?" Mia asked, feeling dense and confused. Why was he still here, distracting her with his gleaming bare chest and strong shoulders?

"Everything!" he said with a kind smile. "I want to know every single thing! Start at your earliest memory if you want, or what you had for dinner, if you've had dinner, or where you're from, maybe? If you can bear to tell me, why can't you fly?"

Mia wanted to fall into his arms and tell him every sordid story but only gestured to her leg. The knee, now that she'd been off it for a while, had gone from stabbing pain to deep, hot throbbing. She knew from experience that would be worse than ever if she put weight on it now. "It healed wrong after I fell," she said shortly.

His face fell into a puzzled expression because that wasn't much of an explanation.

Mia plowed on. "The knee was in pieces, and…I wasn't somewhere I could shift, but it still tried to heal and by the time I finally got to a hospital, the bones had already started to knit into the wrong places. The doctors were already really suspicious and confused. Fixing it would have meant specialized surgery, breaking it and rebuilding it almost from scratch. I couldn't just…tell them what I was, so surgery wasn't exactly an option. It's just what it is, now."

She tried to sound aloof, like it wasn't a big deal, like the sympathy in Jack's eyes didn't break her heart. "I get along fine most of the time," she said firmly. "It's just been a long day and a lot of stairs."

"That's your leg, though," Jack said slowly. "I've seen one-legged birds in our feeders back home that can fly with their flocks."

"I'm a water bird," Mia pointed out. "Have you ever seen a loon take off? They've got a hundred goofy videos online with comical music. We have to run on the water for dozens of feet before we can get enough lift to take off."

It might have looked ridiculous, but it had been so thrilling, that dash across the surface of the water, the excitement of the first strokes of her wings that lifted her up…and then the world stretching beneath her as she reached for the sky.

She didn't realize she was crying until Jack gave a little keen of dismay, scooted closer to her, and gathered her, unprotesting, into his arms. "I'm sorry," she sobbed. "I'm such a mess. You deserve someone who can make you happy, not a downer like me."

Jack stroked her hair and held her close to his chest. For a moment Mia thought he was crying like she was…and then realized he was chuckling.

She drew back in confusion. "What's so funny?"

He let her retreat to arm's length, one hand cupping her jaw and making her skin tingle. "Being hurt and lost and alone isn't the same as being a downer. You just need me to remind you how to laugh."

"You don't get it," Mia said in frustration. "You don't understand. I'm sad and depressed and it shouldn't be someone else's job to cheer me up and put up with my disability. You'd be better off without me." Her loon gave a tremolo of grief and protest.

Jack's face was as close to sober as Mia suspected it got and there was still a warm smile lurking at his mouth. "Have you ever played a game on easy mode and gotten bored?"

"I suppose?" Did he not realize that she was telling him to leave? Was he dense, or just stubborn? Mia didn't care for people who couldn't take a hint. Maybe he just knew that she didn't really want him to go.

"My cousins and brothers and I, we're part of a traveling show. We do a comedy and acrobatics routine, kind of like Cirque du Solei, but not all serious. I thought it would be the greatest job in the world because there's nothing I like more in the world than to make people laugh. But it's like that game, on a level that is so easy, it's just tedious. Those people, they come to laugh, they're ready to be entertained, it's their whole purpose of being there. There's no challenge to it. My talent is completely wasted."

He was a ham, Mia decided. Even now, having what ought to be a very serious discussion, his eyes were twinkling and he was pressing his hand to his forehead dramatically.

"There!" he said in triumph, and Mia realized that she was giggling because he was too ridiculous to bear. "Now that's a smile worth the effort."

Then he was swooping down to claim her mouth with a swift, soft kiss.

Mia didn't want it to end. The rest of her life went away, every frustration and pain was simply gone at his touch, at the sweet, desperate need that he woke in her. It didn't matter that this was only a moment, it was *this* moment, and she felt whole again.

When he finally drew back, she realized that her shirt was unbuttoned and she was panting for breath. She was halfway into his lap, and the towel he was wearing did very little to hide the fact that he wanted her as badly as she wanted him.

"Come on," he said unexpectedly, and to her shock, he rather suddenly stood up with her in his arms.

"What are you doing?" Mia demanded. "Where are we going?" She clutched at his shoulders, momentarily fearing a fall, but he was stronger than he looked and lifted her easily. She had never felt safer.

"We're going into the water," he said merrily. "I've got a hard-on to cool down, and you're going to fly."

~

The warm water of the little bay didn't do much to chill Jack's ardor, not with his mate standing naked and beautiful before him. She'd been game about taking off her clothing and limping out into the shallow waves with him. The dragon at the far end of the beach had given them a thoughtful appraisal and then turned to gaze out over the water as if the sight simply wasn't that unusual.

They stood together in water that surged between waist-deep and up to their armpits. She crossed her free arm over her beautiful, slight breasts, holding him with the other as she kept the weight off of her bad leg. "I don't understand," she said faintly. "I don't know how this could possibly work."

"I'm going to throw you," Jack said. "All you need is lift, a little boost to get you started. If something goes wrong, you'll just fall in the water and I'll come to get you. It's perfectly safe. If I can toss Jonas's lazy bulk high enough for a triple twist, I can fling a bird into the air high enough to catch a draft. Trust me, I'm an expert."

She looked back at him with dark, sparkling eyes, clearly not used to trust. But there was another of those rare, precious smiles lurking behind her doubts, and Jack knew he couldn't fail. "Try it," he begged. He wanted to give this back to her more than anything else he'd ever wanted in his life. "If it doesn't work, we've only gotten wet."

She blushed then, and Jack wondered what kind of wet *she* was thinking about.

She nodded and shifted, bobbing into the water as a sleek, dark bird, her feathers stark white against black in a striking pattern. She tilted and turned in a circle, wings slightly spread as she fought for balance with one good leg, then gave a little trill as Jack put his hands beneath her and lifted her straight from the water.

Lighter than he was expecting, Jack was able to catapult her far up into the air, and for a moment he feared that he'd made a terrible mistake. He was going to meet his mate and then throw her to her death in the space of ten minutes, right in front of the dragon lifeguard.

Then her wings snapped out and she was flying.

It wasn't the fixed-wing soar of an eagle, but it was flight, and she gave a loon's haunting wail as she circled overhead in wider and wider spirals. Jack couldn't understand how a sound could be so sad and so full of joy at the very same time, but he felt utterly full of elation that he'd been able to reunite her with the sky.

He fell sideways and splashed under the surface of the water as a dolphin, adding his own song to hers. It was too shallow within the reef wave break to do fancy jumps and flips, but he could scoot on the surface and swim in circles beneath her.

~

There was air beneath Mia's wings again.

She was free and full of hope and felt like she'd been wrung out of all her emotions for the moment, left like a dry leaf in an updraft. She could still feel the ache in her bad leg, tucked up against her feathers, but it was less the sum of her life and more a small part of her equation.

She'd met her mate—her laughing, sunshine mate!—and he'd let her fly again.

The island beneath Mia seemed to flatten, the steep stairs reduced to a winding path through the resort.

Maybe it really was magic.

Maybe she really could be happy again.

At last, she returned, controlling her descent so that she splashed down with the barest bobble. She shook her head and dived under the waves, then stood as a human, hopping on one leg as Jack reached to catch her with his own human arms.

"I could fly," she murmured into his chest, half sobbing and half laughing. "I could fly again!"

"Darling Mia," Jack said into her wet hair. "Darling, brave, beautiful Mia."

She drew away and looked up at him in wonder. "This doesn't fix me," she warned. "This isn't a magic pill of happiness that erases all the pain and makes me normal and whole again."

"It doesn't have to," Jack told her, and some of the saltwater on her face wasn't ocean. "You should know that I have my own baggage," he told her gravely.

"You do?" she said, alarmed by his serious turn. How much did they really know about each other?

"You met them," he said, straight-faced. "Jonas and Josh and Julie and Jor—"

Mia felt her face split into a smile, free and full of relief and she had to kiss him for his teasing. She wound her arms up around his neck, then hissed in pain as a wave nearly lifted them from their feet and she stumbled getting her balance again.

"I'm only mostly kidding with that one," Jack said more seriously as they waded slowly back to the shore. "I come with a pod, and they're nosy and bossy and will be one hundred percent up in your business."

Mia's smile faltered. "Will they like me?"

"I know they will!" he promised. Then he gave her a sideways glance. "But it doesn't matter if they do. Do you smell that? Have you eaten at the restaurant yet? It's a treat, let me tell you. Are you hungry? I never did get an answer about whether you'd had dinner."

Mia's loon was pleased by the idea that their mate would feed them.

They dried off with his stolen towel and he wrapped it back around himself as Mia dressed and slung her purse over her shoulder. They wandered up the beach with Mia leaning as much on his arm as on her cane, which was not useful in the loose sand.

"I forgot how many stairs there were," Mia said, looking up them.

"I can carry you," Jack offered, then swiftly added, "or we can walk at whatever speed you'd like."

She looked at him thoughtfully, then smiled. "I could use a lift," she admitted. It hurt less to admit it than she had feared.

Jack stooped to pick her up, nearly lost his towel-wrap, and then carried her, giggling into his shoulder, up to her waiting hotel room.

It was a very long time before they made it to the restaurant.

TROPICAL LEOPARD'S LONGING

CHAPTER 1

Darla Grant's heart pounded in her chest.

Being in the hoard always made her anxious, but this was worse than ever before.

This time, everything was at stake.

All around them, treasure gleamed: jeweled golden goblets, chains of silver and platinum, cut gems, loose stones, coins, tapestries with real gold thread, statues carved out of jade and tiger's eye, priceless art in solid gold frames. A raw diamond the size of a dining room table sat on a low dais, surrounded by cut rubies and emeralds that were merely the size of bulldogs.

Everything was sitting on priceless marble columns or displayed on cunning, hand carved shelves from extinct hardwoods. Strings of precious stones and jewels in findings hung across rafters above them like garlands. Drifts of gold and silver coins filled every corner.

A protection spell shivered in the air around them, the faintest metallic haze over everything.

Beside Darla, Liam let out the breath he'd been holding.

Darla shot him a glance, glad to see that he looked awed rather than disgusted. She had tried to prepare him for the sight, but descriptions of the hoard fell short of the staggering reality of it.

She wasn't the only one watching for his reaction.

Jubilee Grant's mouth turned up in a smug smile of satisfaction. "As you can see, marrying my daughter comes with a great responsibility," she said severely. "With *my* blessing on her wedding, her union will satisfy the dragon contract and unlock the hoard in entirety."

Liam looked adorably confused, glancing behind them at the door they had just come through. It had been conspicuously open. "It's… locked?"

"Magic, of course," Jubilee was happy to explain. "My dear, departed husband had a protection spell set over it. He was the last dragon shifter of his line and so disappointed that Darla ended up being a snow leopard shifter. He wanted her to continue the dragon line, much as my father had hoped for me."

Darla gazed forward with practiced serenity. She had never felt like her father had been particularly disappointed in her shift form; certainly not to the extent that her mother had. She wondered how much of her mother's disapproval came from the disappointment that Jubilee herself had grown up with; she had also been the last of a great dragon line, and had also failed to manifest wings and scales.

"The spell was one of the last things he did before he died," Jubilee continued. "Dragons are so protective of their hoards. You know how that goes, of course!"

Liam gave her a dazed smile, nodding agreeably. Neither he nor Darla bothered to explain that Eastern dragons were considerably less motivated by wealth than their Western counterparts. Liam himself was as poor as a proverbial churchmouse.

Would her mother care about that? Darla wondered, her heart in her mouth. Would she approve of Liam as a suitor for her hand, or would she find his poor origins and ordinary shifter bloodline too distasteful to forgive? The alternative… Darla carefully did not look past her mother to where Eugene was frowning thoughtfully at a particularly gaudy dragon statue studded with cut gems.

He was a distant cousin from her mother's family, chummy with her mother and rather more friendly to Darla than she had ever wished he would be. His lingering looks had bothered her even before he had started leaving hints that a marriage between them would be beneficial to the precious family line. When her twenty-fifth birthday—the usual age of engagement for dragons—came around, his hints and his distasteful courtship had grown considerably less subtle.

Only years of training kept Darla from shuddering at the very thought of marrying Eugene and she let her hand tighten in Liam's just a little.

He looked down at her anxiously and Darla smiled gratefully up at him.

"Well, Mother, what do you say?" she asked, trying to look just the right amount of eager. "Don't leave Liam in suspense!"

"He doesn't come from an established dragon line," Eugene was quick to remind them. He had done a poor job of hiding his seething anger behind his social polish since Darla had sprung Liam on them that afternoon. "He doesn't understand dragon honor."

"But he *is* a dragon shifter," Jubilee said, a little smile at her lips.

"A great surprise to my dear mother," Liam said, with a charming little laugh.

"It's a good match," Darla said coaxingly. "And we're very fond of each other." It wasn't a falsehood; Darla was not brave enough to outright lie to her mother, though she had been practicing a series of half-truths that might be convincing in the event that her mother was reluctant to approve the union.

It appeared that she needn't have worried.

Jubilee, despite Eugene's dissent, seemed so taken by the idea of a dragon shifter to marry to Darla that she didn't seem to mind his common origins or Eugene's not-so-subtle protests of the union.

"Madame Nadine told me that Darla would be best suited to someone she'd known a long time," Jubilee said knowingly. "And that she would be the start to a long, healthy line of new dragon shifters. Liam, you are obviously exactly who she meant; Darla's been volunteering at your retirement home for years now! You were so sly not to tell me of your relationship earlier!"

Eugene sputtered unexpectedly. As much as he usually

supported Jubilee's unhealthy obsession with her psychic, he seemed weirdly surprised that Jubilee would follow her advice now.

Darla tried not to feel too smug about thwarting him; he was as clever as he was unsavory, and she knew from his dark expression that he wasn't done trying to get her hand—or the incredible hoard she would inherit once she was married.

Liam was not oblivious to his ire either. He met Eugene's hateful gaze evenly and calmly.

"Oh, yes," Jubilee said, not noticing either of them. "Eugene, this is perfect! You don't have to marry Darla now after all! Oh, everything is falling into place, just as Madame Nadine predicted!"

Darla almost smirked; Eugene had played up marrying Darla as his *duty* so heavy-handedly to her mother that he had no footing against Jubilee's enthusiasm for the new suitor she presented. "Thank you, Mother," she said, casting her gaze down like the very picture of a dutiful daughter. "I'm sure we'll be very happy."

"My thanks, Mrs. Grant," Liam added politely.

Jubilee clapped her hands happily. "Come, let's go talk with the lawyer regarding the dowry, and there will be an engagement party —we can do that next week. I've been researching all the dragon customs in great detail and oh, I know *exactly* where I want the wedding. There's this lovely luxury resort for shifters off the coast of Costa Rica that I've heard the most *wonderful* things about! Eugene, come help me figure out the guest list. All the best people, of course…"

Liam and Darla were the least of her concerns now and Jubilee Grant swept out of the hoard with Eugene simmering at her heels, not even noticing that the two to be married lingered behind.

Darla let out her breath, letting relief wash over her at last. "It worked," she said gratefully. "Oh, Liam, you are a lifesaver."

"I should say the same," Liam said, but he sounded hesitant. "Are you sure about this? You deserve a love match, and you know I can't..."

"She never wanted a love match for me," Darla said calmly. "And this solves so many problems for both of us."

"You don't have to do this for the retirement home," Liam protested. "I could probably find other funding. Somehow."

"You've met Eugene, now," Darla reminded him. "I am *not* just doing this to keep the home afloat. I mean, I could just marry *him* and use my pocket money to keep the center open." The very idea left an awful taste in her mouth.

"Now that I see what you consider casual spending money, I believe you could," Liam said dryly. He was clearly still staggered by the wealth of the hoard. They left the halls of treasure behind to return to the house, going from unimaginable treasure to more pedestrian ridiculous wealth; the paintings here were only in gilded frames, not solid gold, and the decor was more 'tasteful opulence' than 'actual piles of gold.'

"Anyway, it won't be so bad, marrying me," Darla promised coaxingly. "I think we'll get along just fine, and I know this great retirement home where we can grow old together."

Liam smiled at her. "What could possibly go wrong?"

CHAPTER 2

"Have you got a key to cottage fifteen?" the handyman Travis asked, striding into the kitchen with his rattling tool belt. "Scarlet says we're missing one, and you're the likeliest candidate."

Breck Aster, leopard shifter and head waiter at Shifting Sands Resort, looked up from the plates where he was arranging garnish and grinned. "Oh, cottage fifteen? That gorgeous brunette with the legs for miles. *And* her sister. Yeah, I probably still have that." He made a show of searching for the key in his pocket as if there were several to choose from. "Mmm, the stories this key could tell…" He pulled it out.

"I don't want to know," Travis protested. "I *really* don't want to know."

The lynx shifter took the key with distaste and carried it back out of the kitchen held out in front of him as if afraid that it was permanently contaminated.

Breck watched him go with a satisfied smirk that faded as he turned back to give the garnish one final tweak.

Appearances matter, he reminded himself, lifting the plates into his hands and carrying them out to the restaurant deck. Travis didn't need to know that Breck hadn't been using any of the keys he'd been collecting.

"The beef tenderloin," he announced, setting the plate down in front of a fresh-faced blonde woman with a wink. "And the halibut filet for the catch of the sea." Breck's exaggerated appreciation of her boyfriend made him startle and squirm, even after a week of the treatment, but it was a flattered and tolerant embarrassment, not a harassed objection to the attention.

The young woman laughed in amusement, delighted with her boyfriend's discomfort.

"Can I order you anything from the bar?" he offered. "A mojito for the lady? A beefeater for the beef?" These two had been at the resort for nearly a week and he'd figured out their habits within a day.

"Just top off the water," the blonde said regretfully. "We're packing up to fly out tonight."

Breck put his hands over his heart. "The resort will be empty without you," he said dramatically. "My nights will cease to have meaning."

Even the boyfriend laughed at that.

Breck topped off water for all the tables on the deck, smiling at the single woman in blue who was making eyes at him over her sunglasses and steak. He flirted very lightly with her, keeping it silly and over-the-top when she might have been angling for something more, and he escaped back to the kitchen as quickly as the conversation politely allowed.

It was quiet for the time of evening; the resort was in an odd lull. Usually, people streamed in and out at regular intervals with the scheduled charters, groups overlapping. But this time, the entire resort was being emptied to make space for an exclusive wedding of two high-profile dragon families. For the first few days, it would be only the immediate family and wedding party. Then there would be almost a week of extended guests, stuffing the resort to the seams.

The wedding itself was a two day affair, with a ceremony so convoluted and steeped in specific tradition that Scarlet, the resort owner, had diagramed it with visual aids. There was a midnight vigil, hours for recitation of the family lines, formal dances, even a two hour window for a duel of challenge, should there be one.

Everyone was under strict orders to be on their best behavior and the staff knew that Scarlet was hoping that *this* was the event that would tip the resort over into genuine solvency.

Chef was singing something operatic in the back of the kitchen, chopping and banging pans around as he started concocting experimental *hors d'oeuvres* to offer as options for the wedding.

"They'll choose the worst one," Breck warned him, depositing a load of dishes into the sink. "It's inevitable."

"Even my worst is better than they'll find anywhere on the mainland," Chef said expansively, waggling a cleaver at Breck when he snuck in for a taste of the truffles being chopped.

"Your genius in the kitchen is only exceeded by your humility," Breck agreed, licking his fingers.

He washed his hands dutifully and went to freshen up the dessert platter.

By the time the young couple was finished with their meal, the forward woman with the sunglasses had left… leaving her key conspicuously behind.

Breck pocketed it thoughtfully and dismissed the rest of the staff early.

As he finished clearing the last tables himself, he found himself patting the key in his pocket thoughtfully. He was in the longest dry spell of his life, and it wasn't for lack of opportunity. But the endless string of available partners had somehow lost its lustre. Breck found himself searching faces for… something more.

It wasn't that she was too old, or that she wasn't plenty attractive—Breck appreciated beauty in all packages—it was just that Breck felt like he had nothing left to give.

He felt oddly like he'd been giving a little piece of himself away with every lover, never asking for anything in return. And now, at last, he'd been whittled away to a tired, hollow shell that felt like a mask.

He had that mask firmly in place, smiling in apparent self-satisfaction when he returned to The Den.

"Don't tell me," Jenny guessed as he rummaged in the staff fridge for a beer and she grabbed ice cubes from the freezer next to him. "That male model from Italy decided to try your side of the fence, didn't he! He's been eying you curiously all week."

Jenny, an otter shifter and the resort lawyer, and her identical twin, Laura, both had mates living with them in The Den. Their presence had turned the building from an established bachelor pad into more of a community house; Breck and the landscaper Graham were the only single men left living there now.

"All sides of the fence are mine," Breck said with a saucy wink. "And let's just say, he got the courage up to peek over… and liked what he saw."

Jenny laughed, shaking her head. "I'm sure he did, Breck." She kissed his cheek in a sisterly way. "You'll break his heart like all the others," she teased.

Breck checked his watch. "I've got a late evening of heart-breaking lined up in just a tick," he said, too loudly to his own ears. "Just enough time to catch a shower first…"

But he needn't have worried about fooling Jenny; her attention was caught by Bastian, who was groaning dramatically. "My *parents*," the dragon shifter lifeguard was saying in despair. "My *parents* are coming to this awful wedding."

"Did they get over the fact that they didn't get a fancy formal affair for you and Saina?" Jenny asked.

Bastian was too busy groaning and putting his head on his arms to answer, so his mate Saina did for him. "It's hard to tell. There's been echoing silence from them since we eloped, which suits us both just fine. The letter letting us know they were coming was very vague and brief. Dragons, you know." She shrugged with all the nonchalance of a siren. "They never say more than they have to, lest they get caught up in an unintentional contract."

"I love weddings," Breck said as he opened his beer. "They put everyone in the mood to make *connections*."

"As if you needed an excuse," Jenny ribbed him.

Breck gave her a cheeky smile and toasted her with his beer as he left the kitchen.

His smile faded at his exit.

The Den had not been designed as staff housing, but as a luxury mansion for the original owner of the resort. Scarlet had moved them to open up spaces for guests in the hotel building, because so many of the amenities had to be shared and it wasn't structured for individual rentals. Breck sometime wondered what the original plan had been for staff, and what had happened to the owner who was supposed to be living in the lush accommodations.

He took his beer with him to the spa-like shared shower and stood with the hot water spilling down over his bare shoulders.

He had not told Jenny the whole story.

The model from Italy had been three sheets to the wind, finding his courage for experimentation in the bottles at Tex's bar. Even at better times, Breck would not have indulged his desires with such questionable consent. Though he didn't advertise it, and let people believe whatever they wanted, he had a very strict code of honor, and he never poached drunk partners, invited angry liaisons meant to cause jealousy, or propositioned anyone already in a relationship, no matter how willing they were.

He'd given the model a cup of coffee and a kind, private decline that left them both smiling. If Breck's smile was more relieved than anything, he would never have admitted it.

"Don't wait up!" he called as he left The Den a quarter of an hour later.

"Wasn't planning to," Travis retorted cheerfully.

"I don't want to know about it later, either!" Tex added.

CHAPTER 3

Darla stared at the laptop that was open on the tiny airplane tray in front of her.

Two words started the page: *I vow…*

The rest was blank.

This shouldn't be any harder than writing a thank you letter, or a polite invitation response. Finishing school had given her plenty of the applicable skills to use; there were standards to follow, and patterns that should make this simple and straightforward. All she had to do was pick a few flowery phrases and put them in a pleasing order, something she did regularly.

It wasn't even like she was lying about what she was trying to write; she really did want to marry Liam. She glanced ahead down the aisle of the little jet to where Eugene was sitting next to her mother, sipping a glass of wine and exchanging small talk with her.

Darla shuddered. Yes, she really *did* want to marry Liam.

She turned the silver bracelet on her left wrist and fingered the dragon lettering that translated to 'Unbroken Line.'

It was hot against her skin.

If she could have pulled it off, she would have, but it was heavy and seamless, as if it had been forged there. A shackle, she thought bitterly. A magical shackle that only reinforced that she was no better than a broodmare, to be married off and docilely provide children for the honor of the family.

How was she supposed to put *that* in her vows?

Beside her, Liam looked up from his book and Darla realized that she had sighed out loud.

"Having trouble?" he asked kindly, slipping off his headphones.

"So much trouble," Darla confessed. "Have you written yours?"

"I looked up the vows they use at the Elvis chapel in Vegas and changed a few words," Liam said carelessly.

Darla gave him a sideways smile. "You're going to marry me with cribbed Vegas vows?"

"Well, your mother probably wouldn't let me fly Elvis in to perform the ceremony," Liam teased with a dramatic sigh.

Darla giggled despite herself. "It would have been so much easier just to elope to Las Vegas," she said with regret.

"Your mother…"

"My mother would have had a fit of vapors and then she would have figured out how to have it annulled so she could do this whole circus her way anyway," Darla agreed. "I know."

Liam took her hand, and the matching bracelet on his wrist was cool against her arm, like it always was. "We'll make this work," he said gently. "It's going to be okay."

He didn't say that they *had* to make it work, though he could have. He had as much to gain from their marriage as she did… and arguably more to lose if it fell through.

It was a sensible match, Darla reminded herself, twining her fingers into his for comfort as much as for show. She liked Liam and marrying him solved so many of her problems. If it wasn't the love match she'd always dreamed of, it was certainly better than any of the other options before them.

She rubbed her bracelet against her opposite arm thoughtfully, pondering the inscription and the bizarre source.

Several days after their engagement announcement, the bracelets had arrived in the mail. The note enclosed had been a polite decline of the invitation to the wedding by one of the prestigious New York dragon families that Jubilee aspired to be friendly with.

Jubilee had been delighted in the gift. "These dragonrunes mean 'Unbroken Line,'" she explained with the authority vested in her from several weeks of research. "They must be fertility charms."

She had insisted that Liam and Darla put them on immediately and to Darla's horror, they had sealed onto their arms with a permanence that gave Darla cold chills, the seam vanishing.

"Who sent these?" she asked, struggling to mask her horror.

Liam had smiled the same very polite smile that he had practiced for Jubilee, but Darla recognized the same distrust that was plaguing her.

"He's a lawyer in New York," Jubilee had said, comparing the note to her ever-increasing guest list. "A very important figure in dragon social circles there. He would have been quite a catch to have at the wedding, but a gift like this is nearly as good."

She didn't seem bothered at all by the fact that they were now affixed to Darla and Liam with no obvious possibility of removal. If anything, she was delighted by the show of magic.

Darla was not delighted.

They seemed to represent everything inescapable about the impending wedding.

CHAPTER 4

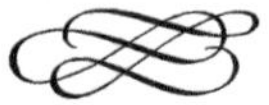

Breck raised his hand and knocked on the cottage door.

He didn't have a key for this door and would never have asked for one. He was, however, carrying a bouquet of flowers.

"Come in!" called a thin voice from within.

He opened the unlocked door. "Mrs. Shandy, you are looking more lovely than ever."

Mrs. Shandy was a hundred years old if she was a week and she was sitting at a little table by the bed. It was one of the smaller cottages, laid out as a simple one-room efficiency. The remains of a meal beside her showed that the rule against food outside of the restaurant had been relaxed for her.

"Breck, my dear," she cackled, waving her hand imperiously across from her. "You're risking Graham's wrath by bringing me those."

Graham, a lion shifter, was in charge of landscaping for the entire resort and he was notoriously protective of his gardens.

"It is a risk worth taking for the smile it brings you," Breck said, laying a gentle kiss on her forehead. "How's the ankle?"

He busied himself, finding a vase for the flowers and arranging them artfully.

"The ankle is healing up fine," Mrs. Shandy said with a smile. "It's the shoulders complaining today. At my age, it's always something."

"I'll have Lydia come give you a rub tomorrow," Breck promised. The swan shifter was in charge of the spa, and was a talented masseuse for both animal and human forms.

"Oh, she's too busy," Mrs. Shandy protested. "I couldn't ask her to do that."

"She'll insist," Breck warned her. "And tomorrow shouldn't be too bad. The first wave of the big wedding party came in just tonight, but it won't be very busy for a few more days. Do you feel like a game tonight?"

"I could beat you a few times," Mrs. Shandy said slyly.

Breck opened the backgammon game between them.

After one lively game, Breck thought that she seemed to be flagging, and he closed up the board.

"When are you going to find yourself a nice girl or boy and get married yourself?" she asked, as Breck helped her up from her chair.

"You know me," Breck said breezily. "I could never settle for one person."

"I know you," Mrs. Shandy rebuked. "You would like people to believe that you are shallow and hedonistic so you never have to get hurt."

Breck held her bathrobe as she shrugged out of it. Naked, she turned and took his face in her wrinkled hands. "When are you going to open yourself up?"

"I love everyone I've ever been with," Breck protested.

"But you never let them love you," Mrs. Shandy reminded him. "Not really." She sighed and patted his face. "Someday," she warned him. "Someday, you will understand what it can be."

Then, she let go of him and shifted. A tall, elegant old greyhound stood in her place, tail waving very slowly. Breck put a respectful hand on her head and the tail waved more vigorously. Then, ignoring the bed, she went to a cushion laid out on the floor by the French doors to the deck. She turned around twice and settled down with a sigh.

"Good night, Mrs. Shandy," Breck said gently. He quietly gathered the dishes and slipped out.

After he returned the tray to the kitchen, he stood on the restaurant deck, looking out over the bar deck, and the pool deck below that. Beyond, the ocean looked smooth and inviting.

Breck slipped a hand into his uniform jacket pocket, and fingered the key he found there thoughtfully. He was… restless. Like he was waiting for something. Like there was something missing.

He watched the moon move halfway across the sky before he sighed and returned the key to the staff lost and found.

CHAPTER 5

Seventeen necklaces glittered on the crisp bedspread. "Which of these did you want me to wear?" Darla asked skeptically. She would have liked a nice single strand of pearls or maybe a silver chain with a simple pendant, but the choices laid out were crowded webs of cut jewels, torcs of gold, and twists of lustrous dragonmetal inlaid with precious stones.

"It's a dragon wedding," her mother sniffed. "All of them. I've done the research and dragon weddings are about showing off *wealth*."

Darla picked up one of the heavier pieces. "I couldn't even walk down the aisle in all of these." She more quietly added, "And I'm not a dragon."

Unbroken line. She was careful not to touch the bracelet weighing on her wrist.

"You're *marrying* a dragon," came the unnecessary reminder. "And you come from dragon blood. You have to show that you're *worth* marrying." Her tone indicated that she doubted that Darla would be able to do that even wearing a small fortune in jewelry.

"Anyway, it's a wedding in strict dragon tradition," Jubilee continued. "Now, let's try on the dresses and see how these layer with them. It's possible you can wear some of them for the rehearsal dinner and the vigil or the dance, instead. And we'll need to pick a headdress for each of them, too."

Darla wished she were the sort of person who could put her foot down. "No," she imagined saying. "I'm not trying on those ridiculous dresses again, and I'm only wearing one necklace, and I'm canceling the vigil, and we're doing a simple, short wedding, or else I'll throw a fit and you won't get any wedding at all."

But that was not her. That was someone braver than her, someone more clever and self-assured.

Instead, she timidly said, "I'm very tired from traveling, Mother, and I haven't caught up to this timezone. Do you think we could do that this afternoon instead? I thought I might lie out by the pool before the sun got too hot."

"Lie out in the sun?!"

She might as well have suggested yodeling or dancing naked in the restaurant.

"Lie out in the sun?" Jubilee repeated incredulously. "Darla, sweetheart, think of your skin! You *know* how you freckle. You don't want to look *common* for the most important days of your life!"

The bolder her might have pointed out that no one would be able to see through the glitter of the ugly jewels to even notice a few freckles. The real her knew that she'd look common no matter how un-freckled her cheeks were kept.

"I was thinking I'd do it as a leopard," she said swiftly, knowing that a sunhat or skin protectant would not reassure her mother. "It's a resort for shifters, after all, so it's completely normal here."

Jubilee looked unconvinced and Darla would have conceded defeat if the earth hadn't given a rattling little hiccup under their feet just then.

The earthquake was brief, doing no more than rattling the paintings on the walls. They fled the bedroom, but by the time they came out into the living area, the earth was quiet again.

Jubilee's eyes were wide. "It's a sign!" she gasped. "An earthquake before a wedding, it must mean something."

"It's a sign that we're in the ring of fire where earthquakes happen all the time," Darla said smartly before she could stop herself. Adrenaline made her feel brave.

Jubilee ignored her, pressing a hand to her chest. "Oh, my heart is hammering. This is dreadful. Maybe this resort was a mistake. We could have done this in the English countryside, or in Italy, perhaps. There might still be time for the rest of the guests to get their tickets changed."

Darla patted her arm awkwardly. "Come and sit down, Mother. It's just a little earthquake, it's not a portent of doom."

Jubilee was shaking her head as she reluctantly took the plush wicker chair that Darla offered. "I should consult with my psychic," she said. "Maybe we're doing the wrong thing." She dug into her designer purse for her phone. "I wish I'd insisted that she come with me. But she doesn't like to travel. Oh, maybe she *knew* something!"

Darla left her mother dialing her phone and muttering about foreshadows and bad signs and returned to her own bedroom. The jewelry on the bedspread hadn't even gotten tangled in the quake. Darla frowned at it, then perked up. Her mother would be occupied for a long while with her psychic, and she hadn't explicitly told Darla she *couldn't* go sun herself in leopard form.

That was as close as Darla was going to get to actual permission, and she wasn't going to squander the chance. As quickly as she could, Darla stripped out of her clothing, leaving it folded neatly on the bedside table. The engagement bracelet could not come off, but it was dragon magic, and would shift with her.

Quick as a thought, she was a snow leopard, plush and graceful in ways she never was as a human. The silver bracelet shone on one wrist. Darla shook that paw, not liking the weight of it, then scampered out the private back door of her bedroom to visit the quiet pool and enjoy the sun and fleeting peace.

CHAPTER 6

The bar deck was quiet when Breck came down following the breakfast service.

Though it didn't tend to get truly rowdy until evening, there was usually a steady stream of shifters through the space. Even if the guests weren't drinking alcohol, the fruit drinks and snacks were popular, and there were games and books, and the fitness center was nearby. There were more shaded tables than were available on the pool deck below, and it was rare that there weren't a few people sitting at them.

"It feels weird, doesn't it?" Tex, bear shifter and bartender, was restocking a cooler with bottles. He passed Breck a ginger ale.

"Reminds me of a couple of years ago, before business picked up," Breck agreed, unscrewing the lid and taking a long swallow. "We used to get lulls like this a lot."

"I suppose it's good that business is brisker now," Tex said. "Job security, and all."

"Not to mention bonuses," Breck chuckled. "Though it would help if you didn't get resort property blown up this year."

"I had nothing to do with the boat blowing up!" Tex protested.

He considered. "Well, very little, anyway. How'd it go with your hot date last night? You were certainly back late."

Breck shrugged. "I don't kiss and tell," he said with a wink.

"Oh?" Tex said skeptically. "When did that start?"

"I am the epitome of discretion," Breck protested with mock innocence. Another time, he might have simply fabricated something. He had an active imagination and a wealth of experience to draw on, and it was always entertaining to make Tex flush and regret asking questions.

But he still felt the restless displacement of the night before and needling Tex held no distraction.

His leopard was agitated; he had the nagging feeling he had forgotten something terribly important.

He took his bottle of ginger ale to the edge of the shade and looked out over the deck. Bright sunlight gave the white tile a luminous character and the pool below glimmered blue. The water features at the near edge of the pool provided a wash of restful sound and the thrum of the ocean beyond was a deep, constant beat.

A movement caught his eye. A snow leopard was coming in the side entrance, padding silently across the tile around the pool. After a moment, it hopped gracefully up onto one of the wide, low benches that were designed for large animals to lounge on. It circled twice and lay down, looking away over the beach below. Something glinted on one of its paws.

Tex, coming to stand beside him and squint out into the bright light, spotted it too. "Well, we've got one guest out and about. Do you mind offering them a water? Laura's up at the spa helping Lydia and I want to finish up here." Newcomers to the resort often underestimated the heat of the sun and their own need for hydration—especially in animal form.

But Breck was already moving, heading down the grand stairs as if he was being drawn by a string.

As he closed the distance between them, the snow leopard's head swiveled towards him. It shifted its weight and rolled to its feet.

Blue eyes met his, blue eyes more beautiful than any sky he'd ever seen. It was a gorgeous snow leopard, with thick, patterned fur. The glint he'd seen was a heavy-looking silver bracelet encircling one of its legs above the paw.

His own leopard rose to his feet in his head. *Ours*, he said firmly. *This one is ours.*

Breck was struck dumb.

This was not a familiar state for Breck. He prided himself on thinking fast on his feet, of being smooth, and he was always ready with a clever compliment or a quick comeback.

But looking into these blue eyes, no words came to his mind.

He wasn't sure he still had mastery of language.

All he knew was that this, *this* was the part of his life that had been missing. This was the answer to every question, the fulfillment of every desire. This was peace and harmony and hope.

This was home.

He ought to kneel, he thought achingly, or offer his hands, or say something. But all he could do with stare, until suddenly the bracelet the leopard was wearing flared to life, glowing warmly and then fading slowly back… not to silver, but to gold.

The snow leopard blinked down at it in surprise, exchanged another glance with Breck, and suddenly wheeled away, fleeing the pool deck on silent, padded feet.

That was my mate, he thought, feeling like there was no floor beneath his feet. He was excited and eager and anxious, and it felt like everything around him was resettling in some new shape.

That was my mate, Breck repeated to himself, his leopard purred, *Ours*! in pure delight.

Then he groaned and let his head fall into his hand. The rest of the staff was never going to let him live this down.

CHAPTER 7

Darla fled, but not back to the three-bedroom cottage she was sharing with her mother and her assistant.

She didn't remember that she wouldn't have clothing on until she was shifting at Liam's door, and knocking frantically.

"Darla!" he said in alarm, opening the door. "What is it? What's wrong? My bracelet went off like fireworks just a moment ago and turned gold, are you *alright*?"

He looked only at her face, nothing else. Darla pushed past him into the room, closed the door firmly behind her, and leaned back on it as if her legs had given out.

For a long moment, she said nothing, trying to catch her breath. It wasn't the headlong flight that had weakened her knees, it was *him*.

The waiter in the crisp uniform had appeared by the pool as if Darla's desire had summoned him. He was tall and graceful, with golden-brown eyes and dark hair, and the way that he had *looked* at her…

"Here, honey, you're shivering. I'll bring you a bathrobe..."

Darla pitched forward into his arms, sobbing. She wasn't worried about her nudity, not with him.

His arms folded around her and his hands rubbed her shaking shoulders.

Hands of a friend, not a lover.

When she could finally stand again, she wrapped her arms around herself and stood looking out over the porch while Liam went to get her a bathrobe.

"Tell me what happened," he said kindly, wrapping her up in the soft terrycloth and drawing her to sit down on the couch beside him.

Darla curled miserably beside him, tucking her head onto his shoulder as he put an arm around her. "I met him," she said into his shoulder. "I met my *mate.*"

Liam froze, then resumed patting her as if she was a restless animal.

In many ways she *was* a restless animal. Her snow leopard was intently focused on going back to the pool, now, and *quickly*. She didn't understand why Darla had fled in the first place.

"Are you sure?" Liam asked quietly.

"So sure," Darla sobbed. "It's just like the stories. I knew, I just knew he was the one, and I… just can't. Because..."

"You don't have to marry me," Liam said firmly. "I'd find another way to finance the retirement home."

"You know I have to marry you," Darla protested. "If I don't, it will be Eugene. He'd challenge for my hand. And my mother would never accept less than a dragon shifter, otherwise. I'd be disowned and she'd see that the retirement home was destroyed, out of spite if nothing else."

"Is it possible your mate *is* a dragon shifter? The lifeguard here is a dragon," Liam suggested, and for a brief moment hope bloomed in Darla's chest.

But no… "He was... a waiter." And he was a big cat, Darla was sure, not a dragon. Something about the way that he walked, and the gold in his brown eyes.

"Oh, not a *waiter*," Liam said in mock horror. "Your mother barely accepted the director of a retirement home for her son-in-law. She certainly wouldn't tolerate a *waiter* in the family."

Even as Darla recognized that he was trying to tease, to lighten the situation, she burst into tears. "She wouldn't!" she sobbed.

Liam held her and let her cry herself out. "What are you going to do?" he asked as she sat up and wiped her face on the arms of the robe.

"I'm going to be eating at the buffet on off hours a lot," Darla snuffled. "Maybe I can pretend to be sick and get special permission to eat in the cottage."

"That might get you out of a few meals," Liam agreed. "But there are going to be formal dinners. You aren't going to be able to avoid him forever."

It would be impossible to eat at the restaurant, to be served by her mate, to not watch him, not want him. She gnawed on her lip at the idea of it, her treacherous imagination supplying the idea of him feeding her food, of licking his fingers…

She drew in a shuddering breath and wiped her face again, nearly scraping herself with the hateful bracelet encircling her wrist. She paused to inspect it, frowning over the cosmetic changes. It had definitely shifted in color, from a cool silver, to a light gold. It felt hot against her skin. Were the markings different? She didn't know how to read dragonrunes, so she wasn't sure.

"Did you talk to him?" Liam asked gently. "What's his name?"

Darla shook her head. "I don't know. I just… I ran. I had to. It was… so much."

"You should talk to him," Liam said. "It's not fair to just avoid him."

Darla looked at him and made a face. "None of this is *fair*," she said sourly.

CHAPTER 8

Breck arrived at the staff meeting several minutes late.

A cold shower had not been optional, but it had not done anything to calm the roiling confusion in his chest, or the desire that his leopard was feeding him.

Scarlet gave him a piercing look, probably taking in his damp hair with the kind of assumption that Breck knew he deserved. He attempted to grin at her like he usually would and guessed by her puzzled expression that it failed.

"Nice of you to join us," Tex hissed near his ear as he took the last seat. "Was it worth Scarlet's wrath?"

Behind them, Travis leaned forward. "Watch it," he said quietly. "Scarlet is going to be pissed if you start drama with the bridesmaids."

Breck was momentarily distracted by the accusation. "I don't start drama," he insisted.

"Start drama with. Sleep your way through. Whatever. If Scarlet catches you risking this contract, she will make a suit from your hide and wear it to the wedding."

A sharp glance back from Scarlet made Travis sit back and all three of them pretended to pay attention to Lydia's report on the spa supplies.

Was the snow leopard a bridesmaid? Breck wondered. The big cat had to be some member in the core wedding party or immediate family, because those were the only guests right now.

It was odd to see a shifter wearing jewelry in animal form, if not unheard of. And he'd never seen any jewelry do anything like that.

And why had they run away?

Breck could think of many possible reasons, but none of them made sense.

Travis leaned forward between Tex and Breck. Tex was playing a tic-tac-toe game with himself in the nap of his cowboy hat.

"You'll want to listen to this bit," Travis said knowingly.

Jenny was standing up. "So, as you know, we've been battling with the owner of the island, Beehag, and his lawyer for nearly a year now about the sale of the island and the fate of the resort. The lease contract that Scarlet has is one of the most complicated pieces of legalese I've ever seen and it references several older documents, including the ones that covered the transfer of the property to Beehag senior on the disappearance—and presumed death—of the original owner of this half of the island, Aaric Lyons."

If Breck had not been looking past Scarlet to see Jenny, he would not have noticed the subtle flinch the resort owner gave at the name.

"Lyons left very specific instructions that the resort was to be continued in the event of his death, and also that his progeny would have first right of refusal on all property sales… including subsequent sales. At the time, Beehag senior's offer to buy this half of the island and continue to administrate the property was accepted by the Lyons family. But if we can find anyone remaining in the Lyons line, *they* get the chance to buy the property at appraised value before Beehag the lesser can sell it to any of these nasty characters he's been scraping the barrel to find."

"I thought the family of the original resort owner was all dead!" Bastian said.

"Possibly not *all* of them," Jenny said with a grin. "The last of the line was a kid named Grant Lyons. He was jailed for manslaughter when he was 18, about fifteen years ago, and he vanished directly following his sentence. I've found some intel that he might have changed his name and moved to America. It's a cold trail, but I know some good people. If we can find him, we may be able to persuade *him* to buy the property. Possibly he would be willing to hold it in trust for us if we could raise the money. At the worst, he could not be a more miserable landlord than our current one."

The room rose in a murmur of speculation that trailed off as everyone looked eagerly at Scarlet.

If Jenny was expecting surprise or warm approval for this revelation, she was disappointed. Scarlet rose to her feet and faced the room with an utterly expressionless face. "Thank you," she said, neutrally. "See what you can find out. Chef, I'd like your report from the kitchen."

The start of Chef's report was drowned in whispers and quiet conjecture until Scarlet loudly cleared her throat and the room went quiet again.

After the meeting had finally been adjourned, Breck remained sitting and let everyone else filter out.

The quiet room did nothing to his peace of mind.

He'd met his mate… and he had no idea who they were. He didn't even know if the snow leopard was a man or a woman.

He only knew that he'd never rest without them again. This wasn't a hunger of his body, but of his heart, and he had no idea what to do with it.

CHAPTER 9

A beautiful Latina woman greeted Darla cheerfully at the entrance to a beautifully mosaic-covered building and drew her into the cozy spa as Jubilee looked around critically.

"You must be the happy bride!"

Darla, stomach already churning with nerves, only nodded. She was half of that, at least. "I'm Darla," she said politely.

"I'm Lydia," the woman introduced herself. "This is Laura. My staff and I will be happy to supply any beauty services you may need while you're here."

Jubilee sniffed, clearly finding the spa barely acceptable.

Alison, Liam's plump mother, on the other hand, was looking around in awe and seemed impressed by the range of services listed by the door. "This is all so lovely!"

Jubilee ignored Alison, as she had for much of the time since their arrival; she clearly considered Liam's mother a charity case and had as little to do with her as she could politely manage. To Lydia, she said, "We're going to want to do a complete facial and deep condition, of course, and we'll want to preview her hair styling and makeup so we can select the right accessories. I've brought several references showing exactly what we'll want." She handed

Lydia a folder of photos. She didn't hand over the velvet-lined jewelry case she was carrying.

"Certainly," Lydia said with a warm smile. She glanced through the photos and nodded. "We can definitely do this. You'll look like an angel! Let's get the deep conditioning started. We can do a massage while that's setting if you'd like; you're carrying a lot of tension in those shoulders, and no wonder! You must be so excited!"

Lydia was so kind and gracious, it was hard not to relax as she settled Darla into a chair by the sink and began brushing out her wavy hair.

The smiling woman with sepia skin who had been introduced as Laura offered Jubilee and Alison mani-pedis, and Darla was glad when her mother accepted for both of them… and even more glad when they were given seats far enough away that they wouldn't easily be a part of the same conversation.

"How are you liking Shifting Sands so far?" Lydia asked as she gently brushed.

"It's lovely," Darla said honestly. "Really, it's gorgeous here. And everyone has been so kind."

They chatted idly about the food and the beach until Darla couldn't keep back the real question that was bubbling up in her chest, even if she wasn't sure how to ask it. "There's a waiter," she said, as quietly as she could, as Lydia leaned her head back in the sink and started running water. "I was wondering who… it's just… I was…" There was no safe way to finish the sentence.

"Oh, you must mean Breck," Lydia guessed with a laugh. "Tall, dark hair, brown eyes, devastatingly handsome and knows it?"

Breck, Darla thought. She'd never heard the name before, but it was suddenly perfect. *Breck.*

Lydia continued as she turned off the water and began rubbing something that smelled delicious into Darla's wet hair. "He's our head waiter, and don't take him too seriously. He will flirt with *anyone*, but he doesn't really mean it."

"Anyone?" Darla repeated, not sure what to make of the emphasis she used.

"He's bisexual," Lydia said casually.

Darla blinked, glad that Lydia had a quiet voice and that her mother was loudly explaining the various spa services to Alison, as if she would obviously need Jubilee's help to understand something of this class.

"Bisexual as in…" Darla had to clarify.

"He sleeps with both women and men." Lydia's fingers never stopped in their gentle scalp massage. "Does that bother you?" Her voice was too kind to be challenging.

"No," Darla said honestly. She knew that it existed, along with a range of other sexualities, it just surprised her that Lydia talked about it as if it wasn't a *secret.*

"He's a sweetheart," Lydia said fondly. "And so funny! I cannot wait until that man truly falls in love, because when he does…"

Laura, who had been giving Jubilee her manicure, chose that moment to walk past the sink to get some supplies from the shelf next to them. "Breck? Settle down? Is it possible?"

"Bisexuals can be monogamous," Lydia said with a chuckle. "And I think that big heart of his deserves someone who can love him back just as much."

To Darla's mortification, the conversation had gotten loud. Loud enough to carry through the room.

"Oh, I saw that waiter, flirting with a *man* this morning," her mother interjected with disgust from across the room. "Has he been bothering you, sweetheart? If he's made an unwelcome advance on you, I'll have that deviant canned. I won't have some sex freak making you uncomfortable."

There was an awkward moment of silence following her mother's judgmental tirade. Darla, her head back in the sink, could see the flush in Lydia's face and down her neck. She wasn't sure if the woman was angry or just embarrassed for her mother's shallowness.

Laura cleared her throat uncomfortably.

But before anyone else could speak, Alison spoke sharply. "Well, Jubilee, *you* certainly won't have to worry about *any* advances with that ugly attitude. Laura, honey, I think my cuticles are soaked enough now."

Someone gave a strangled giggle, but Darla couldn't tell who. She wasn't entirely sure it wasn't herself.

Laura noisily found the supplies she'd come for and returned across the room as Lydia turned the water in the sink back up to full and began vigorously massaging Darla's scalp.

Darla could feel her heart pounding in her throat and tears gathered in her eyes that had nothing to do with Lydia's work. She'd held out some hope that the waiter—her *mate*!—*Breck*—would miraculously prove to be someone who could step into Liam's shoes for the wedding steamrolling down on her and whisk her away to a fairy tale ending.

That hope was ashes in her chest now. If her mother would have disliked him as a lowly waiter before, she would certainly never accept an openly bisexual son-in-law. And even if she had somehow been able to get past *that*, now he had indirectly humiliated her, and humiliation was the kind of thing that Jubilee Grant never forgot or let go of.

CHAPTER 10

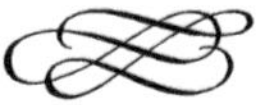

Breck straightened his tie, staring at his muted reflection in the stainless steel refrigerator.

His mate was probably out there now, being seated at the restaurant.

So go, his leopard urged. *Go find them.*

Breck hesitated. His *mate*.

Why had they run away?

Maybe they didn't want to be found.

"If you're done admiring yourself, are you ready for tonight's menu?" Chef was standing with his thick arms crossed.

Breck gave him a sideways smile that must have been a better attempt than his earlier grin at Scarlet. "It's all about appearances," he said with at least a hint of his usual flippancy as he gave his tie one last tweak.

Chef harrumphed. "Baked chicken breasts stuffed with fresh spinach and gruyere cheese, with an olive reduction beside baby red potatoes and peas. The other choice is a homemade vegan pasta with a sweet pepper and truffle sauce."

Breck cataloged the information away without writing anything down. His memory was not eidetic, but he was extremely good at remembering details and never needed to write down orders. "Got it."

"Not too many people tonight," Chef said, turning back to the ovens with his nose testing the air. "You should get out of here early."

Breck hung one of the crisp white napkins over his arm, sucked in his breath, and went to see if his mate was among the diners already seated.

But no one there gave him the lodestone pull that the snow leopard had earlier. Breck swallowed his disappointment and went to do his job.

A few giggling girls wearing bridesmaids sashes reassured him that putting his flirtation on autopilot wasn't failing and a table full of grandmothers gossiping like hens made bawdy counter-offers and winked at him. Finally, he moved to top off the water at the last table, where a young man sat alone near the deck railing at a table set for four.

He was stunningly good-looking, straight from the pages of a cologne ad, with dark hair and features that hinted at Asian ancestry.

"Well, *hello,* handsome," Breck said, automatically turning on the charm. "I'm Breck and I'll be your server today. If there's *anything* I can get you, please don't hesitate to ask. I'd be happy to get you a drink to occupy your tastebuds until the rest of your party gets here."

Only then did he notice the thick pale-gold bracelet that encircled the man's left wrist.

Startled and breathless, he looked up into the man's face.

And was completely confused.

This was not his mate.

The bracelet was identical to the one that the snow leopard had been wearing and too distinctive to be a coincidence. But his own leopard had utterly no recognition of this person and Breck felt no desire for him at all.

Moreover, he had not reacted to Breck's habitual overture.

Breck was excellent at reading people. He could pick up the

faintest signs of discomfort and knew how to recognize the tiniest flicker of interest.

When he flirted with straight men, he often got a mixed reaction —some were embarrassed, some even got angry or defensive. There was almost always surprise, at first, and often curiosity. Gay men usually responded with interest, or at least evaluation. Even gay women reacted to his flirtation, with dismissal. Whether it was challenge, desire, or a brush-off, there was always *some* hard-coded response.

But this man didn't react in the slightest.

He wasn't flattered by Breck's teasing and he wasn't off-put by it. He wasn't… anything.

He simply smiled as if he was amused but not really affected, and moved his waterglass closer to Breck. "I'll wait, thanks. Ah, it looks like they're just arriving anyway."

"Oh, Liam, darling!" A tall, elegant woman wearing far too much jewelry and a sash that read 'Mother of the Bride' simpered in past Breck. "Darla, come sit next to your fiance. Such a fine-looking couple you make. Eugene, you sit here, darling." She fixed her gaze on Breck and gave a stare that passed disapproving straight to loathing. "I'd like a white wine, something dry and not too cheap."

But Breck's eyes were only for the young woman beside her.

She was not quite as tall as too-much-jewelry woman and more lushly curved. Her strawberry-blonde hair was elaborately styled and was heaped on her head with flowers and jewels. The sash she was wearing said: Bride.

And her eyes were the same stunning blue as the snow leopard's.

This was *her*. This was his mate, this was his everything.

The bracelet she was wearing rather suddenly began to glow and she clamped her opposite hand over it in alarm as the twin to it on the non-reactive young man suddenly did the same.

Be-jeweled woman's scowl vanished into astonishment as she looked from Breck to the two oddly-behaving bracelets. "This is amazing!" she said, clapping her hands in excitement. "This is wonderful! I *knew* it was dragon magic!"

Breck was still staring at the bride as his brain slowly caught up with the rest of him.

She was the bride.

His *mate* was the bride.

With effort, she jerked her gaze away from his and slid into her seat next to the man with the matching bracelet. Breck could not dredge up the same amount of self-control and continued to gaze at her helplessly as the depth of the disaster began to come clear in his hazed mind.

"Forget the wine," her mother was saying imperiously. "A bottle of your finest champagne. No! Just water for her! Just in case! Does it mean you're—oh, I can't even say it. But it's just fine, no one will blame you for getting a head start, don't look so mortified."

Breck forced himself to look somewhere—anywhere—else.

The fourth member of their party, a big, weaselly man with dark blonde hair, was eyeing him suspiciously.

"Champagne," the mother was saying imperiously and Breck stared at her for a moment without comprehending.

"Of course," he finally was able to say and, without further courtesy, he fled.

CHAPTER 11

Darla was dizzy and her mother's effervescent words washed over her like surf.

Breck was here and her world was upside down.

She was want and wanton and wanted.

And she couldn't have any of it.

Only Liam's hand anchored her. Liam's hand and the heat of the bracelet on her wrist that seemed to be gleefully and shamelessly proclaiming her desire, to her mother's amusement and Eugene's distasteful diversion.

Then her mate was gone, without so much as a word to her.

He didn't have to say anything.

She knew from his eyes alone that he craved her the same bone-deep way that she desired him.

He must know now that they couldn't be together. She was sitting next to her fiance wearing a ridiculous sparkling sash that proclaimed that she was the bride.

And her mother was going on and on about *sex*.

Liam was doing his level best to maintain the conversation, utterly cool and collected, as Darla floundered trying to find her mental footing again now that proximity to her mate wasn't confusing all of her synapses.

"Oh, look how we've embarrassed Darla," her mother crowed. "Sweetheart, you're going to be a married woman. There's no shame in your desires."

"None at all," Eugene agreed with a smirk that made Darla want to crawl under the table.

"Can we talk about something else?" Darla asked plaintively. She was grateful to see that her bracelet had finally stopped glowing. Liam's had dimmed in unison.

"There are things you should know about being pregnant," her mother said, managing to find a topic more appalling. "Maybe the bracelets have picked up on the fact that you're ovulating."

"I'm sure that's also a topic better saved for a more intimate setting," Liam said firmly, and Darla could have kissed him.

Fortunately, their food was served at that moment. It made Darla's heart fall a little that it was a strange woman, not Breck, who delivered their artfully composed plates of food.

It was better that way, she told herself.

It was best if she never saw him again.

CHAPTER 12

Staring at his warped reflection in the refrigerator door, Breck had forgotten about the champagne, had forgotten about the suspicious man, had forgotten about everything but the perfect heart-shaped face, flushed and forlorn, that would haunt his dreams forever.

His mate.

Here to marry another man.

It couldn't get worse, he decided.

Then he heard familiar heels clicking across the tile kitchen floor, and he knew that it could.

"Breck."

Scarlet's reflection next to his had unnaturally bright red hair and Breck could tell that she was frowning.

He turned to face her.

"I've gotten a complaint," she said without preamble. "The mother of the bride has requested that you not be permitted to serve in the restaurant for the remainder of their contract."

"I'm… sorry," he said, filled with so much regret that it felt like he would fall apart at the seams.

"I am too," Scarlet said unexpectedly. "It's disappointing when you run into that kind of prejudice. I certainly don't agree with her views and I don't like to further them by agreeing to Mrs. Grant's request… but…"

She looked conflicted and Breck suddenly realized that she had no idea that he was the mate of the bride. Mrs. Grant was asking Scarlet to relieve him of duty because he was openly bisexual, not because he was hopelessly in love with her daughter.

And Mrs. Grant *was* paying ridiculous piles of money for exclusive use of the resort.

"I don't want to pull you off duty," Scarlet said firmly, to Breck's surprise. "But it would make my job a lot easier if you could dial things back and act more strictly professional for the duration of the wedding. I know you never cross the line of actual impropriety, but someone who didn't know you might consider your flirtations too forward."

"No," Breck said swiftly. "No, you *should* pull me off the floor."

He couldn't go out there. He couldn't go out there and watch her cozy up to her fiance, knowing that he could never have her. He couldn't serve her food and watch him feed it to her.

Scarlet blinked at his vehemence. "Should I know something?" she asked suspiciously.

"No." Breck dug deep for anything resembling steadiness and took a slow deliberate breath. "She's already made up her mind about me," he pointed out. "And you've made it clear how important this contract is. I've got more than enough staff to cover the floor for now, and Jenny or Laura or Saina can step in when things get busy. You could even stuff Graham in a uniform if things are dire. Watering people isn't much different than watering plants. There are a whole lot of things I can do behind the scenes. I can help Chef in the kitchen. The van needs a new alternator."

Scarlet furrowed her brow at him and Breck realized that he was talking too fast.

"Are you sure you don't mind?" Scarlet asked. "It would simplify things, but I'd back you up if you wanted to keep serving."

"I would too," Chef said in his deep, booming voice, unexpectedly appearing from behind Scarlet. "You're the best waiter I've ever worked with and I hate it when bigots win."

"I'm sure," Breck said, touched by their support. "It's just about making sure things run smoothly."

And he knew there was no way things could run smoothly if he tried to go out there and see his mate being courted by someone else.

It was more likely that he'd give the fiance a black eye 'by accident' and Mrs. Grant would end up demanding his resignation, not just his absence. Maybe she'd sue the resort.

Chef gave a skeptical harrumph. "Well, you can make yourself useful by getting these plates ready," he said. Something started to boil over on a distant stove that called him away down the kitchen aisles.

Scarlet continued to scrutinize him, not looking entirely convinced.

But if there was one thing Breck was good at, it was keeping up appearances. He put on his most charming smile. "You've saved me a fortune in dentistry from grinding my teeth to stumps serving that woman. If this were the kind of place where you tipped, she's the type to tip spare change from her purse on a hundred dollar meal."

He gave an exaggerated shudder and made a show of untying his tie and stuffing it into a pocket. "It'll be nice to have a change from the penguin suit anyway."

Scarlet smiled. If she wasn't entirely convinced, she was at least mollified. "Thank you, Breck. This could have been a very unpleasant situation, and I appreciate how accommodating you've been."

Breck went to help plate food, thinking privately that she had no idea how unpleasant the situation actually *was*.

CHAPTER 13

The next morning, Darla rose before the sun. She had tossed and turned all night, completely unable to find any rest in the perfect bed.

She'd barely been able to eat the night before and her stomach grumbled. If she went to the kitchen before the restaurant opened, she should be able to find something to eat before Breck got there and hopefully avoid him the rest of the morning at least.

She dressed quickly, cursing every creak of the wooden floor, and crept out her back door with her sandals held in her hands. She tiptoed back across the tiny lush lawn behind their house and skirted the noisy gravel until she was sure she wouldn't wake anyone else.

The resort before dawn was hushed and full of fragrant anticipation. The drone of the night insects seemed less than it had been when darkness fell, but Darla decided that she was probably just used to it. In daylight, all the white tile was almost overpowering, but at night, everything seemed to have a moon-like glow.

She found her way easily up to the restaurant. The buffet was empty; her mother had negotiated limited hours on it, deciding that they didn't need overnight service.

There was a light behind the swinging kitchen door, and the

sound of rattling cutlery, so Darla pushed it open and tentatively went in. "Hello," she called quietly, not wanting to startle the cook.

Then her breath left her.

At the far end of the kitchen, Breck had just turned from the sink. He was holding a sponge in one hand, and a spatula in the other, his sleeves rolled up. The sharp waiter's vest was gone and the sheer white shirt was damp with dishwater splashes, leaving little to the imagination.

For a moment, they were silent, staring across the empty kitchen at each other as the door swung back and forth behind her and finally stilled.

Finally, he spoke. "Can I help you?" he asked gently.

He could, she thought. He could lay her down on the floor and help her in all the ways her snow leopard was telling her he should.

She bit her lip. If he could be professional, she could, too. "I was looking for a quick breakfast," she said, as steadily as she could. "I didn't mean to disturb…"

"Oh, I am very disturbed," he said frankly, when she trailed off. He put the sponge and spatula into the dishwater and reached for a towel. "But I am delighted to make you some food."

Darla had drifted several steps into the kitchen without meaning to. "Thank you," she said faintly, as he dried his hands and opened the giant refrigerator door.

"It's the least I can do," he said gently, with his back to her.

Darla took some courage from the fact that he wasn't looking at her. "I guess you know," she said boldly. "And, I'm... sorry."

Breck leaned his head briefly against the door to the refrigerator. "I am, too," he said so quietly that Darla automatically took a few steps forward to hear better. Then he straightened and drew out a plastic-draped plate.

When he turned back to her, he was smiling gently. "But we make the best of what we get. Now, what are you doing up so early?"

There was a stool next to the counter and he gestured her to sit. Darla walked the rest of the way into the kitchen and did so, gingerly. He was being careful to keep distance between them; she was grateful for that. Even this close, she was mesmerized by the way he moved, the breadth of his strong shoulders.

"I… wanted to avoid the waitstaff, actually," Darla admitted. "I didn't think you'd be here this early."

"I wouldn't, usually," Breck said, sounding almost cheerful. "But your charming mother requested that I not serve in the restaurant for a spell, so I've moved to behind closed doors. Chef is having me bake bread this morning." He was bustling around, getting more things out of the fridge, cutting things, putting things back. "Chef's got a mate of his own and he rarely gets a chance to sleep in, so I'm happy to give him the opportunity."

"I'm sorry about my mother," Darla said. "I could talk to her…?"

"I think it's best this way," Breck said swiftly. "This way, we don't have to…" he trailed off, but Darla knew what he meant.

"You're probably right," she agreed. "It would be easier if we didn't…"

He put a glass of orange juice down in front of her. "So, tell me about something else. What do you do for a living?"

Darla waited for his hand to be safely away before she reached for the juice. "I'm an heiress. I don't *do* anything." It came out more bitterly than she intended. "I wanted to go to college, or maybe even trade school, but it was always more important that I attend parties and practice deportment and meet all the right people."

"What did you want to study?" Breck asked, putting a plate in front of her.

Darla had to gaze at it, awed by the spread. Beautiful plump strawberries, a selection of pastries drizzled in icing, a few slices of bacon—cold, but fragrant with salt and smoke—and a fan of sliced cheese and crusty bread.

"This is too much," she said, though her stomach growled in protest. She automatically added, "Won't you share it with me?"

She glanced up and made the mistake of meeting Breck's eyes. He was gazing at her in hunger that had nothing to do with the food before her. He wrenched his eyes away and nodded courteously, settling onto the stool across the stainless steel counter from her as she pushed the plate between them.

They were painstakingly careful, never reaching for the plate at the same time, not exactly looking each other in the face.

"What did you want to study?" Breck asked again.

"You'll laugh," Darla warned him.

"I won't," he promised. He took one of the strawberries. Darla looked at her orange juice to keep from watching him eat it.

"I wanted to fix things," she said. "Electricity, or plumbing, or cars, or something. I wanted to learn to do useful things." She laughed at herself, nibbling on a piece of creamy cheese. "It's ridiculous, of course. I don't know the first things about tools or machines. My car got a flat tire once, and you know what happened?"

"Tell me," Breck encouraged.

"My mother bought me a new car."

Breck did laugh at that and the sound was somehow settling. "Just like that?"

"Just like that," Darla said, shaking her head. "I thought maybe I could change the tire myself, but I couldn't find any of the tools, and I wouldn't have known what to do with them if I had found them. And my mother freaked out because it had left me stranded in the middle of a *terrible* neighborhood. One with *apartments* and children playing in the *street*, of all the horrors."

"I could teach you," Breck said unexpectedly. "I fix the cars around here and I could show you a few tricks."

Darla looked up again and regretted it at once. She could drown in those eyes. "Yes," she said. Her brain caught up with her. "I mean, no." The food went tasteless in her mouth and she swallowed.

"I'm sorry," Breck said immediately. "You're right. I shouldn't have offered."

There was a moment of silence. Neither of them reached for the few things left on the plate.

Breck finally said, "Do you do anything for fun?"

Darla clung to the conversational lifeline. "Mother finds it acceptable for me to volunteer for charities, so I spend a few days a week at a retirement home for shifters. She has no idea what the home entails or I'm sure she wouldn't let me. I think she figures I arrange flowers and maybe fluff pillows and read to people in comas. But it can be really dirty, hard, heart-breaking work and I love it. All of them are so sweet. Mrs. Asher is like a grandmother to me. And Mr. Danby—he's non-verbal, but you can tell that he's still in there, and we play chess. That's... where I met Liam. He runs the home."

She had managed to stop looking at Breck at some point, so she only heard the slight hitch to his breath at the reminder of Liam.

"Do you love him?" he asked, as if he couldn't help himself.

Darla shrugged miserably. "Yes. Not… like *love* love, but he's my best friend. He's my *only* friend. I don't want to leave him in a lurch."

Breck was quiet a long moment. "You'll be happy with him," he said, as if he desperately needed to believe it.

Just a day ago, she would have said that she would have been perfectly happy with Liam. Then she'd met Breck and gotten a glimpse at what happiness *could* be.

"I *have* to marry him," Darla said, and she didn't realize that she was crying until the first tear fell on the counter below her. It made an imperfect little wet circle on the shiny stainless steel. "I'm sorry, Breck," she said, as boldly and honestly as she could. "I wish things were different. I wish we could be together."

"I'd do anything," he said simply. "I'd wait. I'd fight. I'd change. Tell me what to do, and I'd do it."

At the word *fight*, Darla's head rose. "There's a challenge…" she said, barely daring to hope. Maybe she'd been wrong about Breck's animal.

"I'll challenge," Breck said swiftly. "How do I challenge?"

"It's a battle in shifted form," Darla said, heart in her throat. "Your animal…"

Breck looked crestfallen. "I'm a leopard," he said doubtfully. "I don't think I could take on a dragon."

Darla sighed, her brief hope draining away. "It's not Liam you'd have to worry about. He would stand down… but if he did, then Eugene would challenge *you*."

"Eugene? That weaselly-looking man hanging on your mother? What's he?"

"A cave bear," Darla said with despair.

"Oh, a cave bear," Breck said archly. "Is that all." He didn't have to say out loud that he stood no more chance as a leopard against a giant extinct bear than he did a dragon. "Well, is there another challenge, possibly a challenge of *wits*? I could manage that pretty handily. How about a swimsuit competition? You should see me in a Speedo. Even your mother would swoon."

Darla giggled despite herself. "I'm afraid those aren't part of the ancient dragon tradition," she said regretfully.

"Then forget ancient dragon tradition," Breck suggested. "Run away with me. You don't need your mother's blessing to live a life of delicious sin in some little town on the mainland." Darla thought he was trying to make it a joke. A joke too heavy for humor, too intense for levity.

For one short, blissful moment, gazing into his longing golden eyes, Darla wondered if she could… then she remembered. "The retirement home. Without my inheritance, it will go under. Mrs. Asher… Mr. Danby… they'll all have nowhere to go. My mother will be so angry, and she has so much power. I'm afraid of what she'd do to Liam, to his family, to the home, just to punish me for humiliating her."

Breck made a noise that Darla couldn't identify. Anger, maybe, or frustration.

Everything about the situation was *frustrating*.

He was so beautiful, so graceful.

And she wanted him so badly.

Suddenly, there was the sound of singing, something operatic in a male voice from the restaurant.

Panic filled Darla's chest. They couldn't be seen. Surely the attraction that was sizzling between them would be obvious to any observer.

"Chef," whispered Breck, clearly thinking the same thing. "Out the back!"

Darla scampered after him to the back door and there was one beautiful moment when his hand was at her waist as he hurried her outside.

It was quiet behind the kitchen, with just a promise of dawn in the sky. Breck followed her out and, for a moment, they stood close together, not touching. "If I kiss you, I'll never be able to stop," he said regretfully.

"I know," Darla murmured. She wanted him to anyway, but her head knew that the smartest thing to do was simply not to start.

"Good luck," Breck said. "I…" He started to offer his hand to shake and reconsidered, drawing it back reluctantly. He knew as well as she did that any touch would take them down a road they couldn't go.

"Good luck," Darla echoed quickly, then she turned and fled as the singing came closer and there was the creak of a door at the other end of the kitchen.

CHAPTER 14

Breck swept the rest of the Darla's leftover breakfast into the trash and dunked the dishes under the foaming surface of the dishwater just as Chef swept in the door with a deep resounding line of music.

The kitchen was *wrong* without Darla. Even knowing that she couldn't be his, it had been better with her near, being able to talk to her, being able to *feed* her.

Chef broke off his song with alarm as he strolled down the aisle of the kitchen. "Did you set the timer for the bread?"

Too late, Breck recognized that part of the wrongness of the moment was the slight tinge of burning bread in the air. "Oh, hell," he said in dismay.

The bread was not badly burned, but Breck felt wretched. "I'm sorry," he said. "I don't know what happened. I guess I'm... just tired. Not used to this pre-dawn nonsense." He couldn't very well give the real reason for his distraction.

Chef waved him off. "This party is a crusts-cut-off sort of bunch anyway," he said expansively, tapping the tops of the darkened loaves. "The bread inside is fine." But he gave Breck a searching look that suggested he wasn't buying 'I'm tired' as a believable excuse.

Breck returned to the dishes and then chopped fruit, unable to stop thinking about Darla, sitting across the counter with her tousled hair and sweet blue eyes. The way she licked her lips so daintily as she ate, her perfect manners, her gentle voice, the longing in her heart-shaped face...

"Hmmm," Chef said, eyeing the irregular pieces of pineapple he was trimming. "Who is she?"

Breck looked up in alarm.

"Who is who?" he asked as innocently as he could manage.

"Or he," Chef suggested. "I suppose I shouldn't presume."

"I don't know what you're talking about," Breck said firmly, mutilating the chunk of pineapple and nearly taking his fingers with it.

Chef's booming laugh filled the kitchen. "I always knew that when you fell, you'd fall hard. One of the bridesmaids? A groomsman? Not one of the grandmothers!"

"Not a grandmother," Breck said regretfully. A grandmother would have been so much simpler.

"I'm guessing they're quite a firecracker, to damage your calm this badly," Chef chuckled.

No one would call Darla a firecracker, Breck thought miserably. She was a moment of stillness, the reflection of the moon on quiet water, a single perfect note of music.

"You don't have to say," Chef said, voice rich with amusement. "Whoever it is, I wish you luck. And I wish them even more; they'll need it."

Breck nicked one of his fingertips and sucked the stinging pineapple juice from it. "Thanks," he said dryly.

"That pineapple is irrecoverable for fruit bowls," Chef observed, accurately. "Even before you bled in it. Go ahead and finish destroying it and I'll cook it down for a pineapple cheesecake sauce tonight."

Breck sighed and went to wash his hands. The cut had already started to heal over by the time he returned, determined to make presentable fruit pieces.

If Breck had been confident that Darla could be happy, that she'd be better off without him, he could have let her go.

Probably.

His nights would have been an agony of wanting and missing, but he could gone on with his life like nothing was wrong, pretending to flirt, keeping up appearances.

But what else could he do? Ask her to call off her wedding? She certainly seemed to be well trapped in the arrangement.

"You're not doing much better with those," Chef observed over his shoulder.

The second pineapple had not fared any better than the previous fruit. Breck put the knife down in defeat.

"This isn't just some girl," Chef guessed.

Breck exhaled. "No," he confessed. "Not even close. She's…" He couldn't finish.

Our mate, his leopard insisted. *It's simple!*

"Maybe you should just wash some dishes and let me handle the sharp items while your brain is figuring out whatever it is you need to figure out," Chef suggested.

"I don't think there's anything to figure out," Breck admitted. "It's… not something that can happen."

"Ah," Chef said with a smile. "One of those situations. Well, you'd be surprised what your brain can come up with if you give it a chance."

Breck shrugged at him, not convinced, and went to wash dishes.

"Your brain!" Chef reminded him in a sing-song. "Not the other parts!"

CHAPTER 15

The spreading lawn was almost flat, in a resort that was unexpectedly steep and built in many levels, and it was large enough for the hundreds of people who would be seated to watch the ceremony that Darla was dreading.

Already, there was a white archway and a small platform half assembled. Two of the resort staff were busily finishing the rest.

"I want this threaded with flowers," her mother was saying imperiously. "This whole arch! And we should have pots all along the aisle. Oh, do you think this is the right angle? I don't want the sun to be in anyone's eyes."

Scarlet, the resort owner, looked absolutely serene in that way that Darla recognized from the mirror as a polite, trained mask. "The sun will be setting in that direction," she indicated. "But the final part of the ceremony should be just before it is low enough to cause any discomfort. By the time it is on the horizon, everyone will be back in the event hall for the evening reception and dancing."

"Hmm," Jubilee said, standing in various positions experimentally. "But is the view better this way? Maybe we should move the platform."

"No one will be looking at the view, mother," Darla said shortly.

That earned her a surprised look from everyone there, except the guitar player. She had been dutifully, politely quiet while her mother steamrolled everything, up until now. She gave a tiny, apologetic smile.

"Oh, you're right," Jubilee said quickly. "We wouldn't want the view to be better than the view of you, of course! This will do. Come, I want to see the event hall. Are you sure it's *big* enough?"

The two men assembling the archway exchanged amused looks behind Jubilee's back as she and Scarlet left across the lawn, her assistant and the bridesmaids straggling behind.

Darla remained at the half-built platform, staring at the contraption that was going to seal her in a cage.

It could be worse, she reminded herself. She could be marrying Eugene.

It could be better, her snow leopard reminded her. Darla had given up trying to explain why she wasn't marrying her mate, why they weren't together *now*, like her animal insisted they should be.

"Your mother is not very nice," the woman standing with the musician said frankly, with a shake of her head. She had long, untidy braids on either side of her face. Darla had at first thought she had black and white ribbons woven into her hair, but it was actually locks of dark hair mixed with pure white strands.

"She's under a lot of stress," Darla tried to apologize for her. "With the wedding and everything."

"*You're* under more," the woman said critically, giving her a piercing look. She was oddly forward, and strangely shy at the same time. "I'm Gizelle. You've already met Conall." She hung back behind Conall slightly, not offering to shake hands.

"Thank you for agreeing to play at the wedding," Darla told him politely. Her mother had been delighted when she realized that the famous classical guitar player Conall Wright was living at the resort and had been relentless in her attempts to get him to play at the wedding.

He was glancing after the rest of the wedding party and didn't respond.

Gizelle smiled. "He can't hear you," she said in explanation, just as Conall looked back and said, "I'm sorry, did you say something?"

Darla furrowed her brow. "I... thought you could hear now," she said slowly, wondering if it was rude. "I understood that the island had fixed your hearing."

"He's not something to fix," Gizelle said with unexpected defensiveness that gentled into amusement with dizzying quickness. "But he can hear with my ears if he's touching me!" She took his hand and gleefully announced, "He's my mate!"

Conall's tender glance down at Gizelle cut Darla to the heart.

That was what a mate should be.

That was what she would never have.

Her chest feeling very tight, Darla politely repeated what she'd said earlier when Conall couldn't see her. "Thank you for agreeing to play at the wedding." *The* wedding. Not *her* wedding.

But Gizelle was giving Conall a quizzical look. "Are you going to play at *our* wedding?" Then her eyes got big and she clung to his arm earnestly. "Can *we* have a wedding? With cake and a white lacy dress like Jenny's and flowers that Graham doesn't roar about?"

Conall smiled at her slowly. "Are you asking me to marry you?"

Gizelle was still for a moment, then began capering around like a child wound up on Christmas candy. "I am! I am! I am! I will marry you! I will!"

She launched herself at Conall, who caught her effortlessly and lifted her into the air with a laugh of delight. "You will be the most beautiful bride in the world," he said. "And I will be the luckiest groom."

"Wait, wait!" Gizelle cried. "Do I have to wear shoes?"

"You do not," Conall assured her.

"Do I have to wear...?" she suddenly looked around, and whispered the rest into Conall's closest ear.

"You do not," Conall repeated, grinning ear-to-ear.

Darla tried to resolve the musician with the grim, dramatic portraits on the covers of his discs, and entirely failed.

"That's a pretty bracelet," Gizelle said out of the blue, wriggling out of Conall's arms and circling Darla curiously. "It's in your skin."

Darla self-consciously turned it on her wrist, not liking the idea of the bracelet in her skin. It seemed more gold than ever in the bright daylight. "It was an engagement gift," she explained. She remembered too well how it had felt, clamping irreversibly around her wrist.

"What does it do?" Gizelle asked suspiciously, returning to take Conall's hand.

Darla showed her the writing. "That means 'unbroken line.' It's supposed to promote fertility, I guess."

"I don't think you're using it right," Gizelle said with great authority. "That's not how babies work."

Darla flushed but before she could respond, Conall said merrily, "She probably already knows how babies work, Gizelle. And I'm very happy to play at your wedding."

The last part was to Darla, who smiled wanly.

"Did you have a particular song you wanted to request?" Conall seemed all business again.

"I'm sure my mother has already given you a detailed playlist," Darla said more bitterly than she intended.

He stilled and gave Darla a solemn look. "Isn't there something you want? It's *your* wedding."

Darla wrestled with her impulse to insist that it wasn't. "Whatever she has selected will be fine," she said instead, keeping her voice mild and her face a polite, neutral mask.

Conall gave her a knowing look. "If you change your mind, just let me know," he said kindly.

"Thank you," Darla said faintly. "I appreciate that. I'll let you know if I think of anything."

CHAPTER 16

Breck slapped the last of the pans from lunch down into the drainer and pulled up the stopper. Watching the soapy water spin down the drain was a moment of distraction; it looked like Breck's heart felt.

"Restaurant is empty," Chef observed. "Why don't you go wipe down tables and get your grumpy self out of my kitchen."

Breck, feeling epically grumpy indeed, took the advice and a clean rag.

To his surprise, Liam was sitting at one of the tables, looking over the drink menu. None of the other servers were in sight.

"Well, sir," Breck said cautiously, with just the barest trace of his usual charm. "I'm not supposed to be serving today, and the kitchen is closed, but I can't let someone languish without service. May I get you something from the bar? Make you up a sandwich?"

Liam looked at him appraisingly. "You're Breck," he guessed sympathetically.

Breck gave him a wary smile. "The very one," he said, giving a little bow. He had no idea how much Liam knew. Was he just a server who'd rubbed the mother of the bride the wrong way? Or did Liam know more?

Liam glanced around the empty restaurant and then gestured at the seat opposite. "You're Darla's mate," he said quietly.

All of his breath left Breck in a rush and he sank down into the indicated chair. He hadn't said it out loud, and neither had Darla, even if they had both acknowledged it; hearing it made it feel real.

Bitterly real.

"I'm Darla's mate," Breck agreed. "And *you're* her fiance."

"Saying I'm sorry seems insufficient," Liam said regretfully. "Have you two had a chance to talk? Did she explain?"

"About the retirement home? Yes. A little."

"Not just the home," Liam said. "If it were just that, I'd… I don't know what I'd do, but I would never ask her to go through with this if that were the only consequence."

"She told me about the challenge. About Eugene. She doesn't think a leopard has a chance of winning."

Liam looked more uncomfortable. "Eugene is a cave bear shifter, and a mean fighter. And he wants the hoard as much as he wants Darla."

"There's a hoard?"

"Oh, yeah," Liam laughed dryly. "There's a hoard," he said. "Unimaginable wealth. Caverns full of gold and precious gems and lost treasures. Darla is the last of two dragon lines and she is the heir to all of it. She has a regular inheritance, too, stocks and bonds and market things I don't even know. But before her father died several years ago, he had a spell cast over the dragon hoard. It's locked, except to someone of his blood, who is married according to dragon custom with a family blessing. If I had to guess, he did it to give Darla a little extra time to get out from under her mother's thumb, since dragons traditionally marry at twenty-five years. That's why Jubilee has been so meticulous about this wedding ceremony. Dragon contracts are tricky at best, and she wants to make sure every t is crossed and every eye is watching so Darla can unlock her hoard."

"Because her mother certainly seems to have *Darla's* best interests at heart," Breck said sourly.

There was a moment of silence that Breck recognized as Liam

struggling not to insult his future mother-in-law. Without meaning to, he softly asked, "Have you known Darla long?"

"A few years," Liam said kindly. "She answered a call for volunteers at the retirement home." He chuckled. "When I saw her, I thought she was a spoiled dilettante who was going to run away at the first thing that smacked of hard work. I gave her the dirtiest jobs, the most stubborn old shifters, and figured she simply wouldn't show up for the second day of work. But I was so wrong about her. She was an absolute angel for the home. She's gentle with the patients, she's not afraid to get dirty, she works hard, and frankly, she's the only reason the place hasn't already gone under. Even before the wedding arrangement and the dowry, she was paying most of the expenses. She loves them. They adore her."

"Raise your prices?" Breck suggested, not particularly seriously; probably Liam and Darla had already considered all the options that he could come up with. "Apply for a grant?"

"They all pay what they can, but most of them have no family and no money. And we have a lot of… special expenses that would be hard to explain under the scrutiny of a grant. Getting old can lack dignity for simple humans, but for shifters, it can be especially tricky. Not all of them can control their shifting anymore. That's not a problem for an ermine shifter, but a mammoth shifter can't stay in a standard room."

"Do you *have* a mammoth shifter?" Breck asked curiously.

Liam chuckled fondly. "Yeah. He's about a hundred years old and no one can understand a word he says anymore, but he plays a mean game of chess and likes to watch gameshows. He wanders, if someone isn't keeping an eye on him. We had to chase him down the freeway one night and coax him back with gingersnaps. Fortunately, he was mostly just a naked man for that romp; he was a mammoth for the night out in an empty parking structure. I still wonder if anyone watching security cameras saw any of it."

"I can only imagine," Breck said, laughing. "I'd be pouring out whatever I was drinking."

"Or saving it for science," Liam agreed. "I miss those guys," he added. "I'm sure they're in good hands for the two weeks I'm gone, but you get used to all their idiosyncrasies and special needs."

"Have you met Mrs. Shandy?" Breck asked impulsively.

"Is she one of the permanent residents?" Liam asked. "The… ah… very *large* woman with auburn hair? I've seen her at the restaurant a few times."

"That would be Magnolia, also a peach. Mrs. Shandy doesn't make it out of her cottage much these days. You'd probably like her, and I'm sure she'd love a game of backgammon if you've got the time." Breck felt guilty for not making it by himself more often since Darla's arrival had upended his life. "She's a greyhound shifter, in retirement here."

Liam smiled. "I'd love to meet her. Darla's the one who has a million things to do. Grooms are apparently just supposed to smile and show up at the end. The suit fits, I've gotten my hair cut, so they're done with me until the vows."

I should detest this man, Breck reminded himself. *He's marrying our mate.*

But his leopard was oddly unconcerned with Liam. *He's not our rival.*

He's marrying *our mate*, Breck repeated with emphasis. But he knew that neither one of them had any choice in the matter.

"I should get back to work," Breck said, standing. "Before people start showing up for dinner and Her Highness finds out that I've dared to show my face in public."

Liam grimaced. "Sorry about that, as well." He looked conflicted, like he wanted to add something else, but chose not to at the last moment.

"I'm not sorry," Breck said firmly. "We should keep things as simple as possible, and it's simpler when there's distance."

As he turned to wipe down the rest of the tables and gather the last abandoned dishes, he realized that he actually liked Liam. It didn't make anything easier; if anything, he almost wished he had someone to hate, and was disappointed that Liam hadn't stepped into that role.

CHAPTER 17

The next morning, Darla found herself at the back kitchen door she'd fled from, listening to the pans rattle with her heart in her throat.

It was foolish to be here. It was a bad idea. She should be trying to avoid Breck, not steal fleeting moments in his company wishing she was someone else.

But here she was, even earlier than the morning before, her stomach a knot of tension and yearning. She pushed the door open boldly and made herself stride in.

And then she froze, because Breck wasn't there.

The mountain of a chef was already turning at her entrance, clearly expecting someone else. "You didn't have to come in until six," he was saying cheerfully. "But…" He stopped as he recognized Darla. "Miss Grant? Can I help you?"

He was carrying a large tray of bread ready for the oven.

Darla backed up a step. "I'm sorry to bother you," she said politely. She wracked her brain for a reason to be there and stared stupidly for a moment. "Break… breakfast," she finally remembered, stumbling over the sound of Breck's name accidentally on her tongue. That was why she had come the previous morning. She drew herself up. "I was hoping for an early breakfast. If that's alright. I don't want to be any trouble."

"Come in, come in," the man invited warmly. "Have a seat. I need to get these into the oven, and I'll whip you something right up."

Darla thought his look was a bit knowing, a suspicion that was confirmed when she slowly perched on the stool she had used the day before. He set a plate down in front of her with a slice of cold ham and a fresh roll and asked mildly, "You were expecting someone else, I think?"

Darla stared at her food, her stomach an unwelcoming knot.

"You've got something of a pickle then?" the big man said. He settled across from her in the place the Breck had been.

Darla couldn't speak and she tried to will back the tears that pricked behind her eyes.

"It will all feel better on a full stomach," the chef assured her kindly.

She didn't want to appear ungrateful, so Darla took a bite of the warm roll and swallowed obediently.

"See, isn't that better already?"

Darla didn't trust herself to speak yet, so she nodded and took another bite. "Thank you," she said, once she had swallowed that and her stomach didn't seem to want to rebel.

"Everyone calls me Chef," the man said gently.

"Thank you, Chef," Darla said. She could look at him now, and his face was filled with kindness and sympathy.

"Your thanks is the enjoyment of my food," he said with a warm, knowing smile. "Now, is Breck your mate?"

Darla had been taking a tentative nibble of the cold ham, and nearly choked.

"Did he tell you?" she asked, once she had swallowed.

"I put some pieces together," Chef said smugly. "And there's a look you've got. A look like you're in a room with no door. I know that look." His voice was gentle again.

Darla remembered that Breck had said Chef had a mate. "Was it easy for you? With your mate, I mean?"

Chef gave a warm, low chuckle. "It was not," he said. "We both sacrificed a great deal to be together, and I worried for a long time that she would never forgive me for the things she gave up. But mates make it work."

Darla looked at him skeptically. "I'm marrying *someone else*. I don't know how a magical animal instinct is going to overcome *that*."

Her snow leopard gave a wordless grumble of frustration.

"I suppose you have considered *not* marrying someone else?" Chef suggested.

"I did think of that," Darla said dryly. "Many, many times. But… dragon honor is a complicated thing. It's not a matter of just calling it off. For starters, if I don't marry Liam, other people are free to challenge for my hand, and there are far worse choices out there."

"A certain man in your mother's pocket who starts with E," Chef guessed.

Darla couldn't quite keep herself from shuddering. "The very one," she said. "Liam is a dragon shifter, and Eugene doesn't dare challenge him. But Eugene is a cave bear shifter, and he's a mean, experienced fighter. Breck wouldn't stand a chance against him. If he got hurt…" She had to close her eyes.

"And what does Liam say about this?" Chef probed. "Does he know?"

"He knows," Darla said. "He is the only person I've told. He says I don't have to marry him, but he understands the complications. He also stands to lose more than I do if I don't marry him."

"Money?" Chef guessed.

Darla sighed. "He's already spent my dowry to save the shifter rest home he runs. He doesn't *have* it left to pay back if the marriage falls through. He says he could make things work, but I honestly don't see how. All those shifters—my friends!—would be turned out on the streets to die alone and he'd be bankrupt, and it would be my fault."

"You couldn't simply give him the money?" Chef suggested.

"None of it is mine," Darla shrugged. "I have always had everything I wanted, but if I disobey my mother, that all goes away. I am an heiress; I get nothing if she decides to disinherit me. I have some jewelry that I got as gifts, but my car isn't in my name, I don't pay my own rent, my credit cards would be cut off… I think I could be alright with being poor, but I don't know if I could live knowing I chose my own happiness over the safety of other innocent people."

Chef's expressive face was full of sympathy and sorrow.

He opened his mouth to speak, but the timer went off. Darla wiped her face as he went to check the bread, and took a large gulp of orange juice. It felt like a relief to talk about things with someone, even if the problem didn't look any less futile.

The fragrant bread did not, apparently, meet with approval. He put it back in the oven, setting the timer.

"Miss Grant..." he started, when he returned.

"Darla," she corrected. "Please call me Darla."

"Darla," he agreed. "Do you know what you're going to do?"

Darla looked at him with all the steadiness she could muster. Talking over her dilemma had only solidified her resolve. "I am going to get married. I am going to walk down the aisle and recite fifteen generations of ancestors and wear flowers and seventeen necklaces and say vows that will bind me to someone else forever."

"And your mate? Are you sorry you met him?"

Darla's gaze wavered. "I'm not sorry," she said at last. "Even if I only got a glimpse of what might have been, I'm glad I got that much." She sounded more miserable than brave to her own ears.

It could be so much more, her snow leopard wailed.

Chef turned away, and Darla wondered if she'd said something wrong. When he turned back, his eyes looked misty.

"I'm not sorry you met him, either," he said warmly. "Breck's got a big heart, and you clearly do, too."

"Will you… will you tell me about him?" Darla asked hesitantly. Was it foolish, wanting to know more about someone she couldn't have?

Chef smiled at her. "You've probably… heard things," he said knowingly.

Darla's blush betrayed her.

Chef pulled out a wicked knife and began chopping a bin full of vegetables into tiny, perfect pieces as he thoughtfully spoke. "What you have to understand about Breck…. he's not what he'd like everyone to believe. He isn't bothered by people thinking he's a hedonistic heartbreaker, out for his own pleasures, nothing more complicated than a shallow, self-centered playboy. But if you look a little closer, you'll see that he's more than the stereotype he sets himself up as being. He cares more about people than he cares about what they think. He's not afraid to look weak to make someone else feel strong; he'll sacrifice every shred of his own dignity to give someone else their own."

He shook the dirt off of a clump of carrots and cut the leafy tops off. "I've known a lot of people over the years who imagine themselves as heroes, for standing up to bullies or muscling their way to success. But I'm not sure any of them has ever given a fraction what Breck has given, to people he'll never see again, in ways they usually never even recognize. He isn't kidding when he boasts that he could have his pick of partners, but he never selects the most handsome or the richest. He always chooses the one who needs him most. And he doesn't do it for their acknowledgement, only for their happiness."

"Your mother, she only sees the stereotype. Breck's not ashamed of his sexuality, and he's never been afraid to use sex to comfort someone or give them confidence. But don't make the mistake of thinking he's in it for his own pleasure first or that the jokes and flirtation are all there is."

"My mother doesn't understand comfort or confidence," Darla said quietly, absorbing Chef's words. "Appearances have always been more important."

"Then you, of all people, know how much weight to give them," Chef said wisely.

The timer went off again and he got up to remove the bread

from the oven a final time. Darla finished her plate of food while he busied himself preparing the day's food.

"Thank you," she said sincerely.

"Thank *you*," Chef said oddly. "I hope you'll stop in tomorrow morning, as well."

"It's nice to miss the breakfast bustle," Darla agreed. "I think I will."

CHAPTER 18

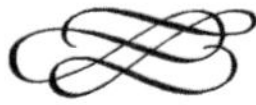

Breck was surprised that Chef trusted him with the bread again after his previous blunder, but he didn't mind the early assignment.

It wasn't like he was sleeping much anyway, and it gave him the excuse not to linger in the common room with the others that evening.

He rose well before dawn and walked in the drizzly darkness to the kitchen, trying not to think about Darla.

He was very unsuccessful at it.

So unsuccessful that he stopped and stared at her for several moments before he realized that it actually *was* Darla, standing at the back kitchen door. Her hair was getting wet and sticking to the sides of her face.

"Chef said I should come early," she said, when he proved incapable of speech. "I… hope I won't bother you."

"Oh, it *bothers* me a lot," Breck said when he could unstick his tongue at last. "But I'm really glad you did." His sense of courtesy finally caught up with him. "You're getting soaked! Come inside and get dry!"

He opened the door and ushered her inside, careful not to actually touch her. He could still feel the impression of her waist on his hand from two mornings ago when he had helped her flee from Chef's approach.

He had to smile, to think of Chef playing matchmaker.

"Does it often rain here?" Darla asked as Breck found her a dry kitchen towel for her hair.

"Usually only at night, at this time of year," Breck said in exactly the same light, polite tone she had used. "Your wedding should have lovely weather."

He wondered as he spoke if it was too tender a topic, if he should avoid it—and the minefield of other subjects that would remind them of the web of promises keeping them apart.

But Darla laughed as she toweled at her hair and perched on her stool. "The weather wouldn't *dare* be less than perfect," she said mockingly. "Cross my mother? Even nature wouldn't do that."

"Ooo," Breck said, "You're living dangerously, challenging nature around here."

The earth beneath them gave a well-timed rumble, brief and minor. Silverware rattled, and the hanging pans swayed for a moment.

Darla's eyes got big. "Do you get earthquakes a lot here?"

"More recently," Breck said. "But only little ones, and Shifting Sands is well-built. Nothing to worry about, I promise."

She smiled trustingly at him. "I feel safe here," she said softly. "With you…"

"Darla…" Breck felt like a pressure was building in his chest, a pressure that had nothing to do with lust or desire, but was still an undeniable yearning. "You said that you had to get married, and I have to let you do what you have to... but… will it always *be* no for us? Because there could be divorce, and I would wait… years if I had to. Lifetimes."

Her trusting smile faded and Breck wished he hadn't spoken because it was replaced with misery.

"You don't have much experience with dragon contracts, do you," Darla said sadly.

Breck shook his head. "I know Bastian avoids making promises," he realized.

"Dragons can add magic to enforce their contracts to make them binding. Like a geas. My marriage will be unbreakable. We will be literally incapable of dissolving it or... committing infidelity."

That sounded pretty final, and Breck felt like he was standing over a yawning pit of misery on a very narrow footbridge. "Well," he said, as cheerfully as he could manage. "At least I can get you a good breakfast before you walk the plank. Any requests?"

Darla's grateful smile was slow and timid. "It was all delicious last time. I've never had such amazing strawberries."

The plate that Breck made her was heaped with strawberries and included sizzling breakfast sausages, balls of goat cheese rolled in herbs, and flaky croissants, with a little chunk of carrot carefully carved into a rose. Darla's delight over the rose was like salve on a sunburn and his leopard was thrilled that they managed to please her, at least that much.

She insisted he share the food with her, again, and Breck sat across from her and watched her hands and wished he could touch them. He had a pang of sympathy for Conall and his mate Gizelle, who had been too afraid to let him touch her for more than a week after they met.

But Conall had tamed her wild heart with his patience, and they were comfortably *together* now.

He and Darla had no such chance, and patience was not their answer.

They had far less than a week.

Breck startled from his seat. "Dammit, the bread!" He turned on the ovens. "First I burn them, now I forget to bake them."

Darla stood up, surprised at his sudden outburst. "Can I help?"

Breck laughed, "No, there's nothing to be done, really. They've already been shaped, they just need to warm up while the oven heats and then I'll bake them. I'm just about twenty minutes behind the schedule, that's all."

"Bread has always been very mysterious to me," Darla admitted, as he took the trays of bread dough from the refrigerator and uncovered them. "It's squishy dough, and then, magically, sandwiches!"

"Crazier than that, it's little colonies of living yeast that we carefully cultivate and then murder," Breck added. "Delicious, delicious murder."

Darla giggled, her eyes crinkling perfectly. "I never would have thought of that," she said in chagrin. "How will I ever eat bread again without thinking of those millions of little extinguished potentials. One of them might have written the yeast equivalent of Shakespeare's plays if it hadn't been baked."

"You might also have eaten a little yeast Jack the Ripper," Breck suggested. "So it probably balances out."

Darla's laugh was the most beautiful sound Breck had ever heard, an unreserved moment of joy that he wanted to bottle.

As it faded, he realized he was staring at her, all the yearning in his heart undoubtedly on his face. "I'm sorry," he said, looking away. "I didn't mean to…"

"Is your leopard driving you as crazy as mine is?" Darla asked softly.

Breck dared to look back and Darla's face was a mirror of desire and despair. "So crazy," he admitted.

"I'm so sorry I can't…" she trailed off in embarrassment.

Breck dredged down for a way to lighten the situation, to lift some of the weight of misery from her shoulders. Humor was always the first thing in his toolbox. "You *should* be sorry," he teased, gesturing to himself. "All this, and you don't even get to touch it! I'll have you know that I'm the greatest lover that has ever set foot on this island."

Darla's eyes got very big indeed. For a moment Break feared that he'd overshot his attempt at flippancy and horrified her instead. Then she burst out laughing and the delighted smile that bloomed over her face was everything Breck had hoped for.

"Seriously," he continued flippantly, "if they gave out trophies for sex, I'd run out of display space for them. I'd have to choose between keeping the 'best beach sex' trophy and the 'greatest floss'.

You know, I'd probably keep that one in the bathroom. Keep my toothbrush in it."

Darla laughed so hard that she had to lean on the counter. "You're impossible!" she said.

"Just highly improbable," Breck joked. "Now I'll need to chop up some fruit for the breakfast service, or Chef will can me the rest of the way."

He did a considerably better job chopping the fruit than he had the day before, despite Darla's distracting observation from across the counter.

She was fascinated by the process and admitted that she hadn't spent any time at all in a kitchen. "I had no idea a mango started out looking like *that,*" she said. "And I didn't know a pineapple had a core you couldn't eat."

"Want to help me wash up some of these dishes?" Breck asked impulsively, when he had laid out all of the fruit dishes and added the mint garnish.

Darla looked shocked. "I've... never washed dishes before," she said hesitantly. "Do you think I could?"

"Darla, my love," Breck said expansively. "I can teach anyone anything. Since I have no chance to teach you all the things I *really* want to, I can settle for showing you how to scrub plates."

She smiled shyly. "I probably shouldn't ask what you really want to teach me," she said mischievously.

"Not unless you want anatomic diagrams," Breck teased. "And those are classes best taught with a hands-on lab." Her blush was everything he could have hoped for.

He managed to tie an apron on her without actually touching her, a feat he took considerable pride in. He showed her how to wash the dishes, aching to press up behind her to demonstrate over her shoulders, and took them to rinse and dry. He was careful not to brush against her and watched her from the corner of his eyes as they worked.

Her look of studious concentration was as alluring as her laughter had been and her strawberry-blonde hair was lightly curled around her face in the steam. She nibbled on her lower lip as she worked and her triumph when Breck approved her work was like a wash of joy.

She got invested in the work and when Breck handed back a plate, pointing out an imaginary fleck, she was at first chagrined, then realized he was teasing her. "There's nothing there," she protested.

She splashed him with the soapy water, laughing, and Breck started to automatically gather her into his arms, only stopping at the last moment, standing very close to her with his hands on either side of her arms… not quite touching her, but desperately wanting to.

They were frozen there a long moment before Breck could wrestle his hands back to his sides. He wanted to apologize, but *sorry* was the hated theme of their whole relationship.

"I should go," Darla said breathlessly.

He was close enough to kiss her with the slightest lean forward and his leopard was doing angry, pacing circles over the fact that they hadn't yet.

"You should," Breck whispered.

"The sun will be up soon," Darla said, not moving. She was gazing up at him, her pupils large with desire.

"If I kiss you, I won't be able to stop," Breck warned her for a second time.

"I know," she mouthed without sound. Breck felt like he could hear her heart breaking in the silence.

He wasn't sure how long they might have stood there, insisting that Darla had to go, if it hadn't been for someone whistling outside the back door of the kitchen. They each took a step back and waited in fear as the whistler passed by without pausing.

Darla released her held breath in a rush. "Tomorrow morning?" she asked longingly.

"I'll be here," Breck promised.

Then she was gone, and the kitchen was achingly empty again.

"I'll be here," Breck repeated helplessly to himself.

CHAPTER 19

Darla didn't realize she was still wearing the apron that Breck had so carefully tied onto her until she was creeping into the back door of her cottage. She tore it off with frantic fingers as she heard her mother stirring in the next room and threw it under the pillow.

No, what if housekeeping found it, Darla thought in a panic, casting an eye around the room. Her luggage wasn't particularly safe from her prying mother and she couldn't think where she might put it that wouldn't be tidied by the staff later. Finally, as her mother tapped on the door, she wadded it up as small as she could manage and stuffed it into her Gucci handbag.

Did it bulge suspiciously? There was no time to reconsider.

"You're dressed early," her mother said, sounding grouchy as Darla let her in.

"The sun wakes me up," Darla fibbed. "I'm not used to it."

"I should complain about the curtains," Jubilee said, twitching them open. "You'd think as much money as we're paying, they could afford better light-blocking fabric. You'd also think they would put coffee machines in each house. I'm going to the restaurant to get a decent cup as soon as they open."

She turned to give Darla an appraising look. "We've got a long day ahead of us," she said. "I want to go over the seating for the rehearsal dinner and talk about the menu with their chef. The food so far has been decent, at least."

Remembering the breakfasts that Breck has served her rather than the meals in the restaurant, Darla agreed wholeheartedly and followed her mother. At the last moment, she grabbed her purse, and the ridiculously large designer sunhat that was supposed to keep her from freckling.

Chef himself came out to spread napkins in their laps and take their breakfast requests, something that pleased Jubilee, who loved to be waited on by the most important people.

"A one-egg vegetarian omelet with sliced avocado and cilantro," she decided imperiously. "Cooked in truffle oil, not any nasty canola or corn. And some of that fresh bread I smell."

Darla squirmed and Chef carefully did not glance at her. "I'm afraid the bread is still baking," he apologized. "We… had a late start this morning."

Jubilee frowned, but Darla put her own order in before she could fuss about it. "Just a grapefruit for me," she said graciously. "And a cup of coffee."

"Of course," Chef said politely. "And a loaf of bread will be brought just as soon as it's ready, fresh from the oven."

"It's good that you eat lightly," Jubilee said with a critical look at Darla after Chef had gone. "I should have had you working with my personal trainer more before we left home. You're looking almost plump."

"The dresses fit," Darla reminded her. "And there's a limit to how much weight I can lose in three days."

Jubilee sighed. "Yes, I suppose we have what we have now." There was no doubting from her tone that what she had was a great disappointment.

Darla's grapefruit was served with their coffees and there was a little carrot rose in the garnish on the plate that made Darla's heart flip-flop in her chest. Her bracelet felt hot and Darla put it in her lap under her napkin before it could start glowing and betray her.

Jubilee caught Chef when he returned with her omelet and grilled him about the wedding menu as she ate, oblivious to the other people who came into the restaurant and were seated. Food continued to be served, so presumably, his staff was making do without him.

Breck, Darla thought. Breck was probably in there helping to make the food. She fingered the carved carrot.

"And no iceberg lettuce in the salads," Jubilee said commandingly. "It's so *cheap*. Right Darla?"

"Of course, mother," Darla said faintly.

She was glad that her mother had irrationally banned Breck from serving. Even just knowing he was close, looking at the rose he had carved, she wanted to squirm in her seat. He'd almost touched her in the kitchen, almost gathered her up in his arms when she splashed him, and she had wanted it so badly.

How much worse would it be, if it were Breck instead of Chef, cataloging her mother's demands, refilling her water, spreading the napkin in her lap...

Darla nodded when she was supposed to, agreed with everything, and finished her fruit with one hand hidden in her lap.

She was keenly aware of the apron in her purse. Her sunhat lay over it, and it wasn't at all obvious, but it felt like it was burning a guilty hole in her side.

Could she simply leave the apron discreetly under the table? How was she going to get rid of it?

Chef finally escaped and it was a server who brought them their loaf of fresh bread.

"Maybe I should call Madame Nadine," Jubilee said thoughtfully. "I really can't decide between a mint reduction on the pork or a tart cranberry braise."

"I like the sound of cranberry," Darla offered, staring at the bread. All those little yeast villains and Shakespeares. She had to smile to herself.

"Mmm," Jubilee said, distracted by the menu she was annotating. "But mint, you know."

"I'd like to have a bit of a rest before we go over the seating,"

Darla suggested. "The heat here makes me quite tired." To say nothing of rising before the sun and spending sleepless nights thinking about Breck's eyes, and his smile, and his arms, and his…

The glow of the bracelet was shining through the napkin in her lap.

"That's a good idea," Jubilee said with a slightly knowing smile, and she gathered up her own purse. She yawned. "I might like a bit of a siesta before lunch myself. I wouldn't be surprised if they gave us decaffeinated coffee, goodness."

Darla gathered up her hat, but left her purse, tucked away off the edge of the chair where it wasn't obvious. It would give her a reason to come back later, when the restaurant wasn't busy, and she'd have a better chance of getting rid of the apron.

And maybe seeing Breck again.

CHAPTER 20

Mrs. Shandy was too shrewd to be fooled by Breck's usual careless jokes and smiles. After he had badly lost two games of backgammon making distracted moves, she put the dice aside and gravely asked, "What's under your skin, young man?"

Breck wasn't sure how he could possibly explain the terrible, restless need that was eating him alive from the inside. "Just resenting my enforced vacation," he said, at least partly honest.

"Oh, piffle," Mrs. Shandy said sharply. "You look like you've got girl troubles, and a whole pile of them. You don't have to tell me what's bothering you if you want to be that way about it, but you should know better than to lie about it to *yourself*."

"I'm not," Breck protested. He was, he thought, being very truthful with himself about the impossibility of his situation.

Mrs. Shandy made a noise of disbelief. "Well be that as it may, I'm sure I don't know what I'm talking about. It's not like I've had a lifetime of romance and relationships or anything."

"Mrs. Shandy…"

"No, no, we're done now," Mrs. Shandy said loftily. "You may take my tray."

She had forgiven him by the time he had gathered up her dishes and swept the floor, and gave him a warm, fragile hug. "You be honest with yourself," she said. "And you let yourself feel, Breck. You open up that big heart and you give yourself permission to be happy."

Breck sighed and stewed over Mrs. Shandy's advice as he walked back to the kitchen with her breakfast tray. He didn't want to feel. That way lay only pain and misery.

He automatically took the main path, his mind busy, until he heard giggling girls and nearly walked into a party of bridesmaids, remembering too late that he was supposed to be staying out of sight.

They greeted him with a range of reactions, ranging from haughty disdain to interested sidelong looks, and he skirted around them without responding. A few days earlier, even under strict orders to stay under the radar, he would have tested their sincerity with flirtation and smiles, but all he wanted to do now was escape.

He thought the rest of his path was clear, and was surprised when he found Eugene lurking near the back door of the kitchen.

"Can I help you?" he asked shortly, his hackles up.

"I'm Eugene," the man introduced with a greasy smile. "You must be the infamous Breck?"

"You're from the bride's family," Breck said flatly.

"Distantly," Eugene said quickly. "My mother was Mrs. Grant's *second* cousin."

This was the man who would marry Darla if Breck challenged for her and lost. For the first time since he had first laid eyes on Darla, Breck and his leopard were in perfect instinctive agreement: this man was absolutely, in every way, their enemy.

So it was unexpected when Eugene seemed friendly. "Hey, I'm really sorry for her interference. She's a little… old-fashioned, you know? And it doesn't help that she's trying really hard to impress the dragon high society with this wedding. I hope you won't lose your job over this."

"Shouldn't," Breck said shortly. He edged past Eugene to go into the kitchen without encouraging further conversation.

To his alarm, Eugene followed him. "Glad to hear that," the man said cheerfully. "Say, have you met the groom yet?"

"Liam?" Breck said in surprise.

"You'd like him," Eugene said jovially. "He's a great fellow. Did you know he was a dragon shifter? Big surprise to his parents. They come from lines of wolf and genet shifters, there hadn't been a dragon in their lines for generations."

"I heard," Breck said, putting Mrs. Shandy's tray on the counter and unloading it. Chef and the few people working in the kitchen were at the other end of the big room, working noisily with mixers. Chef was singing a booming opera over the sound.

"Handsome guy," Eugene said, as if he were sharing a great secret. "And I don't swing that way myself." He laughed a little and seemed to think that Breck should be laughing with him.

Breck gave him a hard look, trying to make sense of this baffling conversation. "Miss Grant is a lucky lady," he suggested, trying to keep the bitterness out of his voice and failing.

"Undoubtedly," Eugene agreed. "But I'm not sure Liam's... heart is in it, if you catch my drift."

Breck rolled up his sleeves in order to wash the few dishes that had accumulated while he was away. "Alright then," he said dismissively.

His unfriendly responses to Eugene's attempts at conversation finally got through and Eugene, frowning, gave up at last and left the noisy kitchen.

It was only after the man had left that Breck realized it sounded almost like Eugene was trying to interest him in Liam. Was he trying to sabotage the wedding by setting them up? Breck chuckled. He could have told Eugene he was wasting his time barking up that tree.

Not only had Liam shown no interest in Breck, Breck was not sure anyone in the world would ever interest him again after meeting Darla.

CHAPTER 21

Darla crept out as her mother was talking over the menu with Madame Nadine on the phone and made her way back up to the restaurant. She paused to make brief, polite conversation with the bridesmaids who were gathered at the bar. They were talking about the cute bartender, and the hunk of a landscaper, and the gorgeous Native handyman, but they changed the topic when she joined them, and she heard them start it back up as she left once she'd managed the minimum social niceties.

At least *they* were enjoying her wedding celebration.

As she had hoped, the restaurant was nearly empty outside of her mother's dictated meal hours.

Nearly empty. Sitting at the table next to the one she had been at that morning was a woman so large that Darla had to do a double take.

No one, she was very sure, had ever insisted on a personal trainer or a diet to this woman. And Darla thought, enviously, that she didn't look as though she needed it.

She was, despite—or possibly because of—her great weight, the most arresting woman Darla had ever seen, health and self-confidence like a crown on her head. The chair she was on seemed barely capable of holding her, but she was holding court as if she owned the place, every gesture full of strength and grace. She had waves of thick auburn hair past her waist and Darla was sure that hours with Lydia and Laura at the spa would never give her such perfect nails.

Chef was sitting across from her, gazing at her in unabashed adoration as they spoke. When he saw Darla, he stood. "Miss Grant," he said politely.

"Sorry, I'm only here to get my purse," Darla said, honestly sorry to disturb them. "I must have forgotten it earlier…"

The large woman turned to see her and her chair gave such a groan that Darla thought it was surely on the verge of collapse. "Ah, you are the bride I've heard so much about," she greeted.

What *had* she heard? Darla wondered, heart in her throat.

"I am Magnolia," the woman introduced, offering a bejeweled hand that Darla wasn't sure if she was supposed to shake or kiss. She settled for giving it the slightest fingertip shake and Magnolia seemed to accept that as her due. "Come, sit with me, darling. Chef was about to run off and abandon me to start the samples for your harpy of a mother."

Chef made a noise, as if he didn't approve of the frank description but didn't want to come out and say so.

"She is!" Magnolia insisted. "She's so strict about when the rest of us can come to the restaurant, Lydia says she's terrible to the staff, and Gizelle is frightened half to death of her, the poor dear." She gave Darla a sly look. "And *banning* Breck from serving altogether. We're all outraged by her self-righteous bigotry."

Darla fell obediently into the chair that Chef had just abandoned.

"Bring the dear thing some food," Magnolia suggested. "Doesn't your mother let you eat at *all*?"

Darla wanted to protest that she'd already had not one, but two breakfasts, but Magnolia didn't let her, waving Chef away imperiously.

Magnolia leaned forward and the table gave a moan under her

weight as the chair creaked ominously. "Now Darla, *darling*," she said in a voice that wouldn't carry past their table. "I understand you're our Breck's mate, and that you can't get out of your wedding, which amply explains why you look like you've lost your best friend and stopped eating altogether, but tell me, isn't he the just the most delicious shifter you've ever seen? Honestly, if I weren't a happily mated woman, I'd have that young man making personal *service* deliveries to my cottage every chance I got. Such arms, he has! And his ass!"

Darla cleared her throat weakly, sure her face was beet-red. Whatever she had expected to discuss with this woman, Breck's personal attributes had not made the list. "He's… ah…"

Ours, her snow leopard insisted jealously. *All ours. Deliciously ours.*

"Very… handsome," Darla squeaked.

Magnolia leaned back and laughed. "Oh, your face," she said kindly. "I didn't mean to make you squirm, dear. I just assumed that you'd be spending every chance you got with the poor man before you had to part ways."

"I can't," Darla managed to say, confused and distressed by the idea as much as she longed for it. "I'm getting *married*."

"You're not married *yet*," Magnolia said pointedly. "And let's face it, darling, the time we have together is terribly short no matter who you are and how much stands in your way. If you have a chance at a few moments of happiness, you take them, and you hold onto them and you do the best with them you possibly can, even if it's not how you thought things might be."

She wasn't looking at Darla, for the end of her words, but over Darla's shoulder, with soft violet eyes. Then her gaze snapped back to Darla. "And dear, if you haven't figured it out by now, Breck knows how to live *now* better than most of us do. You should let him teach you that."

Darla stared back at her, as Chef appeared from behind her with an absolute platter of food: cubes of glistening fruit, croissants, slices of cold meat, exquisite little twists of homemade mozzarella. "I couldn't possibly eat all of this," Darla protested.

"Oh, posh," Magnolia said expansively. "I'll help you."

Which is how Darla ended up eating a third breakfast, listening to Magnolia talk about the beauties and qualities of Shifting Sands Resort, and thinking hard about her choices for the next three days.

She forgot about the apron in her purse.

CHAPTER 22

There was another minor earthquake after lunch. The only loss was a wineglass that fell off the counter in The Den; otherwise it was just one of the tiny rumbles that were starting to feel like just another feature of the resort.

"Who is supposed to be doing these dishes?" Saina asked crossly from the kitchen as she cleaned up the broken glass. "Seriously, there are no clean plates, and it's starting to attract ants." She smashed one with her thumb. "Ew!"

Breck, lying on the couch playing a first person shooter and losing badly, glanced over. They didn't usually have a strict chore schedule, but he was in the habit of cleaning up the kitchen every time he used it. But the past few days, he hadn't been able to dredge up the energy to care if there were dirty dishes, barely interested in feeding himself. "Sorry," he said, sounding unapologetic to his own ears.

"Oh, yuck, this dishtowel is crunchy," Saina said in disgust. "When was the last time these were changed? Breck don't you usually do the shared laundry?"

"Yeah," Breck said, as his character died again. He thumbed off the game, but made no move to get up off the couch.

Saina seemed to finally notice his malaise. "I don't think I noticed how much you do around here," she said as she dumped the last of the broken glass into the over-full trash. "Are you... are you okay?"

Saina wasn't the sort to be sympathetic to self-pity, or to be particularly sympathetic in general, so Breck was touched by the question. "I'll be fine," he lied.

Saina's mouth twisted doubtfully. "You know that mermaids can usually tell if people are telling the truth," she suggested.

Breck hadn't know that, and wondered how many of his outrageous stories she'd known the real truth behind. "I'll be fine," he repeated, not caring if she believed it or not.

To his surprise, she came and sat beside him on the couch. "So, I'm not the most… people-oriented person," she said frankly. "And it's not really siren custom to give a damn about anyone except ourselves."

"Yeah," Breck said, equally honestly. Saina had been an odd fit in their quirky work family, and he was pretty sure that she was the most surprised of all of them how well she had adjusted to the affectionate and cooperative employees who lived in The Den.

"I'm really sorry you got yanked from your work by a ridiculous bigot," Saina said carefully. "And I know that you cared a lot about what you did. So if you want to talk about it or whatever, I'd listen."

Despite the musical lilt to her voice, she said it like she was offering her wrists to be slit, Breck thought, and he was honestly touched by her thoughtfulness. He also knew that talking about Darla wasn't going to fix a thing. "I appreciate the offer," he said sincerely. "But you can't help me with this."

Saina shrugged. "Suit yourself," she said without offense. "I'll do a load of dishes if you want."

"Thanks, Saina," Breck said.

"And Breck…"

"Yeah?"

"Who's your mate?"

Breck sat up straight. "What do you mean?" he said with no hint of his usual smoothness.

Saina looked apologetic. "I've gotten to the point where I can recognize it, like I can tell when someone's telling the truth or not. My magic bounces off of mates weirdly. You're sort of… vibrating with it."

"You can't tell *anyone*!" Breck insisted so vehemently that Saina's eyes got large.

"Alright…" Saina said reluctantly.

"Not even Bastian," Breck added fiercely.

Saina's eyebrows knit in elegant confusion. "Look, I know the staff will tease you about it, but they won't—"

"No one!" Breck was sitting up now, looking her urgently in the eyes. Too many people knew already, and he didn't want any more pity that he already had. Worse, the others might try to figure out who she was and make some futile attempt to solve a problem they didn't understand the messy details behind.

Saina stared at him in silent surprise. "Alright," she finally said. "I won't mention it."

"Thanks," Breck said sullenly, sinking back into the couch with the game controller. "Much appreciated."

When she looked like she might want to talk further, Breck put on the game headphones and tried to distract himself shooting zombies and hellhounds.

CHAPTER 23

By dinner, Darla had still not managed to get rid of the apron. She left it in her purse, but left her purse in her room, shoved beneath the edge of her bed.

"I thought I might sit with Liam tonight," she suggested to her mother as they approached the restaurant and she caught sight of Liam sitting alone. The next night, they would begin the formal dinners; this was her last chance at anything that even resembled privacy.

Her mother, who was already greeting the newest arrivals, had no objection to this proposal, and looked at Darla's wrist suggestively as they parted. The bracelet was dull metal.

Liam smiled warmly as she sat opposite him and let the server put a napkin in her lap and tell her the menu. "You look lovely," he said sincerely.

Darla smiled wanly in reply. "I've spent enough time in the spa today that I ought to," she said.

She spent the meal tensely listening to the conversations around them and picking at the food on her plate, making dutiful conversation with Liam as she wondered where Breck was and what he was doing.

"Would you like to go out for a walk?" Liam invited unexpectedly. "Assuming that you aren't any more interested in the dessert than you were the filet."

Darla looked down at her picked-over steak and put her fork down, only just realizing that Liam had been no more interested in his delectable meal than she had been in hers. "That would be lovely," she said sincerely, feeling guilty. Was she so wrapped up in her own concerns and needs that she hadn't noticed that her friend was suffering, too?

They were stopped no less than five times trying to escape the restaurant, by distant relatives or society friends who wanted to congratulate the happy couple and exclaim over what a *lovely* pair they made.

At last they were alone in the night, the chatter of the diners dying behind them to the drone of the tropical night noises and the whisper of the ocean. Liam took her hand, strong fingers twining with hers and Darla's throat tightened thinking how badly she wished they were someone else's.

"Darla," Liam said, when they had made their way down the stairs past the bar and down again to the pool deck overlooking the beach. "We've got to figure out something better than this. This is worse than my worst fear when we agreed to do this. You knew I wouldn't be able to be what you needed... and you're so miserable I can't bear it."

"Have I done such a terrible job of hiding it?" Darla asked, not bothering to try to deny it.

"Maybe not with everyone else, but I know you a little," Liam reminded her. "And your mate… Darla, you must be in agony."

Darla was keenly aware that someone looking down over the restaurant deck might see… if not their faces, the poses of their bodies, leaning together on the railing looking out over the ocean. Did they look like lovers eagerly anticipating their nuptials? Did they look like friends trying to make the best of a sticky situation? Did she look like someone who wanted a little to jump off the pool deck and see if the fall to the beach would kill her or only hurt a lot?

The thought drew her back in alarm. She'd never had such a

dire thought before. She felt like her brain wasn't her own, like she was losing control. "It's… terrible," she admitted in a whisper. "I feel like I'm inside out, like nothing makes the slightest bit of sense. Like I'm in a toboggan heading down a mountain of broken glass going impossibly fast. I only feel better when I'm near him, even if we… can't."

Liam put an arm around her. That would be convincing, if someone were looking at them through the darkness, even if it was only truly a gesture of friendship.

"Would it be better if you could?" he asked.

Darla froze.

"I don't know of any way out of this," Liam continued thoughtfully. "If you chose Breck, Eugene would challenge, and you'd be back where you started. You run away… and… well, that has problems, too."

But Darla was still locked on the idea of having Breck, even just for a moment. What would it be like, knowing what his kiss tasted like, to have a memory of the feel of his skin, his hair through her fingers, his weight, his smell…

She had to wrestle herself back to the moment with every scrap of her strained willpower.

"And the home," Darla reminded him between gritted teeth. "All those poor people who would have nowhere to go once my mother was done destroying their lives. Mrs. Asher. She's like a grandmother to me. Mr. Danby..."

She wasn't thinking about them. She was thinking only of herself, of her own blazing need, her own terrible hunger, her own aching emptiness.

"Darla," Liam said gently.

She opened eyes she hadn't realized she'd shut and found that their bracelets were both glowing brightly.

That would give any watchers an eyeful, she thought bitterly, as she clamped her hand uselessly over her own.

"Sorry," she said faintly. "I can't… can't help it."

"Darla," Liam repeated. "Would it be better… if you went to him?"

Nothing in the world could be better, she was convinced. And nothing could be worse.

Even if Darla didn't have words to speak, the bracelets, now as bright as beacons, said plenty. *Let him teach you how to live*, Magnolia had said. And oh, she wanted to.

"Past the event hall, you know that white manor?"

Darla crinkled her brows at him in confusion. "Yes," she said hesitantly.

"Go around the back, there's a door on the first floor past the retaining wall. There's a metal lizard on the wall next to it."

Darla stared at him.

"That's Breck's private room entrance," Liam explained. "He's probably there now."

"How did you find that out?" Darla asked breathlessly. Her snow leopard was purring.

"The chef slipped me a note. I… to be honest, I thought it might be an attempt to fix me up with him."

Darla laughed, and was surprised that it was a real laugh. "He knows about me and Breck," she explained. "And Mother being constantly around makes it hard to slip me anything directly."

"There you have it," Liam said with an answering laugh. "More peer pressure."

"I… I just don't know if it's right," she said weakly, feeling what was left of her resistance crumble.

"Oh, Darla," Liam said, sounding as patient as ever. "You have spent your whole life trying to do what is right for *other* people. I think that taking three nights to do the right thing for *you* is fully justified."

Darla raised her gaze to his. "Three nights," she said. "I have three nights left."

"Go make them count," Liam advised. "I'll put a sock on my doorknob per ridiculous custom and everyone will assume you are just being impatient and no one will question a thing."

Darla raised on her tiptoes and kissed him on the cheek. "Thank you," she said simply.

They walked together to Liam's cottage to keep up appearances, and then she was covering her bracelet and scampering through the darkness towards the manor building.

CHAPTER 24

Breck lay on his back in the middle of his bed, staring at the ceiling.

He knew better than to think he was going to sleep that night, and had not even bothered to strip out of his clothing.

He felt like there were bees under his skin.

It wasn't just *wanting*, it was like being incomplete, and he'd never even realized it, only muddled through in ignorance. And now he knew what he couldn't have, had looked into the sky blue eyes of pure love… and as much as the rest of him was sure that it was his, meant for him in every way, his head knew it wasn't.

It wasn't just bees under his skin, it was angry bees, and his angry leopard, who didn't understand why either of them were denying this thing that was so basic and natural.

He could think of nothing else.

The knock on his back door made his heart sink. His room in The Den had clearly been intended for the live-in help; it was less grand than the rest of the house, but had its own tiny bathroom and, most importantly, a private entrance, tucked away at the back of the house. What it lacked in view, it made up for in discreet access. That had been useful for private liaisons in the past, but now he only wished he'd never told anyone about it.

He almost ignored the knock, but his leopard urged him to answer it and he rose wearily to open the door.

It isn't going to be her, he told his leopard as he opened the door. It didn't make sense that it could be her.

But it was, and all the bees inside him went absolutely mad.

"Darla," he breathed.

She was panting and her eyes were dark with desire. The bracelet on her wrist was glowing like cheap rave jewelry and she had her opposite hand clamped over it as if she could cover the light of it.

"You can't be here," Breck insisted.

"I have three nights," she challenged him. "Three nights until I have to get married and I'm bound forever.

Breck felt like a guard dog being tested with a juicy steak. He was supposed to overcome this temptation. Hard as it was—and oh, was it *hard*—he had to turn her away.

"You *can't* be here," Breck repeated firmly.

Then she was moving into the room, putting hands against his chest and hissing at the contact. "I want to be here. I *have* to be here. Show me what might have been."

He wanted to. He wanted to claim her mouth, her sweet body, her very soul. He wanted to lay her down on his bed and show her how to make it sing.

"It's not fair… to Liam," he said desperately. "You are *his*." Saying it out loud made it hurt worse.

Darla paused, then gave a small laugh. "I will never be his," she said, shaking her head. "Oh, I will be bound to him by contract, but I will never… Liam doesn't *want* me. He can't be with me this way."

Breck felt like his brain was moving very slowly. It was very hard to think with Darla's hand burning holes through his thin shirt. "He's gay?" he ventured. It didn't quite make sense.

"He's ace… asexual. He's not interested in anyone, he doesn't like sex at all." Her hands were moving on his chest, fingers barely flexing, like a kneading cat.

Asexual.

"Oh," he said stupidly, thinking of Liam's odd lack of reaction. He'd known there was such a thing as ace, but never knowingly encountered it before. "I thought I was just losing my touch," he had to chuckle. "That actually explains a lot."

I told *you he wasn't a rival*, his leopard reminded him.

"He knows I'm here," Darla said. "He's the one who told me how to get here. Please, Breck, please… once I'm married, I won't be able to do this, ever, and I have three days left that I don't want to waste the way I've already wasted so much of my life. Please, please..."

Breck gathered her face in his hands, the silky sweep of her hair on his fingertips. He leaned close, not quite believing his luck. "If I kiss you, I won't be able to stop," he warned, so close to her mouth that he could feel her breath on his lips. She was straining against his hands towards him and it took all of his willpower to wait there for her spoken answer.

"I don't want you to stop," Darla told him fiercely. "I want you to show me how to live."

Breck's fingers curled and he closed the distance between their mouths with all the hunger he had been fighting since he had first seen her.

She opened her mouth and kissed him back with the fire that Breck had known was lurking beneath her sweet exterior, wrapping her arms around his neck and pressing her body into his.

It was almost too much. He was going to overflow with the need and desire she woke in him. He was going to lose himself entirely in her kiss. He was going to burn away to nothing in the heat of her passion. He was going to...

He was going to embarrass himself if he didn't take steps.

Greatest lover who ever set foot on Shifting Sands, indeed.

Breck caught her face in his hands again and pulled slowly away. "Wait," he growled. "Slow down…"

Darla whimpered and tried to claw him closer to her. "I'm not a virgin, if that's what you're worried about," she said, panting. "And I know you aren't…"

For a fleeting moment, Breck felt guilty. But his leopard reminded him, *Every other lover was worth it, to best learn how to pleasure our mate.*

And pleasure her he would.

Breck turned Darla around in his arms, to her confusion, then bent and kissed her neck from behind, slow and hot, from her shoulder to the bottom of her ear. Her breath hitched as he took the lobe gently between his teeth and reached around her to start carefully, slowly unbuttoning her dress.

With every button, he paused, kissing first one side of her neck, then the other: nibbling, licking, brushing back her hair with deliberate fingers.

She didn't know what to do with her hands, fluttering them helplessly as he coaxed a flush of desire over her fair skin. He licked her shoulder and blew on it, just to make her shiver.

As her dress finally fell from her, she tried to turn, and he resisted her, cupping her breasts from behind and letting one hand trail down her stomach as she squirmed.

"Breck," she begged. "Breck, please…"

He pressed against her so she could feel how badly he wanted her and almost lost his resolve when she ground back against him. One hand caressed her breasts, his thumb over a hard nipple and fingers tracing the place beneath where soft breast met soft flesh. The other hand teased lower, not touching where she wanted it most, but fingering the band of her underwear, circling her bellybutton, touching her thighs.

She writhed and begged wordlessly and when he finally walked his fingers down inside her underwear to find her clit, she gave a little cry and jerked in pleasure and shock. He teased it gently, then slipped his fingers deeper into her, letting his other hand continue to squeeze and caress her breasts. She was dripping wet, and he could just keep the pressure on her clit with the heel of his hand as he stroked into her with his fingers; it was only a few blissful moments before she was going rigid in his arms as pleasure crested over her.

He kissed her as she caught her breath again, and nibbled at her neck and earlobes. He didn't resist as she turned this time, and kissed her deeply.

"I want *you*," she begged through ragged breaths. "I want you *in* me."

Breck had to battle his own desire for the same thing to grin at her. "Patience," he cautioned. "I have only just begun…"

CHAPTER 25

Darla could feel him, hard against her from behind, and knew that if Breck had not been holding her up with one strong arm, her knees would have given out as he brought her to the heights of pleasure and eased her down again.

"I want you," she begged him shamelessly when he had released her mouth. "I want you *in* me." His cock was hard against her; it felt huge through his khaki pants, and Darla was dying to release it.

But Breck smiled at her and his smile was like a promise they couldn't make. "Patience," he said, in that low silky voice that made her even wetter. "I have only just begun."

He laid her back down on his bed—it was a broad bed with generous pillows and a silky comforter that slipped erotically beneath her—and stripped her soaking underwear off of her, cupping the cheeks of her ass in his hands as he did. Then he was kissing her stomach, the underside of her breasts, the top of her hips.

When his lips finally brushed her nethers, she cried out without meaning to, and he was licking and kissing her, agonizingly slowly as his fingers once again spread her. From this angle, he could reach deeper, and Darla squirmed, helpless with need and delight as he thrust into her, raising her slowly to a fever pitch of pleasure.

He didn't let her crest that time, slowing when she might have, and she whimpered and clung to his shoulders.

"Please," she begged. "Please…"

To her delight, he pulled away from her then and unbuttoned his pants. She sat up, panting, because she didn't want to miss a moment or a sight and, when he pulled off his briefs with the khakis, she gave a sharp inhale at the view.

Then he was on her again, leaning her back into the pillows with kisses and caresses as he laid his cock against her, but refused to press in.

Darla could not have said how long he teased her with it, just enough pressure to promise, but never entering as he kissed her mouth rough and nibbled at her neck. He growled at her, the vibration of it shuddering through her skull, and rolled her earring with his tongue.

She begged and tried to press herself up and around him, full of desperation and desire, and he taunted her by pulling away, until she was a tangled ball of need and heightened sensation.

Then, at last, he pressed into her, in one long, slow thrust that joined them on some new level of pleasure and he was trying to shush her with a kiss because she could not help but keen out loud in pleasure.

He continued to thrust, almost painfully slowly, and Darla tried in vain to keep herself quiet as all the nerve endings in her body seemed to burn with bliss.

"Shhh," Breck reminded her, though he looked enormously pleased with himself. He withdrew, making Darla give a little guttural cry of loss, then rolled her over in the bed and pressed into her from behind. Darla stuffed her face into a pillow and screamed as pleasure rolled over her, clawing at the sheets and thrusting herself back against him desperately.

As her senses slowly returned from the overwhelming orgasm and the aftershocks gradually died away, Darla pulled away from Breck and rolled over.

He had a look of intense concentration and desperation and when he buried himself into her again, Darla could feel the way all his muscles were bunched up tight in almost agonized self-control.

"Breck," she said, reaching up to cradle his face. "Oh, Breck."

The sound of his name on her lips seemed to crack him. His weight came down over her as he crushed her into his arms and began to really thrust in earnest.

She cried his name again, arms and legs wrapped around him, and found one last, unexpected wave of pleasure as he made a helpless noise of release and the heat of his seed filled her.

CHAPTER 26

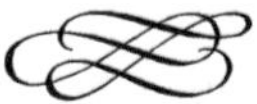

Breck cradled Darla in his arms, tangled in the middle of the mussed bed. A light blanket had been sloppily pulled over them to keep the night chill off their sweat-drying skin.

He would have been content to stay there forever, given the chance, but she stirred.

"I'm *sore*," she said in tired delight, and it made Breck's leopard give a growly purr of satisfaction.

"I'm not sorry," Breck chuckled, nibbling at her neck.

"I hope you haven't left any bite marks," Darla said with a giggle. "Might be hard to explain those to Mother."

Breck turned his nibbles to gentle kisses. "Nothing that won't be gone by morning," he promised.

The words, *gone by morning*, slowed his kisses and made him hold her tighter.

She would be gone by morning.

And two days after that, she would be gone forever.

The languid contentment vanished, like a drop of soap chasing a rainbow film of oil away.

"I shouldn't stay long," Darla said sadly, turning in his arms. "But I'm so glad I came."

"And came and came and came…" Breck teased.

She flushed, and giggled, and buried her face into a pillow to muffle her laughter as it edged to hysterical.

Breck wrapped her up in his arms and tickled her, spurred by her laughter.

Then they lay curled together again and Darla stroked her fingers down his arms as if mesmerized. "Did you grow up here?" she asked quietly.

"At Shifting Sands?" Breck asked. "It's only been open a few years, though it was originally built in the 80s. No, I grew up in Detroit. My parents died when I was young, and my grandfather raised me. He was a steel worker, before the big factory crash."

"Did you get along well?"

"Better than you'd think," Breck said with a chuckle. "He was an old-fashioned Catholic union worker, and I… well, I've always been me. But we were family, and we loved each other even when we didn't exactly see eye to eye."

"Did he… disapprove of you?" Darla asked shyly.

"I always thought he did, but then he got sick, and he was in the hospital, and we had one of those long heart-to-hearts like you see in the movies. He told me that as long as I never hurt people or took advantage of them, there was nothing wrong with enjoying life and he sort of wished he'd done more of it himself."

"Did he… die?"

Breck smiled fondly at the memory. "Not then," he said cheerfully. "Made a miraculous recovery and spent another five years torturing the nurses at his retirement home." He looked at Darla thoughtfully. "He would have been a lot more comfortable in a home with other shifters," he mused.

The mention of the shifter retirement home brought a solemn stillness to Darla's face.

"What about you?" Breck asked swiftly. "Where did you live?"

Darla's voice had a calmness that Breck recognized as practiced. "I went to the finest schools all over the world. Private grammar school in New York. Two finishing schools in Europe, with a semester in China. I can curtsy like a queen and speak French fluently. I know how to dance and host dinner parties and all sorts of useless things, but I don't think I ever *lived* at all before I met you."

They talked into the night, and made love again, and simply lay together not-quite-sleeping.

At last, they had to admit that dawn was coming too fast and Breck reluctantly helped her button her dress back up and find her lost sandals. He put them on for her, worshipfully caressing the curve of her leg as he did, and then walked her out his back door to the edge of the retaining wall at the back of The Den.

They paused there, holding hands, not willing to say their last goodbye, until Darla turned and threw herself into his arms, her face just briefly lit by the light from the house.

"I love you," she said into Breck's chest and he held her tighter until her ribs creaked, kissing her hair. "I have to go," she said miserably.

"I know," Breck barely managed to say.

They shared one last kiss, gentle, almost chaste, and then she turned away and fled away down the path. Breck watched her disappear past a hedge and listened to her footsteps on the gravel until they were drowned by the sounds of the ocean and jungle night.

Then he turned unhappily away… and drew up short at the looming shape of Graham, holding a shovel like he was considering using it on Breck.

"What's your problem?" Breck asked unhappily.

"My *problem* is, that was the bride," Graham said flatly. "The one who's getting married in two damn days. Of all the people you could be screwing…"

Breck was full of anger and frustration already and hearing Graham calling what they'd just done *screwing* was too much.

He balled up his fists and stepped forward. Graham gave a humorless grin, dropped the shovel, and raised his own fists.

"She's my mate," Breck growled.

Graham stepped back in astonishment, his hands falling to his side.

For a long moment, they stood that way. Then Breck let his own hands fall. "She's my *mate*," he said again, in agony.

Graham swore, colorfully, and paced around in a circle. "What are you going to do about it?" he asked when he was back around to face Breck.

"What can I do?" Breck said helplessly. "She's marrying someone else in two days. This… this is all I get."

Graham frowned. "You're not going to stop the wedding?"

"It's complicated," Breck said flatly.

"Good," Graham said unsympathetically.

"Good?"

"If you broke up that wedding, you're not the one who'd pay for it," the lion shifter pointed out. "Scarlet's the one with everything at stake, and she'd lose Shifting Sands. You'd bankrupt the resort. We'd *all* be out on our asses."

The consequences had occurred to Breck, but he hadn't realized that Shifting Sands was that close to the edge. He was mostly surprised that Graham sounded so invested. "Well, Scarlet and the resort are safe," Breck growled. "I haven't got a chance in hell of stopping the wedding."

Graham was quiet, which wasn't unexpected. "Sorry," he finally growled.

Breck wasn't sure what he was apologizing for, but he was sick of *sorry*. "Whatever," he answered miserably.

"Anyone else know?" Graham asked.

Breck gave a humorless laugh. "The fiance. Chef."

"So, probably Magnolia," Graham surmised. "That all?"

"As far as I know," Breck said. "Saina knows I have a mate, but doesn't know who."

"Good," Graham said. "Less that know the better." He turned on his heel and Breck realized that he meant to leave.

"Wait," Breck said desperately. "What do I do?"

Graham gave a dark, rusty laugh as he stalked away into the darkness. "How would I know?"

Breck let him go, knowing that as desperately as he wanted to, there really was nothing he could do but treasure the short time that they had.

CHAPTER 27

"Hello?" Darla called quietly as she came to the entrance of the spa.

It was quiet, with most of the wedding party occupied approving the flower arrangements with Scarlet and the surly gardener, and Darla liked it much better this way. It was cool inside, and she was glad to see only Laura standing at the far window.

"One of my nails chipped," she started to say, then belatedly she recognized the miserable roll to the sepia-skinned woman's shoulders and the ineffective wipe she gave to her face as she turned and tried to pull herself together; she had been crying.

Darla was across the room in a moment, automatically gathering the woman into her arms. "It's okay," she said comfortingly. "Can I help?"

For a moment, she was afraid she had overstepped and been too forward; Laura was stiff and surprised in her impulsive embrace. Then she gave a shuddering sigh and softened into Darla's hug with gratitude.

They sat together on the bench by the window and Darla put an arm around her shoulder and patted her hand kindly as Laura wiped her face on a cosmetic towel and her sobs gradually subsided.

"I'm sorry," Laura said shakily.

"You have nothing to be sorry for," Darla assured her. "Do you want to tell me about it?"

Laura laughed weakly. "It's probably just… hormones. I'm… I'm…" She couldn't quite finish.

"You're pregnant?" Darla guessed, her mother's uncomfortable conversations fresh in her mind. "You just found out?"

Laura took a shaky breath. "I thought I might be for a couple of weeks now, but yeah, just confirmed it."

"Is he going to be unhappy about it?" Darla asked, knowing there must be some conflict to cause her so much grief.

Laura exhaled in a rush, and gave a crooked smile. "He's going to be over the moon… except…" She bit her lip.

Darla let her continue at her own pace.

"There are no kids allowed at Shifting Sands. I… I don't know what we'll do. He's so happy here. I am, too. I can't imagine leaving."

It occurred to Darla suddenly that Breck could be the father to Laura's child, and jealousy threatened to rise up and choke her. Almost as suddenly, she realized that they hadn't used any protection the night before, and that she could get pregnant herself.

"Who is he?" she couldn't help asking, heart hammering in her throat.

The love that bloomed in Laura's face was so brilliant and unabashed that Darla's jealousy and worry felt foolish. "Tex, the bartender," she said almost shyly. "He's my mate." She showed Darla the simple gold band on her left hand. "We got married a few months ago—a double wedding with my twin sister."

Darla had to fight back her own wave of misery, sudden tears welling in her eyes. *This is Laura's moment*, she reminded herself, willing them away and smoothing her face before she looked up from the ring. "It's beautiful," she said sincerely. "You're very lucky, and I'm sure the three of you will figure out something wonderful."

Tears filled Laura's eyes, but these were happier. "The… three of us," she repeated.

Darla smiled at her and nodded. "The *three* of you," she said, squeezing Laura's hand.

Laura gave an excited squeak. "I'm going to have a *baby*!" she said, her tears overflowing.

"It's wonderful," Darla said firmly. "You're going to have a baby, and however it works out, it's going to be amazing."

Laura wrapped her arms around Darla again. "Thank you," she said gratefully. Then she sat up. "Oh lord, I'm a mess. This hormone stuff better get itself in order, or this is going to be a really long nine months."

Darla decided it was wiser not to share her mother's horror stories of pregnancy.

"Now, your nail," Laura said professionally, straightening her skirt and wiping away the last of her tears. "Let's get you fixed right up. That looks like pink angel polish, and the chip isn't bad. We'll just do a quick patch and seal it over."

While Laura fussed cheerfully over the broken nail, Darla looked through the opposite wall, thoughts crowding her head. She had never wanted a child before. Marrying Liam had been a relief from the idea of carrying on the family line like her mother so desperately wanted her to. But somehow the thought of Breck's child seemed like something utterly different. The bracelet on her wrist was glowing faintly, like it did every time that she thought about him, and she rubbed it automatically.

"What is that bracelet?" Laura asked curiously. "Does it always do that?"

"Oh, it's… ah, a fertility charm," Darla said, embarrassed. "It does this… randomly." Thinking about not thinking about Breck had the opposite effect, and it glowed more brightly.

"Well that certainly bodes well for you," Laura said with amusement. "You must be so excited about your wedding."

The bracelet returned to dull metal as Darla made herself smile and she talked politely about the wedding details, feigning the enthusiasm she knew she was supposed to be feeling.

And the whole time she could not stop thinking about the unsettling possibility that she could be pregnant.

When her nail was dry, as flawless and perfect as the others, Laura let her go, giving her a swift hug. “Thank you,” she said warmly. “I’m going to go tell Tex right now.” She was grinning like a loon. “He’s going to be so excited.”

CHAPTER 28

Their second night, Breck met her at the door before she had knocked, drawing her inside with a flurry of kisses and he had undressed her, and himself, before Darla had managed a full breath.

In complete contrast to the night before, they made fast, desperate love right from the start, coupling against the closed door, then bent over the back of a low chair, then on the bed, and when Breck thought he might burst an important blood vessel somewhere, they came together, crying out and trying unsuccessfully to smother their sounds in kisses.

"I'll be back up to speed in short order," he promised, holding her loosely in his arms and breathing in the sultry smell of her. "Don't think the night is over yet."

She drew her hand along his face, and the way she gazed into his eyes made his chest feel too small for the heart inside it. "You are so amazing," she said softly.

Though Breck understood that she wasn't talking about sex, he fled to humor to avoid thinking too hard about how much they'd never have. "I keep telling Scarlet she ought to list me in the sales brochure. The resort would make bank, with a resource like me to pitch."

Darla giggled helplessly, and pinched him. "You're unbelievable," she scolded him. "I'm trying to have a serious *moment* here."

"I'm *serious*," Breck teased her. "Do you think 'sexpert' has a better ring, or should I go with something more humble, like 'Costa Rica's best lover?'"

Darla had to smother her laughter in a pillow.

"The copy writes itself," Breck said, putting his arms behind his head in a pose of satisfaction. "Come to Shifting Sands… and come and come and come…"

Darla decided that her pillow was better served smothering *him.* They wrestled and tickled and kissed until she was pinned helplessly below him and he could kiss and tickle her, and she could only squeak in protest and laugh until Breck had to crush her in his arms and try desperately not to admit that he could probably never be with anyone again after her.

"Tell me about these bracelets," he said, when they were lying quietly together again, slowly caressing each other, trying to memorize all their favorite parts while they could.

It was glowing faintly now, not the blazing light that had accompanied their frantic lovemaking earlier.

"It's… a fertility charm," Darla said hesitantly. "The dragonrunes say 'unbroken line.'"

Breck traced it with one finger. "It's not going to have much luck with me," he said. Something almost like regret settled in the pit of his stomach, though he'd never wanted children before, and he didn't feel like that had changed. But if *Darla* had wanted them…

Darla was giving him an intense look, one that Breck was having difficulty deciphering. "Are you… sure?" she asked. "Liam and I will never… but if I was… if I did, they'd all think… I'd have at least some part…"

Tears were welling up in her eyes, and Breck's chest felt like it might crack. "I couldn't if I wanted to," he said gently. "I've… ah… had a vasectomy. There are no swimmers in there." Discomfort made him ramble forward. "Not an easy thing for a shifter, and harder still to reverse, I might add. I never wanted to be the cause of someone else's burden, and I'd… what kind of dad could I be, really? I'm a waiter at an adults-only resort, and the bonuses around here haven't been great, and I never wanted to settle down… before."

He did now, he realized. He wanted to spend forever with the woman in his arms, and if that had included children, he couldn't have been happier about it.

It was very unsettling indeed.

Darla wiped her tears away fiercely and shook her wrist. "I guess these things are miscalibrated or something then. *Dragon* magic," she said in disgust.

"You wanted children?" Breck dared to ask.

Darla sighed. "Not really," she admitted, to his relief. "I just… thought it might help if I had something of yours… something to carry on with me…"

Breck swept her into his arms and held her tight as she wept, and, though he never would have admitted it, shed a few tears of his own into her hair.

CHAPTER 29

"It's not fair," Darla finally said, when her messy sobs had subsided. "It's not fair to *find* you and have to lose you."

Fair had never bothered her before, she realized. She had always had everything she wanted, been a part of an elite class—moneyed, a shifter… and not just any kind of shifter, but the end of not one, but two prestigious dragon shifter lines. And now that she was at the other end of the fair stick, it suddenly seemed to matter.

"Life is never fair," Breck agreed, stroking back her hair. "But at least we got *this*. Hey, you could write a best-selling memoir about it when you're old and no one cares. Three Nights at Shifting Sands with the Greatest Lover on Earth."

Darla squirmed to look at him skeptically. "I thought you were the greatest lover in the country. And wasn't it the *island* yesterday?"

"I get better with time," Breck said flippantly. "I'm probably better now than when you got here. I might even be the Greatest Lover in the Solar System by tomorrow night." He grinned at her, and wiped away the tears left on her cheeks. "But that probably wouldn't look as good on a book cover. They might think you were bragging."

Darla had to giggle, she couldn't help herself. "Sure, they'd think *I* was the one bragging," she teased him. "How do you do that?" she asked him, sitting up.

"It's a combination of skilled technique and great equip..." Breck started, but Darla poked him in the side.

"Make me laugh, I meant," she scolded him, smiling despite her best efforts.

He sat up with her, and cradled her face in his strong hands, smiling back at her. "I can imagine nothing in the world that I want to do more."

"Nothing?" Darla teased him.

He chuckled, kissed her, and amended, "Almost nothing."

If Darla was very careful, she could think only about *now*, about the feel of his hands on her face, the whisper of his sheets over her legs, the smell of him, the glow of his smile, the warmth of his kiss. She could be here with him in this moment, and be perfectly content.

Her stomach growled, and she blushed.

"Let me go get us a snack from the kitchen," Breck offered.

"If you keep feeding me, I'm going to have seven chins like Magnolia," Darla protested.

"We can all only aspire to be Magnolia," Breck said, giving her a kiss and sliding from the bed. She caught him before he could stand, with a second, deeper kiss that dragged him back down on her. When she finally released him, he grinned at her. "I will *not* be long," he promised.

Then he was pulling on a bathrobe and vanishing out the door.

Darla snuggled back down into his sheets for a moment, inhaling the musky smell of sex and sweat. Then she rose and explored the room restlessly. He had a private bathroom, and Darla smirked at her ruffled, naked reflection a moment before she splashed water on her face and tried to smooth back her hair. She prowled around the bathroom, stroking the lush towels and rattling his lone toothbrush in the holder.

A little chilled in the cooling night air, she decided to find a t-shirt of Breck's to put on, and returned to the disheveled bedroom. A wide, low dresser stood along the far wall, and Darla walked to it and pulled open the top drawer.

The sight that met her eyes froze her on the spot.

CHAPTER 30

Breck was dismayed to find that the common room was not deserted. Worse, most of the staff was there, and they were toasting Tex and Laura enthusiastically.

"I'm going to be a *dad*!" the bear shifter bartender exclaimed, throwing his arms uncharacteristically around Breck. "Come drink with us!"

"I'm… ah, right in the middle of something," Breck said regretfully. "But congratulations!"

"They can come celebrate with us," Jenny suggested laughingly. Several of the others echoed the invitation.

Breck's chest squeezed to realize that wasn't possible and Graham gave him a long, suspicious look as he shrugged them off with a stiffly smiling shake of his head.

"Are you the only one who *isn't* smashed?" he asked Laura bemusedly as he piled a plate with leftovers from the big fridge.

"Not by choice," Laura said, grinning foolishly and toasting with her glass of water.

"Congratulations," Breck said sincerely. "You guys thought about where you'll go?"

He regretted the question at once, as Laura's entire face fell. "I… I don't know," she confessed quietly, with a glance out of the kitchen to where the others were raucously placing bets on gender and shift form. "I guess we'll cross that bridge when we get to it."

"You'll figure something out," Breck promised more confidently than he felt. "Maybe Scarlet will suddenly develop a motherly streak and she'll open a daycare in the event hall. She did let Ally stay over Christmas." Wrench's eight-year-old niece had come in secret for safe haven at the resort and Scarlet had been unexpectedly generous about the infraction of the rules.

Laura giggled. "Can you imagine Scarlet with a baby? They're so messy and unpredictable. She'd want it on a very specific schedule, with very exacting requirements for its feeding and bowel movements."

"You, however, will be a wonderful mother," Breck told her warmly. "I hope you stay here so we can all spoil it rotten."

Laura smiled gratefully. "I'd really like that," she said wistfully.

"However it works out, it *will* be amazing," Breck promised.

Laura chuckled. "That's funny, that's exactly what Darla said."

"Darla?" Breck choked, surprised.

"Miss Grant. You probably haven't met her, with your serving ban, which by the way, is outrageous and everyone is furious. She's nothing like her mother and is really very sweet. Not at all your type, though."

"I don't have a type," Breck said automatically, wondering if it sounded as strangled as he felt.

"Well, you're not her type then," Laura said. "She's lovely, but very much a good little girl: shy, docile, meek."

Naked in my room, Breck thought in chagrin and amusement. *Screams like a siren when she comes… getting married to someone else the day after tomorrow...*

"Anyway, we'll find some creative solution," Laura said brightly. "No situation is impossible."

Except mine, Breck didn't say.

He suffered through another comically drunken hug from Tex,

who had returned to the kitchen to find Laura, and escaped back down the hallway to his room with the plate of food, listening to the happy din diminish behind him.

He was walking quietly and opened the door with practiced silence, then had to stand a long moment, gazing at his mate across the room in awe.

Darla was standing in front of the lamp, so that all of her edges were golden, and her hair was a messy halo of light. She was still naked, and every curve was perfect. She was all woman: plump breasts, round hips, the little roll of tummy that every woman hated and every man adored. Her arms were strong, but soft, and the line of her neck was an invitation for kisses. The mesmerizing sweep of her legs. The perfect tuck of her ass. The dimples of Venus in the small of her back.

Breck looked his fill, trying to memorize it all, to drink her in while he could, reveling in his exquisite thirst for her.

Then he realized that she was standing in front of his open top dresser drawer.

He must have made a noise of dismay; she turned sharply in surprise, cheeks flaming red.

This was it, then, Breck thought in chagrin. This was when she realized that he wasn't the kind of person she really wanted to be involved with anyway. Her wedding would look like a happy escape from an awkward situation now. She may not have been a virgin, but she checked off every box of the stereotype of virginal, and that drawer *definitely* wouldn't fit into her sheltered world view.

Braced for her disgust, Breck put the plate of food on the nightstand. "About that drawer…" he started.

"I want to try *everything*," Darla said breathlessly.

"You can just… wait, what?"

"I don't even know what some of these things are," she admitted shyly. Her cheeks were still red, but it was a delighted flush, and she was licking her lips with interest. "Will you show me?" She turned to reach into the drawer, coming up with a gleaming silver ring… the tamest of the offerings of the drawer.

Breck swallowed hard. "I'm afraid it's a little late for that one," he said, chuckling. "I'd need a cold shower or the funeral of a friend to get me into that right now."

He closed the distance between them and took it from her fingers, pausing to kiss her. "But we could probably make some other inroads on this drawer tonight…" He selected a silk blindfold and watched her smile widen.

CHAPTER 31

Darla was keenly aware of Eugene's eyes on her as they all sat for breakfast. Did he seem suspicious? Or just thoughtful? She had wondered at his easy acceptance of Liam's challenge. Though he'd growled and probably taken his temper out on his staff, he hadn't done any of the things that Darla had been afraid he would, like threaten Liam's family, or work harder to persuade her mother that Liam wasn't acceptable.

She had the uncomfortable feeling he was waiting for something, like he was still planning to spring some last minute nasty surprise on her.

She picked at her omelet until Alison kindly said, "It all kind of makes you want to elope, doesn't it?"

Darla, caught thinking about Breck, stared at her a startled moment before remembering her practiced laugh. "It would certainly be much simpler," she said with a smile. "So many names to remember! The left hand takes the chalice, the right hand takes the flower. Don't drop the chalice on the officiant. The train of the dress always in the right hand. I hope I keep it all straight!"

Everyone laughed, exactly as she meant them to, even Eugene, and the photographer who had been tailing them all morning snapped a dozen candid photos.

"It will be the shifter wedding of the century," Jubilee said in delight. "Did I tell you that I've already been contacted by two magazines who want to run a big photo spread on us? I'm still considering their offers, of course."

Darla smiled wanly as the others at the table congratulated Jubilee and the conversation once more revolved around her mother. Then she caught Eugene's narrow-eyed look again and had to fight to keep her face serene. Did he know? Everyone was giggling over her not-so-secret nights with Liam, but did he guess that it wasn't Liam's cottage she was sneaking away to?

Chef brought her a plate of fruit and rolls, giving her a private wink as she caught sight of a carved rose carrot and blushed. She smiled at him gratefully.

Liam, across from her, gave her a tolerant shake of the head and put his wrist with the bracelet that was starting to glow into his lap, much as she had hers.

After the lengthy breakfast and a parade of formal congratulations from all the new guests, Darla was permitted to escape to the spa, where she could find a few moments of peace with cucumbers on her eyes and let the drone of the other guests fade into the background.

Laura gave her the hot wet towel to remove the facial and shared a knowing look and secret smile with her.

Darla smiled back.

It was ironic that she felt more included in little staff secrets than she did in her own wedding.

"We're going to see that the event hall has been decorated according to my specifications," Jubilee said, interrupting the moment of peace to haul her away from the spa. "And that the dais is completed and the shelter for the vigil doesn't look too cheap. I want everything perfect to start things off tomorrow night."

She had a new audience for her lavish plans, so Jubilee was in her element, extolling in great detail how she had faithfully researched dragon custom to come up with the most authentic ceremony possible. Distant aunts, dragon socialites, and important people from the guest list that Darla had dutifully memorized the week before followed her, chattering about how lovely the resort was and admiring Jubilee's thoroughness. Darla trailed at the rear of the party, watching the photographer dart among them to snap celebrity shots.

CHAPTER 32

"Don't forget," Travis said mockingly. "The bunting has to be exactly 24 inches from the ceiling. From the ceiling, not from the trim." His imitation of Jubilee's voice was close enough to elicit laughter from the rest of the staff working on finalizing the decoration of the event hall. Even Graham, hauling flowering plants in big pots, gave a guffaw.

Breck, at the top of a ladder with the staple gun, a measuring tape, and a roll of the fluffy bunting, defiantly attached it 25 inches below the ceiling.

There, he thought sourly. *Wedding ruined.*

It was the last day before the ridiculous two-day ceremony began, and he was in knots. This was his last night with Darla. His last night before he lost her forever, and dammit, he needed to make it memorable.

But sex didn't seem like the answer.

He loved their bedplay and there was no doubting that she enjoyed it equally, but he felt like there was something more meaningful he ought to be doing. Something she would treasure forever.

"Wedding party incoming!" Jenny called urgently from the door. "They're crossing the lawn now!"

Staff scrambled.

Breck abandoned the staple gun and measuring tape, letting the bunting unroll, and scaled down the ladder hastily.

Travis hissed and pointed to the supply closet as he went to take Breck's place. "Back in the closet with you," he teased.

Breck skidded across the hall and wedged himself in with the chairs and tables and seasonal decorations, just as Jubilee marched in with Scarlet and a contingent of important looking people, gushing over the hall that she had spent the past several days criticizing.

Breck left the door cracked, so he could watch. Beside Jubilee, Alison looked like she'd rather be anywhere. The party with them was the sort Jubilee clearly moved with: rich, blooded society types wearing overstated jewelry and flashy silks.

Then he saw Darla, at the back of the party, drifting behind them looking as dreamy and serene as an expectant bride ought to look. Someone had put the sparkly bride sash on her again.

He watched as the party inspected the work in progress, giving noises of approval over the various decorations and speculating over improvements. Helpful suggestions were offered and Jubilee added a laundry list of things to Scarlet's list as the owner wrote them down without comment.

Darla's eyes strayed back to the far end of the room where Breck was watching from the storage room. After he had scanned the crowd to determine that no one else was looking his way, busy with Scarlet and the others looking at fabric swatches and candles, Breck edged the door open wider and blew her a kiss.

Her eyes opened wider, then crinkled into a helpless smile. It was her real smile, not her perfect society smile, and it gave her dimples.

To his delight, she trailed back to his end of the event hall as the others gathered to leave, ostensibly gazing up at the decorations being hung, but one eye for the storage closet. She stopped nearby, studying, to all appearances, the large Native Costa Rican artwork hanging on the back wall.

Breck pushed the door a little further open, watching the crowd. They were discussing the outdoor decorations now and starting to stream out. The rest of the staff was being dispatched to other tasks, or hauled along with the wedding party. Breck opened the door just a tad further and waved her in enthusiastically.

Smothering her giggles, Darla dashed into the tiny closet and threw her arms around him as he pulled the door shut. "I shouldn't be here," she whispered in his ear as he kissed her neck.

"I'm irresistible," Breck teased her, then she was kissing him back and all he could think was how right this was, and how perfect, even locked in a dark storage room, trying not to let the chairs around them rattle when they accidentally ran into them.

"I should get back to the group," Darla said reluctantly, slowing her kisses.

"Run away with me," Breck said impulsively. "Forget the wedding, forget them all. We could run away to the mainland and live footloose lives on the beach eating bananas and coconuts."

She gave an inhale. "We could steal the boat, sell my jewels…"

"Make love in the surf every night."

"Together," Darla said longingly.

"Forever…"

For one blissful moment, Breck let himself dream.

A tent on the beach, a simple life with his mate, Darla always by his side.

But guilt drew him back. "I couldn't do that to Scarlet and the resort," he said regretfully, remembering Graham's words.

"I couldn't do that to Liam and the home," Darla agreed with the same reluctance. "We'd leave a wake of terrible things behind us, and… I couldn't face my reflection in the mirror if I caused that kind of mess for my own happiness."

"One more night," Breck said mournfully. "We have one more night."

One last kiss, long and lingering, and Darla sighed. "I really have to get back. They'll wonder where I am, and if they caught us…"

"I know," Breck said, but it was another moment before he could let her go, leaning his forehead against hers in the darkness.

They cracked the door and surveyed the fortunately empty event hall, and then Darla slipped out, straightening her sash carefully before walking calmly across the room as if she had simply been enjoying a moment of quiet reflection before catching up with the wedding party.

Breck escaped from the closet when there were no sounds of the party returning and went back to the ladder. He climbed it slowly, looking down over the large room thoughtfully as he picked up the staple gun.

He wanted to give himself utterly to her, and lacking that, he wanted to send her away with some kind of token. Jewelry seemed pointless, and he had nothing that seemed appropriate. Tears in a bottle? Something from his drawer? A letter would surely be too incriminating.

Nothing was right.

He savagely stapled up the next gather of the bunting and scaled down the ladder to move it and put the next section up.

Anything of value he could give her, she'd be able to buy something twice as good for herself. He wanted to give her something… permanent. Something she'd always have. A tattoo, he thought wildly, though he had only the foggiest idea how those worked and had no desire to go ask Wrench for advice on the topic.

Something she couldn't buy… something she couldn't do…

Breck almost fell down the rest of the ladder as the perfect idea hit him.

CHAPTER 33

"Where are we going?" Darla asked in a whisper, giggling, as Breck, after a lingering kiss, did not draw her inside his room, but led her by the hand up past the hotel to the very top of the resort in the darkness. Her bracelet glowed faintly in the darkness.

"I've got a surprise for you!" Breck said mysteriously.

"Is it something from your drawer of goodies?" Darla asked eagerly, already feeling naughty for lurking through the velvet midnight.

"Better," Breck promised. Then he hushed her as they tiptoed past the entrance to the resort. Scarlet's rooms were dark. A small shape disconnected from one of the shadows in the courtyard, startling Darla.

"That's Tyrant," Breck said reassuringly near her ear. "Just a cat, not a shifter."

Tyrant followed them curiously to the door of the courtyard and decided against pursuing them out into the dark drizzle.

Past the low stone wall that marked the top edge of the resort, Breck led Darla to the parking lot, where the resort van seemed to be the only thing waiting for them.

Darla expected to get in and drive somewhere, but to her surprise, Breck took her around to the back of the van. "I'm going to show you how to change a flat tire," he said gleefully.

"In the dark?" Darla exclaimed. "In the *rain*?"

"Do you think flat tires only happen on sunny days?" Breck scoffed. "Of course not!"

He opened the back doors of the van. "Usually you'll find the tools in the back near the tire wells, or in a compartment under the floor here." He showed her where they were cleverly tucked and told her what each of them was.

Then he showed her how to remove the spare tire from underneath the van.

"I'm not really dressed for this," Darla said cautiously, as she meticulously brushed the dirt off of her pants after manhandling the spare to the side of the van. It had at least stopped raining.

"I suppose you will plan your flat tires for days you are wearing coordinating work overalls," Breck teased her.

Darla pinched him, which resulted in being kissed breathless. "Alright, I'll stop complaining," she laughed, drawing away reluctantly. "What do we do now? Do we lift up the van first? On that *jack* thing?" The contraption looked far too small and insignificant for the task.

"A good guess," Breck said. "But no—first you have to loosen the lug nuts. If you try to do that after you've jacked it up, you'll only rotate the tire."

He gave her the tire iron and turned on a flashlight.

"Righty tighty, lefty loosey," Darla said with determination, and she set to work.

The nuts gave her no trouble, between the tire iron and her own shifter strength. Breck stopped her before she removed them completely. "You don't want the tire falling off on you when you jack it up," he reminded her.

"I never would have thought of that," Darla confessed. "I'm so stupid."

"You are not stupid," Breck growled. "Don't ever think that just because you don't know something."

Darla looked up at him. It had stopped raining, but they were both completely soaked. In the faint, indirect light of the flashlight he was holding, he looked big and dangerous crouching beside her. Then he grinned at her and her heart did a little flip-flop in her chest.

"Isn't this fun?" he asked.

"You have a weird idea of fun," Darla told him, but she was grinning back.

It *was* fun, she realized, as Breck started talking about how the van was put together and why you always had to use a piece of the frame structure to jack it up. "Try jacking it up on the body out here somewhere, and it will just crumble when the weight of the van is on it," Breck explained. "That's just plastic. Your user manual will have advice about the best place to put a jack, or you can just look for a good solid piece of frame."

They crawled around in the mud and dirt once the jack was up and the tire was off, shining the flashlight on all the bits and parts of the underside of the van as Breck pointed out what they all were.

Her head spinning with axles and undercarriages and oil pans and mufflers, Darla finally stopped listening and simply gazed at Breck. He was explaining something about exhaust systems and oxygen sensors, and he was so animated and so dear that Darla could barely breathe.

It wasn't just how badly she wanted his touch, it was being with *him*.

It was the way he laughed, and the way he made her laugh.

It was the way he cared more about how people felt than what they thought of him, so entirely backwards from anyone else she'd ever known.

It was being dirtier than she'd ever been in her life, and feeling cleaner.

This was what having a mate could be, she realized, aching.

And she was so glad she'd been able to know that.

Breck glanced over at her and fell silent as he recognized that she wasn't listening. "You… okay?" he asked quietly.

Tears sprang to Darla's eyes. "Yeah," she said honestly. "I am."

He reached awkwardly over in the cramped space to touch her face gently with a dirty finger. "I know it's our last night. I probably should have... fed you chocolate-covered strawberries or massaged you with scented oils, or..."

"This is perfect," Darla said.

Breck's face was an art study of dramatic lighting, the single flashlight casting harsh shadows over the planes of his handsome face. "I wanted to give you something that you could take with you. Something no one could take away."

"You *did*," Darla said, meaning it in so many ways. She drew in a careful breath. "Let's go put that tire on."

They scooted out from under the van and Breck directed Darla in wrestling the spare tire onto the lugs but didn't once offer to help her. He showed her how to put on the nuts evenly using a star shape to keep it balanced and let her lower the creaky jack herself and give the nuts a final tighten.

"You did it," Breck said proudly as she stood back and tried to brush the worst of the mud from her damp pants. "You changed your own tire."

"I did it," Darla realized.

Breck was close behind her, and she shivered.

"Are you cold?" he asked, wrapping his arms around her.

She turned in his arm and looked up at him. The flashlight was wedged in the open van window, pointed at the tire, and it cast the barest light over his face, but her bracelet was glowing bright enough now to reflect in his beautiful eyes.

"You tell me," Darla murmured, rising on her toes to kiss him.

His arms tightened and he met her mouth with his own, hungry and desperate.

They made love slowly, removing damp layer by damp layer, kissing and caressing and whispering things that weren't promises.

She tried to memorize the feel of his shoulders, the way his hair slipped between her fingers, the taste of his mouth. She wanted the feeling of his hand in the small of her back to be imprinted there forever. She pressed her breasts against his kisses, wishing she could bottle the sensation it raised in the hollow of her throat and the pit of her stomach.

The creaky resort van was not the most luxurious of beds, but neither of them cared.

"I love you," she told him, as they joined at last, wedged awkwardly across the back bench. "I will love you forever."

He gripped her harder and made a wordless noise of grief and pleasure and agony that echoed the her own conflicted heart.

"I love you," he told her softly in reply. "I will, always."

It was the only promise they would ever get.

CHAPTER 34

The back seat of a van was not the most comfortable place for two people to lie. Breck's arm was wedged uncomfortably against a seatbelt and, every time Darla shifted in his arms, he got an elbow somewhere tender or a limb went numb.

He still wasn't willing to let go.

These were his last stolen moments with her.

It was nearly morning and she would be occupied for the entire day preparing for her wedding. Tonight she did a chaperoned all-night vigil and the following day, she would go through a ceremony and exchange vows with someone else, completing an iron-clad contract.

So he breathed in the smell of her hair and caressed the soft planes of her body and held her for all the moments he'd never hold her again as the first light before dawn crept up over the island.

"I'm so tired, but I don't want to sleep," Darla said, her voice slow and drowsy. "I don't want to miss a single second with you."

Footsteps crunched on gravel and they both froze.

"I'm telling you, I saw a light up here, they're sure to be this way."

"Mother," Darla whispered in panic, just as Breck realized

they'd left the flashlight on, wedged in the window to illuminated their workspace.

"It's possible she only went for a walk," Scarlet's voice said, sounding perfectly reasonable. Cold chills went down Breck's back. "She may have felt the need to work off some of her wedding jitters."

"Crap," Darla hissed, and she scrambled quietly off of Breck, accidentally kneeing him as she tried to navigate the darkness and the narrow space between seats.

Breck's explicative was no less quiet, but much less polite.

"Sorry!" she breathed.

"Working off wedding jitters isn't what I'd call it," Jubilee said clearly, right beside the van.

Then the van door was yanked open, and she said with triumph, "I told you that pervert was defiling my daughter!" She was holding the kitchen apron that Darla had tucked under her pillow in her hand.

Frozen in the act of reaching for their damp clothing, Darla and Breck stared back at Scarlet and Jubilee.

"So I see," Scarlet said, voice icy.

"Mother…" Darla started.

"*You* will be hearing from my lawyers," Jubilee said to Scarlet, ignoring her daughter. "And if you expect a penny out of me, you'll be informing me of his *immediate* termination."

"Mother…"

"I assure you he will be dealt with."

Breck swore the temperature dropped several degrees with Scarlet's words and there was a building feeling of pressure and power as her green eyes went from surprised to furious.

"Scarlet…" Darla attempted to plead.

She finally received her mother's attention. "Get your clothes on, you shameless hussy," Jubilee hissed. "You are getting married tonight, if Liam will still have you, and you will bless your stars that I'm not tossing all of you into the poorhouse over this."

Darla was pulling on the only clothing she could find and Breck managed to find pants while both women folded their arms and glared into the dim van. "Mother…" Darla protested again as she emerged from the neck of Breck's shirt. "Breck is…"

Jubilee, patience exhausted, reached in and took her firmly by the arm, dragging her from the van. "I don't care *what* disgusting thing he is. You are my daughter and you will do as I say."

Breck reacted to her manhandling with an instinctive growl and surged forward to defend his mate… only to be intercepted by a hand at his shoulder.

He had always known that Scarlet was strong; she had a simmering power that was hard to miss. But he had not expected her to be *this* strong.

Her grip was iron, absolutely unmovable against all of his considerable shifter strength. Breck would have needed to literally rip his muscles from her grasp to be free. His collarbone creaked in protest when he struggled briefly.

He could do nothing but watch as Darla meekly followed her mother away, casting him one agonized look back over her shoulder.

"I love you," she mouthed at him.

Then he was being frog-marched into Scarlet's office and thrust down into a chair.

She settled opposite him and glared across the desk. The early morning light starting to color the sky behind her made her hair look like fire. Green eyes snapped in her shadowed face. "Is this your idea of more *professional?*" she demanded. "Was there some *confusion* about what it is I hired you for?"

"Scarlet…" Breck's shoulder began to throb where Scarlet had gripped it as the blood returned.

"I have been very generous accepting your extracurricular activities these past few years, and I have been very tolerant about your *friendly* behavior. I assumed you understood and respected certainly boundaries, and knew the difference between a harmless vacation dalliance and sleeping with the daughter of a very important client."

"Scarlet…" Breck attempted again.

"She's getting married, Breck! You had your choice of bridesmaids, cousins, society dilettants, even groomsmen… and you had to sleep with the *bride*?" The air in the room was getting hard to breathe. "Did you think about anything before you let your libido loose? Did you once consider what the repercussions would be for letting your cock lead you around?"

Her fists came slamming down onto the surface of the desk and everything on it jumped several inches. "My insurance doesn't cover my staff being unable to keep it in their pants, Breck!"

"I'm not sorry!" Breck roared back.

The office was suddenly silent.

Even the insects and frogs were quiet. Scarlet's fury threatened to choke him from across the desk.

"She's my *mate*," Breck snarled into the stillness. "She's my *mate* and she's going to marry someone else because she's got a bigger heart than this whole island, and I got to spend three gorgeous nights with her and I am not sorry for a single second of it even if it means you toss me out on my ass and I never know a moment of happiness again."

The pressure seeped from the room like a waterbed with a slow leak and Breck might have been able to breathe again if it hadn't been for the pain in his chest.

"She's my mate," he repeated helplessly. "And we'll never be together after this."

If he hadn't expected pity on Scarlet's face, he certainly hadn't expected the sorrow that chased it. Her eyes softened and she let out a held breath like a sigh of wind.

One brave frog gave an experimental croak into the silence.

"Why are you letting her marry Liam, then?" Scarlet asked, and her voice was gentle and full of complexity.

Breck told her. He told her about the home that would go under, and about the formal challenge for Darla's hand that dragon custom required. He told her about the arrangement with Liam, and how he was keeping the odious Eugene from coming forward with his own challenge. He told her about the spell-protected hoard and the magical fertility bracelets.

"Unbroken line," he mourned. "I couldn't even give her children if she wanted them."

Scarlet, who had been listening intently, stood up abruptly. "I can't help you with that," she said. "Nor the challenge for her hand. But the home…"

Breck thought she was coming around the desk, but she stopped halfway, and turned instead to the wall. There was a giant map of Shifting Sands hanging there, half-shrouded in the vines that draped around most of the room and merrily snaked among the beams. "Did you ever wonder where the staff housing was supposed to be?"

"... Yes?" Breck had wondered many times. For many years, they had been housed in the hotel building intended as a budget option for the resort. As business picked up and those rooms were required for guests, it made sense to house the staff in the big mansions along the cliffs that had stood empty so long—too expensive for anyone to rent in whole, too awkward to subdivide into individual rooms.

But he didn't really see what that had to do with *his* dilemma.

Scarlet moved aside some of the vines, revealing a beach past the cliffs where the mansions stood, past the vegetable gardens that Graham snarled at anyone visiting. There was a cluster of buildings drawn there, a sprawling community of small and medium-sized buildings nestled between the jungle and a crescent of sand. It wasn't as grand as the rest of the resort—there were no pools or event halls or restaurants, by the looks of it, but it was nearly as large.

"Are those all cottages?" Breck asked, puzzling over the shapes of their roofs. "Was Shifting Sands supposed to expand over there?"

"Most of them are cottages," Scarlet said. She pointed at one of the larger ones. "This was intended to be a school." Breck could make out playground equipment, now that he knew what he was looking at. "This was a daycare next to it, a little general store, and ...a retirement home." Her finger touched a square building near the center.

For the first time that week, Breck had a stab of hope.

It *hurt.*

"Shifting Sands was intended to be a haven for shifters," Scarlet continued, almost to herself. "It was never meant to *only* be a luxury escape for those who could afford it. It was supposed to be a place for families to work and grow, with the resort to support it. A *safe* place, where they didn't have to keep secrets."

Breck wondered if he imagined the slight bitterness on the word secrets.

"Some of the foundations were poured," Scarlet said thoughtfully. "But the structures were never built." She shook her head. "Money. It would cost a lot of money that I don't have to finish them." She frowned, and gave Breck a piercing look. "How many shifters are we talking about in Liam's center?"

"A dozen, I think," Breck said, dizzy with the idea of it.

Scarlet gave a heavy sigh, letting the vines swing back down over the unbuilt portion of the map.

"I am undoubtedly facing an expensive lawsuit if you run away with Darla and this wedding doesn't go through. I don't think that a return of her deposit would satisfy Mrs. Grant, and I'm quite certain she would not be interested in paying the remainder of her bill. To say nothing of what she would do to our reputation, with her social clout."

She folded her arms and gave Breck a hard look. "We could house twelve people, if their medical needs are minimal and they don't mind sharing a few of the more basic cottages. But if Mrs. Grant takes offense, the resort—*my* resort—is on the line. What are you going to do about that part?"

Breck was silent, chewing over this unexpected turn. "The challenge," he said grimly. "If the wedding goes through exactly according to the dragon custom *she's* insisting on, she wouldn't have a leg for a lawsuit or for backing out of her bill. The challenge is *part* of that custom. She would *have* to let Darla marry me if I won, even if she wasn't very happy about it."

Scarlet's gave didn't waver. "*Can* you win?" She didn't sound as skeptical as she had every reason to.

Breck set his jaw. "I have to."

Scarlet sighed, and shook her head. "Mates," she muttered. "Nothing but trouble." But she said it with a curious warmth to her voice.

Breck stared at her, having to reevaluate her at every level. "You could just fire me," he said. "It would be the safest thing to do. Just send me packing on the next charter and let the wedding to Liam go on."

"Are you telling me how to run my resort?" Scarlet asked tartly.

Breck felt like a band had been released from around his chest. "Scarlet, I could kiss you."

Scarlet scowled back at him. "Hasn't kissing people gotten you in enough trouble today already?"

CHAPTER 35

"How could you?" Jubilee hissed as she dragged Darla away.

"Mother, he's…"

"Oh, don't you even try to defend yourself, you hussy," Jubilee said ferociously. "The way you've humiliated me. Did you think about your family once?" she demanded.

"I'm not…"

"You didn't think about *me* when you decided to ruin your own wedding," Jubilee insisted, her grip on Darla's arm painful as she wrenched her down the gravel path to their cottage. "You only thought about your own base needs, like some kind of common *animal*, like a rutting…"

Darla pulled her arm away fiercely and Jubilee stopped and stared at her.

"Breck is my mate, Mother. I will still get married if you won't compromise and let me follow my heart, but don't think for a moment that I will regret what I did while I could."

Darla was not sure she had ever seen a jaw literally drop, but Jubilee Grant's did exactly that.

"Are you talking back to me?" she asked in astonishment. "Are you *defying* me?"

Darla met her gaze steadily, not nearly as frightened by the act as she thought she ought to be. "Mother, of all the people in the world, I met the man that was absolutely, perfectly made for me, for my happiness forever. You have the power to let me be with him, to find my own happy ending. Will you let me? Will you release me from this engagement and give me your blessing and let me marry Breck instead?"

For one blissful moment, Darla thought that Jubilee might be reasonable, that she really would be able to persuade her mother that she deserved joy.

But at the sound of Breck's name, Jubilee's surprise turned to rage. "I would rather see you *dead* than married to that *deviant*," she spat.

Stunned by Jubilee's vehemence, Darla stepped back in alarm and the hedge behind her prickled her arms.

"If you married him, I would destroy everything you both loved," Jubilee raged. "I would see that this resort was bankrupted, that your precious retirement home was condemned, that Liam and his *entire* family were put out on the streets. I would take every penny you had, you would have *nothing*. You *are* nothing without me, you ungrateful brat, and you will get nothing from me unless you do *exactly* as I say."

Darla gazed sorrowfully back.

She had wanted to believe better of her mother, had harbored some small hope that somewhere deep under the society polish and the greed and the petty rages, there was a woman who still had a heart, who might believe in the generosity she tried to project.

"I will marry Liam," she said, drawing back sharply and holding up an imperious hand when Jubilee reached for her arm again. "I will be the obedient daughter you expect of me and commit myself to the contract you have laid out for me. I will spend two days declaring loyalty to a family that doesn't care a jot for my happiness and join one that at least *acknowledges* it." She went on swiftly when Jubilee might have spoken. "But do not ever expect me to apologize for finding a few moments of joy. I am not sorry for it, and I won't satisfy your shallow need for control by saying it was wrong."

Then she marched down to their cottage, Jubilee trailing in her wake.

Her mother would undoubtedly have had more to say on the matter, but Alison met them just around the corner, so close that Darla wondered if she had heard any of their conversation or Jubilee's terrible threat to have them turned out on the streets.

If nothing else, Darla would be marrying into a far better family.

"I understand we're doing photographs of the dresses today," Alison said cheerfully, choosing not to comment on the shirt that Darla was wearing, or the state of her muddy hair, or the simmering rage on her mother's face. Maybe it was still too dark for her to tell. "I... wanted to see if I could help you get ready."

"We don't need—"

"I would treasure your assistance," Darla said swiftly before her mother could finish. "You could help us select the jewels for my hair, if you please."

Alison glanced at Jubilee's angry face and back so quickly Darla doubted she had seen it. "I'd love to, Darla," she said at once.

"I'll be out of the shower before you can blink," Darla promised.

She took Breck's shirt in with her and spent the time that the shower was heating breathing in the smell of him and the feel of the fabric against her cheek. *Goodbye*, she thought achingly.

Not much later, Darla looked at her reflection at the spa dubiously.

The first of the three dresses was black, to represent (her mother loved to explain) the sorrow of loneliness before the final bond was made. It was embroidered in black and gold silk, textured painstakingly in swirls and patterns.

The second dress, the one she was modeling now, was white and virginal, representing (Jubilee reminded her with new dubiousness) the purity of the bride and the dedication to family and ancestral honor. The photographer had wanted to get it in early morning sunlight.

She certainly looked the role of virgin sacrifice, resplendently beaded in (her mother would tell anyone who would listen) genuine Swarovski crystal until she looked like a snowy Christmas display that someone had hung too much jewelry on. The photography lights they had set up made the whole thing look blinding.

The dress for the third day, hanging beside her, was blood red, representing sacrifice and obedience, and a dozen other things her mother seemed convinced she was incapable of.

I'm here, Darla wanted to say. *I'm sacrificing everything.*

But she knew her mother was still too furious—and too selfish—to appreciate exactly what she was giving up to go on with the wedding.

Jubilee was putting on a good show for the most important of the guests and the photographer, smiling her cultivated smile and giving her cultivated laugh. Darla wondered how she had never heard the falseness that filled it.

"Oh, perfect," the photographer said. "You give me a lovely smile now, and turn a little this way. Let's see the train up over your arm…"

Darla posed, forcing a faint smile that didn't reach her eyes, and wondered how much the photographs would reveal about her breaking heart. They moved out to the gardens for the coveted morning photos, and took shots until the sun was high in the sky.

Then, finally, it was time to model the final dress. "This one buttons up the front," she explained pointedly. "I can get into it myself." Her mother, on the phone with her psychic again, glared at her and left willingly. Alison gave her one last concerned pat and stayed with the photographer outside the spa while Darla went in alone.

The hard-won moment of privacy was interrupted by footsteps and Darla turned to see the only person she wanted to see less than her mother.

"Eugene," she said, completely neutral in tone.

"Don't you look… lovely," he said. "All ruby and ruin."

Though Jubilee had been utterly tight-lipped about Darla's indiscretion, he clearly knew what had happened. Had her mother told him? It didn't seem like she would, but here he was.

"What do you want?" she asked wearily, making herself not hurry to close the last of the ruby buttons.

"I have an offer for you," Eugene said, voice suspiciously silky.

"I'm not interested," Darla said.

"I think you may be," Eugene said, and his smile put cold chills down Darla's spine. "I'm offering you Breck."

Darla's suddenly-numb fingers fumbled the final button. She made herself draw in a breath. "What do you mean?" she said as neutrally as she could.

"It's true, isn't it," Eugene said, his smile widening. "It wasn't just that you slept with the waiter, you're actually in love with him. You think he's your mate."

Darla let herself think about Breck for one brief, happy moment. Her *mate*. She remembered his smiling face beneath the van, his face so unbelievably handsome and dear, lit by the flashlight, as he gave her something no one could take away. Her smile in Eugene's direction was accidentally soft and he took it as an invitation to step closer and settle one of the necklaces over her neck.

"Marry *me*," he said near her ear. "Tell Liam to step aside and let me challenge. Your mother will have to approve the marriage and I'll let you have your little something on the side. He can work in the kitchen, or the garden, or wherever the hell you want, and keep your bed warm on weekends. I get your hand, and half of your hoard. You can spend your half on Liam and his old people, if you want."

"That's not how dragon contracts work," Darla reminded him, shuddering away from his touch. "You know I wouldn't be able to cheat on my husband."

"I could get the contract changed," Eugene promised. "Maybe one that allowed divorce…"

Darla looked at Eugene in confusion. Did he think she was so naive that she thought that would be possible?

"You couldn't do that," she said in disbelief.

"I could," Eugene said confidently. "But only if you marry *me*. You marry Liam, and you're trapped forever."

Darla stared at him. He believed what he was saying. He somehow thought he had the power to make her mother amend the contract. And he thought that Darla would conclude that it was worth marrying him for that chance.

It only hardened her resolve.

She would marry Liam.

She would protect the rest home, and the resort. She would marry her friend and say goodbye to her true love, and it would be worth it.

She'd had more than she could ever have asked for; three nights of love, three nights of perfect happiness with her *mate*.

She could not quite keep the smile of satisfaction that spread out over her face. "Thank you," she said with all of her practiced serenity. "But I'm afraid I have a better offer." She turned back to the mirror and adjusted one of the necklaces so that it weighed at her neck a little less.

Eugene's expression in the mirror was briefly unguarded and ugly. "You'll regret that choice," he threatened quietly as there was a clatter of people returning at the door to the spa. "I will get everything I want anyway, and you'll wish you'd said yes when you had the chance."

"I did say yes when I had the chance," Darla replied with a smirk, equally quiet. "Just not to you."

CHAPTER 36

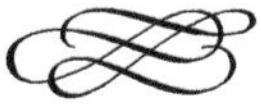

Breck skidded into the Den. "Where's Graham?"

Jenny and Laura, in perfect twin unison, pointed to where Graham was coming out of the kitchen carrying a plate loaded with leftovers for breakfast.

Graham scowled at Breck as he went to sit at the kitchen bar that separated the living area from the kitchen. "Which flower bed have you destroyed this time?" he asked crossly.

Breck ignored the gibe. "I need you to teach me how to fight."

That got him the attention of everyone in the common area. Tex, Travis, Bastian, and Wrench had been playing poker with chore IOUs, and they all folded their cards and put them down.

"What did you *do*?" demanded Laura.

"Shouldn't that be *who* did you do?" Travis teased.

Tex was shaking his head. "Jealous husband?" he guessed.

"Jealous wife?" Bastian speculated.

Graham gave Breck a long, knowing look. "What are you doing?" he asked gruffly.

"I'm getting hitched," Breck said merrily. "If I can avoid getting killed." He gave Jenny a crooked grin. "You might want to go talk to

Scarlet—there could be a big lawsuit pending, but we're hoping not. There's a loophole."

Stunned silence answered him.

"You're crashing the Trayvor-Grant wedding?" Jenny finally said in disbelief.

"You're getting *married*?" Bastian exclaimed.

"You're going to *fight* someone to get married?" Tex said incredulously.

"You're gunna die," Wrench said grimly.

Everyone turned to look at him and the big, tattooed panther shifter shrugged uncomfortably at the attention. "Assuming it's a fight to the death. Otherwise I guess he's just gunna get beat to a bloody pulp."

"I'd prefer to stay in one piece," Breck said, trying to convince himself this was still a good idea. "And I'm hoping you can help me do that."

"Darla's your *mate*," Laura finally guessed. "That's why you've been so *weird* the last few days."

Everyone made noises of mixed sympathy, surprise, and congratulations. No one seemed sure which was most appropriate.

Several moments later, Breck was standing on the back lawn, stark naked, with Tex, in bear form, demonstrating his charge.

"He's a lot bigger than me," Breck said, frowning at Tex's dramatically snarling face. The grizzly was probably ten times the weight of his leopard form.

"Cave bears are bigger yet," Graham reminded him grimly. "But you're a lot faster. And hopefully a lot smarter." He and Wrench were sitting on the picnic bench. Apparently, the imminent death of a fellow staffer excused having a beer with breakfast; they were both holding bottles and looked like nothing so much as the grumpy old critics from the Muppets.

"You gotta be meaner," Wrench advised sagely. "Go for his nose. Won't actually damage much, but it hurts like a sonnuvabitch."

"Might give you a chance to get through to something critical," Graham agreed.

"Don't waste time on the shoulders," Bastian advised. "Too much fat and fur to get through there."

Tex shook himself with a harrumph that sounded proud.

"Well, get out there," Graham said, waving the beer bottle. "Show us what we've got to work with."

Breck sighed and shifted, then, knowing that speed was his only real hope, darted forward and hit Tex's nose with sheathed paws like a boxer.

Tex reared up out of reach and casually back-handed him across the lawn.

Breck rolled back to his feet and circled around behind the big bear, trying to find any part that might be vulnerable. He considered hamstringing him, but even with unsheathed claws, doubted that he would be able to get through the thick fur. Would his jaws work? He didn't want to *actually* hurt Tex.

While he was wondering if he even *could*, Tex turned, a slow, ambling turn, and then gave an unexpected burst of speed for such a big animal, bowling him over and giving an odd little four-legged pounce at the end that completely flattened Breck.

While Breck was still wheezing and trying to catch his breath, Tex shifted back to human. "You okay? I… thought you'd get out of the way faster. Sorry."

He offered a hand to Breck as he shifted to human and helped pull him back to his feet.

"I'm more of a lover than a fighter," Breck gasped.

Wrench took another long swig of his beer. "He's gunna die."

CHAPTER 37

Midnight in the tropics was like a kiss; dark and damp and full of secrets that wanted to be told.

The ocean made a droning rumble on the shore below them and the night insects and frogs sang their songs of longing in endless rounds.

The vigil had been prepared for the usual overnight rain and there was a canopy above them that whispered with the intermittent drizzle. Twists of flowers and embroidered ribbons adorned each corner, reflecting the golden light of the circle of candles.

Darla sat cross-legged in her black dress across from Liam. A single candle sat between them, already half burnt down. Her mother and Alison were seated a short distance away, outside the flickering circle. Alison had sensibly brought a tablet and was reading an ebook that reflected cool light onto her face.

Jubilee had protested, but not strenuously; there was no language in the wedding description that prohibited such an item directly and Alison had pointed out that six hours of sitting out in the middle of the night wasn't going to be a whole lot of fun. Jubilee's restlessness suggested that she wished she'd had the same forethought.

After an hour or so, Jubilee stilled in her chair and a series of quiet snores made Darla put her hands over her mouth to stifle her giggles.

"You laugh so much more than you used to," Liam observed quietly.

"I had a good teacher," Darla said, with a wry smile.

"Are you sure you still want to do this?" Liam asked. "It's not too late yet. And I don't want you to regret all the things I can't give you. Don't do this out of worry for me, or for the home. That's not a good enough reason to trap yourself forever."

Darla smiled at him over the candle. "I'm sure," she said with unexpected serenity. "I've never been more sure. It isn't ideal, and it isn't fair, because *life* isn't ideal, and it isn't fair. But this is the best I'm going to do with the cards I was dealt, and it isn't like marrying you is any kind of… torture. Things could be better, but they could be a lot worse."

Liam smiled back. "As long as it isn't *torture*," he teased.

Darla might have teased him back, but her mother stirred and they were quiet until she settled back into a new position and her snores resumed.

"I can change my own tire now," Darla said with satisfaction. "And no one can take my memories away."

CHAPTER 38

Breck rubbed his arm ruefully as he walked through the dark resort, trying not to watch the spot of bright candlelight at the point where Darla's wedding was starting.

Tex swore he'd been easy on Breck, but the leopard shifter didn't need Graham's scowl, or Travis' worry, or Wrench's dire predictions to let him know that he hadn't showered himself in glory. He probably still had a black eye, though the scratches had at least scabbed over now.

Eugene, he reminded himself, was also a *cave* bear, an extinct kind of giant bear, not just a brown bear like Tex, and an experienced fighter on top of that.

Breck had no chance of winning a challenge against him.

He was going to have to switch tactics, if he was going to make this work, and he had his jaw set now. He wasn't going to let Darla go. He couldn't do it.

And if he couldn't do it with claws, maybe he could do it with his tongue, so to speak.

Eugene's cottage was just past the one Darla had shared with her mother and Breck gave the dark windows one wry glance as he passed.

Eugene opened the door at Breck's knock and greeted him with a smirk. "You look a little worse for the wear. I hear you got canned for banging the bride."

Breck reminded himself that he was there to try to avoid a fight, not start one. "Darla's my mate," he said frankly.

"So I've heard," Eugene said thoughtfully.

"I love her, and I want to challenge for her hand."

Eugene's face twitched and he didn't say anything.

"Promise not to challenge me," Breck said firmly. "And I'll give you half the hoard." Half the hoard was enough to fund a small nation for decades, based on the descriptions he'd heard.

Eugene leaned against the doorframe of his cottage, arms crossed. "Or I could challenge you and have the whole hoard, *and* Darla."

Neither of them had to say out loud that Breck had no chance of winning the challenge.

"It's a dragon contract," Breck reminded him. "You'd have Darla and no one else for the rest of your life. And she *despises* you."

He'd hit a sore spot, Breck realized, at Eugene's narrow expression. Eugene didn't want to be shackled to one person the rest of his life. He wanted all the prizes, and none of the responsibilities. Eugene must not have figured a way out of that part of the contract.

Breck almost smiled. There had been a time not long ago that he'd believed that being restricted to one person would be some kind of imprisonment. Then he'd met Darla, and now he wanted nothing more in the world. Settling down had stopped feeling like *settling*.

"The whole hoard," Eugene countered. "I want the whole thing."

Breck hesitated, thinking about the retirement home and Jubilee Grant's unpaid bill. Scarlet had offered to house the elderly shifters, but he didn't want her footing the expense or losing the resort. And he knew that Darla would forgive him for bargaining away the hoard for their happiness, but not at the expense of the people she loved.

"Darla still has a standard inheritance, outside of the hoard," Eugene explained, voice silky. "Human riches, enough to run a dozen nursing homes and buy a big house on a tropical island. Enough to keep a failing resort afloat. Her mother releases it to her with the wedding."

"But would she release it if Darla marries *me*?" Breck pointed out.

"I can see that she does," Eugene promised.

"How?" Breck knew that Eugene had pull with Mrs. Grant, but that seemed like a tall order.

"I've got her psychic in my pocket," Eugene said smugly, as if he could not help bragging about it. "I'll go make a phone call and Madame Nadine will have a convenient vision that you were the perfect son-in-law all along. Some messages from the crystals or whatever. She's very convincing."

Breck blinked at him. "That sounds… handy," he said neutrally.

Eugene had clearly expected more praise for his cleverness. "Well, can we make a deal?"

"Yes," Breck said promptly. "The whole hoard. It's yours. I promise."

Eugene smiled slowly. "Then I promise not to challenge," he said. "And I'll give Madame Nadine a call, right now."

Breck extended a hand, ignoring his leopard's instinctive hesitation; the big cat still considered this man their enemy. Eugene shook it.

"Well, you'd best get your beauty rest," Eugene suggested slyly. "You've got a big day tomorrow."

He was going to marry Darla, Breck realized, and Eugene no longer mattered in the slightest.

He walked back to his room in a daze.

He was going to marry Darla and he didn't have to ask her to sacrifice Liam's home or put Shifting Sands in jeopardy. He could get word to Liam, if not to Darla, and tomorrow would be the happiest day of his life.

Everything was falling perfectly into place.

CHAPTER 39

The litany of ancestors was the part of the ceremony that Darla had originally been most afraid of, and it was, when the time came, the easiest. The hours of practice meant they fell from her tongue, both of the noble dragon lines that she descended from. She said them slowly, very carefully and clearly, and was conscious of the audience that was avidly watching.

The most prestigious of the guests had arrived last; dragon nobility wearing riches and airs that would have made any other bride pale by comparison.

But Darla knew—mostly by her mother's look of smug satisfaction—that by appearance at least, she held her own. She was wearing all seventeen necklaces, an army of bracelets, and a tiara that would bankrupt a minor museum simply to insure. Her designer dress was alive with tiny crystal beads that made her gleam in the sunlight like an ice sculpture.

At the end of the recitation, there was a murmur of appreciation and the officiant, a gargoyle clergy from Rome, stepped forward and introduced Liam.

Liam's recitation was much shorter and simpler, and elicited no approval at all.

There was a moment of silence.

Darla looked across to Liam, who was looking back at her with a very peculiar expression indeed. One of his eyebrows waggled up and down.

She was still trying to puzzle out what he was trying to communicate when the pompous officiant announced, "Now is the opportunity for challenge!"

A terrible idea occurred to Darla.

She did not realize she was holding her breath until it left her in a rush when the audience behind her began to murmur in surprise and she heard Breck's voice, half-anticipated, half-dreaded.

"I will challenge."

Jubilee gave a muffled squeak of horror, but Eugene pulled her back into her seat when she might have stood in protest.

"You knew," Darla hissed at Liam as she turned in her twenty pounds of jewelry to watch Breck march down the flower-lined aisle towards her.

Her heart gave a lurch at the sight of him, so handsome and so graceful… and so dear. She wanted this more than anything in the entire world.

And she knew she couldn't have it.

"How could you let him do this?" she murmured to Liam.

Liam gave half a shrug. "How could I stop him?"

"You could refuse to concede," Darla whispered frantically. "You don't have to hurt him, just… step on him a little."

"I've got to give him a chance," Liam said quietly. "He said there was a plan."

Breck had drawn up to the platform. "I will challenge," he repeated, his eyes only for Darla.

"Are you sure?" Liam asked, pitched just louder than his whisper to Darla.

Breck's gaze flickered to his. "I'm sure," he said firmly. A cocky smile danced at the corner of his mouth.

"Don't," Darla begged quietly. "You know…" All her reasons crowded her mind: the home, Eugene, the resort, her mother's revenge.

Breck's eyes met hers. "I'm sure," he said, and he smiled at her. "Trust me."

He was so confident, so happy.

So trusting.

Darla remembered Eugene's last words to her the night before… his greasy self-assurance that he was going to get *everything* he wanted.

But before she could stop him, Liam was saying loudly, "I concede the challenge and her hand." He held out his wrist, as an afterthought, and the bracelet opened with a loud snap.

Darla looked down at her own, almost lost amid the jewelry she was wearing, but it was as solid and immovable as ever.

Liam held his bracelet to Breck, who closed it over his wrist. It gave a flare of light and clamped onto him almost eagerly, fading into an unbroken yellow gold, as Darla's did the same.

This invited a wave of speculation from the audience and Breck stepped to Darla as Liam moved back.

"I never want to let you go again," he said, taking her hands.

Darla was watching Breck's face when Eugene stood and shouted, "I will challenge!"

Breck's smile froze in surprise, and he jerked his head to Eugene. "You promised…"

Then Eugene was shifting, pieces of his clothing shredding from him as he charged forward without further warning.

"No!" Darla wailed, but Breck was already shifting and twisting away, drawing the fight away from her. She gathered up her skirts, full prepared to wade in and fight next to him, but her mother took an iron grip on her shoulder, holding her back.

"You can't interfere," Jubilee hissed as the contestant circled each other, Breck staying carefully out of reach of Eugene's big paws. "This is part of the dragon tradition."

"I won't marry him," Darla said furiously. "I won't do it."

"Madame Nadine foretold this," Jubilee insisted. "This is how the dragon line continues."

Eugene charged at Breck, who skirted the attack and dashed beneath the giant paw to circle behind the bear.

"I don't care about the dragon line," Darla said, watching the fight with her heart in her mouth.

Jubilee's eyes narrowed. "You don't marry by the dragon tradition, and you don't get the hoard, either," she reminded Darla. Eugene turned around, growling, to face Breck and charge again.

"I never wanted the hoard," Darla declared out loud. The wedding guests were all watching the battle raptly and ignoring the scene on the dais, many of them backing away with their chairs to avoid being caught up in it. "That was all *you* ever wanted. But I don't care about the money."

"You'll care about it when you're living in a ditch with the old people," Jubilee threatened, only marginally more quietly.

The retirement home. Darla quavered. Without her inheritance…

She steeled herself. She'd figure something out. Plenty of people managed harder things without the piles of money she'd grown up on.

But first… she concentrated on the fight with a sinking heart.

The leopard was obviously badly outclassed by the bear—out-muscled, out-clawed, and the giant bear had clearly been in battle before. Breck led him on a merry chase, able to slip under his big, heavy swings and out-maneuver his charges, but there was nothing he could do to attack in return. His claws were useless against the thick fur and heavy hide of a bear.

His luck dodging finally gave out as Eugene struck him with a heavy paw.

Darla heard a scream she wasn't sure was hers.

CHAPTER 40

Wrench's words rang in Breck's mind as he dodged another swing of Eugene's giant paw.

I'm gunna die, he thought, scrambling to the side of a charge and flanking the bear. If sparring with Tex had taught him one thing about bears, it was that they turned slowly. They charged forward surprisingly fast, and were brutally strong, but they cornered like the old resort van.

He was more outraged than afraid, despite his grim appraisal of the situation. Eugene had given his *word.*

And Breck had been dumb enough—or desperate enough, or hopeful enough—to believe it.

Even knowing it was useless, Breck tried to swipe at the bear's flank with claws fully outstretched.

As Tex had warned, he barely got through to skin; he drew blood, but not enough to do anything more than irritate Eugene, who turned to the best of his ability and charged as Breck darted around him again.

His only real hope was to tire the bear out, to wear him down, then get his jaws in somewhere critical. He went over the vulnerable places they had covered in practice—under the neck, crushing the windpipe or severing an artery... or his eyes. The list was painfully short.

And he had to do it without getting caught in a death-grip himself, or getting hit with one of Eugene's giant swinging paws, and he had to do it fast enough that Eugene couldn't get *his* jaws around one of the many, many vulnerable places on Breck.

The bracelet was not helping.

It was heavy and distracting, and kept catching Breck off-guard with its weight.

And every time it spun on his leg, Breck found himself thinking about the terror and longing in Darla's face as Liam snapped it onto him.

But what he should be thinking about was the bear facing him down, clearly growing more irate by the moment for his inability to put a quick end to the lithe leopard.

A paw the size of his head with claws like wicked knives sailed overhead as he ducked and he darted in to claw at Eugene's nose, mindful of Wrench's advice.

Eugene gave a roar of pain and, before Breck could retreat, struck him with his other massive paw.

Breck tumbled, end over end, as guests shrieked and scrambled back, and knew that the claws had drawn blood. He didn't have time to figure out where his pain was coming from; Eugene was facing him, and already surging forward into a charge.

His leopard drove him back to his feet, but there was no time to flank the oncoming beast, so he dashed straight at it, ignoring every bit of the sparring advice he had gotten.

At the last moment, he sprang, not at the bear, but over it, and his choice was so unexpected that Eugene's ponderous head lifted and snapped at him too late.

He landed on the bear's back, and dug in with all of his claws.

Eugene bucked and shook, trying to dislodge him, and Breck crouched closer and dug in harder. The bear snapped and tried to twist his head back to bite at him, but his neck was too short to reach.

With a sudden surge of hope, Breck swapped ends, as only a cat in a narrow space can, and pounced forward for Eugene's face, raking claws into the sensitive nose from behind and drawing them towards his vulnerable eyes.

As he dug into Eugene's face, he realized that he had forgotten one key thing.

With a roar of pain and fury, Eugene threw himself over on his side, and *rolled*.

Bones creaked and snapped under the massive weight of the angry bear and the breath was forced from Breck's crushed lungs.

Darkness was equal parts fur covering everything, and pending unconsciousness.

Breck! No!

He could hear Darla's voice in his head, like the sweet song of an angel.

Was this what dying felt like? It honestly hurt less than he expected it would; he could feel that his ribs had broken, and that the side of his head was hot and undoubtedly bleeding where he'd been hit by Eugene's claws, but the pain itself was distant and abstract.

I love you, he thought at the imaginary voice of Darla.

His wrist was hot, and hurt worst of all.

CHAPTER 41

Darla's wrist was on fire and she was chucking off her other bracelets, rings, and necklaces as fast as she could.

"You can't go out there," her mother said in shock and horror. "You'll violate the wedding rules! It's not custom!"

"Screw *custom*," Darla declared, and then she shifted. The hateful dress tore with a rain of beads and the remaining clasps snapped, scattering priceless jewels across the dais.

She leaped forward in her snow leopard shape, snarling and springing to the trampled grass where Eugene had pinned Breck.

The cave bear was not expecting her attack; his big head was rolled back as he writhed to crush the leopard beneath him. In a single heartbeat, Darla was on him, closing her jaws around his exposed windpipe.

The temptation was to crush, to kill, to protect her mate at any cost.

But Darla reined in the urge, and just pierced the skin, holding the windpipe in careful teeth and unmistakable threat. The hot taste of Eugene's blood was fiery, like alcohol.

He growled, the vibration rumbling up through her teeth, and Darla bit just a little deeper, growling.

Eugene whimpered then, and shifted into a man. "I yield!" he choked.

Darla closed her jaws just a touch further, taking shallow pleasure in the way Eugene choked and squirmed before she released him and stepped back. She shifted back to human and pushed him out of the way without a single second thought for him.

Breck still lay in his leopard shape, not breathing.

Blood stained the grass around him; thick scratches along the side of his lolling head were still oozing.

Breck! No!

Darla fell beside him, not sure what to safely touch without causing further damage. Her wrist was still on fire and both of their bracelets were glowing.

I love you, Darla heard in her head and she gave a howl of hope and desperation, taking his paw carefully in her hands.

The bracelet gave an explosive sizzle and Darla felt like all of the breath and energy was sucked out of her in one swift motion. She heard a weird crack of setting bones and the sound of Breck taking a labored breath. Her lungs hurt, and the side of her head stung. She closed her eyes against the shock of it and when she opened them again, there was a human hand in hers.

Breck was opening confused eyes.

He coughed, once or twice, and Darla fell, weeping, onto him before remembering that she might hurt him.

Her chest ached, but when Breck sat up and pulled her into his arms, it didn't matter.

"You could have died," she murmured into his perfect shoulders.

"You wouldn't let me," Breck said, wonderingly. He touched the side of her head and Darla flinched. His injuries were mirrored on her, and halved from what they had been.

Then Breck stared at his uplifted wrist in astonishment and Darla did the same.

Their bracelets were gone, replaced by a simple circle of dragonrunes like tattoos around their wrists.

Before they could speculate, Eugene was getting to his feet. "I won the challenge," he said, weaving drunkenly as he held onto his bloody throat. His nose was no longer bleeding, but was still striped with angry red scratches. "I won…"

Darla looked up at him. "*I* won the challenge, you idiot." She and Breck struggled up to their feet, clinging to each other. "And if I hadn't, I still wouldn't marry you."

"You have to!" Jubilee cried from the dais. "It's dragon custom!"

Darla lifted her chin. "I'm not a dragon," she cried in a ringing voice. "I'm a snow leopard, and unlike you, I'm not ashamed of that."

The wedding guests had retreated back from the battle, but had begun to cautiously return. Darla's statement caused a murmur of support; though Jubilee had invited all of the dragon elite that she knew, many of the guests were the more garden varieties of shifters, and most of them had grown tired of the elite dragon attitudes of Jubilee and some of her more arrogant guests.

"If you don't marry according to the custom, you won't get a penny of your inheritance," Jubilee snarled in warning, voice pitched not to carry to their audience.

"I hope the hoard rots," Darla snapped back, as loudly as before. "I don't want your money, and I don't want your blessing."

Eugene was spitting angry. "You have to marry me," he roared. "If I can't have you, no one will. Even both of you can't win against me."

But before he could shift, Liam was stepping forward. "If this is no longer a challenge according to custom, I have no reason to stand back and let you harm my friends," he cautioned with a frown.

"Yeah," another voice added behind them. "We're going to have to back them up, too."

Darla turned. Half the staff of Shifting Sands was ranged behind them, a motley crew in crisp resort uniforms with expressions ranging from amusement to anger. Lydia from the spa was there, arms crossed, and Conall, with Gizelle peering out from behind him.

Even Eugene was not foolish enough to take all of them on.

"You'll be unhappy," he predicted. "You'll be poor and miserable."

"Did your psychic tell you that?" Breck asked with exaggerated pity. "No wait, did you *tell* your psychic to tell you that?"

When Darla gave him a puzzled look, he explained, "He's been feeding your mother ideas through her pet psychic."

"That's preposterous!" Jubilee said in outrage as Eugene started to sputter.

"Is it?" Breck asked. "Check his phone. I'm sure you'll find a familiar number with lots of calls there."

"You dropped it when you shifted," Liam said helpfully, holding the phone in question aloft.

Eugene leaped up onto the dais and tried to snatch it away from the dragon shifter while Jubilee protested his innocence with obviously increasing doubt. Liam held it away, a glint of mischief in his steely eyes.

Darla laughed helplessly. "That explains so much. He just had to have Madame Nadine predict something he could then orchestrate, or pretend to see some private bit of information he'd fed her."

Jubilee looked absolutely furious and Eugene tried more desperately to get his phone from Liam, who was still resolute about holding it out of his reach.

"You've played me like a fool," Jubilee said softly.

"You *are* a fool," Eugene spat, giving up on his phone. "None of this would have been necessary if you had just given me your daughter's hand when I first asked."

"You didn't want my hand," Darla said in outrage. "You only wanted to get your hands on the hoard."

Eugene gave her an ugly leer. "I would have enjoyed having my hands on you, too, you cold b—"

Before he could even finish, Breck had leaped up onto the dais, and in one swift move, punched him in the nose.

Darla's knuckles stung from the blow.

Eugene staggered back, nose streaming blood again, and roared in anger and pain.

An authoritative voice cut through. "As satisfying as I'm sure that was, I think that there has been enough fighting for one wedding. Wrench, Bastian, Eugene appears to need medical attention. Please give it to him *elsewhere*. Travis, Graham, if you wouldn't mind cleaning up the brawling pit. Breck, a word. Mr. Trayvor, Mrs. Grant, Darla."

Scarlet, despite the chaos around her, looked as if she had just stepped out of the spa… and found something distasteful on her shoe. As Eugene quit the scene in ungraceful capitulation with Wrench and Bastian, Scarlet drew the primary wedding party onto the back of the dais out of easy earshot.

"I'm sorry," Breck started. "Eugene promised me he wouldn't challenge. I really did think that I'd be able to pull this off without risking the resort."

Scarlet looked at him sourly. "And I suppose you wouldn't have challenged if you hadn't had that assurance."

Breck grinned, not at Scarlet, but at Darla, making her heart rise in her chest. "Oh, I probably would have had to anyway."

Darla shook her head at him hopelessly, smiling despite herself. Then her smile faded. The home. "Mother, about the retirement home…"

Jubilee knew an opportunity when she saw one. "Marry *Liam*," she said firmly. "We can salvage this wedding and you can save your precious nursing home and the hoard will be unlocked for you."

Darla shuddered. "Mother, please…."

"I don't want to disown you," Jubilee said threateningly. "Don't force my hand."

Darla felt like she had never known her mother, like this was a woman she had never imagined could exist beneath her society mother's glossy veneer.

"I am not marrying Liam," Darla said without hesitation. "I am marrying my mate. I am marrying him without your blessing, without dragon custom, because I would not want your blessing tainting my union with him. You force *my* hand, mother. The hoard will be locked forever and you won't have it either. I will find another way to save the home, because I have no desire to be beholden to you. *Ever*."

She looked at Liam. "I have some clothing, a little jewelry. It's mine, and I'll sell it to protect the retirement home as long as possible."

Jubilee took a step backwards at her defiance, confused and shaken. "You'll regret this," she promised.

Darla looked at her curiously. "No, I don't think I will," she said thoughtfully. Breck slipped his fingers into hers and squeezed.

"Well, *you* will," Jubilee said, rounding on Scarlet furiously. "This is *your* fault, your employee who did this. *You* will regret this. I'll see this resort in ashes. I will sue you into the earth and see that your resort is smeared in every major shifter publication. No one who is *anyone* will ever come here again."

CHAPTER 42

Twice in as many days now, Breck had seen Scarlet get angry.

It was no less impressive the second time, even if it wasn't directed at him this time. Her green eyes were hard and brilliant and her red hair seemed to crackle with energy. The air around them grew thick and hard to breath. Jubilee, perhaps recognizing her mistake, took a second step backwards.

"Do you know what *I* regret?" Scarlet snarled. "I regret letting you run roughshod over my staff. I regret biting my tongue while you treated your *family* like chattel. I regret allowing you to disparage your less fortunate guests by constantly reminding them of your supposed generosity and superior bloodlines. I regret letting you take a contract for service as a license for abuse. I regret pulling my best waiter from service because you were a shallow, bigoted fool."

"You can't talk to me that way," Jubilee gasped, retreating another step. "You can't!"

"Because I'm not a *dragon*?" Scarlet seemed to bristle and, for a moment, Breck actually thought she was going to shift on the spot.

Was she a dragon? No one knew. Maybe she would *eat* Jubilee, he thought gleefully.

There was a moment of tension, Jubilee too terrified to protest further, then Scarlet turned away dismissively and looked at Liam, who blinked several times rapidly at her sizzling gaze but held his ground. "Liam, you may relocate your retirement home and any of your family who need shelter to the resort at your convenience. I expect a complete list of the residents and any of their special needs, as well as an accounting of their personal effects for insurance purposes. We'll discuss the details tomorrow."

Then Breck took the brunt of her flinty stare. "Are we still having a wedding, Breck?"

"Yes," he said immediately. Then, when Darla's hand tightened in his, he turned his gaze to her. "If you want to," he added at once. "I think that technically, you won the challenge, so you probably ought to decide."

Darla's blue eyes got big and Breck wondered if anyone had ever asked her to make her own choices about her life. "Yes," she murmured hopefully. Then she drew herself up taller and met Scarlet's eyes bravely. "Yes," she repeated. "It would be a terrible shame to let this all go to waste," she said practically. "But it won't be *this* wedding."

To Breck's surprise, nearly all of the guests—especially on Liam's side—stayed, helping the Shifting Sands crew put the chairs back in order and right the fallen pots of flowers. Only a few of them retreated from the wedding field. One of the dragon guests did the honor of removing the fuming Mrs. Grant from the resort rather than forcing her to wait for the charter plane.

The gargoyle clergy politely removed himself from consideration for performing the wedding before he could be requested, but he did so graciously. Scarlet offered just as graciously to perform the ceremony, and Darla solemnly accepted that.

Darla's dress was beyond repair, which seemed to give her great satisfaction, and Breck's suit was no better off.

"We could just get married naked," Breck suggested cheekily. "Give everyone one last view of what they'll never get now."

But Darla punched him in the arm, then rubbed herself in that same spot ruefully. "I am going to wear clothing at my wedding, and it will be clothing I choose. And I really want to brush the blood out of my hair. You can wait another hour after all of this, can't you?"

Breck crushed her into an embrace. "I would wait a lifetime for you," he declared seriously.

And it was worth the wait, he decided, watching her walk down the aisle in a bright yellow sundress, the setting sun giving everything a rosy light. Liam was at her side to give her away and Chef was standing at Breck's side. "To make sure you don't run," Chef said with a knowing laugh, but Breck had no interest in running anywhere but Darla's arms.

The ceremony was entirely made up on the fly, with a wedding party comprised of anyone who wanted to be in it. Liam's mother was delighted to be asked to help with a candle-lighting ritual that they came up with on the spot and his grandmothers offered to serve food at the reception.

"We may not know as much about dragons and all the high falutin customs that Mrs. Grant wanted," Alison had said warmly as Breck took his spot on the dais. "But we *know* about mates and Darla deserves all her happiness."

As Conall struck familiar notes of a wedding march, Gizelle capered down the aisle in front of the bride and Lydia and Laura walked more sedately, holding flowers.

Scarlet gave a simple, standard civil opening speech and they lit candles together. "Do you have vows?" she asked then.

Breck, gazing at his bride, realized he should have written something. "Yes," he said anyway. "Darla, I vow to love and treasure you for the rest of my life." This would have been an appropriate place for flowery vows and sweet nothings, but Breck felt that they were all insufficient compared to the promise in his heart.

Darla smiled back at him, her face perfectly happy as Breck had only had glimpses before.

"Breck, I vow to cherish and adore you until end of all things."

"Are there rings?" Scarlet asked.

"No rings," Darla said with a shake of her head. "Just these."

She held up her wrist and Breck mirrored her. The dragonrunes glowed briefly and they clasped hands.

"By the power vested in me by the nation of Costa Rica, I declare you husband and wife," Scarlet said solemnly. "You may kiss."

Darla smiled as he slowly gathered her up into his arms. "You're going to be dramatic about this, aren't you," she guessed quietly, amusement crinkling her face.

"I do have a reputation to maintain," Breck reminded her.

Then he kissed his bride, deeply, devotedly. It was gentle at first, and the audience applauded politely. Then he wrapped her tighter and kissed her harder, and she melted into him. By the time he finally released her, with a tapering series of butterfly kisses, she was panting and weak-kneed and Breck was grinning and breathing just as hard.

There were whistles, then, and more enthusiastic cheers.

"Get a room!" Tex called.

"It's a good thing they waited and got married with clothes on after all," Travis said in a stage-whisper.

CHAPTER 43

Darla had expected to hate her wedding reception.

The food would be too rich, the music too staid, the people too stiff.

But the reception she got was filled with bemused laughter and cheerful music that occasionally ended in, "Gizelle, come back!" as the gazelle shifter forgot she needed to hold onto Conall to allow him to hear his fellow musicians.

A siren sang several songs, the magic in her voice like a caress, and Darla danced around the room in Breck's perfect arms until Liam stole her away and Lydia took a reluctant Breck for a turn around the floor, braving the scowls of the giant tattooed man whose primary job seemed to be terrifying people.

"I'm really happy for you," Liam said honestly, as they danced. "I know it didn't work out perfectly, but you and Breck… you belong together."

Darla had been trying not to watch Breck too obviously, and she looked earnestly back at Liam now. "You have been so good to me," she said sincerely. "And I'm sorry you got dragged through so much for so little."

"It's not as little as that," Liam said generously. "Shifting Sands

Resort will be a bit of an upgrade from the warehouse on Seventh Avenue."

"And no one here will care if a mammoth gets unexpectedly loose in the night," Darla chuckled.

"Graham might," Liam suggested. "If he ends up trampling the gardens."

Darla let Liam turn her and returned to arm's length. "Do you think you will ever find your own mate?" she asked. Then, thoughtfully, "Would you want one?"

Liam looked down at her a little wistfully. "I'm asexual, but I can't say I don't wish I had someone who understands me the way Breck understands you. It's just that the chances of meeting someone with the same *expectations* are passingly slim."

"What are the chances that mates ever meet each other?" Darla challenged. "I wish this for you, Liam. With all my heart I wish it for you."

Liam pulled her into a warm, grateful embrace as the music ended. "You deserve your happy ever after, Darla. I am so glad you got it."

Darla kissed him on the cheek. "Thank you for all you did for me. This could never have happened without you."

"I've already punched one person today, do I have to do it again?" Breck's eyes were dancing jealously as he reached for Darla's hands, but the look he exchanged with Liam was all amusement.

Liam politely handed Darla back to him. "I wouldn't want to put you to the effort," he said archly. "Nor harm Darla's knuckles again."

"That really did hurt," Darla laughed. "Please don't punch people if you don't have to."

"That was just the excuse I was looking for," Breck said merrily. "I'll have to clear my busy schedule of punching people, now."

For a long glorious song, she circled the room in her new husband's arms, marveling at the idea that he *was* her husband, that she wasn't settling, that it wasn't temporary, or something that had to be kept secret.

The resort staff certainly seemed to accept her with open arms; if they had been friendly before, they were like family now that she was one of them instead of merely the meek daughter of a high-maintenance client. When the song ended, Tex trotted her around for another song and gave her all the sage advice that three months of marriage had taught him. She congratulated him on the imminent enlargement of their family and he looked dazzled and turned pink with pleasure.

Next, Travis took her hand for a high energy salsa that left no opening for conversation and before she could look around for Breck afterwards, Chef had claimed her hand for something more staid.

"Thank you so much for everything," she told him sincerely. "I thought I'd try helping in the kitchen if you approve. Breck taught me how to wash dishes and I'd like to know more about cooking."

"You'd be very welcome in my kitchen," Chef told her kindly, and it didn't feel like the kind of polite society lie that Darla was so used to. "Can you carry a tune?"

Darla looked at him in surprise. "I had three years of private singing tutors," she confessed. "They said that I'm not hopeless, but that I'd never have a career of it. Not that my mother would have approved of a *career.*"

They compared favorite songs eagerly and at the end of the music, Chef enfolded her in an affectionate, fatherly hug and walked away humming the introduction to a French opera they both knew.

Graham, the grouchy-looking landscaper, took her on one grim, silent trip around the room, and deposited her back at the bar without a single word.

CHAPTER 44

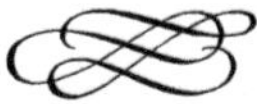

Breck jealously watched as the rest of the staff thwarted his attempts to steal Darla back for himself and found himself on the side of the floor next to Liam, who was clearly feeling uncomfortable about the looks being cast at him by a gaggle of giggling housekeepers. They seemed to think that being a jilted groom called for certain comforts.

"Want to dance?" the leopard shifter asked Liam, as Travis stole his wife from a beaming Tex.

"Will it give the wrong impression?" Liam asked cautiously.

"What's the right impression?" Breck countered.

"Good point," Liam agreed, and they stepped out gracefully. The dragon shifter was happy to take the lead he was accustomed to and Breck cheerfully let him.

"Do you think you'll ever find your own mate?" Breck asked, head swiveling to watch Travis turn Darla.

"Funny, Darla asked me that just now, too," Liam said, his mouth curling up in amusement.

"What did you tell her?"

"That I like the idea of it, and how happy it's clearly made her, but I'm not holding my breath," Liam said matter-of-factly. "Mates seem to have a pretty driving central need… and that's not something in my repertoire. Maybe it's not possible." There was a hint of regret in his voice.

"Do you think that would change, if you met the right person?" Breck had to ask curiously.

"Did meeting Darla make you straight?" Liam pointed out.

Breck furrowed his brow thoughtfully. "I can't think of anyone but her," he said slowly. Then he tried to imagine Darla as a man, and what they might do together. "Nope, definitely still bisexual," he grinned.

"You're kind of baffling," Liam said, shaking his head.

"It's mutual," Breck agreed without judgement.

But he realized that it didn't mean anything about their ability to be friends, and, differences aside, he suspected he'd have a strong friend in this man. He was already grateful for the dragon shifter's friendship with Darla, and admired his generosity with the rest home.

I told you he wasn't our rival, his leopard reminded him.

"I think there's someone out there for you," Breck said confidently. "And this island sure seems to have a way of introducing mates to each other. Maybe they'll show up at Shifting Sands someday and sweep you off your feet."

"Without the sweeping, maybe," Liam said.

The housekeepers were looking pouty and disappointed as they returned to the edge of the dance floor, and Chef stole Darla before Breck could cut in, grinning at him over her shoulder.

Alison was standing there and Breck gave her a courtly bow. "May I have this dance?" he offered.

"I'm not very good," she warned him, but Breck gave her his most charming smile and insisted.

She was better than she had given him reason to believe and became comfortable enough with Breck's lead that they could even converse.

"I owe you an apology for stealing your son's wedding," Breck said sheepishly.

"Pish," Alison said smartly. "You and Darla were clearly meant to be and I'm not sorry not be saddled with Darla's mother for family."

They laughed together over that, and Breck asked cautiously, "Did you... know that theirs was a marriage of convenience?"

"Oh yes," Alison said easily. "I knew Liam was asexual before I knew he was a dragon shifter and he was quite frank with me about their arrangement."

"He says it was a big surprise for you when he first shifted," Breck said leadingly, suspecting a humorous story he could use as leverage later.

Alison laughed. "You know what a teenager's bedroom looks like? Perpetually messy and filled with stuff? Now imagine a very confused dragon stuffed in there, folded floor to ceiling in shimmery coils, with no earthly idea how to get back to human form. We were *expecting* something a lot smaller."

Breck coaxed the story from her, and they laughed together. "It was a crash course in everything about dragons," Alison admitted, as the song came to a close. "Mrs. Grant went on and on about how she researched dragon custom, but she can't hold a candle to the months of study we went through figuring out how to cope with a several-hundred-foot flying serpent who couldn't put a toilet seat down to save his life."

Breck would have laughed, but he was watching Darla being grimly shuffled to the bar by Graham, and he was utterly caught up in a wave of confused emotion: she was so utterly dear to him, she filled him with longing and fulfillment all at once. He wanted to show her off and hide her away to be only his. He wanted to spend forever unraveling the complexity of everything he felt for her, and he couldn't believe that she was *his*.

He was busy watching her instead of minding his feet and he stumbled into Alison before he realized he was still dancing and the music had stopped. "I'm sorry," he said sincerely.

"Your wrist is glowing," she pointed out.

The dragonrunes were pulsing with light and Alison frowned at them thoughtfully.

"Unbroken line," Breck said, rubbing it. "It never did make much sense." He hadn't even been thinking about sex.

"Is that what Mrs. Jubilee Grant said?" Alison scoffed. "Amateur. That part doesn't say unbroken *line*, that says unbroken *bond*."

Breck looked down at it and then across at the gleam on Darla's wrist across the room. She met his gaze through the dancers and smiled sheepishly down at her wrist.

Someone was clinking on a glass in the silence from the music and Alison gave Breck a little push to start walking to Darla as the others parted between them.

The touch of her fingers as they met in the center of the floor was like magic and the marks on both their wrists gleamed like moonlight.

Scarlet was standing with her glass raised and she gave everyone time to find their drinks and join her in a toast.

"We are celebrating a union today," she said warmly. "Even if it's not exactly the union we were planning to celebrate."

The staff and guests laughed.

"Leave it to Breck to steal the *bride*," Travis teased.

Everyone laughed harder.

"Yeah, but then he went and got *hitched* to her," Tex reminded him, sounding horrified.

"Careful, cowboy," Laura warned him with laughter in her voice. "Nothing wrong with doing the respectable thing."

"As if Breck will ever be *respectable*," Bastian laughed. He was in a much better mood since his parents had bailed with the most elite of the dragon shifter society guests.

Scarlet cleared her throat and the joshing died down. "It isn't every day that true mates meet each other, and when they do, it is always worth rejoicing. I am so happy that we could share this day of joining with these two people and wish them all the best in their continuing lives together as one."

Breck kissed Darla to applause and cheers.

"Speech, speech!" Travis prodded.

But Breck wasn't done kissing Darla, and she wasn't done with him, her arms around his neck and her lush body close against his.

"I think that's as much of a speech as we're getting," Scarlet observed dryly. "Cottage fifteen, you two. The rest of you, we'll clean this up in the morning. Please enjoy the rest of the food and take a centerpiece back to your room if you desire."

Breck finally stopped kissing Darla and took her hands in his own. "Let's go somewhere without a peanut gallery," he suggested.

"Cottage fifteen sounds nice," Darla agreed breathlessly.

The night outside was quiet after the noise and merriment of the event hall and Darla's hand in his was warm and perfect. She leaned her head against him as they walked past the abandoned wedding aisle and through the garden towards the pool and the cottages beyond.

"This morning I thought I was never going to see you again," she said softly.

"I thought that very same thing when Eugene rolled over on me and broke all my ribs," Breck confessed. They were still sore.

"Did I fail to impress upon you what a terrible idea it would be to challenge?" Darla scolded him.

Breck stopped walking and faced her. "Eugene swore he would let it stand," he said. "But even if he hadn't, even if I was hopelessly outclassed as a fighter, even if Wrench had been right and I was utterly doomed, I *had* to try. I wouldn't have been alive without you, Darla."

She gave a little whimper. "I know. I *know*. I wasn't alive before I met you."

"I could wish things had gone a little better," Breck admitted wryly. "But I'm not sorry. I'm going to spend the rest of my life loving you, and that's the happiest ending I can imagine."

Darla answered with her mouth, stretching up to kiss him hungrily and run her fingers through his short hair. Breck gathered her into his arms and drew her down to a garden bench that waited beside them. It was much, much later that they made it to cottage fifteen… and Breck knew that there would be music to face from Graham by the time they were done.

HER HELLHOUND BODYGUARD

This story requires an explanation!

At the end of March 2020, two of my most popular series were poised on the brink of hellhound characters taking the stage, and fans were eagerly anticipating them. A reader posted in my Facebook group that they were waiting for ALL the hellhounds, and made up some spoof hellhound titles, including a Shifting Sands release. The timing was too good to pass up—I threw together a cover and a fake description for Tropical Hellhound's Heartache, and posted them for April Fool's Day.

But the joke was entirely on me, because then I had to actually write it…

(This story stands alone and does not significantly spoil any of the Shifting Sands Resort series. It occurs near the end of Tropical Leopard's Longing, just before the epilogue.)

"I'll be *fine*," Christy Ryan protested. "There's no reason to change my plans at this point."

She was packing with one hand, holding her phone to her ear with the other. How many pairs of shorts would she need? The place was clothing-optional...did she really need *any*? She threw in her favorite pairs.

"Someone tried to kill you, Christy! *Kill you!*" At the other end of the line, her sister Betsy was nearly hysterical. But Betsy was often nearly hysterical—it was hard to take that seriously. "Maybe you should go somewhere...safer. Or stay here!"

"Am I really going to be safer if I stay *here*?" Christy asked. "It's not like the police are going to offer me witness protection anywhere but in jail."

"You should have *some* protection," Betsy said firmly.

"I already packed condoms…" Christy said slyly.

Betsy laughed weakly. "That isn't what I meant."

"I know. Look, getting out of town is the smartest thing I could do right now. Things will cool off." Christy hesitated over her shoes. Sandals, for sure, several pairs of heels; Shifting Sands Resort looked *fancy*. She threw in her favorite tall boots. Anything else that she needed, she could buy.

"Maybe you should take a bodyguard," Betsy said pointedly. "What if they follow you? You could have picked an easier mark, couldn't you?"

"It *was* an easy mark," Christy said defensively. "It's not my fault that Slippery Mick was going for the same prize."

"I don't want to know," Betsy sighed. "I never want to know. Just promise me that you'll be careful. And I wasn't kidding about a bodyguard."

"I'm going somewhere perfectly safe," Christy assured her, sighing. She loved her sister, but sometimes she wished that Betsy was as adventurous as she was; she'd always wanted a partner in crime. "It's an exclusive resort, on a remote island off of Costa Rica. I have to take a private charter from Mexico City to get there. I can't imagine being safer! I'll pick up a new burner phone on my way out and give you a call once I'm there."

Betsy didn't seem particularly reassured, but she finally let Christy hang up and get back to packing in earnest.

~

Lorenzo hated answering phones.

There was no hell worse than having to ask the mumbling idiot at the other end of a crackling line to repeat their request, trying to wade through the carefully couched keywords to try to figure out what they were really asking for and answer them in the same code.

No, their business did not coordinate *assassinations*, it was just a bodyguard service. Yes, they were all *hellhounds*. No, they were not *cheap*. Yes, they were *that good*.

But you couldn't just come out and say that directly with most clients. If shifters were secret in some countries, Mexico included, hellhounds were twice that, and there was a tricky balance between advertising services and protecting secrets.

So Lorenzo was surprised when the woman at the other end of the phone very frankly answered his Spanish greeting with clear English. "I need a shifter bodyguard immediately for a vacation to Costa Rica. I'm at the Mexico City airport and my flight takes off in four hours. Can you do that or do I need to shop elsewhere?"

It wasn't worth pointing out that there weren't very many services that were going to be able to satisfy *that* particular criteria.

"We can make that happen, ma'am," Lorenzo assured her in the same language. "I just need some details…" He wrote down her name and number, her flight information, and her destination: Shifting Sands Resort.

Someone was in for a fluff assignment. "I'll call you back with our agent's contact specifics in ten minutes."

"Hey, Purebred," John greeted him.

Lorenzo ignored the jibe. "We got a job. Some rich broad is

leaving on holiday and wants an escort ASAP." He tossed the notes in front of his packmate.

John frowned. "How long?" he asked, pulling up his scheduling software.

"Ten days," Lorenzo said.

"You want a vacation?" John said unexpectedly.

"Me?" Lorenzo scowled in surprise.

"You've done your share of the scut work," John said approvingly. "Think you can be away from the pack that long?"

Was it meant as a dig?

Ten days would have been a long, grueling time for most of the hellhounds to be separated from the pack that kept them sane...but Lorenzo wasn't like most of the hellhounds and all of them knew it.

Probably he was only being offered the job because he was the only one who wouldn't come back strung out like a drug addict in withdrawal from the team if they didn't send a pair. They could do the job for half the cost with Lorenzo.

"Yeah," Lorenzo growled. It beat answering phones.

~

Christy applied her lipstick carefully, trying not to look like she was deliberately dawdling in front of the mirror, and willed her heartbeat to slow. Her suitcase was open on the floor next to her, her make-up kit on the counter beside her.

This bathroom was a quiet one at the very end of the terminal, past a whole section of gates that were closed for construction, and the light was terrible. It was also four in the morning.

A gray-haired lady ambled in and met her gaze in the reflection.

Christy glanced down at her open luggage in alarm, then calmed herself, her hand almost shaking too much to finish her lipstick. She was glad she had already finished her phone conversation.

The woman shuffled further in and found a stall while Christy silently berated herself and finished slowly re-applying her make-up.

It was just chance that Christy had recognized Mick's hired goon at the gate, and suddenly, Betsy's idea for a bodyguard hadn't seemed so crazy. She'd turned on her heel and found the nearest ladies room hoping that the mercenary hadn't seen her. At least her phone got reception...and data.

She wasn't sure that 'shifter bodyguard' was going to get her any hits, so she was surprised and relieved when *Hellhound Proteccion* came up directly in her search. Once she translated it, the carefully-worded webpage sounded exactly like what she was looking for. And fortunately, the man who answered the phone spoke English.

So now she had a bodyguard coming straight to the airport to escort her to the resort and act as hired protection for the week, because she had panicked like a scared rabbit.

And for once, her cat was not giving her any grief about it. *Sometimes, it's smart to go to ground,* she urged. *Better to be safe.*

Christy had a sense of her cat lashing its striped tail, not pleased by the bruise to their pride, and frankly worried.

The expense was definitely going to cut into her profits. Christy reminded herself that this was a *super* exclusive luxury resort. Big money traveled here, and if she was canny, she could still make the trip worth it.

She just had to survive it.

Christy took a deep calming breath and went to pack up her make-up and close her luggage. She had to meet the bodyguard at her gate; she couldn't exactly ask him to come get her in the lady's room. She'd already been in here a suspiciously lengthy time.

It was just happenstance that Mick's merc was there, she told herself. It wasn't likely that he was getting on the charter to Shifting Sands like she was. Probably, he had just been passing by the gate—the Mexico City airport was huge, and busy, an international hub. Even at four in the morning, there were pockets of bustling activity. He could be doing anything here. He was a freelancer, maybe he was someone else's hire today.

She could do this, she thought. No pepper spray, no knives,

because of airport security. But she had her wits, and in not too long, she'd have an impulsively-hired shifter bodyguard. She couldn't be safer.

She zipped her spinner shut and extended the handle, lifted her chin, and marched out of the bathroom, to be instantly accosted by a tall, slim Asian man. She considered clubbing him with her purse, but instinct told her at once that he was harmless, and he only touched her arm to stop her.

"I'm sorry to bother you," he said, as if he genuinely was. "Do you speak English? I'm looking for a woman, an old woman, who went into the bathroom about forty minutes ago."

Had she been in there *that* long?

"She may need assistance," the man said anxiously. "Could you please tell me if she's alright? I'm sorry to ask, but I'm worried, and our flight is soon."

Christy could not simply brush by him and go to her gate after that kind of plea, no matter how easy it would be to pretend she only spoke Spanish; she'd already decided on dark hair for this trip. She glanced at her phone for the time, and nodded. "I'll go look," she said gently. "I saw her, earlier." But she hadn't seen her leave, she realized curiously.

The bathroom was deserted.

Christy went back to the row of stalls and pushed each door open with a hesitant knock, but each of them revealed an empty toilet...and the last one had a puddle of clothing on the floor.

She picked it up, carefully, and recognized the dull-colored sweater from the woman she'd seen in the mirror.

Suddenly suspicious, she gathered the clothing and returned to the fidgeting man outside the restroom.

"Oh *dear,*" he greeted her, his eyes flickering to hers with guilt and alarm. He didn't look exactly *surprised*, and Christy took a chance.

"She's a shifter?"

The man flinched and looked around, then nodded.

Christy looked at her phone again as it gave a little vibration and saw a text from her new bodyguard. Their flight would be leaving soon, and he was coming through security now. She gave the man another appraising look. His shirt was high quality, but well-worn, with the soft lines of someone laundering it in a common machine and didn't iron or starch it. His pants were off the rack. His shoes were cheap. The clothing she was holding was poor-class and thread-worn.

Helping these people would gain her nothing. If anything, it could put her in more danger.

She heaved a sigh. "What's her animal form?" Christy asked crisply.

The hope in the man's eyes was some salve for her lost time. "A mouse," he said quickly. "Thank you. Thank you so much. Her name is Gretta Asher. I'm Liam."

They shook hands briskly.

"I'll go see if there's some small space she could be hiding in," Christy offered.

She did another circuit of the bathroom, crouched low, looking for places a tiny mouse might hide. Another woman in a MexicoAir stewardess uniform came in and gave her a look of horror while she stood up from bending over behind the trash can, where she'd been poking at a dark corner.

Christy made a show of carefully washing her hands, and then came out to give Liam the bad news.

"Maybe she slipped past me," Liam said apprehensively. "I suppose it's possible she went back to the group. She...gets confused sometimes. We had a nurse traveling with us, but we only have one more flight, and this was far as she was contracted. I'm so sorry to bother you."

"Are you on the charter to Shifting Sands Resort?" Christy guessed.

Liam looked surprised and guilty, though Christy wasn't sure why he would, since it seemed like an obvious destination once she knew he was with a shifter. "Yes," he said cautiously.

"Me, too." Christy walked with him to the gate, and found a cluster of elderly women with sharp eyes and a very old man in a wheelchair who appeared to be insensible.

"Did you find Gretta?"

"Who's this?"

"Is she your new girlfriend?"

"She looks single…" This old woman was eyeing Christy's ring-free finger. "Pretty, too."

Christy was beginning to have second thoughts about Shifting Sands. If this was the kind of clientele…

Someone behind her cleared their throat. "Christine Ryan?"

Her bodyguard. Maybe he could protect her from the match-making of nosy old biddies.

Christy turned to see a tall, scowling man in a beautiful suit that was half as handsome as he was, and fell directly into his fathomless eyes as her cat suddenly wrapped claws around her heart and cried, *ours!*

~

It was supposed to be an uncomplicated job. Protect some spoiled rich woman heading to a tropical vacation with delusions of danger, get paid, go home.

Lorenzo had not expected the trust bunny to be quite so tall or self-possessed. He definitely did not expect to find her surrounded by chattering seniors. And he really did not expect her to turn around and steal his soul in a single, green-eyed glance.

Deep within him, he heard a sound like baying, as everything in his world was suddenly bright and focused.

Ours. Our mate.

It was as if everything fell into place at the same time.

"I'm...Christy," she said breathlessly, looking back at him with the same world-upside-down expression that he was probably giving her.

"Lorenzo," he answered in an exhale. "From...ah…" he looked at the staring circle of old women in consternation.

"Is he going to *kiss* her?"

"I thought she was Liam's girlfriend," one of them said in disappointment.

"Where's Gretta?"

"Is that *our* flight?"

A very harried man with short dark hair and Asian features checking the pulse of a man lying limp in a wheelchair looked up in alarm as the charter to Shifting Sands Resort was called for pre-boarding.

"They're missing a woman, about ninety years old," Christy explained, still looking dazed. "Gretta. She was in the restroom, but...ah…" she lowered her voice considerably, "shifted. We haven't been able to find her."

How was this woman even able to have a conversation? Lorenzo was nearly overwhelmed by his hound's circle-turning, tail-wagging excitement. This was their *mate*!

With effort, Lorenzo reined in his excitement and attempted to focus. "A missing person…"

We can help with that! his hound said eagerly. *Help her! Help her!*

"Ah, what kind of shifter?" he asked quietly.

"Mouse." The dark-haired man had been satisfied by his charge's condition and came to greet Lorenzo. "I'm Liam."

Lorenzo shook his hand bemusedly. "Do you have something of hers?"

Liam looked confused.

"I'm a...ah...hellhound," Lorenzo explained. *Mostly.*

Now we are whole, his hound said triumphantly.

Liam continued to look quizzical, but Christy immediately understood and her face lit up. "Finding people, that isn't just fiction?"

Lorenzo shook his head, desperate now to prove himself. "A hell-hound always finds his prey."

"Her sweater," Christy said, handing him a beige cable-knit sweater

Don't fail me now, Lorenzo begged his hound, taking it.

We will not fail, he replied confidently.

It wasn't scent, exactly, that led a hellhound to its quarry. It was a trace of *who,* with a smudge of *where,* and just the slightest memory of *how* and *when,* swirling in the air where they'd been. Once a hellhound had a trail, they never lost it.

"Show me where you last saw her," he said, and to his alarm, six of the old ladies wanted to traipse with them to stand outside the ladies water closet. Liam remained anxiously behind with his wheelchair-bound charge, frantically trying to collect up their abandoned bags.

"It was in here," Christy said quietly.

Lorenzo closed his eyes and the world swam into shadows. It was effortless, this time. It didn't feel like he was fighting for every step. He could walk through walls, breathe fire...for the first time in his life, he was complete.

He opened them at once. "She's right here."

The elderly women immediately began to scramble around, looking behind trash cans and at the baseboards where a tiny mouse might hide, calling, "Gretta? Gretta, dear!"

"We're going to miss our flight!"

"Darla is waiting for us, Gretta!"

"No," Lorenzo corrected. "She's right *here.*"

He pointed at Christy's rolling case.

You'd better be right, he warned his hound. But for once, his hellhound was completely confident.

Everyone stared at Christy's luggage.

"Oh!" she exclaimed. "It was open in the restroom!"

One of the other women started to kneel next to it and reach for the zipper. To everyone's surprise, Christy snatched it away to her far side. "No!"

Swiftly, she added, "Not here. Let me go in *alone* and get her dressed. You stay here. Make sure no one comes in."

Then she was clicking away into the bathroom and Lorenzo had to hold himself back from the impulse to chase her right through the wall into the women's-only sanctuary while the six seniors arranged themselves into a makeshift defensive perimeter.

~

Christy's heart was pounding in her throat as she fled into the women's room and she paused a moment at the sink to splash some cool water on her face.

Bad enough that her hasty new hire was a gorgeous man who set her blood very unprofessionally on fire, he was also her mate.

Her *mate*.

She'd just met her mate.

It was hard to think around her cat's laser-pointed attention. She had very, very definite ideas of what they should be doing, and an empty washroom would suit her just fine, thank you.

But it wasn't an empty bathroom.

Christy tipped her rolling bag onto the side and unzipped it carefully. The top layer looked undisturbed, and she folded back the evening gown and moved aside the make-up bag. There was the lock-pick set, and the jeweler's tools, several false ID cards, and all the utilities of her profession.

Nestled up in a pair of soft gloves was a small brown mouse, still sleeping soundly.

"Hey, hey, Mrs. Gretta," she said, picking up the tiny rodent. "Time to wake up and go for a plane ride."

A few splashes of water finally roused the little creature, and she yawned, stretched, and shifted into a very naked, very confused old woman. "Goodness," she said in alarm. "Who are you?"

Who *was* she? Would her mate want anything to do with her, if he knew what she did for a living?

"Never mind that," Christy said firmly. "You're on a flight that leaves very soon. Here are your clothes."

"Those aren't my clothes," she insisted, and for a moment, Christy thought she was going to have to wrestle an unwilling woman into her pants.

Then Gretta gave a sparkling laugh. "Oh, your face, sweetie! I was gassing you. Let's see those, then."

A stewardess came out of one of the stalls, then, saw Christy helping Gretta step into her leggings, and proceeded to completely ignore them as she washed her hands and fled without asking for explanation.

"That's not Gretta!" the stranger was greeted at the door.

"Let her go, then. Where are your glasses, Maggie?"

"Do you need help, Christy?" one of them called.

"Be right out," Christy sang back.

She helped settle the sweater over Gretta's thin shoulders and swiftly zipped her rolling bag back up.

"Nice lock-pick set," Gretta observed, to Christy's dismay, then she was leading the way out of the restroom.

Christy scrambled to follow, and was drawn up short at the sight of Lorenzo, no less handsome on a second viewing, his dark eyes and his olive skin like temptation given tangible form.

Her *mate.*

They returned to the gate in a daze, surrounded by short, chattering women like a pair of stunned geese in a flock of fluffy hens.

Liam's relief was worth every hassle, and Lorenzo's admiring glances made Christy feel a curious combination of pride and guilt.

The flight attendant was tight-lipped and terribly unhappy with their tardiness, rushing them out onto the tarmac with the other impatient passengers to board the tiny chartered jet.

As they showed their tickets and dragged their luggage through marked airport doors and followed painted lines on the tarmac, Christy was keenly aware of Lorenzo, of his sheer presence. He helped some of Liam's elders with their luggage, utterly unflustered by his sudden advancement from bodyguard to porter.

There was no opportunity to talk to him, and Christy was dismayed when they were all weighed for balancing the plane, and then seated nearly half the plane apart from each other. He was still putting bags in the overhead for Liam's charges as she buckled herself in and put her purse under the seat in front of her.

What would we talk about, anyway? she wondered in despair.

A crowded little plane was no place to tell him that she was a common *cat* burglar.

Then she looked up as a passenger running even later than they had been boarded the plane, and her heart froze in her chest.

Mick's goon gave her a knowing smile that showed too many teeth and moved past to sit a few rows behind her.

~

It was absolute torture walking past his mate without stopping to...to what? Kiss her? Drag a finger down the side of her beautiful face? She watched him with the same hunger that was raging in his veins, and Lorenzo heard her sigh longingly as he passed her to his assigned seat.

Lorenzo made himself march further back in the small plane, heaving the luggage of half a dozen seniors up into the overhead storage space as they giggled and shamelessly admired him.

We can't protect her from here, his hound wailed when he found his seat.

She doesn't need protecting right now, Lorenzo protested. *We're on a tiny plane. Who would hurt her here?*

He had to fold himself uncomfortably into his narrow seat, one knee splayed into the aisle, the other up tight against the seat in front.

Then all of his hackles stood on end, as one final passenger appeared in the front of the plane, the harried flight attendant pointing him crossly to his seat.

Lorenzo knew hired muscle when he saw it, and this was not the savory sort. That alone would have had him on high alert, but then the man smiled at Christy, and although it was a knowing look, it was not a *friendly* knowing look, and he saw Christy shrink into her seat.

Only the steely look from the flight attendant as he tried to unbuckle, and the certainty that the man would not possibly try something in front of so many witnesses in a place with no escape route, kept him in his seat.

His gaze did not flicker once from his forward watchfulness, not when they got to cruising altitude and drinks were served, not when anyone attempted to speak to him, and not hours later as everyone got bored and slept restlessly in the little seats. He almost rose to his feet when the man stood, forgetting that he was still wearing his seatbelt. The man came back in the plane to use the facilities rather than forward to where Christy was reading a tablet, and Lorenzo studied him.

The goon was tall and probably had as much difficulty with the airplane seats as Lorenzo did. He was undoubtedly a shifter, on this flight, but Lorenzo appraised his stride with practiced skill. A fighter, Lorenzo guessed, but a scrapper, not a dancer. The sort to take the damage and try to outlast an enemy. The sort to *cheat.*

Well, it would take more than an average fighter to face him down. Lorenzo cracked his knuckles as the man squeezed past, drawing his attention at the last moment and causing a quick flicker of alarm to crack the mercenary's smug face.

The man took a long while in the restroom, and when he returned, he approached Lorenzo warily from behind.

Lorenzo casually tipped his empty drink cup into the aisle just in front of the mercenary to draw his attention. His seatbelt was already free this time, and in one smooth move, he had the man by the neck of his shirt and was hauling him to his knees between the seats.

It would have undoubtedly captured all of the attention of anyone on the plane who was awake...if one of the elderly ladies had not abruptly woken from sleep and shifted into a bear at that very moment.

The entire plane went dipping alarmingly to the side, as the carefully calculated weight and balance was suddenly off by seven hundred pounds. Most of the passengers shrieked and clung to their seat arms as the pilot struggled to regain control of their craft. Someone who hadn't been buckled in fell heavily into the aisle.

The giant brown bear was the most panicked of all of them, suddenly taking up much more than seat real estate than the single frail woman had, and she struggled futilely as people around her ducked her flailing claws.

Lorenzo took advantage of the moment to snarl into the face of the man who had threatened his mate, showing him just a hint of his true nature with blazing red eyes and a whiff of sulphur at the corner of his mouth. It was as far as he ever let himself shift in front of people.

"You're a *hellhound*?" the man said in astonishment.

More now than ever before.

"Think," he warned the man in a low growl. "Think about what you are being paid and how much you are willing to risk for such a payment. Know that if you harm one hair on my mate's head, I will extract a payment far more dear. I never lose my quarry, my kind does not end a hunt with mercy, and you will suffer everything you have ever dealt five-fold or more at my hands. Think on that and then turn and leave the island the moment you arrive."

Understanding dawned in the man's wide eyes. "Your *mate*...I had no idea, man."

Lorenzo blinked back to his usual dark eyes and swallowed the last of the smoke. "Now you know. Tell your employer."

"We're going to flip over!" someone shrieked. The plane was still wobbling back and forth wildly, and Liam was frantically trying to calm the thrashing bear as he was flung from side to side.

Lorenzo let go of the man's collar and settled back into his heaving seat, just as Liam reached the bear and managed to talk her back into sheepish and confused human form.

Lorenzo met Christy's bright green eyes over the chaos as she craned back to see him, and the mercenary staggered back to his seat in the steadying plane with an ashen face.

~

Christy was one of the first guests off the plane, ushered urgently off by a flight attendant who was clearly reconsidering her career choice, and she waited nervously at the bottom of the stairs. Several alarmed and chattering passengers passed and then Lorenzo was coming down the steps to scoop her into his arms the way that she'd wanted him to from the very first moment she'd seen him.

"That was a helluva ride," she squeaked, not realizing she was trembling until she felt Lorenzo's solid arms around her.

There was a van that looked like it had seen better days being loaded with luggage and guests, and when Lorenzo finally, reluctantly, let go of her, she saw her own bag being put in. "Oh—" she said in alarm, but it was already in the back of the vehicle.

Then she looked up into Lorenzo's face. "I've got things to tell you," she murmured regretfully. "Things you won't like."

"I've got a few things of my own to admit," he said, his voice as thick with contrition as hers.

A black-haired, bronze-skinned man was closing up the van. "Only our elders are staying behind for the next trip," he called to them.

Christy took a look back up the stairs to the plane, confused. Mick's mercenary hadn't made an appearance. She hadn't expected him to make a move in front of others, but she was braced for an uncomfortable accounting the moment she was alone...and desperately glad she had hired Lorenzo for a host of reasons.

"He's not coming," Lorenzo said with a slight smile.

"You…!"

"I *changed his mind* about staying."

Christy felt a wave of relief. "I'm giving your bodyguard service a five star review on Yelp if you keep this up."

"They're going to leave without us," Lorenzo pointed out, grinning down at her.

He put his hand in hers and they ran for the van as the driver started the engine.

The brilliantly red-haired woman who greeted them at the counter when they arrived at the resort gave Christy shivers of apprehension. Possibly, her original plan to use the resort as a seat for her work would have to be shelved. She did not think that the resort owner would be amused if Christy stole from her guests.

The woman introduced herself as Scarlet and asked mildly, "How was your trip?"

"One of the passengers turned into a bear and nearly crashed the plane," Christy said frankly.

Scarlet didn't even blink. "At least it wasn't the mammoth." She gave Lorenzo a steely glare. "I don't have a record for this guest."

"My...bodyguard," Christy said. *My **mate***, she thought, her cat purring so loudly she was surprised that no one else could hear it. She caught herself smiling hopelessly at Lorenzo.

Not the slightest bit fooled, Scarlet raised one eyebrow and didn't comment. "I've got some paperwork I'll need filled out."

She did not so much as double-take when Lorenzo wrote down *hellhound* for his shift form, but she did calmly remind them about the *no predation* rule. Twice.

She gave them keys, the old-fashioned kind on big wooden keychains that made Christy salivate—keys were so much easier to crack than keycards—and showed them on the map where their cottage was. Some of the cottages near the top of the island had been marked in pen: 'private.'

Then they were back outside, in the tropical morning sunshine filled with the most *amazing* smells.

"We could stop at the restaurant if you're hungry," Christy suggested half-heartedly.

"I'm *hungry,*" Lorenzo growled, and she looked up to realize that he had no interest whatsoever in eating.

"Me, too," she agreed with a purr.

The first fork in the path that gave them privacy was excuse enough to reach for each other, and then, at last, at last, his mouth was claiming hers. He pulled her up against him, one hand at the back of her neck, one at her waist.

He kissed her and kissed her, until she was on fire and not at all sure where on the resort map they even were, or where their cottage was, or even what country they were in.

Fortunately, Lorenzo had a better sense of direction. He lifted her up into his arms and seemed utterly prepared to carry her off and leave their luggage on the white gravel walk behind them.

"Wait, wait," Christy cried, against his mouth. "I need my bag."

He groaned, and reached blindly behind him. His questing hand, hampered by the fact that Christy could simply not stop kissing him, finally found the upright handle of her bag, and then he was carrying her and dragging it, unerringly to the cottage that their key fit into.

"Wait," Christy said in sudden agony. "I'm not who you think." She wasn't going to start this all off on the wrong foot. "I'm...I'm not a rich trust-fund bunny."

"No," he agreed. "You're no rabbit. You're a feline, if I had to guess."

"Housecat," she confessed. "Just a housecat, nothing fancy. Tabby stripes and all."

Lorenzo seemed to think that was her confession. "Doesn't bother me in the slightest…"

Christy was too weak from her desire not to kiss him again for a long, lingering moment. Then she sighed and pulled away.

"I'm a thief."

~

Of all the things Lorenzo had expected Christy to reveal, being a thief was not in his top five guesses.

"Expert job on my heart," Lorenzo said dryly, reaching for her again. He and his hellhound were absolutely in alignment on what happened next.

But Christy caught his hands in her own. "No, really," she said seriously. "I...I'm not a good person. My suitcase is full of fake jewels...and some real ones that aren't technically mine, and lock-picks, and fake IDs. I'm a liar. A con artist. I...wish I was something better…"

Lorenzo turned his hands and captured hers in return. "I won't judge," he said honestly. "I'm in no place to judge. I've certainly stolen my share of things...and…" he heaved a great sigh and drew Christy down beside him on the bed. "You tell me, and I'll tell you. How did you get started?"

Christy gave a throaty little laugh. "We were poor, and I didn't want to be. My mom worked so hard raising me and Betsy, that's my sister, and I wanted them to have nice things, and a house where things worked in a neighborhood where graffiti and gunshots weren't the order of the day."

Lorenzo rubbed his thumbs on the backs of her hands. "Are you good at it?"

"So good," Christy said without a trace of false modesty. "It was little things at first, stud emerald earrings from the place I got a summer job doing landscaping, a bracelet here, a watch. I figured out pretty quick that it's hard to carry big pieces as a cat, and hard to fence them, too. I also learned that people think they've just lost something if you take one of an earring but not both, and that prying out a jewel or two is even less suspect.

"I got to the point where I was doing fancy parties, taking one diamond from an earring, then pretending to find the rest of the setting on the floor. 'Oh, it must have fallen out! How terrible!' Easy money. Simple marks. I got selective, only robbing from people who got where they were by taking advantage of others. Mom got a sweet penthouse and a male nurse named Kevin. Betsy has a cottage upstate and her kids have college funds."

"But…" Lorenzo prompted, guessing there was more.

"But Slippery Mick was running a shifter thief ring, and he wanted to be the only game in town. He offered to let me in on his business, but I liked being independent, and I felt like I had standards he wouldn't meet. It started to get...competitive, and Mick had important friends. My fences got scared." She sighed. "I figured it was time for a break from the city. Shifting Sands Resort looked like a perfect place to lie low for a while. I thought I'd treat myself to a vacation, rake in a great haul from all the rich guests, and let things cool off back home."

"But…" Lorenzo prompted again.

"But my latest New York heist went sideways. Mick was after the same prize, and he was pissed when I got it. He holds grudges." Christy shrugged. "I thought I'd lose him for a little while, coming here. I didn't really think he'd send someone out of New York after me."

"He won't do that again," Lorenzo growled. "I'll see to it."

Christy gave a little shiver at his tone, but she didn't look afraid.

"There are things I have to tell you, too," he said reluctantly. "I want you to know."

"You've *done* things?" Christy guessed. "As a bodyguard...as a hellhound?"

"Let me...tell you about being a hellhound. About *becoming* a hellhound. Do you know how we are made?"

"Made? You aren't...just born this way, like shifters?"

"Hellhounds are bitten."

Christy's heart-shaped face, scrunched now in confusion, was every bit as beautiful in every expression she made. Lorenzo had to make himself focus.

"Like...werewolves?" she guessed.

"Yes...and definitely no," Lorenzo said. "Not every hellhound can turn others, and not everyone can be turned. And...it doesn't always go right."

Christy waited with bated breath for him to go on, not interrupting him, but absently stroking his leg. He doubted she even realized he was doing it.

"My mother was a shifter from Brazil, my father was a human from America. I was fifteen, living in Mexico, when they were killed in a train crash."

Christy made a tiny noise of sympathy.

"I fell in with a street gang, at first, but...I didn't want a life of crime."

Christy swallowed and looked guilty.

"I found *Hellhound Proteccion* and what I wanted all fell into place. Legitimate business. A pack to belong to. I worked for them running messages at first, and finally convinced them to turn me. I don't know why I didn't become a shifter like my mother, but apparently, some people keep the potential to be shifters, and have animals that sleep within them, that never wake up. Latent shifters, they call them. "

"You were one of those latent shifters?" Christy guessed.

Lorenzo sighed. Here it came. "Yes. And turning a latent shifter can be...unpredictable."

"What does it mean?" Christy asked. "What did you become?"

"A hellhound," Lorenzo said. "But…"

Her green eyes were so...deep. So trusting.

Lorenzo steeled himself.

And then he stood up and shifted.

~

Christy was braced for something terrible. Tentacles, maybe. Or a giant hellhound with multiple heads, all of them breathing fire.

Instead…

"Oh, aren't you *darling*!" she couldn't keep herself from saying.

He was a poodle, standard-sized, with thick, dark curls cropped short. Big, soulful, flaming-red eyes looked at her under black brows, and silky ears framed his long, narrow nose.

He shifted back and Christy was only slightly disappointed that his clothing came with him. "Darling isn't exactly the usual adjective for a hellhound." He looked like an odd mix of embarrassed and resigned...and just a little flattered. "I couldn't breathe fire, I couldn't walk through walls...and...I never fully bonded with the pack. I've always been...half a hellhound. Until *you*."

Christy felt like her chest was too full for words, and even though she was happier than she'd ever been in her life, there were tears welling up in her eyes like there simply wasn't room for them anywhere else.

"You complete me," he said, his voice hoarse. "*You* are my pack. *You* light me on fire."

"Can you do all those things *now*?" Christy asked in awe.

"I think I could move mountains now," he said, without a trace of hesitation.

Christy knew that feeling. She felt like a better person now that she'd met Lorenzo, and had found herself in his eyes. She could leave her life, and all the things that had come with it, behind and follow him anywhere.

"I'm done with it," she said quietly. "No more thieving. No more lies. No more cons. Just...you and me. Let me start fresh."

His hands were on her face again, her lips on hers, and when he sat beside her on the bed again, she crawled into his lap and kissed him until she was dizzy.

He fell backwards onto the bed and dragged her with him, big hands exploring her shoulders, her back, her waist.

She could not be close enough, could not have enough of his skin, his touch, his warmth. They were pulling desperately at each other's clothing, and Christy realized that she was whimpering and begging.

Every layer that was removed was a new discovery, and they rolled over the wide bed in reckless, joyful abandon, until they were completely naked, their old lives stripped away with every touch as they rebuilt each other anew.

Then he was driving into her and she was crying out in ecstasy and release, clutching the blanket beneath her.

~

"I'm going to miss it," Christy said, holding one of the strings of jewels down off the edge of the bed to catch the low evening light coming in through the window. "Being a thief, I mean. I liked being *good* at it."

Lorenzo was lying on the bed with his arms behind his head, watching the reflections of Christy's jewels against the walls. Her lush curves were bare for his appreciation. "I can think of other things your skillset would apply to."

She rolled back up onto the bed. "Oh?"

"Have you ever thought about bodyguard work?"

She blinked at him. "Seriously?"

"You're shifter strong," Lorenzo said appraisingly. "You're fast and smart. You're observant, which is one of those under-appreciated skills that makes the difference between a muscle and a professional. I could train you."

"What would your pack think of that?"

"If they don't accept you, we could go freelance," Lorenzo said firmly. "You're all the pack I need."

"A hellhound and house cat," Christy mused, a slow smile spreading over her face. "Hellcat Protection Services?"

"I love it," Lorenzo said sincerely. "We'll buy one of those sweet Dodge Challengers and put our company logo on it."

"Wouldn't an unmarked black van be more useful?" Christy teased.

"Protection services!" Lorenzo scolded her in jest. "No kidnappings, no robberies!"

Christy heaved a dramatic sigh. "I suppose," she agreed with mock reluctance. "You know, it isn't just anyone that could get me to go straight."

He captured her face in his hands and kissed her, slowly and soundly. "You never did tell me what it was that you stole from under Mick's nose," he said curiously.

Christy dissolved into laughter. "You won't believe it," she said, shaking her head.

Lorenzo grinned back, bemused by her mirth. "What was it?" he demanded.

Christy reached deep into her bag and pulled out the cause of so much trouble. She poured it, sparkling, from the velvet bag. "It's a diamond dog collar," she said, laughing so hard she could barely hold it up. "I stole it from some jerk who made his money running dog fighting rings."

Lorenzo choked and then roared with laughter. "Just my size," he chuckled. He took it from her hands. "But I think it would look better on you…" He held it at her bare throat and their laughter slowly turned into something more urgent as he buckled it onto her beautiful neck.

He followed it with kisses, dragging his teeth along her pale skin. "You know, you hired me for another nine days and there's no one here to protect you from. You really should get your money's worth."

"Oh," Christy purred. "I think I will…"

The cover that started it all!

TROPICAL LEOPARD'S LONGING: EPILOGUE

"Charter's coming in," Graham called from the back kitchen door.

Chef answered him with the chorus of an opera in Italian and Darla left a warm kiss on the cook's cheek as she untied the apron from her waist. "I'll be back when they're settled," she promised. "It should be before the dinner rush."

Her kiss for Breck, at the back door, was considerably longer, and not limited to his cheek.

"Travis won't hold the van for you," Breck warned her at last, and she reluctantly pried herself away.

"I'll see you soon," she said.

They'd been married nearly two weeks, and it still felt impossible and precious and fragile. Darla kept expecting someone to tell her she wasn't allowed to feel this happy, and to take it all away from her.

Travis was waiting at the van and made a point of looking at his wrist, but his eyes were dancing. The noisy journey down to the tiny island airstrip prevented any real conversation and Darla spent most of it looking at her hands, thinking about how much her life had changed in just a few short weeks.

Her nails were short and practical, without a trace of polish. She was developing calluses from the cutting knives, and her fingers were rough from dishwater. She had sold her jewelry and designer clothing to pay for getting the rest home residents plane tickets and was dressed in a simple resort uniform: a green polo shirt and khaki shorts. Her hair was back in two braids, lovingly—if not expertly—put there by Breck, not styled at a salon.

She rose every morning before dawn, which would have felt ridiculously early at any other point in her life, and made bread dancing around the kitchen with the love of her life.

When the van finally pulled in at the gravel strip, Darla was smiling foolishly.

She could honestly not imagine a more perfect life.

Liam looked considerably less content than she did as he ushered the eight senior citizens from the charter plane.

"It was an interesting trip," he confessed, thoroughly ruffled. "Mrs. Asher got lost in the Mexico City airport, and Mrs. Snaffit fell asleep in her luggage and you have no idea what someone shifting into a bear does for the weight and balance of a small plane. Thank goodness it was on the charter, and not the commercial airliner."

"Interesting sounds like an understatement," Darla laughed. She stepped forward to help Mrs. Snaffit down the last of the steps from the plane. They didn't have a wheelchair for Mr. Danby, who had been sedated for the trip to keep him from shifting into a mammoth mid-flight, but Liam gathered the old man easily into his arms and carried him to the waiting van as Travis assisted the chattering old ladies into their seats.

The seven ladies had a great deal to say about the road to the resort, the heat, the sun, Travis' big muscles, the flowers, and, when they finally saw them, the cottages that Scarlet had assigned to the retirement community.

The resort owner had allotted four houses for the new residents and Travis had constructed a large shelter for Mr. Danby; it was warm enough now that a roof over slat walls would more than suffice, and they had some time before storm season to come up with something more weather- and mammoth- proof.

The hedges between the four building had been removed, so it was a cozy community of homes, all at the same level, situated on a long, seamless lawn. One of the houses had been set up as a common area, with a dining table and chairs, couches, recliners, and televisions. The remaining three cottages were living quarters, and each of the new residents had a private room with a bed and a chair.

The seniors had a great deal to say about their rooms and, after checking Mr. Danby's vitals, Liam and Darla left them to unpack and explore their new campus.

"This is wonderful," Liam said, coming back out into the sunlight. "How did you get it all done so fast?"

Travis, hauling in the last of the luggage, was pleased with the praise. "It wasn't that much to do," he said modestly. "Though I couldn't answer for Graham and the landscaping. He can work miracles with the green stuff around here."

"Speaking of miracles..."

Breck was standing in the doorway of the common cottage. Darla ran to give him a kiss.

"The breakfast crowd was small, so Chef let me out a little early to help Mrs. Shandy get settled in with all our new guests," he explained, putting a hand around her waist.

"Is she fitting in well?" Darla asked.

"They're already planning a backgammon tournament," Breck said with a grin. "I don't think they know what they're up against."

"I don't know," Liam said. "Mrs. Asher can hold her own if there isn't any cheating."

"Welcome back," Breck said, offering a handshake that Liam warmly accepted. "How was the trip?"

"Grueling," Liam said wryly. "I'm glad that it's over."

"How is your mom?" Darla asked. Alison had graciously declined Scarlet's invitation to move to Shifting Sands, but had promised to keep it in mind when—if—Jubilee made good on her threats.

"She's doing great, sends you a kiss." He gave her a sideways look. "How's *your* mom?"

"We got the earnest money back on the warehouse, less fees," Darla was happy to report. "With the rest of the jewelry that Saina fenced for me, we have the dowry to pay back. We'll be free and clear of the whole thing." She played with the cheap fabric of her polo shirt. "There's no word about a lawsuit yet, but it could happen at any time. I think she's been busy having vapors over the fact that Eugene was manipulating her psychic. She hasn't paid the remainder of the bill, of course."

She had terribly mixed feelings. She had spent her life admiring her glamorous mother from a distance, but the real person behind the dazzling image had been so cold and heartless and Darla was only beginning to recognize how controlling she had been.

Liam gave her a look that suggested he understood the depths of her confusion. "I'm hoping for the best," he said simply.

Darla smiled at him. "I'll settle for not awful," she said sincerely.

"I would be perfectly satisfied with 'not awful' at this point also," Scarlet said, startling them all by suddenly being at the corner of the community house.

"I'm sorry for—" Darla started automatically.

Scarlet waved her off. "I'm not blaming any of you for circumstances," she said firmly. "You don't need to continue apologizing." She gave the area a critical look. "I hope that this will suffice for now."

"It's fine," Liam said gratefully. "More than I could have hoped for. Your generosity…"

He trailed off at Scarlet's dismissive wave. "I'm not running a charity," she said briskly. "And I hope I can count on you to keep your charges under control and out of the way until further, more permanent, accommodations can be arranged."

"Of course," Liam said swiftly.

Scarlet's voice gentled. "Once you are settled, I'd like to go over meal schedules and talk about accessibility needs that might still need addressed. I would also appreciate your attendance at our senior staff meetings in the future, as I am assigning you the responsibility for the rest home and I will require you to coordinate your needs with the rest of the resort."

"Yes, ma'am," Liam agreed.

"Just Scarlet is fine. We'll be meeting at one o'clock this afternoon. Darla, I'd appreciate your attendance as well."

"Yes, ma'am," Darla squeaked, drawing to attention automatically. "Er, Scarlet. Ah, why?"

Scarlet looked amused. "Because we've got an important wedding party coming in tomorrow, and I thought you might have some useful input based on your own experience."

Darla smothered a nervous giggle. "I have lots of ideas what *not* to do," she agreed. "Is it a very big wedding?"

Scarlet actually smiled, and Darla wondered if she was being teased. "Very small, actually, and the bride and groom are mates, so we aren't likely to run into the same sorts of problems that you faced."

Breck looked at her suspiciously. "Mates, you say?"

Scarlet gave him a narrow-eyed look and then smiled as she explained, "Mary and Neal are coming back to get married. Amber and Tony are coming as bridesmaid and best man."

Breck gave a laugh of delight. "No one in the world would have thought I'd get married before those two."

"You know them?" Darla said, smiling at his contagious joy.

"Neal was a captive in that zoo across the island that Gizelle came from," Breck explained. "And his mate Mary was a guest here. Tony is our friend from the Shifter Affairs agency. He and Amber were the ones who uncovered the zoo and were key in taking it down."

"So it will be a pretty important reunion, then," Darla guessed. "But probably not a disaster of a wedding like ours was."

Breck pulled her close. "*Our* wedding was perfect," he said in mock offense. He shot Liam a laughing look. "It was your wedding to *that* guy that made all the tabloids."

"Don't remind me," Darla groaned. Photographs from the wedding debacle had made all the major shifter gossip publications.

"I'm expecting far less drama from this union," Scarlet said mildly.

But Breck was making distracting swirls on her neck with his thumb and Darla barely heard her. "I can think of parts of the wedding I'd like to do again," he said quietly. "Maybe not the being crushed by a bear part, but there were some lovely moments afterwards…" He pulled her into a spontaneous dance across the lawn, and Darla laughed and stepped willingly into it as he spun her around and dipped her.

"There were some lovely moments before, too," she reminded him.

"Not so much the night before," Breck said, mouth close to hers. "But the night before that."

"And the night before that," Darla reminded him, blowing on his ear.

"And the night before that," Breck added, kissing her jaw and her nibbling at her neck.

"One o'clock," Scarlet reminded them firmly, and Darla heard her sensible heels click away in exasperation as Liam muttered, "Baffling!" and went to check on Mr. Danby's vitals again.

Breck lifted Darla back to her feet but didn't offer to let her go. "We've got a little time before the meeting," he told her, raising an eyebrow suggestively.

"Want to go recreate one of those nights?" Darla grinned.

Breck's perfect mouth curved into a smile. "There's a tire on the van that needs changed…" he said leadingly.

Then they were running, hand in hand, for the entrance of the resort.

PREGNANCY KNOWS

This story was mostly an excuse to write Gizelle asking questions about babies…

Laura stood up too fast and had to focus hard on fighting down her nausea. The last thing she wanted to do was throw up on Scarlet's shoes. The looming weight of Laura's secret pregnancy had lifted, now that most of the staff knew, but she and Tex still hadn't told Scarlet. The resort owner was in a mood like black ice already; the disaster of Darla Grant's wedding had undoubtedly not been good for her bottom line, there was a pending lawsuit, and the press had not all been flattering. The staff was giving her a wide berth.

An even wider berth than usual.

"I love you, Cowboy," she told Tex, as he put up his "Help yourself at the cooler!" sign. "But your bar smells bad."

Tex looked affronted. "What does it smell like?" he asked, inhaling deeply.

"Like your feet," Laura complained, knowing that she was complaining and hating it. Pregnancy hormones made her feel a moment from weeping, too. "Sweaty cowboy boots. And bruised mint. And that new cleaning liquid. And seventeen kinds of booze."

"I only smell sixteen kinds of booze," Tex teased her kindly. "Pregnancy nose is amazing." He kissed the tip of it and Laura got a whiff of his breath, which would have been inoffensive at any other time. She waved a hand in front of her face.

"I want to walk around with a clothespin holding it shut," Laura laughed. "The people coming off the last charter nearly made me puke." In truth, she hadn't actually thrown up that much since she realized what was going on, but she did get a sick feeling that left her dizzy and without appetite.

"You are looking a little green around the gills," Tex said kindly. "Can I get you a tonic before the staff meeting?"

Laura tested the idea and shook her head. Despite the name, her morning sickness seemed to hit worst in the early afternoon, when the sun was highest and she had the most to do…and her chance of running into Scarlet was the highest.

Gizelle, barefoot, was sitting in the middle of the steps up from the bar to the restaurant, holding something cupped in her hands that she was studying intensely.

"What have you got there, cub?" Tex asked, as they parted to step around her.

"I'm not a baby," Gizelle said gravely. "And I'm not a bear. I have an ant. Did you know that they can lift up to fifty times their own body weight? And there's a caterpillar in Laura that will be a butterfly."

"Ah…do you mean the baby?" Tex asked as Laura put a hand reflexively to her belly. She wasn't by any means obviously pregnant; as weird as her body felt on the inside, she looked no different in the mirror's reflection. Yet.

"I don't remember meeting it," Gizelle said curiously, still focused on the ant that was scurrying frantically around her fingers trying to escape.

"It won't be born for many months," Laura said gently. "You haven't met it, yet." It occurred to her suddenly that Gizelle might not ever meet her baby, at least not while it was young. Scarlet didn't want children on the island, and Gizelle would likely never leave it. "Gizelle, sweetheart, please don't say anything about it to Scarlet yet."

They didn't have a plan for the future yet. Laura hated to ask Tex to leave his bar; he loved it here as much as she did, if not more. But the resort wasn't a place to raise a baby, all alone with no other children, even if Scarlet did decide to allow it.

Gizelle looked up with shining eyes. "There are so many secrets," she observed without judgement. "Old secrets. New secrets. Big secrets. Baby secrets. Do you think that I could have a baby? I have a mate, now."

"Would you want one?" Laura asked cautiously, sitting on the step beside her.

"Do you know how it works?" Tex sat at Gizelle's other side.

Gizelle smiled and laughed. "Yes, of course. Breck explained everything in great detail," she said carelessly. "And Conall always—wait, that's too much information. I remembered!"

Laura exchanged an amused look over her head with Tex.

"I never was a child," Gizelle said, herding her ant carefully back from her wrist to her fingertips. "How could I teach a baby how to be one? What do you do with a baby? There's so much to know."

Since this was a question that Laura had been wrestling with herself, she hesitated.

"I don't think anyone has all of the answers," Tex said thoughtfully. "We just have to make it up as we go, and love it completely. I hope."

Gizelle's head swiveled to look at the bartender. "Wait, you don't know?" she said dubiously. "Don't you remember when you were a baby?"

"No," Tex said in surprise. "No one does!"

"Why not?" Gizelle said in astonishment. "Do you?" She turned to Laura.

"No," she said. "He's right. No one remembers being a baby. You don't start remembering things until you're a little older."

Gizelle looked suspicious, like she thought they might be making a joke she didn't understand. "There's so very much to know," she said with a sigh. "But it ends soon."

"What does?" Tex asked.

"My memory," Gizelle said. Then, abruptly, she stood up and started twisting around in alarm, shaking her sundress and lifting one bare leg after another. She craned to see the backs of each elbow, and contorted into awkward forms as she chased her own backside around in a circle like a dog.

"What's wrong?" Tex asked, rising to his feet in alarm, an arm out to catch Gizelle if she toppled off the step.

Laura scrambled to her own feet and had to sway a moment in dizziness. "What is it, Gizelle?"

"I've lost my ant!" she explained in dismay. She fell to her knees and began poking around in the grass at the edge of the steps. "There are too many, I'll never find him. There are more ants than there are people, more than twelve thousand different kinds, did you know? I'm a terrible mother. He'll get lost! He'll get into the salt! He'll be stepped on!"

"There are other ants," Tex said, trying to comfort her.

"You wouldn't say that about a baby," Gizelle scolded him, peering into the grass.

Laura had to smother a laugh over her earnestness. "No, we wouldn't," she agreed. "But there's a big difference between an ant and a baby."

"That ant is all grown up," Tex pointed out. "Maybe he wants to go live his own life."

Gizelle abandoned her search and came to stand next to Laura on the same step. She was so slight and spent so much time crouched down that it was easy to forget that she wasn't also short. "You'll take good care of your baby," she said confidently. "And I will find a new ant to love and raise." She considered. "What about a bird? Maybe I can catch one! Oh, but the kittens would want it for their own."

Then very suddenly, she bent to put her head very close to Laura's belly, though she didn't offer to actually touch her. "Maybe you will remember," she said. "Remember your ant." Then she straightened. "Can I be his ant?"

"Ant?" Laura said in confusion. Did she mean aunt?

"His?" Tex added hopefully.

"It's a homonym. If I were your sister, I could be! Instead, Jenny will be. Oh! That means that Travis will be an uncle! Do ants have sisters? I have to look it up on my tablet!" Then, in a flash of salt-and-pepper braids and bare legs, she was gone, flying down the stairs and away through the hedges.

As she often did, Gizelle left a moment of dazed confusion in her wake. "Do you think she actually knows it will be a boy?" Tex asked, as they resumed their climb of the stairs to the restaurant. He slipped an arm around her waist.

"Sometimes, she knows things," Laura said thoughtfully. "And sometimes she really doesn't."

"You're worried," Tex observed, because he knew her so well.

"I'm going to miss this place," Laura confessed. "And we can't stay, can we?" She was all but begging for him to tell her differently. He was so proud of his bar, and all their friends were here, even her sister.

"How lucky are we?" Tex said unexpectedly.

"Lucky?" Laura didn't feel lucky. She felt like crying.

They were at the top of the stairs, near the archway leading to the restaurant, and Tex drew her to one side. "So lucky," he said. "It doesn't matter where we are, or where we end up. We'll be together, you and I…and our child. Not everyone gets to do that. Not everyone gets to work at a place like this, and maybe we'll come back someday. But there's a whole big world out there, and we'll find a place where we can fit. Maybe Texas. Maybe California. What's between them, Arizona? New Mexico? I could live there. I could live anywhere with you. We'll visit when we can, and Jenny and Travis can come see us whenever the resort isn't on the brink of falling down or being sued."

Laura hated the rollercoaster of hormones, but this was the good part, the hopeful part. The part where Tex was right, and this was exactly what was supposed to happen and she was deeply, tremendously excited. They were on the brink of something amazing and new, a journey together that was terrifying and…absolutely perfect.

She didn't have to know where they would end up yet; they had time, still. To her chagrin, tears overflowed her eyes.

Tex crumbled and stepped to embrace her. "Oh, Laura, sweetheart, it's okay, it's going to be wonderful, everything will work out exactly as it is supposed to and I love you so much, please don't cry!"

But these were tears of happiness, and Laura fell into his arms laughing. "I know," she said. "I know."

FAKE FUR

In an unfortunate (but orchestrated!) error, a party of guests were booked at Shifting Sands Resort who aren't shifters, and don't even know about them! These hapless humans are from a subculture known as furries*: people who dress and roleplay as anthropomorphic animal characters...and they are expecting that the resort is a haven for other furries like them, not for actual shifters! This occurs during the events of [Tropical Lion's Legacy](), but spoils nothing for that book.*

The resort owner, Scarlet, was so angry that it made Amy's skin itch.

She was still smiling: this serene little smile that couldn't really hide the fact that she was furious. Amy thought she was one of the most beautiful people she'd ever seen in her life, but she was also kind of terrifying, with her perfectly pulled-back red hair and her gleaming green eyes.

There had been some kind of mistake with their reservation, Amy was sure, as Scarlet stepped aside to have a very quiet, intense conversation with a giant, shaggy-haired man wearing a staff polo shirt.

Amy was exhausted from flying for more than a day, and already feeling like this whole trip had been a giant mistake.

She had wanted a vacation so badly, been so desperate to escape her terrible job and horrible boss and her leering landlord and the screaming neighbors upstairs, that she would have agreed to a weirder last-minute trip.

"It's a furry resort," Sonja had told her. "A whole resort just for furries. It's going to be amazing. Like a convention but way, way more relaxing. And Brandon is paying for the whole stay, isn't it just the luckiest thing?"

Amy's first doubts had emerged before she met Brandon. She'd been afraid, at first, that Sonja was going to try to hook her up with her mysterious new friend and benefactor, and she'd been terrifically relieved that Brandon didn't seem particularly interested in her—but then, who would be?

Brandon still made her nervous. He was just…a little too gregarious, a little too generous. Who bought a whole vacation for people he'd just met? Yes, the furry community could be pretty inclusive and Sonja was always raving about how they were the very nicest people you'll ever meet, but there was something about Brandon that made her alarms go off.

Like he had some other kind of purpose to this whole thing and was just indulging Sonja and her friends. Like he knew something they didn't. Amy had a keen sense of 'being used,' and a lot of experience with it, and Brandon checked off all her boxes.

Still, Amy had filled out the forms on the webpage, because she would be going with Sonja and Adam and Donnie, and while she felt like Brandon had his own agenda, she wasn't going to turn down an all-expense-paid last minute trip to a tropical island off of Costa Rica for anything less than sure mortal peril.

"Fox," she'd selected, when the weirdly-worded online form had asked for her fursona, or furry persona. She didn't have multiple suits like Sonja and Adam did, but she had finally finished her fursuit, and she'd spent a month's rent on the articulated head alone. It felt kind of nice to have a place to show it off again; she'd only worn it to one convention so far, which seemed like a crying shame, considering the expense.

Her mother had heard only the worst things about the furry community, and thought the whole point was lots of kinky sex, but Amy's experiences had all been completely innocuous, and she'd found it oddly comfortable to wear a fursuit out in groups of people.

She didn't share Sonja and Adam's single-minded pursuit of costuming, and she wasn't like Donnie, who was utterly convinced that he *really* had a bear's spirit inside of him and used that as an excuse to mostly grunt through conversations and growl at people he didn't like. But she liked them despite their fanatical obsession. Maybe because of it. Even though they were quirky, they were *honestly* quirky, and refreshingly unabashed about who they actually were and wanted to be.

Scarlet, returning from her quiet conversation with a bright, false smile, didn't look like the kind of person who wore costumes. She looked like the kind of woman who always had perfect hair and perfect nails and never, ever sweated.

Unlike Amy, who felt sticky and limp in the unexpected heat.

"I'm afraid we've got a bit of a situation," the resort owner said apologetically. "But I assure you, I am taking care of everything. The hotel is temporarily closed because of an insect infestation. It is too late this evening to get you to the mainland, but we are setting you up with a tent on the beach."

"A tent?" Sonja said reluctantly.

"Insects?" Adam said, with a glance at their bulky luggage. "What kind of insects?"

Amy thought that Scarlet's gaze was a little too knowing. "A small cloth-eating variety of moth. We're having the building tented and gassed as we speak."

Sonja gave a little squeak of dismay.

"Tomorrow morning, we'll take you to a resort on the mainland that has availability; I've already made all the arrangements for you."

Amy knew to the bottom of her stomach that this woman was

desperate to get rid of them. She couldn't figure out *why*, but she was good at reading people, and they were definitely not welcome here.

~

"I am so bored of resorts," Calvin said, slumping down at the table next to his sister. "Seriously, how long am I expected to chaperone you around these places?"

"Until Mummy and Daddy think I'm responsible enough to go on my own," Charlene suggested, taking a sip of something fruity-smelling in a tall glass with an umbrella.

Calvin groaned. "You're saying I'm doomed to an eternity of this?" He tried to flag down a waiter, but there was some kind of commotion at the far end of the restaurant and he failed to get any attention whatsoever.

Charlene wrinkled her nose at him. "I'm not any happier about this than you are," she pointed out. "I'm twenty-two, and I think I can go to a wedding at a tropical resort *all by myself.* All you do is moan and complain and sunburn because you aren't smart enough to put sunscreen on."

Charlene smelled like coconuts and had already developed a glistening golden tan.

Calvin, with his pale hair and freckles, would never be able to achieve such skin pigment, and didn't particularly care.

"Well, maybe if you can stay out of trouble this entire trip and avoid good-looking motorcycle gangsters, I can finally be taken off of big brother duty and go back to my own life."

"You say that like you *have* your own life," Charlene scoffed. But she blushed at the reminder of the motorcycle bad boy she had very regrettably hooked up with on their *last* vacation.

Calvin raised his empty water glass, hoping to get some service, but the staff appeared to have all of their attention on the party at the end of the deck.

Obviously something important was happening; Calvin had enough experience with bodyguards to recognize their I'm-not-as-casual-as-I'm-pretending-to-be stance, and the big woman sitting across from the figure they were flanking had all the graceful self-confidence of royalty. There had already been a lot of noisy toasts, and it sounded like someone was sobbing happily.

Charlene wasn't really wrong, to Calvin's chagrin. He was beginning to suspect that he was being sent out with his sister as much to keep him from moping around the estate as anything else. He'd finished his lackluster degree in business with no more ambitions to take over the family business than when he'd started, and every hobby and entertainment he'd pursued left him cold.

He was the family…maybe not the family screwup, but definitely the family disappointment. There was no passion in his life, nothing but tiresome duties that he dodged as much as possible. "You're lucky," he groused at Charlene. "No one expects *you* to have a life. You're doing exactly what a good daughter of money should be doing, dangling around for an *appropriate* husband to scoop you up."

Charlene gave him one of those brief, piercing looks that always made Calvin aware that there was more to his sister than most people would credit, but before she could retort, she stared past him. "Oh. My. God."

Calvin swiveled to look.

A party was coming into the restaurant, four lost-looking people who were clearly puzzled not to be met by a waiter. After a moment of milling, they seated themselves at a vacant table next to theirs, and Calvin couldn't keep himself from staring, turned around in his chair.

"Those must be the *humans*," Charlene whispered.

The resort owner, Scarlet, had personally warned them not to shift or perform superhuman feats until some non-shifter guests who had accidentally been booked were shipped out the following morning. Calvin had suspected a joke, but it wasn't humor that arrested him.

One of the women was wearing great, fuzzy green ears tipped with white. Her arm was linked in a soft-looking man's, and he was wearing a fitted furry vest. When they turned to take their seats, fluffy tails swung behind them. The second man was wearing a Dead Kennedys t-shirt that was a little out of place at a luxury resort, and had leather bracers on his wrists, but had no other trappings.

It was the second woman that had caught Calvin's attention… and the absolute laser focus of his wolf.

She was curvy and had a golden-skinned complexion that had more to do with genetics than sunlight, with silky black hair to her shoulders. Bangs framed an oval face, and almond-shaped brown eyes were anxiously surveying the restaurant. She was wearing red fox-patterned fuzzy ears of her own, and Calvin caught just the barest flick of a fake tail when she went to take her seat next to the Dead Kennedys shirt guy.

That's her, his wolf said with absolute conviction. *That's our mate.*

"You should stop staring," Charlene hissed at him. "They're just idiotic humans, but it's still rude."

Calvin wrenched his gaze back to the table. *Are you* sure? he demanded of his wolf.

Her, his wolf sang happily.

"Wow," Charlene chuckled, taking a sip of her dwindling drink to cover her amusement. "Just, *wow*. See, this resort isn't *all* boring."

Calvin was breathing like he'd just run a lap around their estate; his entire body hummed with need and he felt like he was awake for the first time in his whole life.

That was…*her*.

Even looking away from her, the image of her face was burned into his memory. She was beautiful and perfect and Calvin had never wanted anything so much.

And she was…human.

Not a shifter.

According to Scarlet, she didn't even *know* about shifters.

"Are you okay?" Charlene's voice suggested that Calvin looked as flabbergasted as he felt.

"Fine," he said faintly. "Fine."

It was a complete lie. He was nothing even resembling fine. He was undone to the very center of his soul, and he knew that there was only one person who could put him back together.

And she was a *human*.

~

Amy was beginning to feel…conspicuous.

"I'm surprised no one else is wearing costumes," Sonja said thoughtfully. "I mean, maybe not full fursuits because it's still a hundred degrees after dark, but where are the ears and tails? I was kind of expecting, you know, a beachside campfire howl or something *themed*." Sonja was wearing her ears, of course, as was Amy. Brandon had chosen not to eat with the group, citing some business that might keep him out late.

Donnie wasn't wearing any furry accessories at all, and Adam's (fake) fur vest was more subtle than the ears, but Amy was still uncomfortably aware that they were getting odd looks from the nearby tables.

It had been nothing but odd looks since they'd arrived that afternoon. Odd looks and conversations that died at their approach. Odd looks, dead-on-arrival conversations, and the most *gorgeous* people that Amy had ever seen outside of a magazine. This was the first place she'd ever been where the actual guests were more beautiful than the brochure photos.

There was a man at the next table over that looked like a movie star. He was wearing khakis and a silk shirt and had a shock of blond hair and absolutely amazing shoulders. He looked away swiftly as Amy sat down, but she got just a glimpse of bright blue eyes that seemed to linger on Amy's retinas.

"I'm starting to think this isn't a furry resort," Amy said nervously, tucking her tail through the bars of the chair. "I mean, no one else seems to be in costume. No one's talking about art or their fursonas or anything."

"Why did they have all that stuff on the registration then?" Sonja asked. "*What's your animal form? What special needs does your animal have?*"

"It was worded kind of funny," Amy pointed out. "Animal form, instead of fursona."

"Maybe it's for real animals who are making reservations," Donnie surmised in a growl.

They all chuckled, even Donnie, because how ridiculous was that?

"It's not really weirder than all those rules about not picking flowers or disturbing the plants," Adam said. "I mean, those were pretty draconian."

"They do seem pretty mysterious about things, though," Sonja said thoughtfully. "Maybe it was some kind of secret code, on the form. Maybe…" she gasped. "Maybe it's human trafficking."

"Human trafficking?" Adam snorted. "Honey, don't be ridiculous."

"Maybe the hotel is where they're keeping all the helpless victims!" Sonja said in a loud whisper.

As much as Amy didn't really believe that the hotel was closed for extermination, human trafficking wasn't even in her top hundred ideas for why they'd shut it down and were trying to get rid of them. "I doubt they're doing anything *that* nefarious," she said. "They wouldn't be so nice about everything and put us up at another resort if… oh!"

Amy bit off her protest as a waiter finally came to their table, looking apologetic…and as incredibly handsome as every other staff member they'd met.

"I'm so sorry for the delay," he said, with a broad grin. "Our chef has finally popped the question to his mate, and we're all in celebration mode."

Sonja craned her neck to look down the restaurant deck. "Oh!" she said in delight, apparently forgetting about the dire deeds hypothetically being committed in the tented hotel. "That's so sweet!" She took Adam's hand in her own. "We're *mates*, too."

The waiter blinked at them, then seemed to take the statement in stride. He cleared his throat. "Ah…of course," he said, with a winning smile. "Congratulations to you as well. Can I bring you some champagne to start with? I'm afraid that dinner itself is going to be a little slow as we get things sorted out, but you are welcome to serve yourself from the buffet at any time..."

Sonja accepted champagne for all of them, though Amy doubted that bubbly alcohol was what she needed after a grueling plane ride through four time zones that had taken more than twenty-four hours with layovers. She was already feeling light-headed and silly.

"I'm going to grab something from the buffet," Amy said, rising to her feet.

"I filled up on airplane nuts," Sonja said. Donnie just grunted.

So Amy went to the buffet alone, feeling self conscious about her plush tail instead of finding the swish of it against the back of her legs reassuring.

If the quality of the food that had been out in trays for an indeterminate amount of time was any indication, the resort restaurant was every *bit* what the brochure had promised. There was a creamy casserole heaped with crunchy topping, and a selection of beautifully spiced vegetables that weren't overcooked in the slightest, mashed potatoes so silky that they made a perfect, snow-capped mountain on her plate, and a pot roast so tender it fell apart as she put it next to the potatoes.

Then she found the salad bar, and wished she hadn't filled her plate quite so full, because everything was fresh and crisp, and there were six amazing sounding flavors of unusual dressing, and piles of fruit so recently cut that the pieces still had juice beading up on the slices.

She turned carefully, not wanting to jostle her precariously heaped plate, and nearly ran into the gorgeous must-be-a-movie-star from the next table looming behind her.

"Sorry," she squeaked automatically, as he moved impossibly fast to catch a roll that made a break for freedom from her tray.

His blue eyes were exactly as amazing as she'd remembered from her brief glimpse, and his shoulders even broader up close. "I was…hungry," Amy said apologetically, feeling like she ought to explain why she had so much food.

"Me, too," he said, and even his rich, cultured voice was movie star perfect.

It also didn't sound like he was talking about *food.*

Amy wasn't sure where to look; he was tall enough that looking up into his face felt awkward and weirdly intimate but if she wasn't looking at his beautiful features, she was staring at the vee his shirt made where it was unbuttoned, teasing at the chest beneath.

"I…uh…I'm Calvin," he said, and when Amy ventured a glance upwards, she was surprised to find that he was *blushing.*

Wait.

He was stuttering and blushing and talking to *her*?

"Where's the tiger?" Amy asked flippantly.

He blinked at her, because it was the stupidest reply she could possibly have come up with. "The tiger?"

"Hobbes," Amy explained. And when he continued to stare at her, added, "...from Calvin and Hobbes? The comic."

"Oh," Calvin said with a desperate laugh. "For a moment, I thought you meant the best man, Tony."

It was Amy's turn to stare. "Tony…the tiger?" She was pretty sure she was missing something.

"He's great," Calvin assured her.

Amy could not smother her laugh fast enough, and nearly upset her entire precarious tray of food onto him.

And if she'd thought that Calvin was devastating looking awkward and blushing, Calvin with a big grin making his eyes twinkle was utterly undoing.

Amy had never wanted to throw her arms around a stranger and kiss them so much in her life. The tray in her hands actually began to tip, and tightening her grip drew her attention back down to it.

"Your roll," Calvin said suddenly, as if he only just realized he was still holding it.

"Sorry," they both said together, and they shared another slow, shy smile as he put the bread down on her tray.

"I'm Amy," she finally remembered to tell him.

"Amy…" he said on an exhale, and Amy had never heard her

name said quite that way before, like he was savoring the two puny syllables.

"Yeah," Amy said unintelligently. "Amy." He said it better than she did.

"I'm Calvin," he said eagerly. He made an abortive move to shake her hand, realizing at the last moment that her hands were full of her buffet tray.

"I know," Amy said with a giggle. "Like Calvin and Hobbes." It was somehow reassuring that he was clearly as nervous as she was. Considering that her heart seemed to be racing in her chest and parts lower were on absolute fire, this seemed like a pretty low bar to limbo under.

She looked behind him and realized that the woman he'd been sitting with was glaring at them. "I…er…think your friend is trying to get your attention."

"Sister," Calvin insisted vehemently. "She's my *sister*."

Was it a little too defensive? He turned to look and Amy took the opportunity to slip around his other side. "I've got to get back to my friends. And…eat, you know. Hungry." It was definitely a different kind of hunger that she was feeling now.

"You could join us," Calvin offered with clearly ill thought impetuousness. His sister looked utterly disgusted and like she would rather have a cockroach at their table than Amy.

"I should sit with my friends," she said reluctantly. "But thanks…"

They parted slowly, exchanging awkward, blushing smiles. Amy almost ran into her table before she figured out how to operate her chair, and she was grateful that Sonja had apparently kept the attention of the table. Only Donnie gave her a suspicious sideways look, and no one found it weird that she ducked her head to her food and ate in silence for the rest of the meal, trying not to stare at Calvin's shoulders as he sat down with his back to her.

~

"What the hell was that, Cal?"

It took every ounce of Calvin's self control not to swivel in his seat and stare at Amy. *Amy*. His mate.

He vacillated between giddy happiness and gaping uncertainty.

What was he supposed to do *now*? He had to catch her before she left, and Scarlet had been explicit about getting the non-shifters off the island in the morning. So he had to woo her...and explain shifters to her, and the whole idea of mates...all before she shipped out in the morning and left an Amy-sized hole where his heart had been. And he could barely talk in complete sentences to her.

"Cal!"

Calvin raised his eyes and gave Charlene a crooked smile. "Sorry. It's just...she's my mate. I should have gotten her number."

Charlene almost never looked shocked. She had perfected a cool, disinterested smile that she used on everyone indiscriminately.

So Calvin felt triumphant when Charlene's jaw rather literally dropped and her eyes flew open. "Don't be ridiculous," she said, once she'd snapped her mouth shut.

"She is," Calvin insisted. He tried to look discretely over his shoulder, but Amy was staring down at her plate like it might bite her if she didn't.

"She's a human," Charlene pointed out. "Not a shifter."

"Hey, you can argue with my wolf all you'd like, but she's the one. My one. My only. Just like the stories, just like Grandmama used to tell us."

"Grandmama was senile," Charlene scoffed.

"Well, she wasn't wrong about this," Calvin said. "I know her. I look into her eyes and it's like coming home. I look at her and..." He tried to smother his wolf; he certainly wasn't going to tell his sister that he was absolutely desperate to know how Amy's skin would feel, what her kiss would taste like, how deep he could... He took a bracing drink of the water a waiter had finally filled.

Charlene wasn't fooled. "If this is you being a disgusting horndog because you've been too busy minding *my* business instead of finding someone you can--"

"It's not just attraction," Calvin protested under his breath. "I love her."

"You literally just laid eyes on her," Charlene said, shaking her head. "And have you missed the point about how she isn't a shifter?"

"I don't care," Calvin said with a second swift glance over his shoulder. Amy was still looking studiously down at her food.

"You'll care when Daddy disowns you," Charlene hissed. "*Quit staring*! Marrying a shifter is like, the *most important* criteria they have. And *oh my God*, she's wearing *fake fur* ears."

Calvin thought they were adorable. They were like a little glimpse of the playful, curious spark that he already knew Amy had behind her shy smile. And the tail, swishing over her perfect ass as she walked away was burned into his memory. "It's cute," he said.

Charlene looked at him like he'd just praised a rabid opossum.

The approach of a grinning waiter stopped her from undoubtedly saying something cutting. "Can I get you folks anything else to drink? I'm afraid our usual dinner service has been interrupted tonight, but the buffet remains stocked, and if you'd like me to dish you up a plate..."

Charlene gave a sigh. "A sandwich," she said flatly. "No cheese. No greasy meat. In fact, make it just veggies. Not too many onions. Mayonnaise and a little mustard. A *little*. Sprouts if you have them."

"And for you?"

Calvin was startled into looking back at him, and was alarmed when he received a wink. "Nothing, thanks." He hadn't lied to Amy about being hungry, but it was a hunger that no sandwich was going to fill.

The waiter actually bowed, and his merriment didn't diminish in the slightest. Calvin caught him humming as he walked away.

"See, Daddy would probably approve of that guy before he approved of some cultish human," Charlene said pointedly.

Calvin started to look back over his shoulder, protesting, "She's not cultish."

"Stop staring," Charlene whispered. "And I've heard about furries. They're…like a religion. They choose their animals by taking tests on the Internet and then have big conventions where they dress up and pretend they're like us."

"They don't know about us," Calvin pointed out.

"An imaginative version of us," Charlene said, rolling her eyes. "Highly imaginative, by the sounds of it." She sniffed. "And the looks of it, too. They'll *talk*, Calvin, if you have a girlfriend like that."

Normally, Charlene's snobbishness didn't really bother Calvin, but he caught himself growing angry with her snotty tone and superior attitude. That was his *mate* she was disparaging.

"I'd rather be with someone who has some imagination," Calvin snarled back. "Someone who has interests beyond improving their tan and buying the latest fashion sandals and gossiping disdainfully about other people who are actually out there living *lives*."

Charlene stared at him, as shocked as he'd ever seen her for the second time since he'd come back to the table.

"It's not like I'm expecting you to be best buddies." He couldn't resist adding, "I'm sure she has better taste than that. But I might have thought you'd be a little bit glad that I just met someone who can make me happier than I ever thought it was possible to be. Call Mom and Dad and let them know that you're on your own now. Because I am going to follow that woman to the ends of the earth if I have to, and I don't give a damn what you or anyone else thinks about it."

Calvin was out of words, so he stood up, shoving his chair back as he turned to go to Amy…only to find that she'd already left.

He stared at her empty chair in consternation, barely registering the inquiring looks from her friends. He considered saying something to them, but what was there to say? I'm a *real* animal shifter and your friend is my destined mate?

He needed a game plan, he realized, walking past their table after only a moment, ignoring Charlene's hiss to come back and sit down and stop making a *scene*.

His feet took him down several winding flights of steps to the bar deck half-tucked beneath the restaurant deck. A man wearing a ridiculous cowboy hat and a shining belt buckle offered him a drink, but Calvin was afraid that he was going to need a clear head to figure out how to talk to Amy; it wasn't any good loosening his tongue if he didn't know what to say.

"No thanks," he said. "I need whatever wits I've got."

The bartender chuckled and gave him an approving nod. This was probably one of the very few bars in the world that *wouldn't* encourage drinking, taking into account the damage a drunk shifter could do and the fact that all the drinks were included in the tab.

Calvin looked out over the railing to the pool...and to the beach beyond that. A grand white tent had been pitched on the sand. That would be where they'd put the humans...and Amy. She must be *there*. His wolf was yearning towards her, full of desire.

But he had to think first, think how to tell her what she must think was impossible. He had to explain to her that he really *was* a wolf, and that she was his fated everything, and had been from his first view of her. Without scaring her, or accidentally convincing her that he was a complete nutcase, or a creepy predator.

"You know how you pretend to be an animal...?"

That sounded condescending.

"So, you've heard of werewolves, right...?"

That would undoubtedly bring all sorts of misconceptions up. There was even a full moon that night.

"How would you like to have sex with a real wild animal?"

Absolutely *not*.

Calvin groaned.

There really was no safe way to do it, he decided, listening to the water crash down the falls at this end of the pool. He just had to spit it out, get down on one knee maybe, declare his love, and explain everything in whatever order it came out.

Hopefully, she wouldn't pepper-spray him.

He gathered his resolve and his breath, but as he stepped away from the railing, a tall, slender man with dark hair came skidding into the bar.

"Have you seen a naked old man?" the man asked in an urgent stage whisper, glancing at the restaurant deck just above where the rest of the human party was presumably still eating. "Or possibly...a mammoth?"

~

The tent on the beach was nothing like Amy had imagined. She had pictured the kind of battered camo tent that she'd stayed in for her long ago Girl Scout camps. Maybe a couple of cots to go under the sleeping bags, if they were going for comfort, and maybe a flickering, battery-powered lantern.

But Scarlet had gone all out on this tent.

It was a sandy white, trimmed on the outside with a flirty little ruffle that whispered in the slight breeze, and it was *huge*. It had an actual door, anchored in a wooden frame that was guyed out with cords marked with colored ribbons so that no one would accidentally walk into them in the dark. Amy knocked, in case Brandon was already there, but she was relieved when it was silent inside, and she cautiously opened the door.

All the breath went out of her as she stepped into the wonderland that had been created for them and actual tears rose up in her eyes. There was a thick plush rug down over the sand, and there were slippers laid out neatly for each of them right next to the door, so Amy wriggled out of her flip-flops and put a pair on.

The room she walked into had a low table that would seat five, with cushions all around it. A pack of cards and a few games were stacked at one side of the table, as well as a few bottles of water, and a vase overflowing with tropical flowers; apparently the resort staff was exempt from the strict 'no picking flowers' rule. There was a comfortable couch at the other side of the space, and the whole room was lit with twinkle lights strung across the ceiling. There was a battery-powered speaker playing gentle music, just barely louder than the surf whispering on the shore.

The tent had been subdivided inside, and each fabric door was pulled aside so that Amy could see that the beds were *definitely* a step above a cot with a sleeping bag.

Each room, easily identified by their waiting luggage, was

decked out with a small dresser draped in lace topped with a little vase of flowers. The bed was on a platform, and when Amy gave it an experimental bounce, found that it was a high quality mattress with a light down comforter and…was it a feather bed? It was soft and decadent and Amy immediately pulled her fabric curtain shut and shucked out of her clothing because she was almost shaking from exhaustion and nothing in the world looked as amazing as that fluffy bed.

… except maybe Calvin's eyes.

Amy woke up in confusion, not sure how long she had slept. It was still full night, she guessed by the quiet and the darkness, and she lay still for a moment and listened.

The surf still beat against the sand, and she could hear a quiet snore…probably Donnie. Beyond that, she could hear the murmur of a voice that she guessed was Sonja, answered by Adam, then they went silent.

Just as Amy thought she might drop back into sleep, she heard something else outside, a snuffling sort of sound that she couldn't resolve.

Wondering what it was drove her all the way awake with adrenaline, as hard as Amy tried to convince herself that it wasn't anything to be worried about. It was highly unlikely that Scarlet had put them up in this nice of a tent in order to feed them to some weird Costa Rican beach monster.

The snuffling sound seemed to fade away.

Amy had finally gotten her heart rate under control again, convincing herself that she'd probably imagined the snorty sound, when she started thinking about Calvin again.

That was not going to help her get back to sleep, she realized quickly, remembering his shy smile, savoring the memory of their conversation, and the way he'd said her name. After a few moments, she rolled out of the amazing bed and put her feet into the slippers. Only one strip of twinkle lights was still on, but Amy found a flashlight on a low table next to the couch. The door to Brandon's room was still open; it looked like he'd never shown up.

She left the flashlight off as she stepped outside, drawing in a breath at the view.

The moon was low in the sky, huge and bright and surrounded by glittering stars in the clear night. The ocean stretched before her, reflecting the moonlight off of rows of wrinkled waves. The air was richly scented, and warmer than she had expected. Amy drew in a deep breath and looked down the beach.

She blinked.

There was an elephant on the beach.

A shaggy, monstrous elephant was meandering around in the surf, and as it turned, Amy realized by the fur and the size of its tusks that it wasn't an elephant at all.

It was a *mammoth.*

Amy gaped at it, nearly dropping her flashlight as her fingers went numb with shock.

And then it got *weirder.*

The mammoth seemed to shimmer in the moonlight and suddenly shrink, and there was a considerably smaller figure, naked and skinny, standing in its place. It was an old man, Amy thought in surprise, all silver in the color-drained light of the moon.

He took a few staggering steps, as if he was unfamiliar with being on two feet, but what was ankle deep to a mammoth was knee-deep or more to a slight, frail man, and he lost his balance in the swirling surf.

Previously a mammoth or not, Amy couldn't let someone helpless drown in front of her. She dropped the flashlight for real and sprinted down the beach, floundering a little in the sand as her slippers abandoned her.

The man was sitting up when she got to him, trying occasionally to regain his feet and failing. Amy paused, just at the edge of the water, trying desperately to make sense of what she had just seen, then bolted forward as he tried to lever himself up and a wave hit him in the face.

She waded out as he sputtered, feeling the sand shift beneath her bare feet as the ocean tried to steal it out from underneath her. "It's okay!" she called gently. "It's okay, I'll help you."

He said something unintelligible over the murmur of the surf, and Amy bent down and got an arm around him.

For a moment, he struggled, as if he thought she was a threat, and Amy thought for a horrible moment that they might both drown. Then he stopped, looked into her face curiously and reached up and touched her hair. He said something Amy tried to make sense of and failed.

"That's right," she said, suspecting dementia (though she couldn't eliminate the idea that it might be her *own* dementia). "I'm here to help. Come on, let's get up."

With her help, he regained his feet, and he leaned heavily on her as they made it to the loose sand, where walking became very complicated indeed.

He was clearly very tired, and much more heavy than Amy had initially guessed. They staggered together for the length of the beach and she was glad when they hit the firmer soil at the base of the stairs going up to the pool.

Her relief was short-lived, as she began to appreciate exactly how difficult it was going to be to get the rather bendy and easily distracted man up the stairs. "Come on, then, maybe the bar is still open, because I really, really need a drink after this."

~

The dark-haired young man introduced himself as Liam, and when the bartender inconveniently vanished, Calvin could not in good conscience let him search alone for a missing old man who, he learned, was senile, non-verbal, and also, by the way, an uncontrolled mammoth shifter.

"Scarlet's going to kill me," Liam was saying in an endless loop as they scoured the gardens and around the cliff staff houses and down the cottage paths together, late into the night.

Calvin could see that an elderly shifter who couldn't control his shifting could be problematic, especially given the moratorium on shifting while the humans were around. His wolf gave a sigh of longing at the reminder of Amy. After they found the rogue mammoth, he could go find Amy. And…what did you even knock on with a tent? She was probably sound asleep. Was it too creepy to sleep on her doorstep? Tentstep?

"Scarlet's going to kill me," Liam said again as they met up again after splitting to investigate two cottage paths.

"I'm sure she won't literally kill you," Calvin tried to reassure him. "I didn't see any signs of him down there."

"She's out so much for having us here," Liam lamented. "This is a really crappy way to repay her."

They regrouped at the empty pool deck, and shifter keen hearing made them both look towards the steps leading down to the beach hopefully.

Calvin's heart did flip flops in his chest, and he guessed Liam's did, too, for different reasons.

A woman was walking slowly up the steps, barefoot and wearing pajamas that were soaked with salt water. Hanging on her shoulder was a wet, naked elderly man trying to eat her hair.

"Amy…" Calvin breathed.

"Oh, thank god," Liam said, and they both hurried to the strange pair.

"He was…he was…" Amy looked shocky, her eyes big and wild and unsettled. "And then he was…and I thought he might drown."

Liam and Calvin exchanged a knowing look. "I'll take him," Liam said, as Calvin said, "I'll take her."

"I couldn't understand him," Amy said, as Liam hooked an arm under the other side of the man. "He's heavier than he looks." Then she laughed hysterically. "Practically an elephant," she wheezed, as Liam effortlessly swept the man into his arms.

She stared at his feat of strength, her burst of laughter dying. "Okay, then," she said in a very small voice

Calvin grabbed towels from the pool caddy and offered one to Liam, who tucked it one-handed around the naked man who was starting to struggle in his arms. "Thanks. I'll get him his medicine and see he gets straight to bed."

Calvin was standing then with a second towel, shyly facing Amy, who was still staring after Liam and the old man.

"He was…he was…"

"I got you a towel."

"Calvin," Amy said, saying his name like it was a lifesaver.

"Like Calvin and Hobbes," Calvin said, because he couldn't think of a single other thing but the way she looked with her pajamas stuck to her luscious body.

"I…he…this has been a very strange night," Amy said weakly. She shivered.

Calvin very tentatively stepped closer and wrapped the towel around her unresisting shoulders. But he was completely incapable of stepping back again, and when she gave a little sob of shock, he slowly, gently wrapped his arms around her.

She went limp in his embrace, and they stood there for a long moment. Her hair had parted and her neck was bare to him. Calvin could not keep himself from kissing it, and she stirred in his arms but made no effort to get away, so he kissed her again, and again, down her neck to the slope of her shoulder, until he had to drag himself away from her altogether, panting.

"I'm sorry," he said. "I'm so sorry, I should have asked, I should have waited…"

They faced each other, Amy clutching the towel around her and starting at him with big eyes shining in the dim light. "I…liked it," she said, her voice small and plaintive. She certainly hadn't tried to get away.

"Can I kiss you again?" Calvin asked.

He edged closer, hopefully, but waited until she gave a breathless little, "Yes…"

Then nothing was going to keep him from her mouth.

~

Calvin was *kissing* her.

Of all the remarkable things that had happened on this extremely remarkable day where Amy had flown thousands of miles to a foreign country and seen a mammoth on the beach, the craziest part of all was that Calvin was kissing her.

Amy was having trouble thinking around the pressure of his lips on her mouth, and the way his chest felt so hard and strong against her. That wasn't the only thing that was hard, she realized between kisses; though Calvin was doing an admirable job of trying not to press his erection against her, it was very obvious and she wasn't doing a very good job of not rubbing herself against it like a cat in heat.

"Amy," he said against her mouth, and it was the same absolutely magical way that he'd said it earlier, like she was something… sacred.

Her arms had somehow gotten around him, and she was hitched up against him with one leg like she could climb him. Then he was lifting her up, as if she weighed absolutely nothing, and she was being carried to a pool lounge in the far corner of the pool deck and laid down on it. They were shrouded by a fringe of potted plants and entirely alone.

This was exactly what her mother had warned her about, Amy had a brief moment of clarity to realize.

A gorgeous stranger was going to ravage her right here, almost in public, and Amy was absolutely, one hundred percent on board with this.

He seemed to realize that they were moving insanely fast when he'd gotten three of her pajama buttons undone and one of them flew off and bounced off the tiles. "I'm sorry, I'm sorry," he said, as if he were hauling himself back by the reins. "I shouldn't be moving so fast, I'm taking advantage of your shock. You're soaking wet, we should get you warm before…"

Amy *was* soaking wet, but she knew he was talking about her pajamas, not her underpants.

"Please take advantage of me," she begged, pulling him back to her with his shirt collar so she could kiss him again. "This is exactly what I want…"

And it was.

It wasn't the three dates she always required herself to wait. It wasn't a good dinner and meeting the parents first. It wasn't a slow, respectful courtship the way she kept insisting on.

She didn't know a thing about this man, but she already trusted him completely.

And if she wasn't going to have wild, impulsive sex here, on the dark, deserted pool deck of a mysterious tropical luxury resort with a gorgeous hunk, when would she?

He slowed, but he didn't stop, kissing her deeply as he got the rest of her buttons off without incident and stripped his own shirt off over his head. He was boundless acres of muscled flesh, with broad, strong shoulders, and just the barest curls over a magazine-worthy chest. Her thumbs over his nipples made his breath hiss in.

"Amy," he murmured, and she could have listened to him say her name like that forever.

He cupped her breasts, and kissed between them. When Amy tried and failed to unbutton his pants, he took them half-off himself, and shimmied her damp pajama pants and soaking underwear down over her hips.

Both of them were bare only to their knees before urgency drew them together and Amy was arching to meet him, and he was filling her and it was awkward with their legs hobbled, and wonderful, and she was clawing at his shoulder whimpering in need.

"Yes, yes, oh, Calvin, yes!" she cried, as pleasure washed over her, and the sound of her saying his name seemed to have the same effect on him that her name in his mouth had on her.

He stiffened and thrust harder, deeper, growling and clutching at her, and a second wave of pleasure rose up in her as he lost himself.

They coupled helplessly through the aftermath, gasping and stroking and grasping at each other, until he collapsed slowly to wrap her in his strong arms.

They lay together a long moment as the sounds of the jungle night slowly came back to her ears, and when Calvin finally rolled off of her, Amy knew a moment of loss so keen that tears came to her eyes.

This was it, she told herself. It was everything she'd hoped for and now it was over and he would get dressed and she would slink back to her fairy tale tent on the sand and in the morning she'd go to the mainland and they'd never even exchanged last names.

Then Calvin was returning with an armful of fluffy towels, and he tenderly cleaned them up and then buried them in a nest of fresh, warm towels as he snuggled back down with her onto the generously sized pool lounge.

Amy didn't question the unexpected turn of events, only sighed into his embrace in delight, resolving to enjoy every moment of it.

~

No bed had ever been as comfortable and welcoming as that barely-padded pool lounge with Amy curled in the middle of it.

"Amy," he murmured, wrapping them both in thick towels.

She sighed happily and moved to give him room on the lounge.

"Am I…am I *dreaming*?" she asked, after a long still moment. "Because you…and…" She stiffened in his arms. "I saw a *mammoth* on the beach."

This was his opportunity, Calvin realized, and when he sat up, she did also.

"Shifting Sands…isn't a normal resort," he said gently.

"It's not a furry resort," Amy said firmly. "And the hotel isn't being fumigated."

Our mate is no fool, his wolf said smugly.

"Right," Calvin said, and he struggled to find somewhere to go from there. "The man you found, he *was* the mammoth on the beach."

Amy gave a little hiss of sucked in breath, then blew it out slowly. "Okay," she said carefully.

"We call ourselves shifters," Calvin said every bit as carefully.

"You're a mammoth, too?"

"No, no!" Calvin hastened to correct her. "I'm a wolf shifter."

"Like a werewolf?" Amy's eyes got wide and she pulled away in alarm. She glanced aside, towards the full, silver moon that was starting to sink into the sea.

"Sort of like a werewolf. But…not really like the stories or movies. I mean, no halfway form, it's one or the other of us. And regular bullets work, they don't have to be silver. No crazy killing sprees, either, I promise!"

She stared at him a long moment in silence while Calvin tried to figure out how to explain his wolf's driving need for her, and what it meant to have a mate. He was sure he was doing a terrible job explaining things and dreaded making it worse.

"Can you…turn me?" she asked at last, her towel clutched around her.

Calvin looked at her blankly. "Turn you?"

"*Bite* me. Turn me into one of you."

Calvin couldn't read the expression in her face, and he probably looked as horrified as he felt. "It doesn't work that way," he said more firmly than he meant to. "It's something you're just born with."

Calvin realized that the expression had been hope when it fell away into something more like despair.

"Of course," she said faintly, and she seemed to shrink into herself, shivering and pulling the towel closer around her as she looked away.

Fix it! his wolf howled, sure that Calvin had said something wrong. *Tell her she's perfect just as she is.*

"You're perfect," Calvin said stupidly.

She looked back, fast and angry. "Don't patronize me. I know what I am."

"You're…perfect," Calvin said again, helplessly.

She stood up and drew away, all the comfort of their coupling drained away. "I'm a *fraud*. You must think we're so stupid. Dressing up in costumes, *pretending*, and all along, you were actually the real thing." She found her abandoned pajama pants and pulled them on roughly, refusing to look at Calvin. Her underwear fell out through a leg and she wadded them up and put them in a pocket as she searched for her shirt. "I feel like an idiot. We've been a *laughingstock*."

"I don't think you're stupid," Calvin protested, standing. He tried to gather her up in his arms again, but she pushed him back.

"You're not a laughingstock!" But he remembered Charlene's snide comments and his heart sank.

"All those suddenly hushed conversations, all the sideways looks. I feel…I feel so betrayed..." She pulled her pajama top on roughly, starting the buttons off-row and not realizing it until she got to the space with the missing button. She struggled with it, hands shaking, until Calvin tried to help her.

"Don't touch me!"

"Amy…" It was the first thing he'd said that gave her any pause at all. But the softness in her eyes vanished into anger almost at once.

"Was it pity? *The poor deluded thing!* Or was it curiosity? *Let's do a* human."

"It wasn't like that," Calvin insisted. "Amy…"

She flinched. "Don't. Just…don't." She gave up on trying to fix the misaligned buttons and turned away.

"Please, can I explain?"

"Leave me alone!"

And then she was flying away down the steps to the beach again, leaving Calvin by the pool with his wolf howling in his chest.

~

Amy couldn't go back to the fairy tale tent. She didn't want to listen to Sonya and Adam whispering romantically together, or Donnie's snores, or possibly run into Brandon coming home late…was he even a furry, she wondered. Or was he one of these shifter things? Had he known when he set up the reservation? Maybe he was a werewolf *hunter*, she thought suddenly and it was everything she could do to talk herself down and not turn back to warn Calvin.

She found herself at the place on the beach that the mammoth had been standing, and she scowled at the sand. The tide was coming in, and all of their footprints had been washed away—human and giant extinct elephant alike.

Like it hadn't even happened.

Like this was all just a crazy dream, a hallucination, her imagination running away with her. Except that she found her flashlight (it didn't work any more), and one of her lost slippers.

Amy wrapped her arms around herself, and all she could think of was Calvin's kisses, his strong arms, the way he said her name… and big, salty tears rolled down her cheeks, because it had been so perfect, and she was so *stupid.*

Everyone here was strong and supernaturally good looking and she was just an idiotic little *furry* playing dress-up, and they all *knew*, and Amy could not wait to leave this horrible place.

She found a place where the beach started to become firm ground, where trees were untangling from the shore, and curled up in their roots for a good self-pity cry before morning finally dawned and she could turn her back on this whole ridiculous, impossible place.

~

Calvin was surprised to find Charlene with her laptop at the little desk in the sitting room of their cottage. "What are you doing up?" A glance at the clock on the wall suggested that it was nearly dawn.

She waved at him crossly to hush and Calvin noticed that she was holding her phone to ear as she said, "Okay, thanks, Daddy. Love you! Kisses!" Then she put down the phone and turned to regard Calvin thoughtful.

Calvin scowled at her. "Why were you talking to Dad at this hour?"

"They're in Italy," Charlene said with a careless shrug. "It's the middle of the day or something."

"That doesn't answer the important part of the question."

Charlene stood. Her height always surprised Calvin, even when she was barefoot. He kept expecting her to be the little kid sister who was always in trouble.

"You look like hell," she said. "Having trouble with your human girlfriend?"

Calvin could only snarl helplessly, not wanting to think about the betrayal and hurt in Amy's eyes when he tried to explain shifting to her.

"Well, you're going to have to fix that part yourself," Charlene said breezily. "But things are all smoothed over with Mummy and Daddy."

Calvin felt like his brain was moving slowly. "What do you mean, smoothed? What's smoothed?"

"They're okay with you having a human mate," Charlene said with a slow, eager smile. "I told them all about her and said they were going to have to get used to the idea, and that if they weren't nice to her, I was going to get back together with Darrel the Motorcycle Jerk."

Calvin stared.

"Did you ever get her last name?" Charlene asked casually. "It's Tasher; I got Scarlet to tell me, and she has a Facebook page, and do you know, furries aren't really as bad as I thought? Turns out they do a lot of charity work. They're big donors to animal rescues and stuff."

"What are you *doing*?" Calvin asked numbly. The idea of his sister bullying the resort owner into giving up a guest's name was faintly amusing.

"I'm trying to be a good sister," Charlene said frankly. "If she's your mate, she's your mate. I shouldn't be…judgy. I..." she looked abashed. "I want you to be happy."

Calvin sank into a chair and put his face in his hands.

"What did you do?" Charlene demanded. "What did you say?"

"I told her I was a shifter," Calvin said weakly.

"And she freaked out?" Charlene guessed.

The memory of Amy's hurt eyes was burned into Calvin's memory. "She thought that I'd slept with her out of *pity*."

"You slept with her before you told her?" Charlene groaned. "Are you a complete idiot? Does she even *know* about mates?"

"I was going to tell her! I tried! She…ran."

She'd run away from him, and Calvin knew that his life would never be complete without her, but he had no idea what to do.

"I'd run, too," Charlene said without sympathy. "You really made a mash of things, big brother. This is going to take a grand gesture."

"A what?"

"A grand gesture," Charlene said matter-of-factly. "A big, showy display of affection to convince her you aren't a complete ass." She said the last dubiously, as if she wasn't quite sure of the truth of it.

"Is this *your* grand gesture?" Calvin asked. "Getting Mom and Dad to be okay with this, I mean."

Charlene sat opposite from him. "Maybe it is," she said wryly. "You've been a good brother. I've…been less of a good sister."

"What do I do?" Calvin asked plaintively, his wolf still howling in his head. "How do I get her back?"

"Well, you can't sing, so no serenades."

"I could play something on my phone, but we…don't have a song." They didn't have anything. Anything but a stolen moment on an empty pool deck and the bone-deep knowledge that there was no one else for him, ever. "I'm so *stupid*."

"You're not stupid," Charlene said thoughtfully. "But you *are* going to have to pull out all the stops for this one. Are you willing to break rules?"

Calvin gave her a hopeful look. "I'd do anything," he agreed.

~

Amy dragged her bag behind her, wishing she had taken the offer by the staff to carry it for her. It was awkward, hauling it through the loose sand towards the dock. She eyed the man wrangling the rest of the luggage, wondering bitterly if he wasn't pretending just a little too hard that it was heavy for him.

Now that she knew what everyone was, she couldn't *not* see it. They were all so strong, and supernaturally graceful, and there was no way that the chef who had brought them their apologetic breakfast wasn't some kind of giant bear shifter. There was a woman sunning by the pool in the early morning light who was almost certainly an otter, and she'd swear she heard a hyena laughing as they ate breakfast.

The boat was already running when they got to the dock.

The resort could not *wait* to get rid of them.

Amy walked briskly ahead of Sonya, Adam, and Donnie, yanking her recalcitrant bag behind her. She hadn't told them anything, and didn't plan to. They were wrapped up in their own little dramas, and she was happy to let them think this was just another fancy luxury resort. Let them continue to believe that there weren't actually people here who had everything that they had always imagined for themselves.

Brandon had never shown up again, and Scarlet that morning had gravely told them all that he had been detained by the Civil Guard for kidnapping, which had led to a great deal of conversation and lengthy explanations punctuated by Sonya mouthing "Human trafficking," and Adam pinching her.

Brandon was the least of the revelations of the island, Amy thought, glancing back to the beautiful resort and the gorgeous verdant jungle that cradled it. An amazing world of magic and enchantment. A world she wasn't a part of, and never could be.

Then she was at the dock, and her bag was rolling easily and there was a tall, golden-haired woman stepping behind her to offer to take a last photo of Sonya, Adam, and Donnie. Amy was too weary to even feel bad that she seemed to be deliberately excluded and she walked down the dock with her bag thunking along the boards behind her, ignoring Sonya's attempt to call her back.

A smiling man in a staff polo shirt helped her down into the boat, handed down her bag after her, then gave her a wink and pushed the boat from the dock with one foot, just as Amy realized that the vessel was absolutely *filled* with flowers.

She held onto the railing in a moment of cold panic as the boat picked up speed away from the shore, and she turned to see that the man at the wheel was familiar even before he shot her a sheepish smile over his shoulder.

"What are you doing?" she cried, over the roar of the engines, staggering to stand beside Calvin.

"It's a grand gesture!" he shouted back, then he turned the engines down. "I hope," he added. "I mean, I know there's kind of a fine line between crazy stalker and crazy romantic gesture, and I'm really hoping I've walked it."

"Well, you definitely got the *crazy* right," Amy protested. "Does the resort *know* that you cut all these flowers? You're probably going to lose your room deposit."

"I don't care," he said fiercely. "I needed to catch you before you left, because if I let you go without explaining, I was going to regret it for the rest of my life."

Amy stared at him, filled with longing and confusion and despair. "You already explained," she said achingly.

"Only part of it," Calvin said. He fiddled with the controls and set the boat to idle. "Please, let me tell you the rest. And if you still want to go, I will take you right back to the dock and never bother you again."

"My friends probably think you're part of a human trafficking ring," Amy said seriously. "So this better be good."

"I love you, Amy."

All of the breath left Amy in an incredulous rush. "We just met…" she said weakly, because the statement left her knees feeling boneless and everything else in her body was on fire.

"Shifters, they…we have a chance to meet our one true mate, the person who is going to make us happiest out of anyone else in the entire world. It doesn't always happen, but when it does…it's this. It's knowing who you are, right down to the amazing, courageous, brilliant core of you, and loving every part of you."

"Like…love at first sight?" It was a fairy tale. It was impossible. Like this whole crazy, impossible island.

"At first sight and forever," Calvin said softly. "I will love you if you want to go back to the shore and never see me again and leave my life empty and alone. I will love you until the stars go cold and the ocean rises and swallows the land. I will never be complete without you."

The smell of all the flowers was making Amy dizzy. "This is crazy," she breathed.

"Be crazy with me," Calvin begged. "Oh, dammit, I was supposed to have music on for this part." He fumbled with a phone and turned on "In Your Eyes."

Then he dropped to his knees. "I don't have a ring, I don't have a plan, I just know that I want you to be with me forever. Give me a chance?"

Amy could not help but laugh, slightly hysterical and tears streaming from her eyes. "When you go for a grand gesture, you really go all out," she wept and chortled.

Calvin's face went hopeful. "Is that a yes?"

"Are you really asking me to marry you?" Amy asked incredulously.

Calvin's face lit up. "Yes. Absolutely yes."

"This is insane," Amy said, but she made no protest as Calvin stood and swept her into his strong arms. "I don't even know what last name I'd have…"

"Montgomery," Calvin said, kissing her gently.

Amy let her arms slide up around his neck. "Amy Montgomery," she said, savoring the sound of it. "You know, this could have backfired terribly?"

Calvin kissed her again. "I had to take the chance," he said. "You are my one, my *mate*."

It was crazy, Amy thought, but crazy had never felt so perfectly right as being in his arms, with his mouth on hers, his body hard up against hers.

"Yes," she said, and she meant it with all of her soul.

By the time they made it back to shore, Sonya was having hysterics, the owner of the resort was at the dock looking like a thunderstorm and sort of feeling like one, too, and Amy's mouth was bruised with kisses.

~

Sonya and the others were placated by Amy's cautious explanation about Calvin, skipping the part where he was a wolf shifter and she was his mate and concentrating more on the love. Charlene did a great deal to smooth things over, and managed to charm not only Sonya, but also Adam and Donnie; she had a gift for making ridiculous things sound utterly sensible and she and Sonya were exchanging sewing tips by the time the furries left in the boat.

Amy stood on the dock and waved after them.

"Do you know, it never once occurred to me not to believe you," Amy said later, lying next to Calvin in his bed making circles on his chest with one of her clever fingers.

"That I love you?"

"That you're a *wolf*."

"You had just seen a mammoth on the beach," Calvin pointed out. "I suppose that I wasn't that much of a leap of faith." He sat up. "I could show you."

Amy sat slowly up with him. "I'd…like that," she said carefully.

Calvin thought she sounded more wistful than jealous or angry. "Let me just…" he stepped off the bed and seamlessly *changed*.

"Oh," she said, staring at him. "*Oh*."

He paced to stand beside the bed where he would be the closest, and she crawled to the edge of the bed to look down at him. "You're beautiful," she said in awe. He nuzzled her, then licked her, and she laughed in delight, slipping off the bed to put her arms around him and snuggle with him. "It's like a dream come true," she said with a contented sigh.

Curled together, Calvin shifted back. "I don't want you to ever feel like you're less because I happen to have a mangy, smart-ass dog in my head with me."

"I like you in both shapes," Amy said. "And you are amazing enough for both of us."

He leaned down and kissed her, slowly and deeply. "I have my work cut out for me," he said.

"What work is that?" Amy asked, tangling her fingers in his hair.

"Convincing you how completely perfect you are." Calvin heaved a sigh. "It might take me years of telling you every day."

"I'm very stubborn," Amy agreed.

"Just do one thing for me," Calvin said, smiling.

She smiled back. "What's that?"

"Wear your ears?"

She froze, and for a moment Calvin wondered if he'd made a terrible error. "I love them," he hastened to say. "They're so whimsical and adorable and brave and they sort of sum up everything about you."

"It isn't…weird to do here? I mean, now that I know? Because it's…fake?"

Calvin brushed a lock of hair from her face. "Darling, this is a tropical island for people who have voices in their heads and can change into animals. There's a periodically rampaging non-verbal mammoth. The lifeguard is a dragon. Weird is what they serve for lunch."

"Embrace the weird?" Amy said, a tentative smile blooming over her beautiful features.

"I love the weird," Calvin assured her. "Please be weird with me forever."

Amy stood up, padded over to her open luggage, and pulled out her ears. She smoothed the soft, fake fur carefully back into shape and after considering for a moment, placed the headband over her head.

"Yes," Calvin sighed. "That's *you*."

Amy walked to the mirror in the corner and examined her reflection. "Alright," she agreed, perfecting the shape of one of the ears. "I should probably put clothing on before we go to dinner," she chuckled.

"The resort *is* clothing optional," Calvin said suggestively.

"I think that if I go like this, we won't be eating much food," Amy chided.

Calvin stood and walked to stand behind her. "There are other hungers to feed."

Amy tipped her head back and got him in the face with one of her ears. "Oops," she giggled.

Calvin gathered her into his arms anyway. "You'd be fake *without* them," he said. "This is who you are."

Amy turned in his arms. "I feel like the Velveteen Rabbit," she said wistfully.

"I thought they were fox ears," Calvin said, mystified.

"It's a story, about a stuffed rabbit who became real…because someone loved it. I feel like I'm…real now, like your love brought me to life. I may never be able to change into an actual animal, but that's not as important as having someone who really sees me, and loves me exactly as I am." She smiled. "And having a pet wolf, that is kind of like a dream come true."

"A pet?" Calvin said in mock outrage. "You are not putting a collar around this neck."

They both considered that statement after he'd said it out loud. "Well, maybe," he conceded, as she said, "It could be fun..."

"I'm getting hungry," she said, after their laughter had faded. "And I *am* going to wear clothing to the restaurant."

"And the ears?" Calvin said hopefully.

"And the ears," Amy agreed.

A NOTE FROM THE AUTHOR

An author isn't supposed to have favorite characters, but Gizelle is totally mine. I hadn't originally planned to give her her own book, but when readers starting asking for it, it fell into my brain almost in whole. I knew from the beginning that she had a tragic backstory, but I tried to tell it with care and sensitivity. And Breck, dear Breck! I loved his entire book, from the very first doom to the very last kiss. Thank you for joining me at Shifting Sands Resort for these stories. The answers are all ahead!

I would love to know what you thought—you can leave a review at Amazon or Goodreads (I read every one, and they help other readers find me, too!) or email me at elvaherself@elvabirch.com. I really enjoy hearing from my readers and I especially love finding out what your guesses for what Scarlet's true nature were before you got to the big reveal!

If you'd like to be emailed when I release my next book, please visit my webpage and sign up to be added to my mailing list at elvabirch.com, where you can find a list of all my books. You can also follow me on Facebook or join my Reader's Retreat on Facebook!

MORE BY ELVA BIRCH

A Day Care for Shifters: A hot new full-length series about adorable shifter kids and their struggling single parents in a town full of mystery and surprise. Start the series with Wolf's Instinct, when Addison comes to Nickel City to take a job at a very special day care and finds a family to belong to. Funny and full of feeling, this is a gentle ice-cream-straight-from-the-container escape. Sweet and sizzling!

~

The Royal Dragons of Alaska: A fascinating alternate world where Alaska is ruled by secret dragon shifters. Adventure, romance, and humor! Reluctant royalty, relentless enemies…dogs, camping, and magic! Start with The Dragon Prince of Alaska.

~

Suddenly Shifters: A hilarious series of novellas, serials, and shorts set in the small town of Anders Canyon, where something (in the water?) is making ordinary citizens turn into shifters. Start with Something in the Water! Also available in audio!

~

Lawn Ornament Shifters: The series that was only supposed to be a joke, this is a collection of short, ridiculous romances featuring unusual shifters, myths, and magic. Cross-your-legs funny and full of heart! Start with The Flamingo's Fated Mate!

~

Birch Hearts: An enchanting collection of short stories and novellas. Unconstrained by theme or setting, each short read has romance, magic, and heart, with a satisfying conclusion. And always, the impossible and irresistible. Start with a sampler plate in Prompted 2 for fourteen pieces of sweet-to-sizzling flash fiction, or the novella, Better Half. Breakup is a free story!

Shifting Sands Resort: A complete ten-book series - plus two collections of shorts. This is a sizzling shifter romance set at a tropical island resort. Each book stands alone but connects into a great mystery with a thrilling conclusion. Start with Tropical Tiger Spy or dive in to the Omnibus edition, with all of the novels, short stories, and novellas in my preferred reading order! Shifting Sands Resort crosses over with Fire and Rescue Shifters and Shifter Kingdom.

Fae Shifter Knights: A complete four-book fantasy portal romp, with cute pets and swoon-worthy knights stuck in a world of wonders like refrigerators and ham sandwiches. Start with Dragon of Glass!

Green Valley Shifters: A sweet, small town series with single dads, secret shifters, sweet kids, and spinsters. Low-peril and steamy! Standalone books where you can revisit your favorite characters - this series is also complete with six books! Start with Dancing Bearfoot! This series crosses over with **Virtue Shifters**, which starts with Timber Wolf.

SHIFTING SANDS RESORT COMPLETE TIMELINE

Shifting Sands Resort shares a world with Fire and Rescue Shifters, and Shifter Kingdom. This is a complete timeline of all three series, with short stories in their appropriate order. This is not at ***all*** *the order I would recommend reading them the first time, as many of the short stories spoil the subsequent books!*

Steps (Tropical Tails)
Roots (Tropical Tails)
Run (Tropical Tails)
Treasure Sense (Tropical Tails)
A Recipe for Happiness (Tropical Holiday Tails)
Firefighter Dragon
Firefighter Pegasus
Royal Guard Lion
Royal Guard Tiger
Firefighter Griffin
Tropical Tiger Spy
Other Duties as Assigned (Tropical Tails)
Locked (Shifting Sands Omnibus Vol 1)
Tropical Wounded Wolf
Unlocked (Shifting Sands Omnibus Vol 1)

Firefighter Sea Dragon
The Master Shark's Mate
Tropical Bartender Bear
Tropical Lynx's Lover
The Storm (Tropical Tails)
Tropical Dragon Diver
Tropical Panther's Penance
A ChristMOOSE Story (Tropical Holiday Tails)
Dance Lesson (Tropical Tails)
The Betting Pool (Tropical Tails)
Firefighter Unicorn
Tropical Christmas Stag
Scarlet and the Christmas Kittens (Tropical Holiday Tails)
(the epilogue of Tropical Christmas Stag)
Lift (Shifting Sands Omnibus Vol 3)
Firefighter Phoenix
Tropical Leopard's Longing
Her Hellhound Bodyguard (Tropical Tails)
(the epilogue of Tropical Leopard's Longing)
Pregnancy Knows (Shifting Sands Omnibus Vol 3)
Tropical Lion's Legacy
Fake Fur (Tropical Tails)
Reunion (Tropical Tails)
Pickled Magnolias (Tropical Tails)
(the epilogue of Tropical Lion's Legacy)
Tropical Dragon's Destiny
A Will and a Wedding (Tropical Tails)
A Hoard of the Their Own (Tropical Tails)
Of Course (Tropical Tails)
Perfect Match (Tropical Tails)
All in the Timing (Tropical Holiday Tails)
(the epilogue of Tropical Dragon's Destiny)
Unreliable Senses (Tropical Tails)